KINGS
BE.

Carl Johnson returns to Brighton after two years exile in Los Angeles to discover that the presumed suicide of his wife, Rose, was the work of his gangland boss, Jack Fossey.

The mysterious Johnson enlists the help of his old friend, Michael Rossi, to help him resolve the increasingly bizarre affair, vowing that his will be his last deed before beginning a new life.

The meek and alcoholic Rossi is suddenly pulled into a dark and violent world where his courage and self-belief are tested to the limit. He is further tormented by a series of vivid and terrifying nightmares that seem to foretell the future.

Then Rossi begins to doubt his sanity when he meets the ghost of a man Johnson has just killed . . .

KINGS OF THE BEACH

Mick Casey

JANUS PUBLISHING COMPANY
London, England

First published in Great Britain 1998
by Janus Publishing Company Limited,
Edinburgh House, 19 Nassau Street,
London W1N 7RE

www.januspublishing.co.uk

A CIP catalogue record for this book
is available from the British Library.

ISBN 1 85756 318 2

Phototypeset in 11 on 13 Bembo
by Keyboard Services, Luton, Beds

Cover design Nick Eagleton

Printed and bound in Great Britain by
Antony Rowe Ltd, Chippenham, Wiltshire

DEDICATION

For the original Beach Boys:
Brian, Carl, Dennis, Mike and Al

1

It was the moment Michael Rossi always dreaded after one of his almighty binges; the moment when he pulled back his living-room curtains and the hot sun hit him with without mercy. It invaded his dark, cosy little haven with an unrelenting brutality, casting a huge spotlight on the scattered debris from the night before, showing it up in all its true ugliness.

He had to be mad, for he had done this all too often lately, always promising himself that this time would be the last time. But then drunks are the world's best at making and breaking promises, and Michael knew what he had become. He hadn't quite graduated to alcoholism. He had yet to wake up on a park bench, rummage through a dustbin for his first shot of the day, or piss himself in his sleep. But he had reached the point where he could no longer comfort himself with the age-old excuses. The trembling hands and sporadic muscle seizures were disturbing proof of the mushrooming disease.

Michael knew what was wrong, and that was why he was gripped by guilt. He hadn't suffered a bereavement or lost his job. He wasn't overdrawn at the bank and being strangled by his mortgage. Indeed, in his quest for street credibility, he would feign financial difficulty by regaling the guys at the office with tales of how the cash till across the road had spat his card back at him for the umpteenth time. He would gain comfort from these lies, because they made him feel like a rebel. They provided a false but pleasant taste of the dangerous life, a life he had never known.

The heavy drinking was the result of plain, ordinary boredom, the backlash of a lifetime of conformity. On the surface, everything was fine. Michael Rossi was thirty-nine years of age, single, the archetypal Mr Average. Blond haired, blue-eyed and athletically built, he wasn't classically handsome by any means, but a fair looker all the same. Girls warmed to his engaging personality, but they were usually homely girls in search of true love and marriage. Michael, in his increasing restlessness, yearned to have raw sex with a seasoned prostitute and tell the guys at the pub that he had a social disease.

He had never rocked a boat in his life. At grammar school, he had been the classic average pupil, never gaining exceptional grades, but always working hard and passing the necessary exams; and always secretly longing to emulate the school villains who had the balls to backchat teachers, skip homework, and fart out loud in assembly.

Adventure appealed to Michael, but it scared him too, keeping him firmly in the bland centre lane of life, where danger never threatens but where the boredom kills you anyway.

Now, with his fortieth birthday just around the corner, he held a boring job in a boring town, and longed to be rescued. Twenty years of doing the football pools had convinced him that he wasn't destined to become an overnight millionaire. That was for people who didn't know what to do with large amounts of money and never really wanted it in the first place. He despised those nauseating, happy-go-lucky pieces in the tabloid papers, where Bert the knob twiddler would win a million and vow to be back on the factory floor first thing Monday morning.

Michael's own system was based on an incredible knowledge of football and hours of studying form, and he hadn't even come close to hitting the jackpot. Was it God's way of making some kind of point, to let a moron win a million pounds? The popular press and those awful early evening quiz shows seemed to adore morons; people willing to reveal intimate details of their private lives and make utter fools of themselves in return for half an hour in the national spotlight and the chance of a microwave oven.

One of the reasons Michael had dropped out of mainstream journalism was because he had been suffocated by trivia during his long stint on a local newspaper. One favourite story, which he took a rather perverse pleasure in relating to friends, was of a Mrs Kerr, who insisted the paper did a story on her pet dog, Happy, who could apparently bark in time to 'Land of Hope and Glory'. (He couldn't.) Then there was the retired postman who took great pride in his ability to twitch his ears without moving the rest of his face. Actually, the only things that didn't twitch were his stupid ears but Michael dutifully wrote the story. Shortly afterwards, he resigned. The world was going to hell and he had spent eleven years writing about musical dogs and geriatric ear twitchers.

The boredom and the sense of aimlessness had set in, and soon became compounded by worry and then sheer panic as thirteen months of unemployment followed, much of it his own making. He applied for all manner of jobs during that awful period in limbo, anything and everything that was radically different from what he'd been doing. In truth, he no longer knew what he wanted to do. At one point, he'd applied for trainee management with a hamburger chain. Why on earth had he done that? He was pushing thirty, too damn old to start at the bottom all over again, couldn't even stand the smell of hamburgers.

Finally, on a cold and rainy day in London, he found himself sitting an exam for executive officer in the Civil Service. Another pointless pursuit. Michael was a placid plodder, but not *that* much of a placid plodder. Arriving early, he slipped into the local pub for a few pints of beer and could have quite comfortably remained there for the rest of the afternoon. Feeling pleasantly hazy, he sauntered across to the examination hall, took his seat, and was suddenly confronted by a little dictator with a microphone who seemed to take an immense pleasure in informing everybody of the rules and regulations.

The clock began to run and Michael looked down at his paper, which was full of those infuriating brain teasers that are death to a man with alcohol in his blood. He didn't give a damn what the answers were, because he thought the questions were stupid anyway. When he failed the exam by an embarrassing margin, he regarded it as one of his finest achievements.

Who was he trying to fool? He had been a journalist right from the start, and, like it or not, that's what he did best. He had a novel on the drawing board, and one day he would be writing for himself, outrageously wealthy and acclaimed as one of the true greats. Then he would emigrate to his beloved Northern California, where the inspiration would surely flow like good wine; to San Francisco, Monterey, Big Sur or Salinas.

Michael loved America, having travelled the country extensively during those golden days when he was still living with his parents and didn't have to worry about a mortgage. He had watched baseball games at Yankee Stadium, listened to jazz in New Orleans, had ridden the cable cars in San Francisco, and had never got it out of his system. One day he would go back. That was his dream.

In the meantime, he would toe the line and keep plodding away. For the past five years, he had been staff writer for a trade magazine in Horley, Surrey, not far from Gatwick Airport. In fact, as far as Michael was concerned, Horley's proximity to Gatwick was about the only thing it had going for it. The job was pleasantly interesting but safe, the story of his life. In fairness, it had its compensations. Horley is about thirty miles from Brighton, where Michael lived in a pleasant ground floor flat, just two minutes' walk from the railway station. There was a stopping service to Horley which left Brighton at 7.26 each morning, allowing Michael fifty minutes to read his paper, have a sleep, and work up a passable air of enthusiasm for the people at the office. They all liked Michael. He was that easy-going guy at the end of the corridor who always smiled and acknowledged everyone and never seemed to suffer a bad mood. They didn't know of his raging desire to heave his computer through the nearest window, jam the fax machine and flood the toilets.

The job also offered the occasional trip abroad, to Germany or Italy or France to see over a factory, but many of these sojourns were known as 'jollies' in the trade, where work took a back seat to having fun. This enabled Michael to indulge his love of drinking, and it was a pleasant escape. But it wasn't enough. It wasn't nearly enough.

Now it was a hot Saturday morning in June of 1994, a little after eleven o'clock, and the sudden rush of sunlight didn't bang home with quite the normal impact as he held his breath and clumsily swished back the curtains. He had the cushion of a three-week holiday, which meant that there wasn't the usual obligation to become a normal human being again by Monday. He had decided to

4

forfeit a holiday abroad, having recently had his flat extensively redecorated, and he was depressed about that. But three weeks in Brighton was still better than three weeks in Horley. If the mood took him, he could simply spend those three weeks in a state of permanent drunkenness. He could live with his hangovers as long as he could recover from them at leisure. The worst part of being a drunk was getting up at six in the morning, climbing into a suit and having to act responsibly.

Yet Michael was a man tortured by his conscience. He was an incurable worrier who experienced tremendous and long-lasting guilt over his unorthodox behaviour. Here he was, with no obligations or responsibilities for the next twenty-one days, and he still couldn't get drunk without feeling remorse. He winced as he surveyed the wreckage of the living-room. His prized collection of records and tapes, which he valued dearly and treated with such care, was scattered all over the room, out of their sleeves and cases, and Michael dreaded the task of matching them all up again. The telephone was off the hook, a filthy ashtray full of cigarette butts beside it. On the floor was a half finished meal and his open diary. He vaguely recalled calling somebody in the early hours, but who had it been and what had he said? His inability to remember things like that always alarmed him.

His large pine table, situated directly in front of the window, resembled a miniature bar. There was an empty rum bottle, a half full bottle of Scotch, and four empty glasses. Christ, he'd been switch-hitting between rum and Scotch and he couldn't even remember drinking the rum. He didn't eat much when he was on a binge, and now his head was banging and there was a terrible emptiness in his stomach. Common sense told him to go into the kitchen and get something to eat, but the Scotch on the table was begging for attention. He'd drink the rest of that first, smoke a few cigarettes, listen to some gentle music on the radio and then clean himself up.

Promises, promises . . .

2

Michael had no girlfriend at present and few interests. He was fast becoming a hermit at weekends, dividing his time between long walks, penning his novel and drinking. But drunk or sober, he enjoyed his regular Saturday morning walk down to the sea. He had lived in Brighton since early childhood, when his family had moved down from South London, and he loved the town. Its cosmopolitan mix reminded him strongly of San Francisco, and he never grew tired of the rich variety of people. Brighton was a great melting pot of yuppies, hippies, students, actors, street entertainers, young people, old people, and out-and-out eccentrics. Whatever the season, whatever the weather, the town was always bubbling, and he loved its laid-back and easy feel.

Michael had worked out many different routes to the sea from his flat and enjoyed the weekly task of deciding which one to take. He would avoid the centre of town today, because the tourists would be swarming over it. Churchill Square and Western Road would be jammed. He always made a point of avoiding crowds when he was feeling fragile and edgy. There was a touch of the claustrophobic about him, and, being a naturally fast walker, he could feel his blood rising whenever his path was blocked. His favourite route was one that took him through a network of little back streets into Brighton's Lanes area. From there he would cut through to East Street and on to the sea front. Sitting on the Palace Pier was usually therapeutic when he felt this way, preferably close to Horatio's Bar, where he could opt for the hair of the dog if his pains didn't subside.

He hadn't cleared up the mess in his flat before he'd left,

promising himself that he'd attend to that later. There was also a pile of washing up and laundry to wade through, and the fact suddenly occurred to him that there was nothing in the freezer in the way of a meal tonight. Shit, he thought. That meant a visit to the supermarket, where he would get hot and frustrated and feel like clobbering someone at the checkout. Hot-tempered mothers and their screaming children, little old ladies who didn't know which way to go, people who pulled out their cheque books and cards to pay for two items ... Michael hated supermarkets.

He had begun to feel better as he made his way down Trafalgar Road, beneath the station, but the thought of having to make that detour to the supermarket filled him with gloom again. To hell with it. He'd leave that until late afternoon, when it wouldn't be so hectic. He wanted to get out onto the pier and breathe the sea air, and hopefully find himself again. He had three weeks to fill, three weeks to make considerable headway on his novel, and he kept telling himself that he had to use that time constructively. No more reckless drinking, no more lost days and nights. That was the plan.

Brighton was experiencing the first days of what would prove to be a long and hot summer. As Michael turned out of East Street, the Palace Pier looked magnificent in the shimmering heat, thick with people, like a giant honeypot besieged by bees. In stark contrast, the sad and crumbling West Pier away to his right was a pitiful spectacle, its rotting domes attracting only birds. Michael paused for a moment and looked up the road towards Hove, wondering if he'd ever be wealthy enough to afford that kind of property. Everything about Hove seemed remarkably sophisticated, clean and correct. He'd once used a public toilet there near the beach and thought he'd walked into somebody's living-room by mistake.

He lingered on the street corner for a while, fighting the temptation to wander right and sink a quick pint in Doctor Brighton's, one of his favourite watering holes. His throat was horribly dry and he was now sweating profusely, a combination of the heat and last night's alcohol. With rare self-discipline, he turned left and made for the Palace Pier, where he bought a Coca-Cola and sat in the shade. Sipping his drink, he tried to focus his thoughts on anything that would take his mind off his discomfort. He looked at fat women and fat men, their bottoms bulging out of tight and gaudy shorts, and wondered how people like that cultivated such self-confidence. He looked up the coast at Brighton Marina and wondered when the hell they would finish work on it. Then he dozed off, and was beginning to feel rather pleasantly divorced from it all when a gruff voice said, 'Michael Rossi, this is your life.'

Even in his bewildered state of mind, Michael recognised the voice instantly, and he could scarcely believe it. As his eyes snapped open, the vision before him suddenly made the whole world seem a better place. Standing right over him, immaculately dressed and as devilishly handsome as ever, was the only man he'd ever wanted to be: Carl Johnson.

'Carl?' he spluttered. 'Is that you?' He realised the stupidity of the question as soon as Johnson's sun-tanned face registered a look of mock disgust.

'No, it's bloody Al Pacino,' Johnson said heavily. 'Your eyes look terrible. Are you going blind?'

'Christ, Carl!' Michael cried. 'Jesus Christ, I don't believe it!' Jumping up to embrace Johnson, he suddenly froze as pain exploded through his head. Johnson grabbed him by the arm and said, 'What's the matter, kid? You're not having a stroke, are you?'

'Hangover,' Michael said, holding his head. 'I had one hell of a session last night. What are you doing here? I don't understand.'

'I'll explain all that,' Johnson said. 'You fit for a drink?'

'Yeah, I think it's the only cure.'

'Come on then.'

They crossed the road and walked up to Doctor Brighton's, a cosy pub tucked around the corner from the Hospitality Inn on King's Road. Johnson was in a buoyant mood, yet he was clearly preoccupied and Michael detected the air of tension immediately. Johnson was one of those naturally charismatic men who exuded electricity when he was simmering over something. Michael hadn't seen him for so long and had so many questions to ask, yet Johnson seemed to be deliberately engaging in small talk.

Inside the pub, Michael slid behind his favourite table near the window and smiled to himself as Johnson eased his way up to the crowded bar and got served immediately. Typical, Michael thought. The waters always seemed to part for Johnson. He was truly a child of fortune. Or was he? Two years ago, his whole world had seemed to crumble at once. His wife, Rose, long troubled by depression and mental illness, had walked down to the beach late one night and drowned herself, not far from the West Pier. Her death devastated Johnson, whose already turbulent relationship with his rebellious teenage daughter, Janice, became unbearable.

Entrusting Janice to the care of a long-time girlfriend, Wendy Barnes, Johnson had mysteriously left for Los Angeles soon afterwards, without so much as a word to Michael, his greatest friend. Since then, nothing until now. Not a letter, not a telephone call. But that was Carl Johnson. Michael had been his most trusted friend for well over twenty-five years, since they were first thrown together by fate at grammar school, yet there was still so much about Johnson that he didn't know. Right from the start, Johnson had been a shadowy, almost ghostly figure; a smiling, joking teaser who would tantalisingly reveal parts of his make-up and then draw back and leave you guessing the rest. Like Michael, he was a transplanted South Londoner, the same age and from a similarly humble background. Yet now he drove the best cars, wore the best clothes and owned various properties in different parts of the world. People would come running at the snap of his fingers, yet, as far as Michael knew, he had never worked a nine-to-five day in his life. Once upon a time, Michael had asked him what he did for a living and Johnson had winked in his mischievous way and said, 'A bit of this, a bit of that . . . enough to keep me occupied.' Out of respect, Michael had never asked him to elaborate, but he knew in his heart that the man he idolised wasn't a legitimate businessman. That was part of the excitement.

Yet it was an excitement tinged by fear, a fear that Michael had first experienced in the school gymnasium the day they became friends. Michael had been a painfully shy boy, easily intimidated by teachers and pupils alike. In the dressing-room, after a frenetic game of five-a-side football, a singularly vicious bully by the name of Paul Black blamed Michael for the loss of a goal. A fierce argument ensued, and Black, ever the diplomat, made his point in the form of a right-hand smash to the nose. As the blood pumped from Michael's face and splattered down his shirt, Carl Johnson seemed to emerge from nowhere. Suddenly, Black was shrieking, his testicles firmly in the grip of Johnson's left hand. To this day, Michael still vividly recalled Johnson's chilling words. 'You ever do that again,' he told Black, 'and I'll squeeze these until your fucking nose bleeds.'

The whole room fell instantly quiet and Michael was mesmerised by Johnson's electrifying presence. Johnson's brown eyes, lifeless like a shark's, complemented his flat, emotionless voice, and Michael could feel the adrenaline charging through his body. He was strangely thrilled, yet equally scared. From that day on, Johnson was a giant in his eyes, and there was a period during that dreadfully uncertain stage in his teenage life when Michael felt sure he had to be homosexual.

Carl Johnson seemed to have it all. At a time when every other kid was afflicted with acne, Johnson already looked like a budding film star. Academically, he was never more than an average student, but that was of little importance to Michael. The sports field was the great yardstick by which schoolboys judged one another, and Johnson had no equal in that department. He was the school's star rugby player and an excellent cross country runner and cricketer. Normally, such perfect students are vilified by their classmates, yet Johnson was a hero because he also possessed the ultimate qualification, that of being the best streetfighter. He never claimed to be, but it was an unwritten rule of the jungle that Carl Johnson was the one guy you never troubled.

He didn't take to too many people, preferring to keep to himself, and Michael regarded it a supreme compliment when Johnson took him under his wing. They drifted apart frequently when they left school, as Michael pursued his career in journalism and Johnson periodically vanished. It was the way their relationship was to continue over the years, with Johnson disappearing for long periods and then emerging dramatically from the shadows like Harry Lime in *The Third Man*. Yet the strong bond between the two men was never broken, and Michael always wondered what Johnson was up to during his lengthy absences. He was best man when Johnson married the tragic Rose, and shortly afterwards Johnson and his bride moved into the kind of home that Michael would only ever get to dream about.

Once, in a rare, unguarded moment, Johnson had told Michael, 'This will probably sound ridiculous, but you're the best friend I've ever had. Don't ever forget that. You know I don't bullshit about these kind of things.' He said that after being away for six months, yet Michael didn't doubt that he meant it and treasured the compliment. For while Johnson was tight-lipped about his livelihood, he had always trusted Michael implicitly in all other matters.

Now, once again, Johnson had crashed back into Michael's life, and Michael felt like a schoolboy again as he sat in Doctor Brighton's, excitedly anticipating what his friend might have to say. As Johnson walked back to the table with the drinks, he looked as though he'd just strolled out of a scene from *The Godfather*, and Michael hoped this wasn't an omen. Johnson was dressed in a cream suit and waistcoat, silk shirt and tie, and his thick black hair was swept back to perfection. Michael noticed that he still wore his wedding ring.

Johnson plonked down two pints of lager on the table and then placed a smaller glass in front of Michael, which contained a dark brew that set his stomach churning again.

'There you go, get that down you.'

'What the hell is it?' Michael asked, gingerly fingering the glass.

'Fernet Branca. Tastes like shit, but it settles the stomach. Drink it straight down.'

Michael reluctantly obeyed, and as the thick mixture slid down his throat and into his stomach, he made a face and shook his head.

'So what were you celebrating last night?' Johnson chuckled.

'The fact that I'm thirty-nine and bored rigid.'

'It's really that bad, is it?'

'It's worse, Carl. Yesterday was the last straw. If I don't get out of this job soon, I'm going to turn into one of those nuts who suddenly goes out and murders a whole town.'

Johnson offered him a cigarette. 'Yeah, I can see you're dying to tell me about it.'

The cigarette tasted foul as Michael took a hearty drag, his tongue still heavily coated from all the booze. But the pleasant jolt to his lungs made him persist. 'I had to go to Birmingham yesterday,' he began, hesitating slightly as he wondered if he might be boring Johnson. His own mundane life seemed to be on a different planet by comparison. 'An hour on that stinking train from Brighton to Victoria, getting kicked around like a football on the tube ride to Euston, and then the Intercity to Birmingham broke down at bloody Peterborough.'

'Sounds riveting,' Johnson said teasingly.

'And all because some technical services manager wanted to give me the ins and outs of his company's latest waste disposal unit. Three hours he kept me. I know everything about waste disposers, Carl, and I hate the bloody things.'

Johnson began to laugh, which relaxed Michael and enabled him to see the funny side of it. 'Anyway, I've taken three weeks' leave. To hell with it. I usually save all my leave 'til the end of the year, then end up losing it. Our wonderful company doesn't allow you to carry days over. I think it's because it confuses Mrs Jackson in administration. She's one of those people who finds it difficult to chew gum and fart at the same time.' Michael paused uneasily. Johnson was nodding gently and smiling pleasantly as if he understood, but Michael didn't want to overdo it. It occurred to him that he had been whingeing about his misfortunes to too many people of late. 'Anyway,' he said, somewhat embarrassed, 'you don't want to hear about all this. Tell me about yourself, for God's sake. Somebody told me you'd gone to Los Angeles for keeps. You left without even saying...'

'Yeah, yeah, I'm sorry about that, Michael,' Johnson said quickly. 'I've, got some business interests out there and I just wanted to get away. I was pretty screwed up after Rose's death, as you can imagine...' He trailed off, though there was no emotion in his voice. Indeed, his dark eyes were burning fiercely, and he seemed to be looking straight through Michael at some hidden tormentor beyond.

'Yes, I know,' Michael said, feeling awkward. 'Are you back to stay?'

'No, just to tidy up a few loose ends. I only got back yesterday. I'm staying at the Grand. I sold the house some time ago. I want to

12

try to make my peace with Janice. I want her to come back to California with me. I've bought a place out there.'

'How is she?'

'I don't honestly know, Michael, that's what's worrying me. I wrote to her all the time from LA and she replied about three times. When I spoke to her over the phone, all I got was one-word answers. She still seems to blame me for everything. Talking to Wendy hasn't been any better.'

'You mean Wendy Barnes? Wasn't she . . .'

Johnson gave a little grin. 'Yeah, my ex bit on the side. She wasn't the greatest choice for a guardian, but I thought I could trust her, you know? She's telling me everything's okay, and that Janice needs time, and all that crap. But it's weird, Michael. Wendy just never sounds right, as if she's not quite there. I'll kill the bitch if she's let Janice drift. I called her again yesterday and this morning. No answer. I set them both up in a little bungalow in Greatstone. It's a quiet little town down the road from Folkestone, but it's such a bloody long and awkward drive from here. I'll do that tomorrow. Shouldn't be too bad on a Sunday.'

Michael didn't know what to think or say. Never had Johnson opened up to this extent. 'Carl, if you were worried, you should have called me. You know I'll always help if I can.' He was struggling for the right words and it was all coming out wrong as usual. For all the years they had known each other, there were still times when Michael fumbled for words in Johnson's presence, like a boy dating his first girl.

'I know, I know,' Johnson said soothingly. 'It's all very complicated and I didn't want to involve you in all my troubles. But now I need a friend – a genuine friend.' He sipped at his lager and toyed with the glass for a few seconds, then leaned back slightly, cocking his head to one side and looking Michael straight in the eye. It was a mannerism of Johnson's whenever he was about to say something weighty and it never ceased to fascinate Michael. It always reminded him of the old joke about how Marlon Brando adopts a similar posture when sneaking a look at his cue cards. Thoughtfully, Johnson said, 'There are a lot of things you don't know about me – a lot of things I've never been able to tell you for various reasons.' He stopped for a second, as if expecting some sort of response. 'I need your help, Michael. There's a lot happening in my life at the moment that's very confusing and very dangerous. I need somebody to ride shotgun with me, somebody I can trust.'

The word 'shotgun' set off a little explosion in Michael's stomach, like shifting wind. He hoped that Johnson was speaking metaphorically. In any event, he had suddenly been yanked into Johnson's dark and mysterious world, and even though common sense told him to make a quick excuse and return to his life of drudgery, he was hooked.

'I'm going to lay my cards on the table and tell you everything you ever wanted to know about me,' Johnson continued. 'And you'll either hate me for the rest of your days or you'll help me. If you help me, you'll never have to suffer another train journey to Horley. I'll bring you out to California and you'll live like a bloody king.'

Michael could feel the adrenaline rising again. It was as if an angel had suddenly descended from Heaven and turned his life around with the wave of a wand. It was all too good to be true. 'Jesus, Carl, what are you about to tell me?' he asked nervously. He noticed his hand was trembling as he picked up his lager, but this time it was fear, not the booze.

'I won't delude you,' Johnson said firmly. 'I'm not offering you something for nothing. The first part of the deal isn't going to be pleasant. You'll see a side of life that you've never seen before and things are likely to get hairy. If you get a dodgy stomach when you cut yourself shaving, you may as well forget about it right now.'

Michael felt a strange thrill, but he was also confused and afraid. For so long, he had yearned to prise Johnson apart and find out what lurked beneath the surface, and now it was happening too fast. Johnson was hitting him with everything at once and Michael didn't know how to respond. He felt like a man who had been invited to an inconvenient dinner party. He didn't want to go, but in the heat of the moment he couldn't find a viable excuse.

Johnson laughed and said, 'You look as if a bomb's hit you!' He gulped down the rest of his lager and tapped Michael on the arm. 'Listen, don't say anything right now. Let's go back to your place and I'll tell you all about it.' He jumped up, itching to go, and Michael was fumbling again, struggling to keep up.

He looked up at Johnson and said, 'I've got to go to the supermarket first. I've er ... I've got nothing in the fridge.' It sounded so trite and inconsequential after Johnson's quietly sinister performance, and Michael felt his face reddening.

'Forget it,' Johnson said with an easy smile. 'I've arranged all that. Come on, I'm parked up the road.'

3

It was the moment he put the key in the door that Michael was jolted back into the real world, remembering with sudden panic the dreadful mess he'd left behind. He wanted to make an excuse, suggest they go somewhere else, anything but open that door and suffer humiliation.

Turning the key, he mumbled, 'I'm sorry about the mess.' The door opened into a narrow little hallway, where there was a trail of discarded clothes, empty bottles and cigarette ends. The kitchen at the end was a picture of equal horror, a bombsite of piled dishes, baking tins, bin liners on the floor and a spilled rubbish bin. Michael couldn't even remember how he had created such devastation. The place reeked of alcohol and stale tobacco.

Depressed and ashamed, he closed his eyes and turned sharply right into the wasteland of his living-room, dreading Johnson's reaction.

'Jesus Christ, what have you been doing in here?'

'Things are a lot worse than I told you, Carl,' Michael said. 'I've been having a really bad time of it lately.' He felt awful as Johnson paused in the hallway for a few seconds, surveying the damage. Then he followed Michael into the living-room, shaking his head slowly. Pointing at the floor, he asked, 'What the hell's that?'

Michael looked down at a mushy mess on a plate and said, 'I think it's a pizza.'

'Christ, it looks like the original prototype. How long's it been there?'

'Only since last night, I think. I er . . . I can't honestly remember.'

Michael wanted to justify it all, but he couldn't. It was shameful and inexcusable and he was lost for words. Only now, in somebody else's company, did he realise how hard and how fast he was falling. Sensing his desperation, Johnson said, 'Okay, let's clear this shit up before we do anything else. And open some windows for God's sake, before we both get pissed on the smell of the stuff.'

Taking off his jacket and throwing it on the settee, Johnson set to work with all the speed and magic of Mary Poppins, attacking the scattered garbage with a clinical efficiency that made Michael dizzy. Still partially hung over and feeling faintly sick, Michael fumbled around in slow pursuit, and the two men barely exchanged a word in the next half hour.

The transformation was incredible, reminding Michael how bright and attractive his little flat was and how damn lucky he was to have his own place anyway. Guilt and more guilt. It chewed at his insides all the time. Johnson made coffee and they sat on the settee and talked. A gorgeous sea breeze was blowing through the large sash window, but it was of little comfort to Michael. His head had begun to bang again and every muscle in his body ached. He sipped tentatively at the bland instant coffee, his hands still unsteady, wishing that he could pep it up with a shot of whisky.

'So tell me,' Johnson said, 'would you rather inhabit a nice room like this or live in that other pile of crap?'

Michael shook his head wearily. 'I've got to stop doing this, Carl. I know what the cause is, but I can't believe I sink to these depths. I start off by buying a bottle to unwind, and then I stand at that table watching the people go by, and everything's okay for a while. Then I . . . I just seem to get lost. I get depressed and angry and I just seem to destroy myself. Sometimes I don't touch booze for days at a time, but then it drags me back like a bloody magnet. It's like a bizarre form of punishment. It's as if I have to kill half of myself to keep the other half going.'

'It's known as quitting,' Johnson said matter of factly. 'You've given up the fight, Michael, and you can either pull yourself together or sink for good. Booze never solved anybody's problems.

17

'I know, I know.'

'Listen,' Johnson said, more gently, 'I know it's easier said than done, and I know the last thing you want to hear when you're down in the dumps is a bloody sermon on clean living and responsibility. But you mustn't ever give up, Michael. Quitting's not the answer. You don't want to be remembered as a loser, do you?'

Michael wanted to express his feelings, but couldn't find the right words. That dreadful word, 'quitting', cut him like a knife, and like every quitter he wanted to believe that he had a viable excuse. Awkwardly, he tried to explain himself. 'I can't stand the boredom. I don't know how it all came about, but I feel as if I'm stuck out in the middle of the desert. I hate the weekdays and then get bored at the weekends. I've lost interest in everything. I used to play golf and go fishing and do all sorts of things, but not any more.' He broke off and sighed in frustration. He had so much to say, but he was already rambling hopelessly.

'So do something about it,' Johnson said with sudden hardness. 'Damn it, Michael, you're whingeing like a bedridden old man who can't get out of the house anymore. You're thirty-nine, single, and you've got no responsibilities. If you don't like your job, chuck it. If you don't like your mortgage, sell the damn flat. It's not as if you're going to drown. You're a talented man, for God's sake.'

'I can't,' Michael said, exasperated. 'What would I do?'

'Whatever the hell you want to do,' Johnson snapped. 'I gave you an alternative in the bloody pub, didn't I?' He jumped to his feet and angrily pointed a finger at Michael. 'Listen, don't give me self-pity, it turns my stomach. My father used to drink to forget and then he'd start whacking my mother around for his recreation. I've offered to change your life, but I'll only help you if you're willing to help yourself. I don't need a manic depressive piss artist in tow.'

Michael nodded but couldn't think of anything to say. He knew Johnson was right and he had no defence. He wanted to take the heat out of the situation and pacify his great idol, who was now raging at him with a fury that he had only ever reserved for others. Reaching for a mutual interest, Michael asked, 'Did you see that piece on Brian Wilson in *Mojo*?'

Johnson was peering out of the window with his hands on his

hips. 'Yeah,' he said bluntly. 'And right now, you're doing a bloody good impression of the man Brian was.'

When the two men were boys, Brian Douglas Wilson, from Hawthorne, California, was the boss. Founder and creative genius of the legendary Beach Boys, Wilson's music had cemented their friendship. Michael used to love Sunday lunchtimes, when he would wander up to Johnson's house for their weekly record session. The music was always too loud, yet Johnson's long-suffering mother, Anne, a kind, sweet woman of saintly patience, rarely complained. The gorgeous smell of Sunday roast filled the house, and Brighton magically became Southern California as the two boys created their own Surf City. It was the lull before the storm, with Johnson's temperamental father safely ensconced in the nearest pub. Michael hated Johnson senior for his hypocrisy. Cunning and devious, he would never throw a tantrum in company. He would play the kind and faithful husband with sickening insincerity, yet Michael still felt fear in his presence, having seen his brutality on Anne Johnson's frequently marked face. Carl Johnson had had to grow up quickly, protecting his mother as best he could. He handled the situation with remarkable maturity and never seemed intimidated by his father. Typically, he never discussed his home life to any great extent, though he once remarked to Michael, 'I've been telling Mum to leave the bastard for years, but she keeps hanging on.'

Yet the imminent arrival of Johnson's father and the uneasy atmosphere that hung over the dinner table could never detract from the magic that had gone before. The Beach Boys were the kings of the hill, better than the Beatles, the Stones, Presley or any of them, and Brian Wilson was only just a notch below God. But the California dream had turned sour for Wilson, and he had only recently fought his way back to health after years of drug abuse and mental illness.

Michael felt an uncomfortable alliance with Wilson, and it went beyond his love of the great man's music. He, too, had lost his way, punishing his mind and body with all the wrong things in an effort to blank out reality and postpone tomorrow. The days of sunshine and innocence now seemed so far in the past. Michael couldn't even pinpoint where it had all gone wrong. Everything good in his life had slowly dissipated. The simple pleasures did nothing for him anymore. He dreaded getting out of bed in the mornings, and the long hot days of summer felt like repeated slaps in the face.

'Help me, Carl,' he said faintly. It was as if somebody else had said it, for he wasn't the kind of man who could easily confide in other people. Johnson was still peering out of the window and said, 'I don't know how some women can carry that kind of weight around.'

'What?' Michael said. He wondered if Johnson had heard him.

'That woman over the road. Talk about "Here's me tits, me arse is coming".'

Michael had been thrown and was suddenly feeling highly emotional. 'Carl...' he began, but the words wouldn't come a second time.

Then Johnson turned and stood right over him. 'The question is, Michael, do you want to help yourself? I can't pull you out of this. I can work your corner, but it's your fight.'

'Are you serious about California, Carl?'

'Have I ever lied to you about anything?'

'No,' Michael said, shaking his head. 'No, never. I want to get better, Carl, honestly. I just want to get out of this nightmare I'm in. If that means giving up all I know and starting again, I'll do it. I just can't go on living this kind of dreary, rotten life. It's eating me away just as much as the booze.' He paused and said, 'I just wish I wasn't so weak. Jesus, the crazy things I do to give myself courage when I'm depressed...'

Johnson sat down in the armchair opposite and gazed out of the window, as if bored with the conversation. Then he looked straight at Michael and said, 'What do you mean?'

'The only time I feel really strong, really confident, is when I'm high on booze,' Michael said. 'That's the way it is for most people who drink, I suppose. But it feels so good, Carl. All my fears, all my hesitance, goes out of the window. I do anything I can to keep that feeling going, even though I know it's not going to be there when I wake up in the morning. I can feel the strength seeping out of me as I begin to reach the end of the bottle. Then it's a feeling of fright –

20

almost panic.' Now Michael was talking more to himself than to Johnson. 'I got off that train last night, hot and tired, and it was the same Friday night ritual – slogged up the road and straight into the off-licence to buy a bottle of Scotch. They do bloody well out of me in there. Always the same routine. I get home here, put the Scotch out in the kitchen while I get changed, and then get into it. It was insufferably hot last night, and I was stripped to the waist, and there was this wonderful breeze coming through the window. And I was sipping the Scotch and I could feel all the tension and the worries slipping away. I always watch tapes of my heroes at times like that. I've got a tape of Roberto Duran beating Iran Barkley for the middleweight championship. What an amazing man Duran is – devil-may-care, larger than life. He doesn't seem to give a damn for anyone or anything. Christ, I wish I had that kind of strength.'

'Michael, you can't be somebody you're not,' Johnson said. 'Whisky or anything else won't change that. Duran's Duran, and you're Michael Rossi. The booze makes you feel like shit the next morning and your problems are still there. Where's the point in that?'

Michael nodded. Johnson wasn't telling him anything he didn't know, yet he needed something to rid himself of the terrible emptiness inside, if only for a couple of delightful hours. 'I wish I could be braver, Carl,' he said. He was struggling again, unable to explain his torment. 'I wish I wasn't so damn passive and easy going and apologetic all the time. I've never been tested. I've never had to confront true fear. I've never been mugged in an alley, or challenged to a fight, or ... or anything like that. And if it ever happened, I'm frightened I'd run away from it. Christ, I never even had a real fight at school. I think I'd just feel a lot better if I could have a fight and win it. Just punch some bully in the mouth and prove to myself I've got balls. Oh, I don't know. I know what I'm trying to say, but ...'

'There are all kinds of fights,' Johnson said. 'You don't have to throw a punch to prove your courage.'

Michael spread his hands in desperation. 'Yes, but don't you know what I mean?'

'I know what you mean,' Johnson replied kindly. 'You're a quiet, placid man by nature, and you interpret that as weakness. Bullshit.

You could get mad for five minutes and knock out Mike Tyson, but you'd still be a quiet and placid man. You can't change your make-up. But if you want a damn fight, I'll give you a fight. Wait here.'

Johnson sprang out of his chair and marched off down the hallway, into the kitchen. Michael's heart began to race. He heard the bang of a cupboard and the clinking of glasses, and Johnson returned holding a full bottle of Scotch and two tumblers. 'I bet you didn't even know you had this,' he said, holding up the whisky. 'I found it amongst last night's debris on the kitchen floor. Bloody good Scotch too. You certainly know how to piss away your money.'

Michael watched, confused, as Johnson opened the bottle and almost completely filled each of the large tumblers. 'Carl, if this is the cure, you've lost me.'

'Make the most of it,' Johnson said, handing Michael his glass. 'The fight begins when you've finished it – because it's going to be your last. You can drink it fast or drink it slow, but once it's gone, that's it. That's your test of courage.'

'Forever?' Michael almost squeaked.

'That's up to you. First, you've got to prove you can live without it. Give your system a couple of weeks to clean itself out. If you can't manage that, then you can either get treatment or go back to killing yourself.' Johnson sat down again, raised his glass and said, 'One last treat before we go to work.'

Michael played it as he always played it when he knew there was nothing left in the locker. He took small, careful sips, savouring every delightful kick as the nectar burned his tongue and slid deliciously down his throat. 'So tell me about it,' he said, smiling weakly. 'If I'm going to go straight, I need some motivation.'

Johnson smiled and his manner suddenly softened. 'How much notice do you need to give your employers?' he asked.

'Four weeks. Why?'

'Right, I want you to take this holiday, go back and do your four weeks, and then come out and join me in California. I'll pay for your flight and take care of all the arrangements. I'll drive you up to Monterey and show you my restaurant.' Johnson was smiling broadly now and Michael was excited again.

'You've got a restaurant?'

'It's only recent. My latest acquisition. My new purpose in life. And you're going to be my assistant manager.'

Michael was open-mouthed, his foggy mind still trying to make sense of all this. 'Carl, it sounds great, but I don't know the first thing about . . .' Johnson let out a big laugh, and reached across and clamped a hand on Michael's knee. 'God damn it, Michael, live! Screw 'em all, man! I'm giving you the chance of a lifetime. I've bought a house up there. You can come and live with me until you find a place of your own. I can't face living in Los Angeles any longer. I'd stay healthier if I sucked on an exhaust pipe for the rest of my life.'

Michael chuckled, but felt uneasy. There was more to come, the bad news, and he had been kept in suspense for long enough. 'What is it you do, Carl? You haven't been in the restaurant business all your life.'

Johnson suddenly looked very serious and leaned back in his chair. 'No, I haven't' he said bluntly. 'You damn well know I haven't.'

'You're one of the bad guys, right?'

'And you've always known that,' Johnson grinned.

'Well, yes, I suppose so. It's just that we've been friends for so long, yet I feel that I've only really got to know you today. I've always had my suspicions, but I didn't feel it was my business.'

Johnson got up and started pacing. 'I understand that, Michael, and I appreciate it. You're not the only one who's trying to go straight, you know. Dirty money didn't buy that restaurant at Monterey. It was the only honest deal I've done in my whole life.'

'I believe you,' Michael said.

Johnson playfully mussed Michael's hair as he moved across and sat on the settee beside him. He took a deep breath, and for the first time ever, he seemed a little nervous. 'I've booked a room for you at the Grand. All expenses paid, as they say. No sense in being on your own tonight. There's an old friend of ours I've got to meet. Steve Cody.'

'From school? *That* Steve Cody?'

'That's the one.'

'He wasn't exactly a friend,' Michael said. 'It was him and his mates who stripped me stark bollock naked one February morning and hung me from the rugby posts.'

Johnson giggled and said, 'Ah, that was just Steve's way of expressing affection for somebody. He's a typical bully, but he's got his uses.'

'How did you meet up with him again?'

Johnson got up, retrieved his glass of whisky from the table, and drank the remainder straight down. 'We've been working together for a while. You've heard of Jack Fossey, right?'

Michael suddenly felt a little jittery again. 'Yeah, vaguely,' he replied sarcastically. 'Unofficially, he's the king of Brighton. And his influence extends far beyond that, from what I've heard.'

Johnson grinned. 'Tut-tut, Michael. You should know the lingo by now. He's a legitimate businessman. And he's spread his legitimate business everywhere. That's the main reason I've been out in Los Angeles. It wasn't all recuperation.'

Michael was so stunned that he completely forgot about preserving his last precious glass of whisky. He gulped down the last large measure all at once, but it did nothing to stop his insides jumping. 'So you and Steve...' He didn't finish the question, because he knew the answer.

'Steve's one of Jack's heavies, if that's the right word,' Johnson explained. 'I'm Jack's chief troubleshooter, if you like. I negotiate, wheel and deal, and take care of all the awkward problems.'

'How long?' Michael asked, his voice catching in his throat.

'What?'

'How long have you been ... well, doing this kind of work?'

'Years. Too many years. Listen, I'm not going to sit here and try and justify it. Crime never ran in the family and I never wanted for anything. I just wanted to make money and live a comfortable life, and I didn't want to break my back doing it. I watched my old man slog his guts out from nine to five all his life, just for a piss-poor pension. It made him as miserable as hell and he died within a year of retiring. Mum followed him a year later and that was their life together.'

'Be honest with me, Carl,' Michael said. 'When you say

troubleshooter . . . have you ever killed anyone?' He rather expected Johnson to muddle his way around that question, but the answer came straight back with chilling bluntness.

'Yes.'

Michael nodded, but couldn't think of an appropriate comment. It was worse than he'd ever imagined. He had pictured Johnson as a latter day Butch Cassidy, who perhaps robbed a few banks here and there, conned a few people, but never greatly harmed anyone. But Jack Fossey's name had destroyed that romantic image. Jack had become an almost legendary figure, especially in his native Brighton, where everybody had their favourite Jack Fossey story.

Business entrepreneur, tireless charity worker, and a pillar of the community, Jack had perfected the art of dignified outrage when questioned about the shadier side of his formidable business empire. Tales abounded of tenants being brutally evicted from his various properties, arms and legs being broken, links to narcotics and prostitution, and corpses surfacing in the unlikeliest of places; all smoothly explained away by Jack's large and slick public relations machine.

This was the man Johnson worked for. How much blood had he spilled on Jack Fossey's behalf? Did he push drugs? Did he beat up whores who didn't toe the line? Michael didn't know what to think or say. What frightened him most, even now, was his inability to dislike Johnson. Like a student of the Wild West who admires Billy the Kid and Jesse James, yet can't justify their violent crimes, Michael was captivated by Johnson's charisma. He had fallen into something of a trance, all these thoughts spinning round in his mind, when Johnson's voice jerked him to attention again. 'If you've got something to say, Michael, say it.'

'What *can* I say?' Michael said, with a nervous laugh. 'I can't condone what you do, but I can't suddenly hate you for it.'

'Will you help me?'

'Christ, mate, I don't know. I don't even know what you're planning to do. You said in the pub you had some loose ends to tie up. What did you mean by that?'

Johnson nodded sombrely. 'I don't know the answer to that question myself yet.' He paused for a few seconds and there was emotion in his voice as he stared down at the floor. 'Rose didn't kill herself, that's all I know. That's why I'm meeting Steve. He called me in Los Angeles and told me to come home as soon as I could.'

'What exactly did he say?'

'He couldn't say too much over the phone. He reckons Rose was murdered. He sounded shit scared. He said he'd explain when I got back. He called me again this morning to confirm the meet. I told him you might be coming along.'

'Murdered?' Michael said, dismayed.

'That's what he told me. Like I said, I don't know any more. So what about it, Michael?'

Michael looked at his empty glass and cast his eyes around the small living-room that would soon be silent and lonely again if he chose to stay. He was on the brink of possibly his only great adventure and he could either risk everything or go back to a life of safety and dullness. He decided to answer quickly before he gave himself the chance to pull the words back. 'I've never stayed at the Grand before. I'll pack a bag.'

Johnson had been staring vacantly at the same spot on the carpet for the past few minutes. Now he lifted his head, the hint of a smile on his face, and the steel back in his eyes. 'It's going to be bloody dangerous,' he said, almost with relish.

Michael shrugged. 'If I stay here, I'll die from booze and depression anyway. If I catch a bullet with you, at least it will be quick. What about this flat?'

'What about it?' Johnson asked, puzzled.

'Well, I'll have to think about selling it if my future is in Monterey.'

Johnson waved a hand dismissively. 'Don't worry about it. I'll take care of that when the time comes.'

'Yes,' Michael said, breathless, 'I thought you probably would.'

4

For the first time in ages, Michael felt wonderfully free and relaxed as Johnson took huge detours and changed the short drive to the Grand into a rambling tour of all their old haunts.

The car windows were down, a jumping jazz number was playing on the radio, and the engine's delicious roar made Michael feel quite superior as he sat proudly up front and took everything in. Johnson's Porsche was one of his great loves, a 1971 green 911e, which, like most Porsche drivers, he drove expertly and lovingly.

Central Brighton was teeming with people in various states of dress and undress, as the temperature hit ninety. The town was one big fashion show, awash with colours as Brighton always is on a summer's day, and Carl and Michael giggled at the various characters as they turned out of Queen's Road and swept down North Street into the Old Steine area, towards the seafront. The hot air was thick with the wonderful smells of goodies cooking in restaurants, sun tan lotion and perfumed girls.

Michael suddenly realised how marvellous he felt. He couldn't remember the last time his body tingled with the joy of simply being alive. He had no desire to get drunk on a day like this and every desire to experience the new and vibrant world into which he'd been thrown. He didn't know what the following days would bring, but even though he was still consumed by an exciting fear, he knew he wanted more.

They arrived at the Grand at around three o'clock, and Michael sat in the cool of the lobby while Johnson parked the car. They checked in and Johnson suggested they grab some rest, as Steve Cody wasn't due until four.

The heat had made Michael tired, but he couldn't sleep, so he killed time by taking a shower and reading a book. A friend at work had loaned him Kerouac's *Doctor Sax*, and Michael was too stubbornly proud to admit that he couldn't make head nor tail of it.

He was reading about the mysterious darkness of Rosemont Avenue and praying for a break in another eight-mile sentence, when Johnson rang and announced that Cody had arrived. Michael felt nervous again and wondered if Cody would approve of his presence. When Johnson opened his door, he was dressed only in underpants and drying his hair. As Michael looked past him, he saw a tall and well-built man staring out of the window, and his eyes were immediately drawn to the man's rapidly balding head. Surely this couldn't be Steve Cody, the vainest boy in school, whose proudest possession had been his shock of brown, wavy hair.

Johnson said, 'Meet the guy who hung you from the rugby posts.'

Cody turned round, and Michael couldn't believe how he had changed. Some twenty years had elapsed since they'd last met, and Michael had been stupidly visualising the classmate who had tormented and infuriated him. At eighteen, Steve Cody looked like a budding film star, slim and handsome, with no shortage of girlfriends. His vanity knew no bounds, and if a wisp of wind disturbed the precious hair it would send him into a major depression for the rest of the day. The prospect of baldness terrified him, and he did everything possible to nurture and cherish the sacred locks.

It hadn't worked. He still had a thin layer of hair, heavily greased and harshly swept back, but most of it hung over the back of his collar. He wore a mighty moustache, as if to compensate for the loss of hair on top. However, Michael had to concede that Cody's dress sense, like Johnson's, was superb. He was sweating heavily in a classic three-piece suit, but this was business, and it dawned on Michael that high-class villains, like high-class boardroom executives, have to look their best for all occasions. There are certain things about people that never change, however, and Cody's smile had always been more of a smirk. He was smirking now and holding out his hand.

'Nice to see you again, Michael,' he said. 'Hope we didn't leave you hanging up there for too long. No lasting damage to the old wedding tackle, I hope.'

Still the same cocky piss-taker, Michael thought. He forced a smile and made a joke, and looked uneasily at Johnson, eager to be rescued.

'It's okay,' Johnson winked, as he started to dress. 'I've explained everything to Steve. He knows you can be trusted.'

Michael wasn't so sure. Cody was the sort who hid behind a smile. Outwardly, he was ever the joker, but you never really knew what was going on inside the man. 'I thought you were one for the quiet life, Michael,' he said. 'What made you come out of your shell?'

'I asked him to,' Johnson said bluntly, and Michael felt pleasantly triumphant as Cody's smirk was replaced by a look of fearful respect.

'You became a writer, then,' he said, with much more humility. 'I always told Carl you'd be a journalist. You were always good at writing.'

Michael just smiled and nodded and said, 'Yeah, that's right.' He really couldn't think of anything else to say. This was the other familiar aspect of Cody's character – his sincerely insincere side. Michael recalled a playground incident at school, when Cody had almost blinded him with a stray shot from a catapult and then promised him everlasting friendship if he promised not to report the matter.

The atmosphere in the muggy room was horribly uncomfortable. Johnson appeared tense and edgy, and Michael was plagued by doubts again. 'Let's take a walk along the beach,' Johnson said.

Not a word was exchanged among the three men as they crossed the road, walked down onto the beach and began to stroll towards the Palace Pier. Michael noticed that Cody was sweating more profusely than ever and looked very nervous, as if timing the right moment to say his piece. The beach was packed with people, and Michael hated it as always. Most of them appeared to be typical day

29

trippers; pot-bellied men supping pints of lager and gorging themselves on hot dogs, and overweight mothers with fleshy thighs vainly trying to discipline their hot and bothered children. Only the local eccentrics appealed to him, such as Loony Lou, as Michael affectionately called him, who must have been all of seventy. With silver hair flowing down his back and a silver beard touching his chest, Lou was never without his personal stereo, purple shorts and purple socks. In the foulest of weather, he still wore the same ensemble. Michael often wondered if it was an indication of his own mental state that Loony Lou made more sense to him than any of the others.

He was watching Lou cruising past the paddling pool, crashing guitars blaring from his headset, when he heard Johnson say, 'Who the hell did it?' Michael glanced at Cody, who looked faintly sick.

'Let's get away from these bloody people, Carl,' Cody said irritably. 'Just let's get to a quieter spot.'

They walked up the steps and back onto the promenade and Johnson looked thunderous. 'Let's sit down,' he suggested, pointing to an empty bench. He lit a cigarette and stared thoughtfully out to sea, as Cody sat down close to him. Michael, still feeling like an intruder, sat a little further away, nervously anticipating the inevitable explosion. 'Who did it, Steve?' Johnson repeated. Cody was mopping his face and neck with his handkerchief, but the sweat kept coming. 'The old man,' he blurted, as if saying it quickly would somehow soften the blow.

Johnson was devastated. 'Jack? I don't fucking believe it. Why?'

'It was an accident,' Cody said nervously. 'Dennis told me.'

Johnson looked suspicious. 'So how come he told you? Why would Dennis betray his own father?'

'He wants to do a deal with you, Carl.'

Johnson nodded. 'He does, does he?'

Cody put a hand on Johnson's shoulder and said, 'I'm sorry, mate, I really am. I've been dreading telling you this. I've been trying to find the right way, but . . .' He spread his hands in desperation.

'What do you mean, an accident?' Johnson asked. He was raising his voice, making Cody feel even more uncomfortable.

'Carl, keep it down, for Christ's sake.'

'Get on with it, Steve. What the hell happened? What did he do to her?'

Cody was wincing, his eyes darting in all directions at the passers-by. 'Carl,' he fumbled, 'I know how much the old man means to you . . .'

'Just tell me!' Johnson snapped.

Cody looked at Michael uneasily, clearly unhappy about his presence. He paused for a few moments, waiting for a smartly dressed old man to shuffle past. 'You know he always had a thing about Rose,' he said uncomfortably. 'He was always . . . well, you know, cuddling her and patting her in that oily way of his.'

'Yeah, I know,' Johnson said. 'He cuddled and patted anything in a skirt. What are you saying – he raped her or something?'

Cody sighed impatiently and rubbed his face. 'Listen, Carl, I'm sorry, but I just don't think Michael should be here. This is business. This is heavy stuff.'

Johnson clenched a fist in frustration and said, 'Just tell me what happened, Steve. Michael stays, so keep talking.'

Cody shakily lit a cigarette and coughed. 'He and Dennis dropped in on her the night after you left for Scotland with Janice. He brought her a bottle of vodka.'

Johnson groaned and lowered his head. 'Oh Christ, she'd only got home from the clinic the day before.'

'I know,' Cody said sadly. 'According to Dennis, Rose was really down in the dumps. The old man kept giving her all that crap about "one little drink won't hurt" and she kept saying she couldn't. Denny told me he started to feel really uncomfortable. He said the old man had told him they were only dropping in to see how Rose was. Then Jack gets out the vodka and some glasses, and Dennis knew something ugly was going to happen. He kept telling Jack they should go and they got into a big argument. Rose broke it up and Denny said he was leaving and went home. He was staying at the old man's place that night, and Jack woke him up at about three in the morning. He staggered in drunk and Denny said he was absolutely soaked through. I mean, it's rare for the old man to show any emotion, but Denny reckons he was in a blind panic. Then the old man slumps down in a chair and starts crying. Denny kept asking what was wrong, but Jack couldn't pull himself together...'

'Get to it, Steve,' Johnson said quietly. His head was still bowed and the sudden greying of the sky in the last five minutes or so reflected the terrible mood that prevailed. Michael saw what he thought was a raindrop gently explode on Johnson's shoe, and then realised with a strange horror that it was a tear. For one rare moment, Johnson was broken, and Michael couldn't handle it. He glanced briefly at Johnson and then looked out to sea, swallowing hard. He felt sadness and anger and a raging desire to go out and kill Jack Fossey, even though he had never met the man. To his shame, he also felt cheated. He and other mortals were allowed to cry, but not the Carl Johnsons of this world. If the hero falls off his horse, who's left to save the day?

'Are you okay, Carl?' Cody asked.

'Yes, I'm fucking okay,' Johnson spat, clearly furious with himself for losing control. 'Did the bastard drown her?'

Cody shrugged. 'He told Denny it was accidental. They drank vodka all through the night. Rose was out of her brain and told the old man she wanted to go down to the beach and take a swim. So he takes her down by the West Pier and he ... well, it just happened. He was pretty far out himself by that time, and he just got emotional and told Rose he loved her and all that. She was in the water with her clothes still on, and the old man followed her in and just got carried away. Rose panicked and started screaming and...'

'And he killed her,' Johnson said.

'Well, not exactly. Rose tried to swim away from him but got into trouble. She started gasping for air and ... well, I suppose it was the booze and being frightened ... she just went under and never came up again. Anyway, that was Jack's version.'

'And the bastard left her to die. It amounts to the same thing. Uncle Jack's highly proficient at destroying people.' Johnson faced Cody with red and watery eyes and said, 'You've never seen that side of the old bastard, have you? You've only known him since he adopted his kindly grandfather image.'

'He still scares the shit out of me,' Cody admitted.

'So he should. I remember one time, about fifteen years ago, when he had this kid called Eddie working for him. He was only about twenty-one, twenty-two, just a bloody errand boy. He made a mess of a certain job – it was so damn trivial, I can't even remember what he did now – and the old man called him in. He had a hamburger bar in Preston Street in those days, and we were going over some figures in the back room. So the kid comes in and starts apologising profusely – the poor little bastard was almost crying – and the old man tells him he can't tolerate mistakes. All that heavy shit, you know? It was like he was reading a script. "Put your right hand on the table," he says. And the kid just did it, like a bloody lemming. And the old man reaches inside his overcoat and pulls out this hammer, and smashes it down on the kid's hand. I'll never forget the noise it made and the kid's screams. In a weird sort of way, it was almost comical. He pulled this hammer from his coat like Tommy Cooper used to pull rabbits out of a hat. A fucking hammer, for Christ's sake.'

The mental picture of a man's hand being crushed suddenly made Michael feel terribly sick, and he quickly looked for somewhere to run to. But there was no hiding place, just thousands of milling people and the brutal heat that made him feel worse by the second. He remembered that he hadn't eaten again this morning, and the once soothing whisky was now having its revenge. He was beginning to sweat heavily again and silently cursed his commitment to refrain from drinking. The awful feeling of wanting to vomit was complemented by a sudden rush to the bowels, yet he was damned if he was going to embarrass himself in such tough company. Hearty swallowing and the application of muscle pressure in the appropriate places enabled the crisis to quickly pass, as Johnson concluded the chilling story.

'I've broken bones and I've killed men, Steve. But I remember that above everything else. It was so utterly cold and pointless, and you only had to look into the old man's eyes to see he was enjoying every moment of it.'

'What happened to Eddie?' Michael asked.

Cody looked at him as if he had gatecrashed a private party, but Johnson just grinned and said, 'The old man told him to piss off, so he went home to his mum and dad and worked in his dad's bakery. Best move the poor little bugger ever made, if you ask me.'

'What do you want me to do, Carl?' Cody asked.

'Kill the bastard,' Johnson said.

Cody looked horrified. 'What ... what, you mean, *me*?'

Johnson looked at him wearily. 'I was being sarcastic, Steve. I'll take care of that problem, all in good time. So Dennis wants to speak to me, does he? What's he up to?'

'Best he tells you that, Carl,' Cody said.

Michael wondered why Cody had ever entered such a vicious line of work, since he was the same old bully boy. At school, he had been no less cunning and crafty, masquerading as a street tough, but only picking on those he felt sure he could beat. There had once been a pitiful misfit called Elwick, a brilliant academic who was barracked unmercifully for his dislike of any form of physical activity. It was the old grammar school mentality. If you didn't excel at rugby and participate in shower-room obscenities, you didn't belong. Most of the other boys would tease Elwick but leave it at that. Cody, however, took a sickening pleasure in applying beatings and various forms of humiliation. Then came the day when he met one of his own ilk, a brooding thug called Bigsby, and Michael witnessed the incident across the crowded recreation area. For no apparent reason, Bigsby walked up to Cody and began pushing and punching him. Michael had never forgotten the look of horror on Cody's face, nor the embarrassing manner in which he had practically begged Bigsby for mercy.

Now Cody was a bully in a suit, refined and mature at first sight, yet there was little real difference between the man and the boy.

'Do you know Nino's restaurant in Preston Street?' Johnson asked him.

Cody nodded. 'I've never been there, but I know it.'

'It's small, and nice and quiet. Not far from where the old man's place used to be, which is rather fitting. We can talk there. Book a table for three for about ten tonight.'

'Okay. The old man's in Glasgow until late Monday.'

'Good. I've got some other things to take care of first, anyway. Go on, you'd better get going.'

As Cody got to his feet, he looked uneasily at Michael again and said to Johnson, 'Are you two going to stay here for a while, then?' He was clearly afraid he was going to miss something important. Johnson didn't answer. Cody hovered for a few seconds, then nodded uncertainly and made off towards the Palace Pier.

Johnson and Michael sat quietly for a few minutes, with Johnson brooding and Michael struggling for something appropriate to say. 'I'll see what Dennis has to say tonight,' Johnson said thoughtfully. 'It's best you don't come along, Michael. Can you find something to do tonight?'

'Sure, no problem.'

'I don't mean get pissed, okay?'

'I won't,' Michael smiled. 'I don't want to fuss, Carl, but . . . well, are you all right?'

Johnson nodded and smiled softly. 'Yeah, I'm all right. I want to see Wendy tomorrow, Michael. I'm greatly concerned about Janice. Perhaps you'd be good enough to come along with me. Janice and me share the same characteristics and we always need a referee.'

'Sure,' Michael said. 'What about Jack Fossey, Carl? What are you going to do?'

'I've got a few ideas. Steve was right, you know. The old man has been like a father to me. I trusted the bastard, Michael – a lot more than I ever trusted my real father. He once called me the son he'd never had, in front of Dennis. I mean, he's never got on with Dennis. Christ, it was embarrassing. Dennis is a soft sod, but I've always felt embarrassed for him when we've been in Jack's company. The old man just humiliates him.' Johnson sighed and bowed his head again. 'Poor Rose. We tried everything to get her off the drink. Hypnotism, even stomach implants. She could never quite get the monkey off her back. That's why it's important to me that you beat this problem of yours, Michael. I've seen the absolute misery it can cause, what with Rose and my old man. Janice didn't help. She was a difficult kid from the start and that just put more strain on Rose.' He grinned weakly, and said, 'Stupid, isn't it? I'm in a business like this, and I can't even control my own daughter.'

'Does anybody else know she's staying with Wendy?' Michael asked.

'No. Not Steve or anyone. I send them both money regularly. Wendy works as a part-time cleaner, just to get herself out. Janice is still at school, or at least she was. She likes the boys too much, that's my worry. I told Wendy to keep a tight rein on her, but . . . Anyway, I'll call her again when I get back to the hotel. They're probably out shopping. That's what they like to do on Saturdays.' Johnson gave Michael a hard look and asked, 'Are you sure you're going to be all right yourself?'

'Yes, why?'

'Because you're sweating like hell again and it's not the heat.'

'I don't feel so good, actually,' Michael said. 'I think I might have a sleep for a couple of hours when we get back. I'm not going to drink, Carl, honestly. I'm determined not to.'

Johnson nodded. 'Okay, I believe you. Come on, let's get something to eat. That's what you need more than anything else.'

5

Saturday evening, and Michael couldn't drink. The thought filled him with gloom. His promise to Johnson gave him strength, and he was determined to honour it, but how he yearned for a cold beer or a slug of whisky. Just one. It was eight-thirty and he didn't know what to do.

He set off in the direction of the West Pier, still dwelling on Cody's tale of Rose and Jack Fossey on that mad and tragic night. He looked out at the sea, quiet and serene at this time, and tried to picture the drama unfolding. There was something about the sea that haunted and frightened Michael. He thought of Dennis Wilson, the Beach Boys drummer, who had been buried at sea after a drowning accident in 1983. For Michael, there was no romance in that. The sea struck him as a terribly cold and lonely burial ground, and drowning a terrible way to die.

He trudged along aimlessly, studying the happy, mischievous faces of the Saturday night revellers, and wishing he could be a part of it. Alcohol had become his lifeblood, and life without it was grey and tedious and frightening. He now felt terribly detached from the world around him, having forgotten how to enjoy himself by natural means. At least the sweating had stopped, and the evening air was pleasantly cool.

Yet as he walked and pondered the events of the day, Michael was tormented by fear and doubt. He had committed himself to this adventure while still fired up from his last whisky. Now the magic had worn off, like all quick cures for all evils, and he could feel his courage slipping away at the same time.

Johnson was right. Why pretend he was somebody he wasn't? Normally, he had trouble surviving the average day. Now he couldn't even make it through the evening. Yet in one devil-may-care moment he had thrown his hat into an arena populated by violent men incapable of guilt, who smashed through their problems with hammers and guns.

Michael had drifted quite a way past the Cannon bar, one of his favourite watering holes, when he reached breaking point. He was infuriated by his doubts and indecisiveness, the feelings of weakness and humility that were the price of withdrawal. He stopped and looked back at the Cannon, at all the happy people sitting outside, with their beers and wines and whiskies sparkling under the lights.

Tomorrow, when the jitters had hopefully subsided, he would walk into a pub and order a coke or an orange juice, anything but booze. He would beat this problem, but not by running away from the source of it. He adored pubs for their atmosphere, their smells, and their rich mix of people. He loved to sit in a quiet corner, drinking beer and studying the characters around him, listening in to their conversations. It fuelled his inspiration as a writer and provided a glorious escape from the harsh world outside. The way Michael saw it, if he gave up pubs as well as booze, it would be an admission that he couldn't handle the problem.

He was tempted to make a start now, but his trembling hands advised him otherwise. There was nothing more embarrassing than getting to the bar and being unable to lift your first pint off the deck. It had happened the first time in the company of his boss, a kindly man named Alf Jardine, when Michael's hand had not so much trembled as vibrated and he had slopped beer everywhere. The sweat was pouring out of him and he pleaded chronic flu. Alf Jardine smiled and sent him home, and never discussed the matter further. But Alf was a worldly, wise old bird, and Michael knew he had been found out.

The seed had been planted in his brain and his first pint of the day had since become another great obstacle in his life; even on those rare occasions when he hadn't drunk excessively the night before. He knew that much of it was imaginary, but it had become such an immense barrier that it preyed on his mind from the time he woke up in the morning. At lunch time, he would meet up with Alf and a few of the other guys at the office for a few beers in the local snooker club, and he would feel the shakes coming on beforehand and start counting the minutes. This necessitated a quick visit to a favourite boozer in a conveniently discreet spot, where Michael would gulp down a fast pint to give himself confidence. He had perfected this routine, telling Alf that he had to pick up some cigarettes and would join the gang later. And it depressed him. He hated himself for it.

Reluctantly, Michael turned and walked on, crossing the road and heading straight for the West Pier. He had a curious liking for this decaying old lady, and it saddened him that such a grand landmark had been allowed to deteriorate. It was actually two piers now, one section having fallen away, yet Michael found it strangely beautiful, more charismatic in its own peculiar way than the glamorous Palace Pier, which throbbed with life. The West Pier, eerie and dying by the minute, stretched out to sea like a giant ghost.

Michael surveyed the rotting structure for a few minutes and then walked down the steps and onto the beach. Most of the day trippers had drifted off home and the beach was now relatively empty. A gang of kids was skateboarding on the lower promenade, risking life and limb hurling themselves from a makeshift ramp, and further up the beach people were dotted about in various states of repose, some looking as if they'd died.

Michael found himself a quiet spot and sat down. He had never fallen in love with Brighton beach. It was all stones and pebbles and shingle, not the kind you found in Beach Boys folklore. He held out his hands and they had seemed to steady a little. There was an empty beer can by his side, and he was thinking how bloody cruel life could be when a voice behind him boomed 'JESUS!'

Hypersensitive in his current state, Michael jumped violently and turned just in time to see a mountain of a man about to fall on him. He quickly rolled to one side as the man fell face first into the stones with an almighty crunch. For a few moments he didn't move a muscle, and Michael stared at him anxiously. The big fellow must have been all of 6' 6", and his heavily bearded face was pressed flat against the stones. He had a mane of yellow hair like General Custer, and he was dressed in a long, black trenchcoat, faded jeans and trainers. He was obviously a man of the road, but was shabby rather than dirty, and didn't appear to have hit rock bottom yet. There was no discernible smell, no sign of fleas. Clutched firmly in his right hand, despite his heavy fall, was a half full bottle of Scotch. At least the man had his priorities in order and Michael admired that. Skilful drunks might break their bones, but they never break their bottles.

Nevertheless, Michael didn't need this. The hulk beside him was too close to home, too frightening a reminder of the kind of man he could so easily be. He was about to get up and quietly walk away, when the big fellow began laughing uncontrollably. He lifted his head and squinted at Michael.

'Sorry, old son, I lost my balance. Pissed again, I'm afraid.' His voice was deep and gruff, probably from too much smoking. He had a South London accent, and Michael thought he looked and sounded vaguely familiar. The big fellow rolled over and awkwardly struggled up into a sitting position. He held up the bottle and said, 'Christ, I had a few before I even started this one. Some days you just get the taste for it. Neil Franklin...' He extended a big shovel of a hand, and Michael gingerly shook it, wondering if he'd catch something.

'Michael Rossi.'

'Pleased to meet you, Mike. Wanna drink?'

'No, I can't,' Michael said quickly. 'I mean, I er...'

Franklin chuckled knowingly as he rolled a cigarette. 'Got some problems yourself, right? Shit, you don't have to explain it. I can't talk.' He smiled, revealing surprisingly clean teeth. Behind the rough beard and dishevelled appearance, Franklin was actually quite a handsome man. Michael guessed he was around forty-five or forty-six. His blue eyes were his most striking feature, bleary from too much drink, but still penetrating. Michael had definitely seen those eyes before.

'To be honest with you, I'm not finding it easy,' Michael laughed. Suddenly, he felt comfortable in Franklin's presence. It was a relief to confide in a fellow drinker, even though he wasn't in his league.

'Well, you're one step ahead of me, kiddo,' Franklin said. 'I've never even tried to jack it in. It'll probably kill me, but what the hell.' He took a hefty swig from the bottle and made a face. 'This isn't my favourite, mind you. Too bloody harsh. I'm a malt whisky man when I've got the choice.'

Michael gestured at Franklin's coat and his thick sweater beneath. 'Aren't you hot in all that gear?'

'Hot as shit,' Franklin said, coughing as he took his first drag. 'But I can't afford a fuckin' wardrobe to hang 'em up in.' The air filled with the delicious smell of Old Holborn as he exploded into laughter again and playfully elbowed Michael in the shoulder. 'I'm sleeping in my sister's spare room at the moment. She's got a place up at Clifton Terrace. She lets me stay there when I'm in Brighton. I used to live here, but I haven't been here for some time now. My sister feels sorry for me, silly cow.' His speech was slightly slurred, but he was coherent and worldly wise.

'Do I know you, Neil?' Michael asked. 'I don't think we've met before, but I've seen you somewhere.'

Franklin grinned and asked, 'Are you a sporting man?'

'Well, I do a fair bit of freelance writing on it . . . boxing, golf, and football mainly.'

Still the penny didn't drop, until Franklin said, 'My fighting name was Neil Shannon.'

Michael clapped his hands. 'My God, that's it! Neil Shannon! I saw your last fight on TV in . . .' He stopped, quite unintentionally, as he looked hard at Neil Franklin for the first time and remembered Neil Shannon.

'Yeah, I know what you're thinking,' Franklin said. 'What the hell happened, eh?'

'I'm sorry,' Michael said awkwardly. 'I didn't mean . . .'

Franklin waved a hand. 'Forget it. I didn't exactly turn out the way I wanted to. No point in bullshitting about it. Just don't blame the fight game for all this, okay? I'm not one of those dumb bastards who can't tell shit from clay and I'm not punchy. I became a piss artist all by myself, but there's nothing wrong with my brain, mate.'

He paused to take another slug of Scotch and continued. 'Listen, I was a big, mean looking fellow with a big punch. So the media hyped me up as some sort of monster who'd crawled out of the sewers and had a single aptitude for killing people. I could never stand all that bullshit. They even changed my surname because they reckoned Franklin was too boring and conservative. The fact is, I went to a poncy grammar school and did bloody well there. Could've gone to university.'

Michael had no reason to doubt Franklin's credentials. He was very obviously a highly intelligent man with deadly insight. Michael liked him. 'What went wrong, Neil?' he asked. The question wasn't meant to sound so blunt, but Franklin didn't seem offended by it.

'So many things,' he replied, his voice now tinged with sadness. 'I drifted in with the wrong crowd right from the start. Didn't need to. I had a perfectly good and sound upbringing. I just got bored easily. School bored me ... being shut in classrooms all day long, running here and there every time a bloody bell rang. I knew I could never work in an office, even though I got good grades in my exams. I didn't want to plod away like that until I was sixty-five. I had the get-rich-quick disease. Make a bundle and get the hell out, you know? I just wanted to have fun, Mike.'

The more Franklin talked, the more he intrigued Michael. There was an almost mystical quality to the man, as if he'd just dropped out of the sky.

'So you took up boxing,' Michael said.

'Yeah,' Franklin laughed. 'That was really the beginning of my disreputable life. I did pretty well in the amateurs. Reached the regional finals of the ABAs in 1967.'

'I know,' Michael said excitedly. 'You floored Tony Williams three times, and then they gave him a majority decision.'

'By Christ, you know your stuff,' Franklin said, impressed. 'Yeah, that's what pissed me off about the amateurs. Most of the judges were either blind or stupid. That was why I decided to turn pro. Some mistake that was.'

'I was only about twelve at the time,' Michael said, 'but I really thought you'd go all the way. You had a lot of trouble with your hands, didn't you?'

Franklin smiled. 'Yeah, I had brittle hands, but that was only part of it. I also had a lousy Jack-the-lad manager whose great ambition in life was to produce a British world heavyweight champion. Except he knew bugger all about boxing.'

'Leo Wright?'

'Leo Wright. It was all a game to Leo, a pleasant little hobby between building up his leisure empire.'

For the first time, Franklin showed anger. He held out a massive hand and clenched it into a fist. 'I made boxing my life. But I hooked up with Leo and he was no fight manager. You've seen my record, Mike. He threw me in over my head right from the start. I was fighting world-class Yanks after only a dozen fights. That's not unusual now, what with the scarcity of talent, but it was then.'

Michael nodded. 'It was a shame, Neil. Even against top talent like that, you gave a good account of yourself. With proper guidance . . .'

'Yeah, I know, I know,' Franklin sighed. He had obviously been told a million times how good he could have been. 'I just lost heart in the end. Started skipping training and staying out late at nights, drinking and whoring and messing around. Spent all the money I ever earned. I finally chucked it in 1976. I'd been treading water for years, and I was tired of getting smacked in the teeth and going nowhere fast. Leo threw me in with a New York puncher called Rory Pritchard, who beat the crap out of me for five rounds before the referee finally tumbled I was getting killed. I had to travel all the way to Buffalo to suffer that experience. I thought, bollocks, that's it.'

Michael studied Franklin's face. He had a small scar above his left eyebrow and his nose had been slightly flattened, but there were no visible marks of his former trade. Fuelled by his beloved Scotch, he seemed to be warming to his role of storyteller. He was like something out of Steinbeck's *Cannery Row*. Once great and now fallen, but a character forever, the kind of man you could listen to all day and night.

'Don't get me wrong,' he continued. 'Leo had a good heart. He wasn't a malicious man. I mean, he never screwed me where money was concerned. The emotional old sod even cried in my dressing-room after the Pritchard fight. He just knew nothing about boxing. And he knew a lot of shady people. That's how I got into trouble after I quit the fight game.'

'I lost track of your career after you retired,' Michael said. 'Until about 1978 when you...' He didn't quite know how to say it, and Franklin was amused by his attempt at subtlety.

'When I was banged up for five years,' he interjected. 'Mike, you're a polite man, but there's no need to overdo it. I've never been afraid to acknowledge the truth. It was 1979, actually.'

'I've never known all the details,' Michael said. 'What happened exactly?'

'I knifed a guy. I didn't kill him. Didn't even mean to knife him, for that matter. By that time, I was living down here. I had a flat in the Seven Dials area. My life back in London had started going wrong when I retired from boxing. That's when I started hitting the bottle. I didn't know what the hell to do with myself. I just stayed at home and drank. Drank away what little money I had left. One morning, Leo paid me a surprise visit and found me stretched out on the floor with three empty bottles. He couldn't get over it. He cleaned me up, poured coffee down me, and wished me a happy birthday. I asked him what he was talking about. I didn't even know it was my damn birthday.'

Michael felt a sudden chill. He could have been listening to an account of his own experience with Johnson earlier that day. In a strange way, he found that hearing about such a thing was even worse than living it. He remembered a Christmas office party about ten years ago, when he got badly drunk and had to be helped onto his bus home. Once aboard, he had proceeded to literally crawl up the stairs. Surprisingly, he remembered every detail of that incident, yet what had hurt him most was returning to work a week later and hearing the different accounts of his drunken adventure from his friends.

Franklin yawned and rubbed his eyes, and wearily planted his bottle in the stones in front of him. 'Better knock it off for a bit. I have to go through the motions of being respectable when I'm staying with my sister. Anyway, Leo gave me this big lecture on life in general and told me I'd kill myself if I didn't get off my arse and do something. And he was right of course. He suggested a complete change of scene and I thought that was a good idea. There were too many distractions in London. Too many friends and too many invitations to go out and party. He told me he had this long-time friend in Brighton and that this guy would fix me up with a job. So I thought, what the hell, and made the move. Jesus, Mike, if only I could turn back the clock. You know who the friend turned out to be?'

Michael, totally mesmerised by now, simply shook his head.

'Jack Fossey. You must have heard of Jack Fossey.'

Michael could scarcely believe it. It was as if all this was meant to be. 'Yes, I've heard of him,' he said, trying to mask his surprise.

'So had I,' said Franklin. 'Stories, rumours, the usual shit you hear about villains. Leo told me that most of it was myth, that Fossey was an old-fashioned bad guy who looked after his mother and never bothered the man in the street. Fossey took me on as his minder, and I figured it would just be a matter of looking fearsome and occasionally giving someone a smack. Then he got me to start leaning on certain people, you know? He had people all over town paying him protection money, and I became one of his collectors. I mean, my heart was never in that kind of thing. I could never just hit anyone for no good reason. There was this Indian guy – Indian or Pakistani, I don't know – who ran this paper shop not far from the station. He had a lot of guts and I admired him. We used to go through the same performance every time. He'd cough up the money eventually, but not before he'd gone through his usual routine of slagging Fossey off. Called him all the names under the sun in that funny little accent of his. He knew he could get away with it with me.

'I think he sort of liked me, if that's possible. Then one day he just freaked. I went in there and his two little kids were playing up – being a nuisance and running around the shop and all that – and his old lady was pregnant again. That was the first time I'd ever seen his wife, and he suddenly let rip at me, calling me a bastard and a bloodsucker and everything. The next thing I know, he's waving this bloody great knife at me and his old lady's screaming at him to put it down. I was telling him to calm down, but Christ, I'm no shrink. Then he took a swing at me and slashed my arm and there's blood splashing everywhere. All those years in the ring, and I get my worst cut from a five-foot shopkeeper. I managed to wrestle the knife off him, but he was berserk by that time. He was picking up packets of cornflakes and jars of stuff and hurling them at me, and then he jumped on me. I brought the knife up instinctively – I swear to God it was a reflex action – and he ran straight onto it. Straight in the gut. That's how it happened, I swear. Thank Christ, I didn't kill the guy. It was touch and go for a time, but he pulled through. Fossey let me hang for that.'

'What do you mean?' Michael asked.

'The bastard completely disowned me, that's what I mean. Him and his shit son, Dennis, who kept telling me how highly the old man regarded me.' Forgetting his promise of a minute ago, Franklin picked up his bottle and took another long pull. 'I mean, I did the honourable thing in court. Had to. The Indian wasn't one of those scared witnesses. He found his courage when he had a go at me in the shop, and there was no stopping him after that. He sprayed Fossey's name all over the court. I kept denying I knew Jack, lied my balls off for the old man. He'd always seemed to like me, told me I'd always have a place in his set-up, and I reckoned it would be like it is in the movies. I'd do my stretch, be a model prisoner, and then I'd be looked after when I got out.'

Franklin shook his head. 'Nothing. Absolutely fuck all. I should have left it at that, but I was bitter, and like a fool I went to see Fossey when I got out. I was raging, and I didn't give a damn how powerful or influential the guy was. I walked into his office and he greeted me as if I'd never been away. All the old greasy charm. I'm sure that guy's got grease for blood. He knew what I was there for, and I heard the door click behind me, and two of his favourite henchmen were standing there, looking terribly sombre. Kenny Carter and Dave Richards. A real pair of bone brains and nasty bastards with it.

'I figured I was in for a spanking anyway, so I told Fossey what I thought of him. He stopped smiling and you should have seen the look on his face, Michael. It was something beyond ordinary anger, or even fury. The guy looked as if he wanted to literally tear me apart. Then one of the others cracked me over the head and I was only vaguely aware of what was going on for the next few minutes. They were dragging me down the stairs, and my head was only just starting to clear when the bastards went to work on me. I caught

Richards with a wild punch, but I didn't stand a bloody chance. They beat the shit out of me. I ended up in casualty, lost a ton of blood. I couldn't believe it when I first saw my face in the hospital. I'd have scared the crap out of the Phantom of the Opera. The doctor told me I was lucky to be alive. They'd broken bones in every part of my body. I still get aches and pains even now.'

'Didn't you report it to the police?' Michael asked.

Franklin gave him a funny look. 'What, and get killed the next time around? Nah, you can't fight them like that, mate. I'd love nothing more than to get Fossey in a room on his own – not to mention that dick-head son of his – but I can't take on his army.' He shrugged and looked out to sea, a sad and haunted look on his face, as if wondering how things had ever come to this.

'Tell me,' Michael said, 'did you ever know Carl Johnson?'

Franklin turned his head quickly and looked surprised. 'Yeah, I knew Carl. He used to help me out a lot. Gave me money when I was down in the dumps. Used to come and see me at my sister's place. Bloody good man, Carl. Tragic about his wife. Rose was a lovely kid. What made you ask?'

'Oh, we were friends at school,' Michael said, being purposely vague. 'I haven't seen him for some time, but I heard he works for Fossey.'

'Yeah,' Franklin smiled. 'I could never understand why a smart man like Carl stayed with Fossey. Mind you, the old man loved him. Carl could do no wrong in his book.'

'What does he do?'

'Carl? Don't know what he's doing now, kiddo. It's been so long since I last saw him. I was never that close to the inner sanctum, anyway. Carl was like a ghost, though. He seemed to have pretty much of a free hand. He'd come, he'd go, and you'd hear all sorts of rumours.' Franklin made a motion, like a man firing a gun. 'Troubleshooter mainly, I think. Any awkward customers, and Carl's the guy who's called in to bang 'em out. That's what I heard, anyway.'

Michael nodded, taking in everything, and turning it all over in his mind. He stayed on the beach chatting to Franklin until around eleven that night, feeling wonderful as Brighton's lights twinkled and a cool breeze blew in off the sea. Franklin had been his antidote. Michael had survived these crucial hours without a drink and his hands had steadied again. To his surprise, the fears that had gripped him in the early part of the evening had also gone. Franklin had given him courage, and he was again filled with that childish and primitive desire to go out and cut Jack Fossey down for all the misery he had caused.

Just before Michael got up to go, Franklin tapped him on the arm and said, 'Listen, don't think I'm always like this. I have my good days, you know. I've still got some nice clothes back at my sister's and I don't get pissed all the time. The doctor diagnosed me as a binge drinker. I go on benders and then straighten out again – sometimes for weeks at a time.' He looked appealingly at Michael, as if feeling that he'd betrayed himself by his earlier admissions.

Michael smiled. 'That's my problem too, Neil. Don't worry about it.'

Franklin shivered and said, 'It's the dreams I can't stand, Michael.'

'Dreams?'

'Nightmares, more accurately. I've been having them on and off for about two years. Must be the booze finally getting to my brain. I mean, terrifying bloody nightmares, you know? You forget normal dreams after a while, but these things I get . . . they linger in my mind for days. I never believed in all that crap about recurring dreams, but there's one I get that's nearly always the same. Never exactly the same, you understand. There are always variations. But the basic scenario never changes.' Franklin stopped and took a drink, his blue eyes glazed as if he'd suddenly been knifed. Michael waited for him to elaborate, but nothing came.

'What scenario?' he asked, feeling suddenly intrusive.

Franklin answered him immediately, yet he was talking to himself now, oblivious of Michael, oblivious of everything. 'I'm lying on the beach just down there, and I'm always conscious of . . . of having been injured in some way. I'm bleeding, always bleeding. The blood's running into my eyes and I can't see properly. It's night time, but I'm sweating like hell. I'm trying to get to my feet and my body won't respond. It's as if I'm being held down. Then I suddenly see this guy out at sea. I'm wiping the blood out of my eyes and struggling to see him, and he seems to be waving at me. Waving, or doing something with his arms. Then everything sort of magically snaps into focus. It's like my eyes are a camera, zooming in on this guy. He's staring straight at me, his eyes wide open and almost shining like lights. He looks absolutely terrified and I'm scared shitless myself. And then I'm on my feet and running up the beach, terrified, and the blood starts running into my eyes again and I can't see in front of me. That's when it usually ends, and it's the same every time. I'm sitting up awake again and the sweat's running off me like water. God alone knows what it's all about. Perhaps I'm finally going mad.'

'Is it a face you recognise?' Michael asked.

'No. I mean, it's a face, but I'm only ever conscious of the eyes . . . that look of sheer panic in those eyes. He's frightened of me and I'm frightened of him. Ah shit, it's got to go away eventually.'

'Probably.' Michael smiled. 'Are you going back to your sister's tonight, then?'

'Yeah. Don't worry about me, kiddo. I'll stay here for a while longer, then make my way back. Look after yourself, okay?' He grabbed Michael's hand and shook it vigorously. 'I might be around here tomorrow. I don't know yet.'

'I hope we get to see each other again,' Michael said. He wanted to go further and tell Franklin how much he liked him, but remembered how so many previous first acquaintances had faded back into the landscape. Some people, however nice and for whatever reason, simply don't want to see you a second time. Nevertheless, Michael hurriedly took out a scrap of paper, wrote down his telephone number, and said, 'Listen, if you want a chat any time, ring me. I mean it.'

Franklin took the note and simply nodded and smiled and looked out to sea again; alone once more with his whisky, his thoughts and his nightmares.

Michael felt strongly linked to Franklin as he made his way back to the Grand Hotel that night, convinced that their meeting had been no accident. Perhaps it was because, against all logic, he felt considerably happier and more relaxed than he had done in some time. From somewhere, carried on the breeze, he could hear Scott

Joplin's hauntingly beautiful 'Maple Leaf Rag', that gorgeous piano sounding more beautiful than ever.

For once in his life, Michael was looking forward to tomorrow.

6

Carl Johnson had always had mixed feelings about Dennis Fossey. In a sense, Dennis was one of life's quietly tragic characters, yet not a man to be entirely pitied. Single, wealthy, and blessed with classic dark looks, he certainly looked the part of the dream heir to his father's throne; a villain who looked like a saint. His thick, brown sun-streaked hair was parted in the middle and framed a handsome face, and his twinkling brown eyes turned many a woman's head. Slim and muscled, he'd have made a perfect leading man in any Hollywood production.

However, the image belied the truth. Dennis looked tough and tried to act tough, but he was weak and vain, not a leader of men. He reminded Johnson of a manufactured boxer. The physique and the charisma were mightily impressive, but they couldn't mask the weak links or the lack of fighting instinct.

In that way, Dennis was the antithesis of his father. Weakness was a trait which Jack Fossey either couldn't or wouldn't understand, the reason why his only son had always been an embarrassment to him. All his life, Dennis had been pushed, bullied and humiliated by his father, punished constantly for not living up to the old man's expectations. It was one of life's familiar scenarios, the upshot being that Dennis Fossey was a frightened boy in the body of a thirty-eight year old man.

Johnson sympathised with him in that respect, yet he shared Jack Fossey's contempt for Dennis's inability to stand up and hit back. That contempt was now growing by the second as he faced Dennis across the table at Nino's, and listened to the

51

childlike carping of a weak and shallow man.

Dennis had a plan, Dennis was going to assert himself and at last take his revenge. But Dennis was still a whinger, a coward pretending to be brave. Johnson picked half-heartedly at his tagliatelle, growing more impatient by the second. It was his favourite meal here, but everything was sticking in his throat on this rotten day. Even Nino's itself, which he had long liked for its relaxed atmosphere, seemed to be suffocating him tonight.

It was around half past ten and the atmosphere was funereal anyway, since he, Dennis and Cody were now the only people there. Cody was sitting next to Dennis, nodding solemnly at his every word between great gulps of food, and Johnson wondered which man was working the other with the foot pump. Dennis had told the story of Rose's death and was apologising for what seemed like the umpteenth time. He seemed full of remorse, his voice faltering every once in a while as the weight of guilt apparently overwhelmed him. It was a show of emotion which was two years late and not entirely convincing.

What irked Johnson especially was Dennis's failure to look him in the eye. Dennis would address a certain spot on your shoulder as he spoke, and Johnson could never determine whether that habit in people was due to shyness or deviousness.

In the meantime, Cody was loudly slurping white wine and pigging his way through his meal with his usual lack of grace and etiquette. That was another habit that infuriated Johnson. Cody ate food as if it had just been invented.

'I just wanted to get all of this out in the open and do something about it,' said Dennis.

'For me, or for yourself?' Johnson enquired curtly.

'Come on, Carl, give me a break.'

'Two years,' Johnson said. 'You waited two fucking years before you finally found the balls to tell me the truth, and now I'm supposed to say "Wow, thanks Denny, and what can I do for you?" You're pathetic, Dennis. I know the old man never made things easy for you, but you've hardly helped yourself over the years.'

'All right, all right,' Dennis snapped, slamming down his knife and fork. He leaned across the table. 'Don't you think I'm ashamed of all that, Carl? But Jesus Christ, the old man never gave me a chance from day one.' He was beginning to shout, as many mice-like men do when their frustrations finally boil over, and Johnson raised a hand. He summoned the waiter, a young and handsome man in his twenties, who had been casting anxious looks at the impending storm on table three.

'Son, could you fetch Nino for me, please?' Johnson asked.

'Yes, sir,' the waiter said nervously, as if expecting one of the three men to bury a knife in his waistcoat.

'Just hold it down for a minute,' Johnson told Dennis.

Nino soon emerged from the kitchen area at the back. He was a short, balding, rotund man with sad eyes and a thick moustache which did nothing for his natural hang-dog expression. His sombre visage cloaked a razor sharp wit. 'Hey, Carl, how are you?' he enquired cheerfully, but without a hint of a smile. He was the real McCoy, yet he almost sounded like somebody impersonating an Italian.

'Fine, Nino, fine. Listen, can you close the place up? We've got some serious business to discuss.'

Nino looked even more despondent and gestured around the restaurant. 'On a Saturday night when business is so good?'

Johnson grinned. 'I'll recompense you, don't worry.'

Nino shrugged and spread his arms and said, 'What the hell. The economy's dead and people aren't spending money anyway. These days they buy a takeaway and watch a video Saturday nights. How can I compete with Clint Eastwood and a bucket of Kentucky fried?' He waddled over to the main door, which was open to let in what little breeze there was, and shouted back over his shoulder, 'Sandro, you can go home now. Go out the back way.'

'Thanks, Nino,' the waiter said, an out-and-out cockney, 'I'll see what me girlfriend's up to.' The young man headed off and Nino waddled back and shrugged again.

'You hear that?' he said to Johnson. 'The kid looks like Robert De Niro and talks like Michael Caine. He was brought up in Lewisham and he's taking refresher courses in Italian. I'll leave you guys to it. Don't wreck the furniture.'

Nobody spoke for a while and then Dennis took a slug of wine and said, 'He bought me a pair of boxing gloves for my fourth birthday.'

'Who?' Cody asked, puzzled. He was stuffing his mouth with the last of the bread rolls, crumbs falling down his shirt every time he took a bite.

'The old man. His idol was Rocky Marciano, so he decided he'd rear a heavyweight champion of his own. He was always forcing me to do things I didn't want to do. He's still got a picture of me in those boxing gloves. A four-year old kid with proud daddy standing beside him. It's pathetic.'

Johnson shifted restlessly. 'My heart bleeds for you, Dennis.'

Dennis slammed a fist on the table, making Cody jump. 'It damn well ought to. The old man never gave me a chance. I never had the freedom of choice in anything. It was always what *he* wanted. You think I'm weak, but I was under the gun from the day I was born. My childhood stank. He bullied me all the time, physically and mentally. He treated me like he treated his enemies. If I stepped out of line, I got whacked – damn hard. The man was an ogre. He built an empire and he expected me to be as good as he was. You can't put that kind of pressure on a kid, Carl.'

'All right,' Johnson said angrily, 'but you've been a man now for years, and things still haven't changed. You still jump whenever the old man snaps his fingers.'

Dennis shook his head. 'Things are about to change, Carl, for the benefit of all of us. I told you that.'

'Listen to Denny, Carl,' Cody said.

'Yeah, I'm listening,' Johnson sighed. He motioned at the crumbs on the table in front of Cody and said, 'Clear that shit up, will you?' Cody, looking surprised and hurt, began to collect the crumbs into a neat little pile.

Dennis slumped back in his chair, like a losing fighter about to give it one last try. 'Carl, you can think whatever you like about me. But I'm sick of the way things are and I'm going to change them. I'm not going to spend the rest of my life under my father's thumb. I've lived a lie for the last two years and I just can't take it any more. The night Rose died . . . I should have learned my lesson then. The old man showed me a side of his character I'd never seen before. I mean, as stupid as it sounds, I imagined he'd never cried before in all his life, not even as a kid. I'd seen him drunk before, but not to the point where he fell apart.'

'Yeah, Steve told me,' Johnson said bitterly. 'Were they tears of remorse, or was it just the booze?'

Dennis shrugged and shook his head. 'It was crazy, unreal. There's never a day when I don't think about it, Carl, and that's the truth. I heard this frantic banging at the front door and the old man just fell on me when I opened it. We both fell to the floor and he was in a terrible mess – absolutely soaked through and reeking of alcohol. Then he started ranting and screaming at me to close the door. He was panicking and punching me on the shoulder and going mad. I picked him up and bundled him into the living-room. I sat him down and asked him what the hell had happened. That's when he started crying, and I couldn't believe what I was seeing. I didn't know what to say or what to do. I felt so bloody awkward and embarrassed. I kept telling him to pull himself together and tell me what had happened, but he couldn't talk for crying. Then he bolted out of his chair and staggered over to the drinks cabinet. He was so pissed, he put his face through the window and cut himself to pieces.

'I shook him like hell and told him to tell me what was wrong. His forehead and cheeks were badly cut and his blood was spurting all over my shirt. I told him I'd better call an ambulance and he grabbed me and said he'd cut my balls off if I did. I mean, my own damn father threatened to cut my balls off. That's when he told me the story. That's when he told me about Rose. And yes, Carl, I was shit scared. The old man actually grabbed me by the throat at one point and promised he'd kill me if I ever told. He was crying his eyes out, bleeding like a sieve, hurling abuse . . .'

Dennis paused for a second, narrowing his eyes and working his hands like a photographer sizing up his next picture. 'He pressed his face right up to mine and all I could see was this mask of blood and this contorted mouth spitting obscenities. I vowed then I'd get even with the bastard. He hasn't mentioned the incident since. It's as if it never happened. But that hasn't changed his behaviour towards me. He deserves all he gets.'

Johnson was listening intently to all this, chin in hand, nodding occasionally, never taking his eyes off Dennis.

'Shortly before the old man left for Glasgow on Thursday,' Dennis continued, 'we had this big row. He was laying down orders and just generally being a shit, and I snapped. I mean, he's slipping, Carl. He's living in another age and the organisation's suffering. He's losing respect from our friends everywhere. I had it out with him and he went berserk all over again. He started all that pushing and shoving crap again, and I just couldn't take it any more. I hit him on the chin. I didn't plan to, it just happened. I knocked him flat on his back and I've never seen him look so shocked in all his life. I thought he was going to get up and rush me, but he got to his feet very slowly and just stared at me. He was fuming, but it seemed ages before he spoke. Then he told me I was finished – as his son, his heir, and all that melodramatic shit. He'd have probably given me the kiss of death if we were Italians. He said he'd discuss it further when he got back. He said big changes were going to be made and I wasn't going to be a part of it. In the meantime, I'm unofficially confined to Brighton.'

'My, my, the worm certainly has turned,' Johnson said.

'You can think whatever the hell you like, Carl,' Dennis said impatiently. 'I've told you the story. That's it. That's the way it is.'

Cody, ever the tough talker and too much a fan of American cop series, leaned right across the table as if there were two hundred other people in the restaurant, and said in a low voice, 'The old man's a liability, Carl. He's got to go, unless we're going to become a bloody laughing stock.'

'All right, all right,' Johnson said wearily. Turning to Dennis, he asked, 'What do you mean, you've been unofficially confined to Brighton? Are Jack's boys watching over you?'

Dennis nodded. 'A couple of the old guard, Kenny Carter and Dave Richards. I've seen them around from time to time. I haven't seen them tonight.'

'Yeah, well, that's not so bad. Carter and Richards couldn't find each other if they were in the same room. So now that we've finished commiserating with each other, Dennis, what do you intend to do about all this? Steve said you wanted to deal with me.'

Dennis looked uncomfortable once more, and made a face as he picked up his glass of wine and quickly put it down again. 'Steve, make us some real drinks, will you?'

'Yeah, sure, Denny,' Cody said. 'Scotch all round?'

Johnson and Dennis nodded, and Cody went to the bar directly behind them and poured three straight Scotches as noisily as only Cody could. Johnson lit a cigarette and exhaled heavily as Dennis stared hard at the table, waiting for the shot of alcohol that would make the next few minutes a little easier. Johnson was tired and furious. He was sick of the business he was in and contemptuous of the people who were a part of it. He missed Rose and now he was becoming increasingly worried about his daughter. Where was she? And where was Wendy? There was probably a simple explanation, but it was still something else to worry about. He had called them again from the hotel, and still there had been no answer. He wanted to drive to Greatstone right now, but everything was happening at the wrong time. He thought of his restaurant at Monterey, and of Janice and Michael and himself living the quiet life, far away from the grey and vicious present. Then Cody slammed the drinks on the table and it was business as usual again.

Dennis quickly picked up his glass and closed his eyes as he drank. The man who would be king, Johnson thought. He could imagine Dennis needing a drink before committing himself to having a shave.

'Do you want me to stay, Denny?' Cody asked.

Dennis nodded. He looked up at Johnson, as if trying to assess the degree of resistance he might meet, and said, 'I want the old man out of the way, Carl. I want to take over. Steve has been putting out feelers and most of our people are with me. They all feel the same way. It's only the old farts like Carter and Richards who think like my father any more. All that bullshit he gave me about big changes ... he's incapable of change. He's a dinosaur, Carl, and we're all going to become extinct if we carry on like this.'

Johnson shrugged. 'Well, that's great in theory, Dennis. But some of those old farts are still highly dangerous men. They're fat, rich and comfortable, and they won't take kindly to some young idealist rocking the boat.'

'So was Ceausescu, and look what happened to him,' Dennis said.

Johnson nodded. 'Yeah, they shot him. So have another swig and elaborate, Dennis.'

Instinctively, Dennis reached for his glass, then pulled his hand away. 'You can't stop taking the piss, can you, Carl?'

'I just want you to say what you came here to say,' Johnson said.

'We clear up the crap and make a fresh start, that's what I'm saying. Steve said the old man's a liability. He's more than that. He's an embarrassment. It's a different business these days, Carl. You might have to whack a few guys here and there, but you don't do it out in the open. If you wanted a diplomat, would you go to my father? I was up in town with him a few weeks ago, and he threatened to take a baseball bat to a traffic warden who'd given him a parking ticket. He still keeps an old starting handle in the boot of his car, for Christ's sake.'

Johnson couldn't mask a smile. 'Well, he never pretended to be Henry Kissinger, Dennis.'

'Come on, Carl, it's more than that and you know it. He's reached that point in life where he can't look forward any more. He's basing his business decisions on whether he likes the people he's dealing with, instead of what they're offering. He's dismissive of anyone who's younger than he is.'

'You wouldn't believe some of the deals he's been turning down lately, Carl,' Cody added. 'He's still a tough character and he still scares the crap out of people. It's not that he's perceived as being weak, just outdated. He's not progressive any more, and certain people are looking at our operation and wondering if we can still hack it.'

'The business with the Hardy brothers is a classic example,' Dennis said. 'It goes back ages, and right from the beginning you were telling the old man to help Bob Thompson stamp them out. They're pissing all over Bob on Tyneside, and Bob's good for us. With a little discreet help from us, he could swat those guys like an elephant swats a fly. We could put an end to all that embarrassment and earn a decent bit of pocket money into the bargain.'

'So what's happened?' Johnson asked.

Dennis made a 'what do you think?' sort of gesture. 'Bob approached the old man again just before you came back and he still won't play ball. He's convinced the Hardys are a Mickey Mouse outfit and no problem. Bob's been thick with the old man for years, and now even he's asking me what the fuck's going on.'

Johnson nodded. 'Okay, so you want the old man out of the way. I can't envisage him pottering off to the local retirement home, so I assume you're talking about a permanent arrangement.'

'Exactly. I want him rubbed out, terminated, killed . . . whatever the fashionable term is these days.'

'You want to kill your own father.'

'I want *you* to kill my father.'

Johnson sneered. 'That's more like the Dennis I know. Why me?'

'Because it's what you're best at and you hate the bastard as much as I do.'

Johnson noticed Cody smiling to himself. Cody loved this kind of thing, as long as he wasn't directly involved.

'Why not give yourself the satisfaction of pulling the trigger?' Johnson asked.

Dennis shook his head. 'I'm not going to justify myself to you any more, Carl. Are you interested or not?'

'I don't know, Dennis. I'm still waiting to know what it's worth.'

Dennis smiled and said, 'Personal motivation isn't enough, then?'

'Don't be bloody flippant,' Johnson snapped.

'Denny's only joking, Carl,' said Cody. 'He's going to write you a blank cheque for this one. Right, Denny?'

Dennis looked Johnson straight in the eye for once and said, 'Tell me what you want and you've got it. That's how much it means to me. Any amount of money, any job you want in the organisation. You can have a say in all major decisions, and you'll still have the freedom to operate in your own way.'

Johnson looked hard at Dennis and recalled a conversation he had once had with an old, disillusioned beat copper in Southwark. Johnson had been caught urinating against a garden wall after a party at a friend's house. He'd never forgotten the incident. It was half past two in the morning, unbelievably quiet, not a soul in sight. And the old boy had emerged from nowhere like a ghost, at that dreadful point when a man has committed himself and can't stop.

'No excuses,' Johnson said, out of panic rather than bravery.

'No bloody staying power, son,' the policeman countered with a wry smile. The two men got talking and discovered a mutual love of boxing. Both admired Stanley Ketchell, the legendary middle-weight champion.

'Ketchell died way back in 1910,' the policeman said. 'I'm surprised a youngster like you knows so much about him.'

'Boxing's always been in our family,' Johnson explained. 'My dad's got a huge collection of old fight magazines. There are some great stories about Ketchell.'

'Who shot him, then?' the policeman asked teasingly.

'A jealous farmhand called Walter Dipley. Stan was flirting with his girlfriend.'

'That's right. That was the only time Ketch had sat with his back to the door.'

'With his famous blue gun on his lap,' Johnson added. 'And Dipley opened the door and shot him with a .22 calibre rifle bullet.'

'That's right, son, that's right,' the policeman said proudly. 'By God, you know your stuff.'

The two men continued to swap anecdotes, the policeman completely oblivious of Johnson's urine snaking around his boots. The old fellow was two months away from retirement and glad of it. When Johnson asked why, the policeman gave a tired smile and said, 'It's different, son. It's not the world I used to know. I know it's natural to see things with a jaundiced eye when you get to my age, but it's more than that. Some of the young prats who are running the show these days ... you wouldn't believe them. Bright young idealists who've got no idea what's going on out there. University graduates, some of 'em. They're beat bobbies for five minutes, and the next thing you know they're running a division. I had one under my wing some years ago. A couple of thugs started on us late one night. Two against two, and my man pissed his trousers, took a glancing belt on the chin and passed out. He's a superintendent now and a self-made celebrity because of his tough stance on crime. Iron Man, the local media call him. Piss-pants I bloody call him.'

Johnson wondered where the old policeman was now. Older and more disillusioned, watching the news every night and telling his wife how coppers did it in his day. Or possibly, and more mercifully, dead, swapping yarns with Stanley Ketchell.

Was Johnson getting old before his time, or just downright cynical? He was only a year older than Dennis, and the same age as Cody, yet he felt a generation apart from them. They were children with weak bladders and Johnson had to pretend to take them seriously. He felt like the next messiah as the two men glanced at him in great anticipation, waiting for his answer.

'That's what I want,' Johnson said.

'What?' Dennis asked.

'Just my freedom. I'll hit the old man. Not for you, or the boys, but for Rose.'

'That's fair enough,' Dennis said, surprised that it was all as simple as that. 'Listen, Carl, the old man's always given you plenty of room to manoeuvre. That's not going to change. What about money?'

'You don't understand,' Johnson said, shaking his head. 'When I say freedom, I mean freedom from all this. This is my swan song, Dennis. After this one, I don't want to know about it any more.'

Dennis nearly spilled his drink. '*You?*' he almost squeaked. 'Christ, Carl, you're kidding.' He exchanged uncertain glances with Cody and both men started laughing.

'Pull the other one, Carl,' Cody said, playfully punching Johnson on the arm.

'I'm serious,' Johnson said. 'I've had enough. I want to walk away and I don't want a bullet in the back.'

Dennis sat back in his chair and spread his hands. 'But why?' he asked, incredulous.

Johnson shrugged. 'Maybe I'm one of those old farts you were talking about. Once upon a time, I liked your father, Dennis. I probably shouldn't have, because he was always an evil bastard, but I did. Now he's the one person I've only ever truly hated. But I can't work for anyone else. It's a changing game and I don't feel a part of it anymore. Besides, there are other things I want to do.'

'Yeah, but Carl . . .' Cody began, but then trailed off. He was looking at Johnson as if Johnson were Billy the Kid and had just announced that guns and violence had nothing on peace and love.

'Listen, don't blow this out of proportion,' Johnson warned. 'There are no strings, no bleeding heart statement about a troubled conscience. I've had enough, it's that simple.'

Dennis, suddenly very sensitive, said, 'It's me, isn't it? Come on, you can be honest about it.'

'I've never been anything less,' Johnson said. 'Yes, that's one of the reasons. I don't think you're fit for it, Dennis. I don't think you're strong enough. I can't work for a man I don't respect. You want your father dead, but you don't want to commit patricide. You want to rule the roost as long as the blood is on somebody else's hands. Sorry, but you'd make me nervous. If I fell out of favour, I wouldn't know when or how the axe would fall. At least the old man would have come for me direct.'

'And that's your opinion, is it?' Dennis said, quietly smouldering.

'That's my opinion. Is it a deal, or not?'

Dennis thought for a moment and asked 'How and when?'

'That's up to me,' Johnson said. 'He's back Tuesday, and I've got some other things to clear up first. We've got some breathing space. When I've done it, I'll let you know.'

Dennis nodded slowly, and took a sip of his whisky. 'Who's this Michael Rossi guy you've been hanging out with?' he asked.

Johnson glanced at Cody, who looked uncomfortable and lowered his eyes.

'Rossi's an old friend. He's no part of this.'

'He knows the old man killed Rose. Steve told me.'

'And that's all he knows. He won't be involved when it happens. Listen, I trust Rossi like no other man alive. He's no concern of yours.' Johnson looked at Cody and said, 'If I'm driving past a rugby ground and I see Rossi hanging from the posts, I'll know where to come.'

Dennis didn't look at all happy, but finished his drink. 'All right, Carl, it's a deal. I wish you'd think again, but if you want out after this, nobody's going to come looking for you.'

Johnson got up, fixed his eyes on Dennis, and said, 'If they do, Dennis, I'll come looking for you.'

'So now we just sit back and wait for the explosion,' Cody said, the familiar smirk on his face.

Johnson gave him a quietly contemptuous look. 'Tell me,' he said to Dennis, 'is Steve here due for a promotion?'

'Yeah, why?' Dennis replied, frowning.

'Oh, I just wondered. Just wondered, that's all.'

7

It was on that hot and sticky Saturday night, in the splendour of his room at the Grand, that Michael had the first of a number of dreams that were strangely linked with the unfolding events in his new life. He had always dreamt vividly, whether under the influence of alcohol or not, and there were times when he was actually afraid of falling asleep at night. He had never taken drugs, but had read of the many effects of LSD, where people could experience the greatest joy imaginable or the worst nightmares. Michael's dreams veered and staggered from one extreme to the other, and he never knew what to expect when he laid his head on the pillow. It infuriated him that he couldn't even retreat into sleep without being teased and tormented.

He had drifted away that night with the 'Maple Leaf Rag' on his brain, thinking about the amazing Neil Franklin. Then he was peering out of a bedroom window at the Hyatt Regency hotel on Sunset Boulevard, at kids skateboarding on the side-walk, at pretty girls, at a gang of Mexican guys in T-shirts and cut-off jeans spraying beer at each other; and at an old man of the road pushing his belongings along in a supermarket trolley and swigging from a bottle concealed by the obligatory brown paper bag.

The bedroom was bathed in sunlight and Michael felt wonderful. He looked across at the bed where Johnson was lying in just a pair of shorts, drinking beer and smiling.

'Nearly time, Michael' he said. 'Fifty minutes, man. Fifty minutes, and we'll be saying hello to the great Brian Wilson.'

'I can't believe it,' Michael said. 'I stayed here ten years ago. I can't believe I'm back. It's almost...'

'Too good to be true?' Johnson said. 'You're worrying again. You're in paradise and you're still worrying. Brian's going to walk into that record shop and we're going to get his autograph.'

Michael smiled, but as the sun suddenly went in and rain clouds gathered, so his spirits sank. He felt menaced, knowing somehow that these glorious moments were a prelude to something sinister and frightening. He wanted reassurance from Johnson. He wanted to know that everything was going to be all right. 'Do you honestly believe we're safe now?' he asked.

Johnson winked, reached under the pillow and pulled out a silver gun that resembled a miniature cannon. He grinned as he pressed the chamber lovingly against his ear, pulled back the hammer and listened to the click as if it were music. 'We're safe, Michael. Know what I call this? Barbara Ann, after the Beach Boys song. She's got me out of some scrapes, I can tell you. Nobody can touch us any more, Michael. We're the kings of the beach.'

'Are you never afraid?' Michael asked. 'Of anything?'

'All the time. I'm afraid of getting to Monterey.'

'What? What do you mean?'

'Never mind. I'll tell you one of these days.'

Michael was distracted by screams and whoops of joy from down on the street. The old man with the trolley was performing a jig, his arms outstretched, his dirty, bearded, smiling face raised to the sky. The kids and the Mexican guys and girls were cheering and laughing. The most beautiful rainbow Michael had ever seen was shining over the throng, like a protective field. 'Carl, look at this,' he said excitedly. 'Jesus, look at this!'

As Johnson hurried over to the window, the old man began to discard his dirty coat and trousers and threw away his weather-beaten hat. He ripped the beard from his face, spun round in a full circle, and was suddenly attired in vaudeville costume, straw boater, and cane. He was staring straight up at Michael and smiling hugely.

'Jesus,' Michael said, 'it's Neil Franklin. Look, Carl, it's Neil Franklin!'

Franklin threw away his cane, cupped his mouth with both hands and shouted, 'It's all right, Michael. Everything's all right now. The nightmares are over. The face has gone. I haven't had a drink in three weeks, Michael. Look at me! Don't I look great?'

He did look great. As great as Michael felt. The sun was out again, the clouds had dispersed. Everywhere on Sunset Boulevard there was joy and happiness.

8

Sunday was another punishingly hot day, but the long and meandering drive to Greatstone was delicious, with the car windows down and the sound of the Beach Boys coming out of the speakers. Michael held out his hands at one point during lunch, and for the first time in weeks they weren't trembling.

'Worth the effort, eh?' Johnson said.

'Yeah, it's a nice feeling,' Michael smiled.

They had started out at around nine o'clock and now they were dining at a modest Italian restaurant in Hastings. 'I've never been sure whether I like this town,' Johnson remarked. 'Too bleak. There always seems to be something missing.'

He had been quiet up to then, saying only the odd thing here and there during the drive. He always chewed the skin around his fingernails when he was deep in thought, though he seemed to be in good spirits. Earlier, Michael had asked him how the meeting with Dennis and Cody had gone, and Johnson had simply smiled and said, 'Not so bad. Nothing you should know about.' He was obviously preoccupied, and hadn't asked Michael how he had spent his evening. Michael hadn't encouraged the conversation and had simply settled back to enjoy the ride.

'I phoned the bungalow again this morning,' Johnson said in the restaurant. 'No bloody answer again.'

'There must be a simple explanation.'

'Yeah, I'm sure there is, kiddo. Anyway, you look ten times better than you did yesterday. I'm not torturing you by supping this wine, am I?'

'No, I'm okay, honestly. Listen, I met an old friend of yours on the beach yesterday – Neil Franklin.'

Johnson was surprised. 'Christ, I haven't seen old Neil for ages. He moved out of Brighton when the booze finally got him. He just drifts around these days.'

'Yeah,' Michael said, 'he was hugging a bottle of Scotch, and he looked pretty scruffy. But he seemed quite happy.'

'He's a strange man,' Johnson nodded. 'A real Jekyll and Hyde case. He'll wreck himself like that for weeks on end and then go back to being a model citizen again. Always heads for the beach when he's drinking. Falls asleep there sometimes. The sea'll get him one of these days.'

'You look after him though, don't you? He spoke highly of you.'

Johnson looked embarrassed, shrugged and said, 'Yeah, when he was in Brighton. But like I said, it's been a long time. Neil's a good bloke. He never really got the breaks. Life's been pretty cruel to him.'

'I know. He told me all about his fighting days and ... well, his relationship with Jack Fossey. He hates Fossey.' Michael wondered if he should have mentioned Fossey, but Johnson didn't seem concerned.

'Yeah, Jack really screwed Neil,' he said quietly. 'I always felt bad about that.'

'Has he ever told you about the dream he keeps having?'

'The man in the sea with the spooky eyes? Yeah. Probably John Barleycorn. I saw him shortly before Rosie's funeral. He told me about it then. Take him with a pinch of salt, Michael. Neil's heart is in the right place, but his mind's somewhere else when he's in that kind of state. He sees and hears all sorts of things.'

Michael sat there and wondered. Franklin had had a profound effect on him and Michael wasn't usually wrong about such things. He shared his mother's gift for being able to read people and sense the unusual. He just felt that Franklin was destined to play a prominent role in his immediate future life. 'It's a funny thing, Carl,' he said, wondering if he was wise in persisting with the subject, 'but I had this incredible dream about all three of us last night. It was probably all the events of the day whirling around in my head, but it was so real.'

'That and the withdrawal symptoms,' Johnson chuckled.

Michael smiled. 'Probably. You said something really strange though, Carl.'

'When?'

'In the dream. You said you were afraid of getting to Monterey, but you didn't explain. We were in the Hyatt Regency on Sunset Boulevard. I stayed there some years ago.'

'Yeah, you told me,' Johnson said. He was suddenly frowning and looking hard at Michael. 'What else did I say?'

'Nothing. Just that you'd tell me about it one day.'

'Christ,' Johnson said, shaking his head.

'What's wrong?'

'That's strange. I have this recurring dream of my own from time to time. I don't know what the hell it all means, but I'm living somewhere up in Vermont for some reason. It's a beautiful place, absolute paradise, but I'm always conscious of being bored. I get in my car and it's on my mind to drive to Monterey, to see all those places Steinbeck wrote about. But I never get there. I get a little further each time, but I never get there. It's as if I'm being warned off it. I got as far as Arizona once and then I got the weirdest feeling and just turned around and drove back again. Figure that one out if you can.'

9

Michael loved Greatstone. Although he had paid fleeting visits in the past, he had never fully explored that gorgeous, winding stretch of the Kent coast that runs from Romney Marsh to Dungeness. He had read the adventures of the legendary Doctor Syn, and heard of the miniature trains that carry such magical names as Southern Maid, Hurricane, and Green Goddess.

A long-promised visit to Greatstone, with all its roaring natural beauty, had been another victim of his drunkenness, a 'must do' item that had been shoved onto the back burner. As he and Johnson passed a pub called The Pilot, near the Dungeness lighthouse, and turned into the coast road, Johnson remarked, 'Pity we couldn't come in from the Romney Marsh end. That's really beautiful.'

Yet Michael had all the beauty he needed. Perhaps his own recent lifestyle was influencing his thoughts and impressions, but for him the power and bleakness of this stretch of the coast were its most attractive qualities. Even on this gentle day, it was quietly menacing. The tide was out and the great sandy beach was seemingly endless. The summer wind was making the telephone wires sing and carrying the excited screams of children on the beach. Michael was reminded of small town America, of places like Old Orchard Beach in rugged Maine, where he once swam and ran and drank beer without a care in the world.

'They'd be putting up skyscrapers here if the climate was constant,' he remarked.

'God forbid,' Johnson said. 'I love this place, Michael. I can think straight when I'm here.'

'Where's your daughter's place?'

'Dunes Road, about a mile or so up ahead in Littlestone. There's a pub called The Jolly Fisherman up on the corner. We'll have a drink first. I have to psyche myself up before a session with Janice. It's like training for a bloody fight.' Johnson laughed, but was obviously tense. 'She's got no drive, no get-up-and-go,' he complained. 'God alone knows what she's going to do in life. She's got no ambition at all. I write her letters all the time, asking her what she's up to. I'm lucky if I get a reply. When I do, her spelling's bloody atrocious.'

'Why don't you both get along, Carl?' Michael asked. 'Is it just a personality clash?'

'That and a million other things,' Johnson said wearily. 'Like I said before, we're so alike ... both stubbornly proud and prickly. If we happen to be in the same mood, it's like two lorries colliding. But that's only the tip of the iceberg. I'll tell you about it in the pub if you really want me to bore you to death.'

The Jolly Fisherman was packed with locals and holidaymakers in their shorts and sandals, reeking of sun tan lotion and digging eagerly into their beer and food. Johnson and Michael managed to grab a spare table, and Michael pondered on how spending time in a pub quickly loses its appeal when orange juice is your companion.

'There's a lot I can't blame her for,' Johnson said, going back to his daughter. He turned his nose up as he took a sip of his whisky and didn't seem at all comfortable. 'I was never there half the time when she was growing up. And when I was, we'd argue like hell. I've never been any damn good at being a father. I left all that to Rose, and then Janice blamed me when Rose started drinking. And when Rose died, well, that sealed it. Janice was always a wild kid, but she seemed to lose her stability altogether after that. And yours truly here was to blame for everything. She actually ran away on two occasions. I found her once, curled up and crying her eyes out, on Euston Station. Christ knows what would have happened if some freak had found her first.'

'How old is she now?' Michael asked.

'Seventeen. You met her once, didn't you?'

'A long time ago. She was pretty.'

'Yeah, she's a nice looking kid. But she's got Rose's suicidal streak. I hate to say it, but even if Rose hadn't ... well, I mean, I think she might have ended up taking her own life anyway.'

'But surely when you tell Janice the truth,' Michael said, 'about Rose's death, I mean, surely she'll realise that ...'

'Maybe, maybe. Do you know what's really ironic? You remember Steve saying yesterday how Janice and me had gone to Scotland the weekend Rose died? That was the first time we'd really ever done anything together. Janice had wanted to see Scotland again. We spent a holiday on a farm up there years ago. It was Rose's idea that we should spend a weekend together, as a sort of way of getting to know each other and thrashing out our problems. We stayed with an old mate of mine called Jeff Murray, who has a cottage in Dumfries. We used to work alongside each other during my early days in this racket. Anyway, I figured Janice might open up a bit in a different environment. It didn't work out for either one of us, quite honestly. We were both uncomfortable about it. It was all very civil, but neither of us could get our words out. I curse myself for that now, Michael. It was up to me to take the initiative and I didn't. It was a terrible experience. I remember us going for a long walk and we barely exchanged a word. I bought her lunch and she seemed to relax a bit as the day went on. She actually started smiling a bit and telling me a few things about herself. And I still felt so awkward. My own daughter, and I was absolutely tongue tied.'

'When did you find out about Rose?' Michael asked.

'Three o'clock on Sunday morning. I'd left Jeff's number with Steve Cody. You know what Steve's like. It took him ten minutes to give me the message. Even now, I can't really tell you how I felt. Just numb at first. Completely numb. I wanted to drive back right there and then, but Jeff talked me out of it. We went into the kitchen and he got some Scotch inside me, and ... well, we just talked for a few hours. I can't remember much of what I said. I was just sort of rambling. In a strange sort of way, Janice snapped me out of it. I woke her up at around seven and she was totally hysterical. I realised I had to get a grip on everything. I just held her tight and cuddled her. She cried and cried.

'Jeff drove us back. Janice eventually fell asleep on the back seat. I couldn't cry, Michael. That's what I remember most. I felt devastated, but I couldn't cry. I just stared out of the window the whole time. The journey never seemed to end. Christ, it was awful . . .'

10

Johnson decided to walk to the bungalow and left the car at The Jolly Fisherman. Michael liked Dunes Road, even though it seemed endless in the brutal heat. Long and wide, and flanked with bungalows of different shapes and sizes, it was incredibly quiet, populated only by two or three kids, riding up and down on their bicycles. The jingle of an ice-cream van rang out in the distance and the smells of freshly cut grass and Sunday cooking permeated the air.

They walked very nearly to the end of the road, which led to open fields and woodland, before Johnson tapped Michael on the shoulder and said, 'This one here.' He pointed to a large and attractive bungalow to their right, painted sky blue, and with a plaque on the wall that read 'Cabinessence'. It was the title of an old Beach Boys song, and Michael chuckled and said, 'Like the name.'

Johnson grinned. 'I thought of Dylan's "Subterranean Homesick Blues", but it didn't roll off the tongue in quite the same way.'

The main door was on the side of the bungalow at the bottom of a gently sloping drive, and there was no answer when Johnson rang the bell. Michael noticed that he seemed almost relieved by this.

'No thudding music,' Johnson said. 'She can't be in.' He kept pressing the bell, and Michael suddenly noticed an old man standing at the top of the drive. He nudged Johnson and asked, 'Is that your neighbour?'

'Never seen him before,' Johnson said. 'I don't know anybody around here. They hardly ever come out.'

'She's not in!' the old man cried, as Johnson and Michael walked up to meet him.

'Do you know where they went?' Johnson asked.

'I'm talking about Janice, mate,' the old man replied. 'The other one's gone – that Wendy.'

'What do you mean, gone?'

'Gone, left. About a week ago, according to Janice. They had this almighty ruck. I could hear 'em from next door. Screaming and shouting at each other they were.'

'Shit,' Johnson said.

'Are you one of her visitors?' the old man asked.

'Visitors?'

'She used to get plenty of visitors – Wendy, I mean. Like a bloody procession sometimes it was.'

'Was it now,' Johnson murmured.

'Yeah, all sorts of different blokes. I said to my missus, she must be one of those homeworkers who stuff envelopes and that sort of thing.'

'Yes, I'm sure,' Johnson said. 'Listen, I'm Janice's father...'

'Oh Christ, mate, I'm sorry. You mean Wendy's your...'

'No, no, she's not my wife. She was just looking after Janice for me. Any idea where Janice is?'

The old man shrugged. 'She never talks to me that often, but she told me she likes The Railway Bell. Up the road, near the holiday camp. I think she's got some mates there.'

'Yeah, I know it,' Johnson said. 'Thanks.'

'She seems like a nice girl,' the old man said. 'I offered her some of my tomatoes once, but she didn't seem very interested in tomatoes.'

'Well, er, thanks anyway,' Johnson smiled, making to leave.

'Do you need any manure?' the old man asked.

'What?'

'Manure. The missus and me have got bags of it. We collect it over there in the fields.'

Michael couldn't help but feel amused as he watched Johnson frowning deeply and looking utterly perplexed. The great leveller with heroes, he thought, is that they are often thrown by the most mundane and innocent things in life.

'I'll pass this time, but thanks anyway,' Johnson said, and as he and

Michael began the trudge back to the car, he turned to Michael and asked, 'What the bloody hell's he asking me about manure for?'

Michael had that awful urge to laugh, until he stepped back into the car and felt the static coming off Johnson as they drove the short distance to The Railway Bell. Michael's gut instinct told him that an ugly incident was imminent, and he began to tremble like any untested man faced with possible violence. These 'mates' of Janice could be snot-nosed, wiry little teenagers. They could also be the kind of genuinely hard men who had struck fear in Michael's heart since the dressing-room incident with Paul Black.

Michael glanced at Johnson for inspiration, but there was nothing there. Just a cold, unattached man driving a car, exuding an electricity that couldn't be tapped. Michael wanted to say something funny to lighten things up, but he was completely frozen. His whole body began to thump, and now he was praying to God that he wouldn't shame himself and run like hell for the safety of the beach when Johnson stopped the car.

The Railway Bell looked innocuous enough as Johnson parked and turned off the engine.

'Do you want to talk to her alone?' Michael asked hopefully.

'Nah, it's okay, you can come with me,' Johnson said, as if he were doing Michael a massive favour.

Inside, the noisy and smoke-filled Railway Bell was almost full, despite its great size. The bar area was massive, yet Johnson and Michael could barely move forward. To their left, a bald, fat man in braces and carpet slippers, who looked like the victim of a time warp, was vamping away at the piano, cigarette hanging from his mouth and ash tumbling down his shirt. He was attempting to play 'New York, New York', but it could just as easily have been 'Roll Out The Barrel'.

Johnson nudged Michael and pointed to the right. 'There's some daylight over there by the pool table,' he said. 'That's where she's likely to be.'

They pushed their way forward, and through the heavy smoke Michael was confronted by the kind of scenario he had been dreading. The pool table had been commandeered by five hefty bikers, and they didn't strike Michael as the kind who simply dressed to look the part. Their girls were looking on, chewing gum and looking bored and aimless.

'Is she here?' Michael asked nervously.

'Can't see her.'

Johnson caught the eye of one of the bikers, a towering hulk with 'Eddie' tattooed on his right arm, who looked as if he'd been chiselled out of a mountain. 'Excuse me,' Johnson said, 'do you know a girl called Janice Johnson?'

Eddie proceeded to play his shot, and without raising his eyes, mumbled, 'Who's asking?'

'It's private,' Johnson said bluntly, but not threateningly.

Eddie straightened up, smiled sarcastically, and said, 'Sorry, mate, can't help you.'

'I'm her father and I'm asking you again,' Johnson said.

Michael felt his heart racing again as Eddie's colleagues suddenly began to look serious, closing in around their leader like a pack of faithful wolves. They all looked pretty much the same. Bearded, brooding and vacant. Then Michael turned, and saw a rakishly thin but very pretty young girl with long black hair stop directly behind Johnson with an alarmed look. She looked as though she hadn't slept properly for days, but her darkened eyes and drawn face couldn't mask her natural beauty. She was dressed in a black leather jacket and leather trousers, and a black T-shirt with a skull and bones design.

She tugged at Johnson's jacket, making him spin round fast, and said, 'Dad?'

With a mixture of relief and anger, Johnson said, 'Janice, where the hell have you been?' There were no kisses or cuddles, no tears. Both looked incredibly ill at ease. Janice shrugged at her father's question, blushing and guilty.

'I've been around,' she said. 'I didn't know you were back.'

'Since Friday, and I've been calling you constantly. What happened to Wendy?'

From behind, Eddie took a few steps forward and tapped Johnson on the shoulder with his pool cue. 'She's happy, Pop,' he said. 'Why don't you do us all a favour and disappear?'

'Yeah, piss off,' said one of the girls, displaying the predictable degree of intellect.

Now Michael knew for sure that something nasty was going to happen. Yet he was gaining a curious strength from his nervousness. His whole body was pounding, but not through fear. His hands were steady and his mind alert. He studied all five bikers carefully, anticipating their first move. He didn't know what he would do, but he was ready. Strangely, he was now almost relishing the confrontation.

Johnson turned only partially, and said to Eddie, 'Get that damn thing off my shoulder.'

'Dad, don't start a scene,' Janice pleaded. 'Eddie's a friend.'

Johnson looked horrified. Jerking a thumb over his shoulder, he said, 'This piece of shit's a friend?'

With frightening quickness, Eddie drew back the cue and raised it over his head. Before Michael could shout his warning, Janice screamed, 'Dad!'

In one movement, Johnson spun round and caught the cue in mid-air as it came crashing down. Snatching it violently from his opponent's grip, he cracked it across Eddie's knees, causing him to yell out in pain. Just as quickly, he crashed the butt end against the side of the big man's head. In an almost delayed action, Eddie staggered back and fell heavily to the floor.

Johnson was quick to seize his advantage, the other bikers momentarily stunned by his savage attack. As the music stopped and people screamed and hustled to get out of the way, Johnson quickly felled two more with single, whiplash blows of the cue, breaking it in the process. Now only two of the bikers were standing, and Michael, frozen to the spot by the violent suddenness of it all, turned to see a bearded face crashing into his own. He felt himself reeling back from the vicious butt, yet incredibly there was no blood. He felt he was going to fall, but kept his balance, and his pain and confusion quickly turned to fury. He was conscious of nothing else in the bar as he instinctively met the charging biker with a blow to the face. His opponent, taller and much heavier, stopped at once, his expression a picture of disbelief, as if such a thing couldn't happen to him.

Michael felt no pain in his fist, no sense of surprise at what he had done, nothing but the glorious pumping of adrenaline. As the biker swayed to one side, Michael swung his arm again, the blow cracking off his opponent's chin and dropping him on his back across the pool table. Michael looked up to see the remaining biker bouncing heavily off the jukebox and crashing face first to the floor, with Johnson moving in on him like a boxer ensuring that the kill had been completed.

Michael glanced at the girls, who had backed into a corner and were still mechanically chewing their gum. He couldn't believe their coldness, their utter detachment from it all. They had expressed no panic, no indignation, not even a token supportive gesture. It was as if their men went through this routine every lunch hour of the week.

Johnson nodded his thanks to Michael, then glanced quickly around the bar. 'Janice ... where's Janice?'

Michael scanned the stunned faces but couldn't see her.

'Come on, let's get out of this dump,' Johnson said.

'What about the guv'nor?' Michael asked. 'Do you think he's called the police?'

'He won't call the police,' Johnson said firmly. 'It isn't that kind of place, trust me.'

As they approached the door, Michael braced himself again as a group of formidable looking men hurried towards them. He counted seven, the leader being an older man who looked as if he had experienced some bruising battles in his time. His face was rough and scarred and set in an intimidatingly grim expression. But this turned to a look of near panic as he caught sight of Johnson.

'Christ, Carl, it's you,' he said nervously.

Johnson was furious, but kept his voice low. 'What the hell took you jokers so long?' he growled. 'I didn't invest in this place to attract scum like that, Colin.'

Clearly embarrassed, and very obviously frightened, Colin struggled to justify himself. 'Carl, me and the lads ... I mean ...'

Fortunately, Johnson was in too much of a rush to make a big thing of it. 'Never mind,' he snapped. Gesturing at the carnage behind him, he said, 'I don't want those bastards troubling anyone again. Tell them what will happen if they do. Then get them out of here. Trash their bikes and tell them to walk.'

'Right,' Colin nodded, looking relieved that he'd escaped so lightly.

Michael watched all this with immense fascination. Being in Johnson's company at times like these was thrilling. Was there anybody the man didn't know, anybody he didn't control in some way? The Railway Bell was a seemingly ordinary pub on a bleak and sleepy stretch of the Kent coast. What was Johnson's involvement in this place and why? Michael didn't really want to know. He was simply content to soak up the wave of glorious excitement that was washing over him.

Johnson said no more. He gave the humbled men one last glare of contempt, clearly reflecting on a poor business investment, and said, 'Come on, Michael.'

Outside, Johnson looked around frantically for Janice. He threw Michael a bunch of keys and said, 'Take the car back to the bungalow and wait for me. She's probably down on the beach somewhere.'

'The Porsche?' Michael gasped.

Johnson looked at him irritably and said, 'Michael, you've just decimated a man twice your size. Don't tell me you're scared of a car.'

'I'm not scared,' Michael said indignantly. 'I've just never driven a bloody expensive thing like . . .' Having acquitted himself so well, he suddenly felt inadequate again and it infuriated him.

'Drive it,' Johnson said. 'It's just another car.'

Michael watched Johnson as he hurried across the road and started to run, until he hit the bank of stones that swept down to the sand and disappeared. Colin emerged from the pub with two of his aides and said, 'You okay, mate?'

'Yeah, I'm okay,' Michael said. The men began to push the bikes around the side of the building, presumably to some discreet burial ground. 'What about those other guys?' Michael asked.

Colin winked, but didn't smile. 'They'll be on their way in a while. They're just being educated at the moment.'

11

Johnson slid down the stones and onto the soft sand, where, it seemed, the whole world had congregated. He looked right towards Dungeness, trying to pick out the leather-clad figure of his daughter from the scantily-clad hundreds. Nothing. Johnson was a classic dresser, and, for a man of his relatively young age, savagely contemptuous of modern fashion. Christ, he thought, she shouldn't be too hard to find. Who the hell dresses in all that leather gear on a day like this?

He looked left towards St Mary's Bay, through a forest of roasting bodies and screaming children. And there she was, down by the seashore, dawdling along as if hoping to be caught, her head down and the water lapping over her feet. Johnson started to jog, weaving his way through the people, and he was less than fifty yards from her when she turned and saw him and began to run. She veered and staggered along the shore, as if half drunk or half stoned, and it didn't take Johnson long to catch her. He grabbed her by the wrist, and she began slapping at him with her free arm and screaming to be let go. The tussle was so fierce that they briefly toppled over and fell into the water, before she exhausted herself and slumped into her father's chest, sobbing uncontrollably.

Everyone on the beach seemed to be looking at them, but Johnson was well accustomed to coping with unwanted attention. He had learned that few people intervene on such occasions. There were the usual would-be toughs who flexed their muscles and thought about playing the hero, but the hint of danger was usually enough to hold them back. Jack Fossey had instructed him on such matters when he first began to learn his dangerous trade. 'Never look anybody in the eye,' Fossey had advised. 'Walk away briskly, but never run. People won't trouble you if you look like the kind of hard bastard who knows what he's doing.'

Johnson was one such man. He possessed that kind of frightening aura that lesser men try to assume for a couple of hours after watching their movie heroes.

Soaked through, he pulled his weeping and bedraggled daughter up the beach in the direction of some deserted sand dunes. He practically threw her down onto the sand, which prompted her to cry even louder. He pulled off his jacket and sat down beside her, brushing his hair back harshly and looking out to sea. Inside, he was raging. He felt hate and rejection, yet he didn't know what to say. He forced himself to look at Janice as she sat there with her head between her knees, her face and arms and most of her legs covered by her gorgeous mane of black, wavy hair.

She was almost Latin looking with her dark complexion, a petite and stunningly attractive girl, but broken and burning out fast. During their brief encounter in The Railway Bell, Johnson had been shocked by her jaded appearance. What in God's name had been going on in his absence? He quickly looked for needle marks as she lifted her head to wipe away her tears, but could see none. She had stopped crying, but hung her head again and said nothing.

Finally, in exasperation, Johnson asked, 'Why the hell did you run away from me? Why do you hate me so much?' He was stunned by the force and bitterness of his daughter's reply.

'Why can't you just piss off and leave me alone?' she spat. 'Whenever you're around, some kind of fuckin' disaster happens. You drove my mum mad and put her in an early grave. Isn't that enough for you?'

In a purely reflexive action, Johnson cuffed her round the head, making her yelp. 'Where did you learn to speak like that?' he asked furiously. 'Your blockhead friend back at the pub? Don't you ever speak to me in that kind of language.'

But his own anger only fuelled Janice's rage. 'Why?' she laughed.

'What are you going to do, kill me? That's what you do to people you don't like, isn't it? I know all about you, Dad. I know all about your noble profession.'

The word 'Dad' was delivered with cutting sarcasm and Johnson had to restrain himself from striking her again. 'Is that so?' he said, but the hard and knowing look in her eyes told him that lying would be futile.

'Do you honestly think I'm scared of you?' she asked, now meeting him eyeball to eyeball. 'I mean, how much more damage can you possibly cause? You didn't give a toss about me from the word go . . . swanning off for days at a time and thinking everything was okay because you brought me back a present. You turned Mum into an alcoholic bag of nerves, and now you've just beaten the shit out of one of my friends. Did that make you feel good, Dad? What did you do, break his legs? Put him in hospital?'

Johnson was fuming. 'He was about to smash a snooker cue over my head, you silly little bitch. Would you have enjoyed that any more?'

'Yeah, maybe,' she yelled. 'Maybe I would. What did you do to him? Where is he?'

'He's walking home. The exercise will do the bastard good. I don't want you seeing him again.'

'Oh, just like that, eh? Father has spoken and screwed up my life again. *You're* the bastard.'

'That's enough,' Johnson growled. His eyes were now blazing, and Janice, fearless as she felt in this wild exchange, knew instinctively to pull back. She turned away from her father's chilling stare and bowed her head again, gripping her left wrist as she tried to contain her fury.

Johnson looked out at all the people frolicking in the sea – fathers and mothers, brothers and sisters, happy families. He wanted to be in Monterey right now with Janice and Michael, he wanted everything to be right and peaceful again. For years, he had handled his rich and turbulent life with such coolness and discipline. He had conducted the most delicate negotiations with some of the toughest men alive, and coldly killed without ever feeling a troubled conscience. Now everything was ragged and out of control and it had nothing to do with worn nerves. It was guilt that was cracking Johnson's armour. Guilt and a burning anger that he could no longer smother.

When Janice spoke again, it was in desperation, not temper. 'How could you make me live with her?' she asked in a quiet and near broken voice. 'How could you screw a cheap prostitute like her for all those years behind Mum's back?'

Not wanting another flare-up, Johnson avoided the question and said, 'I went to the bungalow earlier. The old man next door said she'd left. What happened?'

Janice met her father's eyes again with a look of contempt that enraged him. 'Christ, you haven't got a clue, have you?' she said. 'You think you're so smart and so sharp and you just don't know what's going on, do you?'

'So tell me!' Johnson shouted. 'I've had enough of your cynical, smart-arse shit, Janice. Just answer the bloody question.'

She nodded slowly, and the dark and determined look she gave her father reminded him so much of himself. She wasn't going to back down this time. 'You think I'm cynical do you?' she challenged. 'You think I'm just being smart? Your so-called friends have violated me, Dad. They've raped me in every sense of the word. They've made me feel cheap and filthy and useless. I'll give you all the gory details, if you really want to hear them. Then you can tell me what a spoilt, ungrateful little bitch I am.'

These words disturbed Johnson, for he knew at once that Janice wasn't just giving him self-pity. He knew he was about to be rocked by more shocking truths, that his ignorance of the facts was greater than he'd imagined. 'Come on, kid, tell me,' he said softly.

Suddenly, her anger subsided, and she was a lost little girl again, desperate to confide in someone. Johnson took her gently by the hand and said, 'The old man next door ... what's all this he's been telling me about men coming to the house?'

'Wendy was running a bloody brothel,' Janice said.

'What?'

'Come on, Dad, you're a man of the world. They didn't come to read the meter.'

Johnson shook his head. 'I got her off all that nonsense years ago.

84

That's how she made her living. She used to pick guys up to support her drug habit.'

'Well, her habit came back as well. She never did it in front of me, but I knew she was snorting cocaine. She was okay at first, we became quite good friends. Then she started doing all that and it was terrible. Absolutely terrible. All those weird guys coming to the house ... we had so many terrible fights about it. I mean, Wendy was so stoned half the time, she didn't even know what she was saying. It just got worse and worse. She kept stealing the money you sent us. We were always rowing about that. I can't sleep any more, I never seem to want to eat. I haven't been to school for weeks. I just used to leave the house and spend my time up the pub. That's where I met Eddie. You shouldn't have done that to him, Dad. I know you don't like his sort, but at least he was kind to me.'

Johnson breathed out heavily, trying to take everything in. 'Janice, I swear to God, I didn't know any of this was going on. I thought Wendy ... well, I mean, she'd been off the drugs for years. I genuinely trusted her. Whenever I called her from LA she said you didn't want to talk to me. She just kept giving me all this crap about giving you breathing space. What happened to all my letters? You only wrote back to me once or twice. You should have bloody told me about all this.'

'Oh, come on, Dad,' Janice snapped. 'Of course I didn't want to talk to you. Look at how we parted. You virtually disowned me. Then you entrusted my life to some tart I never even knew.'

Her words were sadly true. Janice was the only person on earth who could pierce her father's icy coolness and let loose his temper. He dumped her before departing for America as if she were a passing girlfriend who had become a nuisance.

'Tell me honestly,' Johnson said, 'did she involve you in any of this? With men and drugs and all that?'

She shook her head quickly. 'No, honestly. She never involved me in all that. Most times she took the guys out.'

'There's more, isn't there?' Johnson said. 'Why did she suddenly leave?'

Now all the fire had gone out of his daughter and she was looking vulnerable and guilty. 'Look, Dad, I needed help. I had to turn to someone. I thought that Uncle J could . . .'

Johnson froze and his anger nearly spilled over again. 'Oh, shit. You stupid little . . .' He bit his tongue, seeing from her bowed head that she would not resist him this time. She was limp and broken and began to cry again.

Uncle J. It had always been her nickname for Jack Fossey. What further evil had the bastard done? It seemed the man Johnson had once idolised had stained his whole family, his whole life.

Johnson rubbed Janice's back gently and said, 'I'm sorry, love, I didn't mean that. I just felt it best that nobody else knew where you were. I wanted to get you away from Brighton and the kind of people I do business with. I have to know what happened, Janice. So much is going on. So many terrible things. I'll explain it all to you, but you've got to tell me everything you know. It's tremendously important.'

She frowned and asked, 'What's going on, Dad?'

Johnson leaned close and said, 'Janice, you've got to believe me when I tell you that you and Michael Rossi are all I have now. I can't trust anybody else any more. Especially Uncle-bloody-Jack. What did he do?'

She smiled, but it was a sad and pitiful smile. 'Yeah, I like Michael. I remember him well, he was always nice to me. He'd never hurt me, I know that.'

'No, he wouldn't,' Johnson said softly. 'Janice, what did Jack Fossey do to you?'

'I rang him early last week. I was at the end of my tether, Dad. Wendy and me had this terrific fight the night before. I got home late and the noise coming from the house was unbelievable. I mean, this really thundering music you could hear from halfway up the street. Eddie dropped me on the corner, and when I got to the house Mr Green was ringing our bell . . .'

'Mr Green?'

'He's the old man you spoke to today. He's really quite sweet, actually. He was more concerned than angry. I said I'd sort it out and told him to go back indoors. The whole house was shaking. I could hear Wendy smashing things, and when I went in her room she was really freaking out. She was throwing things and yelling and crying and swearing, and she just … she was mad. I asked her what was wrong and shouted at her to stop, but she didn't even know I was there. There was cocaine on the bedside table and all over the carpet and a bottle of Scotch that was nearly empty. Then she stopped suddenly and I've never been so bloody frightened. Her eyes were like saucers and she just stood there staring at me. I tried to reason with her, but she started throwing things at me. She threw this vase and it missed my head by inches.

'I tried to turn the music off, but she threw herself at me and knocked me to the floor. Christ, I thought I was gone. I thought she was going to kill me. She was calling me a bitch, a slag, a slut, every foul bloody name you could think of. She tried to strangle me. She had her hands around my throat and I managed to kick and shove her away. I couldn't get my breath and I thought she was going to come at me again, but she got up and ran out of the room. She'd smashed the room to pieces – absolutely smashed it to pieces.'

Janice paused for a few seconds as she dreamily picked up sand and let it run slowly through her fingers. 'I turned the music off,' she continued, 'and I ran after her. I didn't want to, I was scared. But I had to stop her. I had to find some way of shutting her up. I chased her into the kitchen and she grabbed a knife off the draining board and backed into a corner. I was terrified now. She rushed at me and missed, and I knocked the knife out of her hand. I grabbed her and swung her as hard as I could, and she hit her head on the cupboard and fell down. I thought I'd killed her at first, but then I could hear her breathing and moaning. I thought about calling an ambulance, but she didn't seem badly hurt. I didn't know what the hell to do. I was afraid she'd start all over again when she came around, so I dragged her back to the bedroom and locked her in.

'I was bloody exhausted. It must have been about one o'clock, and I fell asleep for a while until Wendy woke me up again. She started banging on her door and screaming at me to let her out, and it seemed to go on for ages. I just pulled the covers over my head and prayed for her to stop. The next thing I knew, it was seven thirty and everything was quiet. It was a bloody miracle no one around here called the police. It looked as if it had snowed in Wendy's bedroom. I've never seen so much cocaine in all my life.'

'Did you clear it up?' Johnson asked.

She nodded. 'Yeah, the best I could. I phoned Uncle J at around eight o'clock. I didn't want to, honest. I just didn't know what else to do. I told him what Wendy was up to and that I had no one else to confide in. He flew into Lydd Airport and drove down from there.'

'Who did he bring with him?'

'I don't know. There was a car outside, but I couldn't see who was in it.'

'Nobody else came into the house?'

'Nobody. I went into Wendy's room straight after I phoned Uncle J, and she was just waking up. She started crying again and hugging me and telling me how sorry she was. By that time, I was sick of it all. I just wanted her out of there. I didn't tell her Uncle J was coming. She assured me she was okay, so I told her to take a bath and get dressed. I made some coffee and we just talked after that. She gave me all this bleeding-heart crap about how useless she was and begged me never to tell you what happened.'

Janice broke off and laughed to herself. 'Christ, when Uncle J rang the doorbell, I thought all my problems were over.'

As he braced himself for the most chilling part of the tale, Johnson suddenly felt closer to his daughter than he had ever done. Never had he felt so emotional, not even when Rose died, and he didn't really know what to make of it. He hated to feel vulnerable, yet he was oddly relieved to find that he could still be touched after such a cold and violent life. He wanted to kiss and hug his daughter, yet right now she seemed too fragile to even touch.

'Tell me what happened,' he said softly.

'I felt so relieved when he first arrived,' Janice recalled. 'He'd always been the kindly figure I could trust, right from when I was a little girl. He'd always made a fuss of me. I knew what he did, of course. I knew he was really a bastard. But I always saw him as the sort of honourable criminal you see in films. The kind of man who always protects his own kind, no matter what. I suppose that sounds ridiculously bloody naive.'

'Not really,' Johnson said. 'I always thought he was a man of honour, a man of morals. A psychopathic bastard, but a man of morals.'

'He seemed like a giant when he walked through the door,' Janice continued. 'He was immaculately dressed, and just seemed to ooze power. He kissed me and asked me what was wrong with his little girl. I trusted him totally. Then he changed like the weather when I took him into the living-room and he saw Wendy. He didn't introduce himself. He just asked me to close the door and wait in my bedroom. Wendy looked terrified. She asked me who he was, and I was going to tell her, but Uncle J asked me to leave again and said everything would be all right. God alone knows what he said to her, but he was in there for a good thirty minutes and I didn't hear a sound.

'Then I heard doors slamming and noises coming from Wendy's bedroom. I went out into the hall and Uncle J was standing there smoking one of his bloody great cigars. He smiled and patted me on the head in that patronising way of his, and told me I had no need to worry. Then Wendy came storming out of her room with her suitcases. I don't know why, but I tried to stop her and say sorry, and she just erupted again. She swung the cases at me and started abusing me at the top of her voice.

'That was when I first saw the frightening side of Uncle J's nature. He clamped his hand on the back of Wendy's neck, and the look of pain on her face made me want to be sick. I mean, she couldn't even bring herself to scream. He told her to go and wait in the car. He said she could do it quietly, or he could rip her tongue out. I knew he wasn't bluffing and I got really scared.

'He pushed her out the front door and she fell over in the drive. I was panicking by then. I told him I just wanted Wendy out of the house, but I didn't want her hurt. He shut the door and that was the last I saw of her. He was all sweetness and light again and said he wanted a few words with me inside. I can't explain it, but I felt then that something dreadful was going to happen. I was still in my nightie and he was leering at me like he used to when I was a little girl.'

Johnson could bear it no more. His whole body had gone cold, shivers running through him in waves. He shook his head and banged a fist into the sand. 'Jesus, what the hell did the bastard do to you?'

Janice was now almost trance-like, her eyes glazed and unfocused. 'He sat down next to me on the sofa and took my hand and started rubbing it. I asked him what he was going to do to Wendy, and he told me I worried too much. "Greatstone doesn't suit Wendy," he said. "This is far too quiet a place for a lady of her lifestyle." He said the car outside was his own special cab and that his driver could take anyone anywhere. I can remember his exact words. "She'll be no trouble where she's going," he said.

'He was smiling at me all the time and I was terrified. I told him I'd better get dressed and he said, "Oh, don't worry about that". He gave me all this soft soap about how much he loved me and how he's always regarded you as his real son – all this bullshit about being a father to you since Grandad died. He told me he'd always look after me as long as I looked after him.'

Tears began to course down Janice's face again as she forced out the last of the bitter story. 'He put his arm around my waist and started stroking my hair, and I told him to stop it. I couldn't believe he was actually doing it. He told me not to be silly ... that everything would be all right and not to make a noise. He scared the bloody hell out of me. It was his eyes as much as anything else. I've never met anyone else with a look like that. Never. The bastard started fondling my breasts and I just balled up my fist and hit him full in the face. It was like hitting a rock. If I hurt him, he didn't show it.

'He went completely quiet for a few seconds and then went mad. He dived at me and grabbed me hard by my hair and pulled my head back over the arm of the sofa. I thought he was going to rape me. Then he pulled out a knife and pressed it against my throat, and I was so frightened I started choking. I nearly blacked out. I really thought he was going to cut me up. He told me I had to learn to play the game, that it would be tragic for a girl to lose her looks at my age. He told me to think about it and then let me go. Then he left as if nothing had bloody happened. He just winked at me and said, "Not a word to Daddy, or Uncle J will be really upset". He's sick, Dad. The bastard is really sick.'

Angrily, Janice pulled an envelope from her jacket pocket and thrust it into her father's hands. 'He said that if I played the game, he would always look after me – that there were worse ways to make money – and he gave me that.'

Johnson opened the envelope and counted ten fifty-pound notes. 'Five hundred quid, Dad,' she said in a breaking voice. 'That's how much that shit thinks I'm worth.'

She collapsed into her father's arms, and Johnson could no longer hold back his tears as he gripped her little body with all his strength. 'Stop it,' he said. 'Don't talk like that.' He passionately kissed her head, her face and her neck, and cradled her head as she sobbed. It had taken him this long to discard his iron mask and express his love for his only child, the only person left in the world he could truly call family. There was only Janice now, and he realised that he could never let her go again.

'When he left, I cleared up Wendy's room,' she said softly. 'I was pretending it hadn't happened. It took my mind off it. I was pretending it hadn't happened . . .'

Time and time again, she repeated these words to herself. 'I was pretending it hadn't happened . . .'

A chilly wind was now blowing in off the sea and Johnson shivered again as he hugged his daughter. Yet despite everything – the wounds he had suffered on this tragic afternoon, and the tears he was ashamed of shedding – his resolve was suddenly stronger than ever. All his old strength, all those qualities that set him apart from the rest, were rushing back.

Now he would cut down Jack Fossey and anybody else in his way. And then walk away from this brutal and bloody business.

12

Greatstone, to Johnson, was a blissful step back in time, where everything seemed a little saner and healthier. It was a place where people still said 'Good morning' and observed the common courtesies. The weather could drive the pampered to despair – serene one day and savagely cruel the next – yet this rough and unapologetic slab of the Kent coast was always a welcome and safe haven for Johnson. It was the quietness he loved most, the chance to cleanse his mind and body of all the clogging filth of his trade. He resented the intrusion of troublemakers, which was why the incident at The Railway Bell had so infuriated him. It had been an invasion of his own paradise, a reminder of the ugliness of his everyday life.

It was the quietness he cherished later that afternoon as he stretched out his legs on Janice's bed, and gently supported his daughter by his side. Her bedroom was in the back of the bungalow, and apart from the cries of seagulls – one of Johnson's favourite sounds – there was only the gentle ticking of the small clock on the bedside table.

Both were emotionally shattered, but he kept his promise and told her everything he knew. The truth about the death of her mother, his own evil doing over the span of twenty years, and the monster of a man he had served. He hid nothing from her, not even his murderous intentions where Jack Fossey was concerned. More tears were shed, more bitter words exchanged between them, but Johnson held Janice close to him throughout, sensing that there was a bond between them at long last.

The poison out of his system, he brightened and told her about his restaurant at Monterey and the new life he had planned for them. To his surprise, Janice seemed genuinely excited about this and asked a great many questions. Exhausted, she fell asleep in his arms for about an hour, and Johnson felt a wonderful sense of relief and peace of mind as he listened to the seagulls and gazed out at a cloudless blue sky.

Michael had wandered off to the local supermarket to buy food and wine, and he was preparing lasagne when Johnson and Janice came into the kitchen at around six o'clock. It was a large kitchen with a pine table in the centre, and the three of them ate and talked together for nearly three hours until Janice grew tired again and went to bed. Initially, she had been shy of Michael, having met him only once before when she was a little girl, but had quickly warmed to him as he repeatedly teased her and made her laugh. This pleased Johnson. It had been so long since he had seen his daughter laugh so freely. He went into her bedroom to kiss her goodnight, then returned to the kitchen and poured himself another wine.

Michael was sipping cola and feigning the look of a man who had been condemned to death.

'Cheer up,' Johnson said. 'The way things are going, we could both die anyway.'

'It's getting really dangerous now, isn't it?' Michael said.

Johnson nodded. The chit-chat over dinner had been trivial and pleasant, yet Michael had felt the frightening tension. 'What happened today?' he asked.

Johnson was drained, but he patiently related Janice's story, pausing every once in a while to suppress his anger. Michael was having trouble understanding it all.

'Is this all part of some bizarre plan, or is Fossey just going out of his mind? Why would he do these things to you? You're supposed to be the kind of son he prayed for.'

'Yeah, he's always spinning that line,' Johnson said. 'He gave Janice all that old crap. I can't believe all this is happening, Michael. I reached a point this afternoon when I honestly thought I'd lost my way. I couldn't think straight, I couldn't come to terms with my feelings ... everything was upside down. I never felt as close to Fossey as he did to me, but I always had a strange respect for him. To my knowledge, he never did me down. We were tied together in a peculiar way. We knew each other. We got along. Christ, I was only nineteen when he took me on. Twenty bloody years ago...'

Johnson covered his face with his hands and sighed. 'Christ, I've got to focus on all this. I feel as if I'm watching some sort of sick video. I'm on the outside and I can't get in.'

'Tell me what I can do, Carl,' Michael said. 'You know I'll help you in any way I can.'

Johnson raised his glass to his friend and said, 'You've already done more than your fair share, Michael, and I'm grateful for that. But I'm advising you right now to step aside. You know I'm going to kill Fossey, and I might have to take out a few of his soldiers as well. As much as I appreciate your enthusiasm, I can't drag you into all that.'

Michael started to protest, but Johnson clamped a hand on his shoulder and said, 'Listen, there's something you still don't know. Last night, Dennis Fossey offered me the world to bump off the old man. He wants to take control of the organisation and he claims he's got majority support.'

'Christ, you're joking,' Michael said. 'From what you told me, I got the impression he was a wimp.'

'He is. That's why he wants me to do it for him. For the record, I'm doing it for myself. Once I've done the old man, I'm severing my ties with the Fosseys. Dennis has given me his assurance that I can walk away without having some sort of convenient accident, but I don't trust the bastard. He's a weak man who thinks power will make him strong. The silly prick could end up getting killed himself if he doesn't play his cards right. He finally found the courage to answer the old man back and capped it all by whacking him on the chin.'

'Wonderful,' Michael said. 'He's really come out of his shell, hasn't he?'

'He's rigged up an almighty bomb, Michael, that's what he's done. It's war now. Apparently, the old man's disowned him and Dennis is being shadowed by a couple of Jack's minders.'

'Anybody you know?'

'Yeah, a couple of guys called Kenny Carter and Dave Richards. They're dimwits, but they do know how to make people disappear.'

'What about Steve Cody? Where does he stand in all this?'

'He's thrown his lot in with Dennis, but Steve's no threat to me personally. He's just happy to cling to the shirt tails of whoever happens to be king of the hill. Power and responsibility frighten the shit out of Steve, but he likes to be close to those who have it.'

Michael still felt disappointed. Brimming with confidence after his adventure in The Railway Bell, he wondered if Johnson still doubted his nerve. 'I'm not afraid of getting involved, Carl,' he said eagerly.

'I know. You proved that today. Don't think I'm dumping you, Michael, because I'm not. There are still some important things you can do for me. In fact, I have one special favour to ask of you.'

'What's that?'

'Listen to me first.' Johnson lit a cigarette and said, 'Jack Fossey's in Glasgow and he'll be back Tuesday. I know what I'm going to do and how I'm going to do it. I've got to see him anyway to update him on things. You and Janice are the only two people left on this earth I can trust. When the time comes, I want you both well out of the firing line. In the meantime, we've still got another day to prepare ourselves, and that's where you can help me out. You're obviously on a high right now. You've got your confidence back and so far you've done it without the sauce. Do you think you can keep it going?'

Michael laughed and made a face. 'I think so. So far, it's not as bad as I thought it would be. Abstinence is boring, but it's not killing me. I keep reminding myself of the positive aspects. It's nice to wake up feeling good in the morning. It's nice to have a clear brain. More than anything else, it's great to feel like a human being again. Don't get me wrong. I'm aching for a glass of that wine right now. But I'm incapable of just getting plain drunk. I lose myself completely, for two, three, four days at a time. I stop eating, I stop bathing, I stop shaving. I stop doing all those boring but necessary little things that hold a man together. I feel as if I'm in hell. It's become a matter of pride, Carl. I've quit on myself so often in the past. I can't spend the rest of my life running away from every little problem. You've done me a great favour in sticking by me. I won't forget that. And I won't let you down.'

'I'm glad,' Johnson said. 'You certainly seem a lot happier and a lot more alert. Tell me, do you feel ready to move back into your flat?'

'Sure, I'll check out tomorrow if you want me to. I've wasted tonight anyway.'

Johnson shook his head. 'It's nothing to do with that, Michael. The Grand's my treat, I told you that. In more pleasant circumstances, I'd ask you to stay on for a few days. Look, this favour I mentioned . . . I wondered if you'd be prepared to look after Janice for me until all this blows over. You seem to get along well with her, and I want a place where she'd be safe. To my knowledge, we've got no one on our backs at the moment, but if things get dangerous I'll get you both out of there. Can you do that for me?'

Michael shrugged and said, 'That's fine with me, as long as it's okay with Janice.'

'Just try to make sure she eats and sleeps properly,' Johnson said. 'And keep her away from your mustic system. I don't know if she's changed since she left home, but she can't seem to hear music unless it's caving the roof in.'

Michael laughed. 'Yeah, I was no angel myself when I was her age. I think she'll be okay, Carl, I honestly do – once she's away from all this, I mean. Behind the rough clothes and the rough talk, she seems a nice kid.'

'Yeah, I could have done worse,' Johnson said. 'I think I got to know her a little better today. I think she's grudgingly conceded I'm not quite on a par with Hitler.'

'We drive back to Brighton tomorrow, right?'

'Right. As early as we can.'

Johnson seemed to drift away for a few moments, biting the skin around his fingernails and staring at nothing in particular. Michael, still very much stage-struck, studied him in awe out of the corner of his eye. Johnson had openly admitted to being confused and uncertain, yet the air of invincibility was still there. Michael wondered how such a man could switch guises with all the ease of an accomplished actor. Johnson could be cold and clinical, warm and charming; ruthless and unmerciful in his work, emotional and compassionate in his private moments. He was a true chameleon, mesmerising at all times.

Michael had to ask him something. 'Do you ever have nightmares, Carl? Do you ever wake up in the mornings feeling scared? I know it's a stupid question, but I'm not a strong man like you. You just seem to be able to rise above it all and come back even stronger.'

'And you have to drink yourself silly and watch old Roberto Duran fights,' Johnson said. He laughed and gave Michael a playful dig.

'What's so funny?' Michael asked. 'I'm really intrigued.'

'You're right,' Johnson said, 'it *is* a stupid question. Of course I wake up feeling scared. And you wouldn't believe some of my nightmares. Why do you always interpret fear as a weakness, Michael? It's fear that makes a person strong. There are no true supermen. Some of the toughest guys alive are scared shitless of spiders and being shut in elevators. You just have to live with it. Fear is always there. It's not something you can run away from.'

'What scares you, Carl?'

Johnson smiled thoughtfully. 'The things I've done . . . some of the terrible things I've been a part of. There are certain things that never go away. You just can't bury them. Years later, they come back and grab you by the balls in the middle of the night.'

He drained his glass of wine and said, 'Let me tell you something that might help you to cope with your own fears. I was twenty-three years old when I killed for the first time. And I killed a man I liked. It will prey on my mind for the rest of my days. He was a big, gentle bear of a man called Ernie White. He had this great craggy face, biceps like bloody boulders, yet he seemed almost embarrassed by his size. He was a typical South London character, the sort of guy you could write a book about. He ran his own betting shop in Lewisham and he was the worst bookie I ever met. He'd known Fossey for years, they'd been close friends at one time. Ernie's trouble was, he was hopeless with money. His shop did a pretty good turnover, just because of its location, but he was a chronic gambler himself and just pissed away all his profits. He started hitting the bottle and then turned to Jack for help. He was paying protection money to the local mob and falling behind with his payments.

'Fossey was good to him at first. He kept Ernie afloat and never asked for any of the money back. The bastard could be curiously charitable like that, if it was somebody he liked. But Ernie carried on gambling and drinking and Jack finally lost his patience. He demanded repayments on a a monthly basis and it seemed to scare Ernie. He seemed to pull himself together for a time. He met his payments and the old man didn't have to push him.'

Johnson rubbed his eyes and sighed. 'It didn't last, of course. Ernie fell back into his old habits and that's when it turned nasty. He owed his own people, he owed Jack, and he just couldn't do it. I was still learning the ropes at that time, and when Fossey decided to turn up the heat, he suggested I get some experience. Jack employed an animal around that time called Charlie Cantwell. I'd never seen Cantwell in action, but some of the other boys had told me he was a real psychopath. Fossey wanted to put the frighteners on Ernie, and told me Cantwell was the man for such occasions. "I want you to drive up to London and keep Charlie company on this one, Carl," he said. "He's a fucking maniac, is Charlie. All he knows is how to put the shits up people, but he might teach you a few things. Mind he doesn't go too far though. If dear old Ernie loses his hands, he won't be able to count my money."

'Fossey loves to talk like that. It's all part of the power game, proving what a tough bastard he is. He told me the other boys in the firm nicknamed Cantwell the Torch Singer. Of course, I was supposed to ask why, which I did, and Fossey told me this story about one of his local clients who incurred his wrath by getting brave and making a stand. He sent Cantwell along to see the guy, and Cantwell pulls out this blow torch and threatens to fry the guy's balls. The guy passed out and was never any trouble after that. That was Cantwell for you. I got first-hand experience of how he worked when we went to see Ernie.'

Michael's stomach had begun to churn and he was now consuming his cola with a rare eagerness. 'Christ,' he said between gulps, 'I

98

can just picture it. I know those sort of guys don't have hearts, but don't they have stomachs either? If I'd been holding the blow torch, I think I'd have passed out before the victim.'

Johnson smiled and said, 'Yeah, I was nearly sick myself when I was with Cantwell. Fossey was right. The man was a maniac. There are different ways of applying pressure. None of them are pleasant, but there are different ways. You can scare the hell out of people without literally frightening them to death. Charlie only knew one way.'

'What the hell did he do to Ernie White?' Michael asked.

'What he did was what probably pushed Ernie over the edge for good. I mean, his life was already out of control, but after that he just seemed to completely give up on himself. Drank like a man who couldn't wait to die. Cantwell was frightening in the car on the way to Ernie's place that night. You could see him getting pumped up by the second. He kept telling me about his past jobs, the guys he'd carved up, his methods of doing it, all that shit. He actually carried a black bag like a bloody doctor, full of his own little weapons. I was the new kid on the block, and he took great pleasure in trying to impress me. He boasted about the scars on his face and the way he looked, which was like the devil, quite frankly. He wore one of those stupid pony tails, long before they became fashionable, yet nothing looked stupid about Charlie – just evil. The only thing he never told me about, and I never asked him about it, was his right eye. He could see out of it, but there was no colour to the pupil. It was just a watery, greyish sort of white, as if it had been punctured. Everything about the bastard was terrifying.

'Ernie had closed up when we got there. There was nobody else around. Cantwell didn't engage in any small talk. As soon as we walked in, he asked him for the money. Ernie was drunk and a little braver than usual, and he protested that Charlie wasn't Fossey's normal collector. They said a few things to each other which I can't remember. Then Cantwell said, "You want to go to the toilet, Ernie, don't you?" Ernie sort of shook his head and Cantwell grabbed him by the collar and shoved him forward. There was a small, dingy toilet out back, and Cantwell pushed Ernie into it and told him to take his clothes off. Ernie started to panic and complain again and Charlie gave him a backhander. Charlie wasn't a big man, and it seemed a pretty innocuous sort of blow, but Ernie crashed back against the wall and slid to the floor.

'That was the first idea I got of Cantwell's physical strength, bearing in mind Ernie's size. Charlie was screaming now, telling Ernie to get all his clothes off. It was Charlie's mood swings that were so scary. Once Ernie had stripped off, Charlie suddenly became serene and spoke to him very softly. He told him to sit on the toilet and then gave him this quiet and bizarre lecture on how to manage his money and remain loyal to his friends. He sounded quite kindly, and kept patting Ernie gently on the back. He told him about his late father, who used to be a butcher and struggled to make a living. That was the moment, I knew it straight away. That's when I braced myself for the worst. Charlie said, "He left me all the tools of his trade, the old man did," and he opened the awful black bag he always had with him and drew out a meat cleaver.

'I saw the look of terror on Ernie's face, and then he screamed out as Charlie grabbed his prick and held it across the toilet seat. It was the most awful scream I've ever heard. I saw Charlie's arm raised, the cleaver in his hand. He had his back to me, blocking Ernie from my view, and I just heard the chunk of the cleaver going into the toilet seat. My head was spinning and I remember closing my eyes, expecting to get spattered in blood. Charlie stepped to one side, and I saw Ernie pitch forward and fall to the floor. Charlie started laughing like a madman. He slapped me on the back and said, "The crazy bloody sod really thought I was going to do it." He'd pulled Ernie's prick away at the last moment and Ernie had fainted out of fright.

'Charlie put the cleaver back in the bag, and then pulled out a felt pen and wrote on the wall "Don't forget – invest your money wisely". Then he said, 'Let's go, Carl.' I said to him, "Are we just going to leave him here?" and Charlie said, "Yeah, the most he can catch is a cold. He's pissed now, son, but he'll sure as hell be sober when he wakes up." And so we left the poor bugger there.'

Michael was feeling faintly ill, but once again found himself strangely drawn to this dark and morbid world. 'I thought you were going to say that Cantwell ordered you to finish Ernie off,' he said.

Johnson shook his head. 'Nah, Charlie never got anybody else to do his work for him. He enjoyed it too much. Fossey asked me how things had gone the next day and I didn't bullshit him. Cantwell scared people, but he wasn't the right kind of man for the kind of operation Jack was trying to build. He was a dinosaur from another age and I told Fossey that. I asked Jack to make me Ernie's regular collector. I told him I could make everything right, and that it would save us a lot of potential embarrassment. Better than Cantwell going in there and leaving a bloodbath behind him.

'The old man seemed shocked by my front, but he was impressed and gave me the job. I made a point of befriending Ernie and winning his trust, and for the next few months he paid me without any trouble. I'd always spend a little time with him, have a coffee and talk about the fights, the horses, football and all that. But I suspected it could never last. Ernie seemed fated. He was just a big, simple lumbering guy who couldn't cope with life. He lived with his sister, who suddenly died – or so he claimed – and he started crying one day and told me he could no longer afford Fossey's rates. I told him he knew the score, but he missed a payment, and I explained his troubles to Fossey and asked the old man to give him a break.

'Jack really gave me a tough time. I got him to agree, but I knew I was only buying a little time, and that my own neck was on the block. I can remember the fat bastard sitting there behind his desk, smoking one of his fat cigars and saying to me, "You sort this out, Carl. I've got great plans for you, son, but I'm beginning to wonder if you've got the balls for this line of work. Maybe you're more the office type." He gave me this big speech about how times had changed, how it wasn't good business to spill blood on the street any more. But Ernie was one of his generation and only understood the old way of doing things. He wondered if he ought to send Charlie Cantwell back in there with his meat cleaver and take Ernie's dick off for real. Looking back, that was the pivotal point in my career.'

Johnson got up, walked across to the kitchen window, and gazed out at the garden. 'The next time I visited Ernie, he was high but not drunk. It was an early evening in July. He was out back in his office, drinking Scotch and fumbling around with his takings for the day.

He always hung around for ages in that dingy office after closing. The shop had become his whole world. I had a gut feeling this was it, that all this shit couldn't go on. Ernie was maudlin and confused, and when I told him of Fossey's ultimatum, he started breaking up and crying again.

'I suggested we go for a drive and talk it over, and he perked up a bit. I was thinking of the absolute worst now. We drove out of Lewisham and into Blackheath, and all the time Ernie's asking me if I know what it's like to lose a sister, to be bled dry by a bastard like Fossey, to be a loser. Christ, it was pitiful ... pitiful and almost comical. I mean, he's sitting there taking slugs from his bottle of Scotch and lecturing me on the demon drink. He was raving by that point, totally out of his head.

'I drove towards Shooters Hill where there are a lot of woods. There's an entrance to the woods just over the hill, where you drive down a little road into a parking area. It's usually very quiet and the woods are all around you. I parked the car and told Ernie we'd take a walk and have a chat. There was only one other car there and I couldn't see any people. Ernie was hugging his bottle like a mother hugs her baby, and he fell flat on his face at one point and started giggling. He was annoying the shit out of me, but I didn't want to upset him even more.

'We got deep into the woods and Ernie was really getting morose. I'd seen him drunk before, but not that drunk. It was making him aggressive and abusive, and he was really slagging off Fossey. Then he talked about suicide. He said it was the only way out, the only way he could get everyone off his back and find peace with himself.

'God knows, Michael, I tried. I tried my damnedest to bring him to his senses. I told him to kick the booze, to straighten himself out, that I'd help him as best I could. I kept trying to punch home the dangers of messing with guys like Fossey, but Ernie was long past understanding the simplest of things.'

Johnson turned around to face Michael, leaning back against the kitchen door. 'I remember the moment of truth so vividly. It's difficult to explain, but it was almost surreal. We came to this little clearing, and the sun suddenly came streaming through the trees. Ernie had staggered away from my side, and the light was so severe for a few seconds, I could only make out his silhouette. His right arm was raised and I could see something flashing in his hand. I thought it was his bottle, and that one peculiar moment seemed to last forever, as if time had stopped. Then the sun died, and he was standing there like a big statue, holding up this carving knife and crying like a baby. Jesus, man, the tears were pouring down his face and running off his chin.

'He was looking straight into my eyes. No man I've ever met has looked at me as intensely as Ernie did at that moment. "I'm not scared of dying, Carl," he said. He started waving the knife at me and said, "This is the way I'll do it. I'll rip my throat out and make it nice and dramatic. Old Jack will love that."

'It was then I think I felt true fear for the first time. It was clear his mind had gone, that he'd finally lost his sanity. He lowered his eyes and just stared at the ground, rambling to himself and whimpering. It was a horrible sound, the kind of sound a dog makes when it's ill-treated. I moved towards him. I honestly just wanted to comfort him and try to work something out. I was reaching for his arm when he lifted his head and gave me that look again.

'I saw the knife coming down at me and just managed to block it. Ernie tripped and crashed into me, and we both fell over. He was yelling and thrashing and trying to get at me with the knife, and I was holding on to his wrist for dear life. He dropped the knife and got his hand free, and started punching me in the face. I was seeing white spots and everything was spinning like mad, and I only knew I couldn't afford to lose consciousness.

'I saw the knife on the ground. By then, it was just a question of instinct, of survival. I grabbed it and stuck it into Ernie's side as hard as I could. His body sort of jerked upwards, and I pulled the knife out and rammed it into his stomach. I'd often wondered what it felt like . . . to stab a man. Yet I didn't seem to feel anything in the heat of the moment. Just Ernie's blood running over my hand. His face was right over mine, his eyes wide, as if they were going to burst out of their sockets. I pushed him off, and he just rolled over as if he'd fallen asleep.

'It was all so strange. I'd just killed a man, yet my first reaction was to look around for other people. I heard some kids shouting in the distance, but I couldn't see anyone. I heard thunder and it started to rain pretty heavily.

'I dragged Ernie's body as far into the bushes as I could. I was panicking for the first time, because I was trying to do all the right things. It was really raining hard, and I rubbed my hands in a bunch of leaves and managed to get most the blood off. I tucked the knife in the front of my trousers and buttoned up my jacket, but it didn't hide all the blood. I wanted to run like hell, but I remembered some advice Fossey once gave me about never running, and I started walking briskly.

'The walk back to the car seemed endless, but I was lucky. I saw some woman walking her dog as I neared the car park, but she was well away from me. The curious thing was, all my nervousness left me once I got into the car. I remember being very cool, very deliberate . . . almost too calm. I didn't drive straight off. My raincoat was on the back seat, and if ever I was grateful for that raincoat, it was then. It was one of those bloody great long things like the old gunfighters used to wear. Perfect. I put it on and I can even remember combing my hair and checking around for any telltale signs. I couldn't believe that I could be so meticulous and so calm at such a moment. I looked at my hands for any blood I'd missed, and they weren't even trembling.

'Then I started the drive back to Brighton. I didn't really think about what I'd done. I don't remember thinking about anything in particular. I was in a trance, yet I knew exactly what I was doing. It was the oddest sensation. And for doing that, I became Jack Fossey's golden boy.'

Johnson sat back down, shook his head gently and added, 'To this day, Ernie White still haunts me in my sleep. Maybe one of these nights he'll take me to the woods and put a knife in me.'

'I think I understand fear a lot better now,' Michael said, very quietly.

Johnson nodded grimly and sipped at his wine.

'What about the repercussions?' Michael asked. 'I mean, what happened?'

Johnson smiled. 'The police put it down to a gangland killing. They knew Ernie was paying off all sorts of people, but they couldn't prove anything. Fossey made things good with the local mob and everyone pleaded ignorance. He protected me well. He always did, I must say that.'

Michael laughed nervously and said, 'Christ Almighty, Carl, you've certainly met some characters in your time. Charlie Cantwell sounds like a composite of every psycho who ever lived.'

'He was the only man who ever truly frightened me,' Johnson acknowledged.

'Yeah, I bet nobody ever picked on *him*. Is he still around?'

'No. He just got too inventive and too wild for his own good. He became an embarrassment. He had to go.'

'What's he doing now?'

'Nothing much,' Johnson replied. He finished his wine, and, without a hint of show, added, 'Charlie was my second scalp.'

13

Michael couldn't get to sleep that night. At home, back in noisy Brighton, he would lie in bed at one in the morning cursing the comings and goings of cabs, the slamming of doors, and the arguments of drunken lovers in his busy street. But Johnson's bungalow was too quiet, to the point of being eerie. Not a sound, not even the distant cries of restless seagulls. But Michael knew that the silence was really incidental. The giddy pace of the last two days had left him bursting with energy and he simply couldn't relax his body.

He no longer felt a part of the world he had known for so long. It was as if Johnson were some kind of giant mythical figure, leading him through a fantasy land at breakneck speed.

Everything Michael felt right now was contradictory to his placid and retiring nature. He had listened to harrowing tales from Johnson and Neil Franklin, and been involved in the kind of bar-room brawl that would have done justice to his Wild West heroes. Fear still gripped him like a vice, churning his stomach all the time, yet it was a drug and he craved for more. His brain was racing, spewing out so many thoughts and images that he felt elated and exasperated all at once.

Finally, he dropped off to sleep, and what followed was his second vivid dream in as many nights, which would make him wonder if he were seeing the future in some terribly twisted form. For this second dream was cruelly deceptive, its initial aura of happiness and tranquility being ruthlessly smashed. There was no hope, no rainbow this time, no dance of joy from

Neil Franklin. It was paradise turned sour, horrifically ripped apart.

Michael, Johnson, and Franklin were seated at a large, round table on the soft sand of Carmel Beach on California's Monterey Peninsula. Michael loved Carmel, having been there on several occasions in the past, and his dreams frequently took him back to that glorious stretch of the Northern California coast. The three men were laughing and joking and chatting about their favourite things, dressed in spotless white suits and waistcoats and white shoes.

The table was an absolute picture, adorned with delicious foods, bottles of wine and champagne, and pitchers of gleaming beer. Right in the centre, there was a vase of the most beautiful red roses Michael had ever seen. But the roses were too red, the sky too blue, the seagulls too white. The whole scene was a breathtaking picture of summer, but too perfect, a fragile façade about to crumble. Michael felt wonderfully happy and relaxed, yet he seemed to sense the approaching storm as he revelled with his two friends.

He was discussing one of his favourite Beach Boys songs, which was ringing out so loud and beautifully in his head. 'It's called "Celebrate The News",' he was patiently telling the others. 'I played it last night for the first time in ages, and I can't get it out of my mind.'

'Yeah, that's a great one,' Johnson said. 'That was the flip side of "Break Away", wasn't it?'

'I think so,' Michael said. 'It's that great crescendo at the end I love, where Dennis says "Come on, come on", and their voices come in waves. Absolutely brilliant.'

They toasted 'Celebrate The News', then the Beach Boys, Clint Eastwood, Jack Nicklaus, and any other heroes who came to mind. 'Let's drink this lot and go back up the road to Pebble Beach,' Franklin suggested. 'That's where Nicklaus won the US Open back in 1972.' Then he came out with the kind of inane remark that finds its way into even the most realistic of dreams. 'You know, back in '75, I caddied for Jack when he won the Greater Iceberg Eskimo Classic.'

'I want to go to Morro Bay,' Michael said. 'The Beach Boys sang about Morro Bay.'

'Yeah, we'll stop off at Big Sur along the way,' Johnson agreed. 'Joan Baez lives at Big Sur, I think. I think I'll ask her to marry me. I'm bloody lonely without Rose.'

In a quiet but slightly desperate voice, Franklin said, 'We've got to go somewhere. We've got to get out of here. It's going to rain. I know it's going to rain.'

'Hey, Neil, take it easy,' Johnson laughed. 'You haven't been seeing faces in the water again, have you?'

Franklin now looked extremely frightened, and Michael felt his stomach sink as the great blue sky turned dramatically grey and the wind began to blow. 'The face came back in my dreams last night,' Franklin said. 'Those awful eyes were burning through me worse than ever. But there was more this time. He was holding a body under the water.' He swallowed hard and looked at Johnson. 'It was a woman's body, Carl, I'm sure of it. I saw the head come out of the water and there were these terrible choking sounds. That's it, you see. It's me who's frightening the face, not the other way around. I'm a witness, Carl. I think it's Rose. I think I'm seeing Rose being killed.'

Now all the laughing and joking had stopped, and Michael was paralysed with fear. At this point, he no longer seemed to be a part of the dream, but a helpless spectator, standing some distance back on high ground, with a panoramic view of the increasingly dark and stormy scene. Johnson's face came into close-up, looking horrified. Michael was conscious of holding himself tightly as the wind whipped his body and the sea welled into a rage. Then Johnson was on his feet, grabbing Franklin by the lapels and shouting above the commotion, 'Tell me! Tell me!'

Then Michael saw it. A hideous figure standing waist deep in the water, covered in seaweed and slime. It was motionless, as if waiting to be challenged, its face a mask except for the terrible eyes that had put the fear of death into Franklin. They were focused directly on Michael, who suddenly felt his breath being sucked out of him. He was trying to attract the others' attention, but he couldn't find his voice. He saw a body floating away from the figure and Johnson was shouting, 'Rose! Rose!'

In the next instant, Michael was standing alongside Johnson, who was brandishing the formidable gun called Barbara Ann that he had toyed with in the first dream. Franklin was still sitting at the table, glaring out at the figure in terror, seemingly unable to move.

'It's Fossey, I know it's Fossey,' Johnson yelled above the howling wind. 'I'm going to kill that bastard.' He was taking aim when the figure raised an arm and pointed at Franklin. Michael looked back, and Franklin was on his feet, knocking his chair over behind him and wiping blood from his face.

'Don't let him get me, Michael,' he shouted. 'Please don't let him get me.' He turned and began to run, zigzagging in his confusion and panic. A huge bank of fog had descended further up the beach, and within seconds it had completely enveloped him.

Michael jumped as the explosion from Johnson's gun thundered in his ears, and the figure in the sea was staggering back, blood oozing from its chest. Johnson fired again, and the figure fell back into the waves and disappeared from view. 'I can't see him,' Johnson said. 'Where the hell is he?'

Michael could see nothing through the foam and spray of the crashing waves, which now seemed to be swelling to ridiculous proportions. The figure and the woman's body were lost and Franklin had vanished like magic. The fog that had engulfed him was moving slowly and ominously towards Michael and Johnson, and Michael had never felt so scared. 'Everything's wrong, Carl,' he shouted. 'It's all wrong. Jesus Christ, what's happening?'

But Johnson wasn't listening. Obsessed with his mysterious prey, he continued to wave the big gun from side to side, ready to fire again. 'He's still alive, Michael, I know it. He's out there waiting for me.'

'Let's go,' Michael pleaded. 'It's too dangerous, it's not worth it.'

'I *can't*,' Johnson said in desperation.

He walked down to the shore and into the water, and Michael was rooted to the spot, powerless to stop him. Johnson was now a man possessed, seemingly oblivious of the giant waves that began to swamp him. The huge bank of fog was nearly upon Michael when the blood-soaked figure suddenly surged from the waves and clasped its hands round Johnson's throat, dragging him under. As the fog started to cover Michael, he saw the two bodies bob up again, engaged in a tremendous struggle. He tried to run to Johnson's aid, but still couldn't move his legs. The fog was smothering him, and he clutched his head as the terrific noise of the wind and the sea forced him to his knees.

He was waiting for the axe to fall, in whatever terrible way, when everything stopped; the great din replaced by a frightening quietness. As he kneeled in submission, he felt the hot sun on his back, warm and caressing. He opened his eyes, fearing the worst, and looked out at a calm sea, sparkling in the brilliant sunshine. There was no sign of Johnson, the figure, or the woman's body. It was the too-perfect summer's day again; no fog, not a hint of wind. Michael wanted to cry, convinced he was going out of his mind. He got to his feet and looked left and right. Nothing. No form of life, not even a solitary seagull.

But there was a presence that made Michael turn around. Franklin was back in his chair at the table. He seemed to be staring straight at Michael, his legs crossed, his hands resting in his lap, his face and his white suit horribly caked in blood. The once picturesque table was now a picture of death. The bottles and glasses were smashed, the roses dry and shrivelled. 'Neil,' Michael cried. 'Neil, are you okay? What happened?'

He ran back up the beach, stopping within inches of the table when he realised that there was no life in Franklin's eyes. Michael placed his hands on the table to steady himself, as he began to weep uncontrollably. Through the mist of his tears, he saw Johnson's great silver gun glittering amongst the glass fragments, and he sensed at once why it was there. He gripped the heavy gun firmly and turned to face the sea. The figure was there again, now pointing a finger at Michael. This time, Michael experienced no other feeling but rage. The soft sand was now flat and firm under his feet, a strip of about ten feet wide, leading straight to the shore.

'Celebrate The News' was ringing in his ears again, giving him a magnificent surge of strength, as he broke into a run. Shot after shot crashed out of the gun, and the crimson-stained figure was flying back into the water when Michael awoke breathless and soaked in sweat.

14

Monday was an anti-climatic day, an itchy day. On Tuesday, Johnson would clash with Jack Fossey and the tension was now unbearable for Michael. He hadn't had a drink for nearly two days, yet he felt so high that it frightened him.

The drive back to Brighton was laboriously slow and the atmosphere in the car tense. Over breakfast that morning, Johnson had told Janice that she would be staying with Michael for a few days, and it was clear that she wasn't pleased at the prospect of being constrained and chaperoned. It was another uncomfortably hot day, and they stopped halfway at a country pub for a cold lunch and drinks. Johnson was putting on a happy face for Janice, but Michael could see that he was tight and distracted.

They sat outside in the back garden and Johnson ordered a ploughman's lunch, but ate only half of it. He went through four cigarettes in fairly quick succession, though he seemed thoughtful rather than nervous.

Janice, not wishing to upset her father, but clearly wanting to express her frustration at being made a prisoner, suddenly piped up 'What about going out, Dad?'

'What?' Johnson said.

'You said all this business might take a few days,' she elaborated. 'We can't just stay in Michael's flat all the time.'

'You're going to have to, Janice,' Johnson said. 'I've got an old friend called Micky Lyle, who's helped me out in the past. He's a freelancer, not one of Fossey's men. Micky will get you anything you need. You stay in the flat at all times, understand?

I don't trust Dennis, or Cody, or any of them anymore. Just do this for me, Janice, please. Don't for Christ's sake go sneaking off on your own. I know you've only got the two bedrooms, Michael. Micky can sleep on the floor somewhere. Sorry to put you out like this.'

'On the contrary, I still feel I'm not serving much of a purpose here,' Michael said.

Johnson smiled and tapped him on the shoulder. 'Don't be silly, I'm just happy to have you around. I'll sleep at your place tonight. I'll just feel more comfortable if I'm with you and Janice. Steve reckons the old man will be back late tonight. He usually sits around listening to his opera until about two or three in the morning, so I'll call him and set up a meeting.'

'Opera?' Michael said, disbelievingly.

'Yeah, he's one of the latter day converts. He saw Pavarotti in concert on TV and was hooked. He thought the guy was an Italian middleweight before that.'

Johnson's joke broke the feeling of uneasiness for a while, yet Michael could feel the static between father and daughter. Johnson was deeply worried for Janice, and she for him, yet they were kindred spirits who became emotional cripples when trying to express their feelings for one another.

At the dinner table in Michael's flat that evening, Janice asked her father how he planned to 'do it'. She couldn't bring herself to look into his eyes.

'Do it?' Johnson said edgily, knowing exactly what she meant.

'Kill him,' she said. 'How are you going to kill Fossey?'

Surprisingly, Johnson seemed to draw strength from the awkward question. 'You ought to see that restaurant of ours at Monterey,' he said, squeezing her hand. 'That's what I keep thinking about, Janice, and I want you to keep thinking about it too. I can't sit here and make you promises about tomorrow. It wouldn't be fair. But I just have a feeling deep down that all this rotten business is going to work out okay. I'll leave you a little something before I go tomorrow. Something to cheer you up.'

She kept her head down. 'You haven't answered my question, Dad.'

Johnson let go of her hand, and while his tenderness was still there, the steel returned to his voice when he said, 'I know how I'm going to kill him. I know exactly. Now let's eat.'

15

Johnson was up at six the next morning, feeling tense but confident. A methodical and meticulous man, he even went about such mundane tasks as washing and shaving in a precise and orderly manner. He was brisk in such matters, but never rushed himself, religiously adhering to his same reassuring routine. It gave him a sense of calmness and enabled him to concentrate his mind on the day ahead.

Once dressed, his last quirky little habit was to place a cherished silver dollar coin in his right trouser pocket. He had picked it up on the street in Lake Tahoe some ten years before and had carried it everywhere with him ever since. He sometimes chuckled to himself about his little superstition, since it had never brought him any outrageous luck.

When Michael drifted into the kitchen, still in his pyjamas, Johnson was sitting at the table drinking coffee. He looked immaculate, as usual, and his appearance reflected the sombre occasion and its likely consequences. Dressed in a black jacket, black slacks and blood red shirt, his hair was swept back more severely than usual and his whole body somehow looked even leaner and harder.

Michael caught him by surprise. Johnson was tucking his gun into its shoulder holster and gave a look of mock disgust at being caught. Pulling out the gun again, he handed it to Michael and said, 'Here, have a quick look. I haven't got time for a question and answer session on the prudence of carrying a firearm.'

Michael gingerly took hold of the gun as if it were about to explode in his hand, and Johnson chuckled. 'It only misbehaves if you pull the trigger.'

'Smith & Wesson,' Michael said, reading the legend on the barrel.

'Nine millimetre semi-automatic,' Johnson elaborated. 'Micky Lyle got me that one.'

'How much do these things cost, Carl?'

'Depends who your supplier is,' Johnson smiled, taking back the gun and placing it in its holster.

Michael made fresh coffee and sat down, still trying to wake himself up. 'It's bloody early isn't it?' he said. 'When are you meeting Fossey?'

'Nine-thirty. I've got some other things to do first.'

'When did you call him?'

'About one o'clock this morning. The oily bastard made me want to throw up. I swear to God he would have kissed me if we'd been in the same room. He wants to discuss his problems. Get dressed as soon as you can, Michael. Micky will be here at about eight. I want to be out of here before Janice wakes up.'

Micky Lyle didn't arrive at 'about eight' but exactly on the hour. Michael could now feel the whole affair taking on the air of a precisely planned military operation, and his admiration for these mysterious, shadowy men was growing ever more.

Micky didn't possess Johnson's charisma, and at first glance he was a disappointment to Michael. Shortish, sandy-haired, and casually dressed in a T-shirt and jeans, Lyle looked as if he'd come to fix the plumbing.

On closer inspection, Michael knew he was in formidable company. Lyle was stockily built, but there wasn't an ounce of fat on him. Michael noticed the Popeye-like width of his forearms and a faded scar that ran from the middle of his left arm down to the wrist. His face, if not handsome, was certainly striking. His watery, pale blue eyes were mesmerising, his snub nose almost cute. But it was a tough face that had obviously taken its share of punishment. Lyle's voice was soft, his nature shy, his handshake crushing.

Johnson issued final instructions to both men, then motioned Lyle over to him as he headed for the door. They exchanged quiet words for a minute or so, but Michael couldn't hear what was being discussed.

'I'll be in touch, Michael,' Johnson said. And then he was gone. Lyle turned to Michael, clapped his hands and said, 'Got anything to eat?'

16

Jack Fossey was a sprightly and hugely energetic sixty-two-year old, despite a great bulging stomach and a face so severely ruddy that it constantly looked on the verge of bleeding. Jack loved life and all the delicious trappings of wealth and power. Loud, rambunctious, and blissfully oblivious of his many shortcomings, he had barnstormed through life in his own crude and straight way, constantly aspiring to be a better person than he was. He was a poor South London boy made good, who loved to mix with the best people, yet had never quite mastered the social graces. Jack was a thundering and intimidating man who invoked fear and respect among his own kind but was a social embarrassment to those he sought to impress the most.

Even within his own empire, he had begun to lose his magic, becoming a parody of the lean and vicious young man who had ruthlessly sped to the top. The years had caught up with Jack. Once a dedicated follower of fashion, with his finger firmly on every pulse, he was now one step behind in every department. He had the slicked-back hair, the red braces on his trousers, and the mobile phone, but he was no yuppie. He had great plans for the future, but was no longer a visionary. In his heart of hearts, Jack knew he was floundering, but his fierce pride wouldn't allow him to let go of the helm. He was a local legend, and it was his fearsome reputation that kept him at the top. He was still a strong man, but a sad man whose lust for a fight was waning by the day.

Jack's only son and child, who had been a failure right from the start, had betrayed him and struck him in the only daring act of his useless life. The young tigers in the organisation were getting restless and ready to make their move, and the old guard offered little hope. The likes of Charlie Cantwell had been too brutally efficient for their own good, yet were leagues ahead of the current generation.

Jack Fossey missed the old days, the old characters, the old and simple way of doing things. The excitement and the adventure had gone. Now everything was bland and clinical and diplomatic, and everybody looked the same.

Jack had reached that state of boredom where he was changing the habits of a lifetime in an effort to revive his interest and keep himself fresh. For many years, since the early seventies, he had spent his mornings within the reassuringly secure confines of his formidable estate on the outskirts of Hove. He would often conduct business in his dressing gown and pyjamas, sometimes until as late as two in the afternoon. He loved sitting behind his great desk in his expansive study, busying himself on the phone, seeing a steady stream of business associates, and issuing instructions to his soldiers. Then he would dress and be chauffeured into town to take up his public role as president of the Southern International Corporation, a suitably versatile and multi-faceted concern which had its fingers in every kind of pie.

But all this had changed, and Jack's Brighton office was now his castle. He hadn't realised how big the house was until his beloved wife, Lilian, had died in 1982, or how cold it could be since Dennis had left. Lilian was a warm, kind, old-fashioned lady, a happily housebound wife out of the old mould, the perfect companion to an incorrigible bigot like Jack. He had loved the way she fussed around him, attending to his every need, and organising his day-to-day affairs with smooth and gentle precision. Even the infuriating Dennis had added a certain warmth to the house, if only in the same way as an obedient puppy.

Besides, there were certain people Jack now liked to keep at a distance; and while his office in the central part of town was large and lavish, it had come to feel safer and more intimate. He had everything he needed there, as well as an eager-to-please secretary called Jenny, who reminded him of his Lilian in her younger days. A picture of Lilian sat directly in front of him on his desk, while the walls were adorned with pictures of Jack the community man, flanked by mayors, boxing champions, and schoolchildren.

Jack had taken to arriving at the office at around half past eight to nine, giving himself a good hour or so to read the newspapers and generally compose himself before getting down to business. Today, as the early morning sun filled the room, he felt more upbeat and cheerful than he had in some time. His schedule had been punishing for the past few weeks, and the phone call from Carl Johnson in the early hours had lifted his spirits. In a cold new era where Jack was surrounded by dense young turks who needed to be fed like computers, and old troupers who had grown fat and lazy, Johnson represented professionalism, intelligence, and common sense.

Jack had taken him on and watched him mature over the years, and Johnson had exceeded his greatest expectations. Jack now treated him as an equal. He could talk to Johnson, confide in him, drink with him. He admired Johnson for his toughness, his fairness, and his love of adventure. Carl was Jack's kind of man, a wonderful antidote to the current image-conscious breed, who drank mineral water and expressed greater concern about their hairstyles than the job at hand.

Jack had cleared the decks for Johnson's visit, briefing Jenny on what had to be done, and farming out the day's business to the appropriate people. Johnson had suggested a brief update on business affairs, followed by a leisurely day visiting their favourite haunts. Jack was suitably attired in a beige summer suit, and couldn't wait to escape. He had a husky, booming voice, and had never quite grown accustomed to an intercom. When Jenny announced Johnson's arrival at nine-thirty promptly, Jack thundered, 'Bring him in! Bring him in!' like a man trying to attract a friend's attention from the opposite end of a football stadium.

Now Johnson had to act as he'd never acted before. For as long as it took, despite the hatred burning within him, he had to step back into his old role of 'Jack's boy', and play the old pals act with utter conviction. The hardest part was the first act, when Jack, in time-honoured tradition, ambled up like a great bear and gave him a powerful and emotional hug. Johnson clasped the big body and inhaled the familiar, overwhelming smell of after shave. Only Jack could apply Aramis with such reckless abandon as to make it repugnant.

'How's my favourite boy, then?' he asked, gripping Johnson by the shoulders and giving him a hearty shake.

'I'm fine, Jack. How's things with you?'

'Bloody awful,' Jack replied, letting out another roaring laugh. 'Sit down, Carl, sit down.'

Jack moved his huge frame around his desk and dropped down into his seat. 'God, it's great to see you,' he said, with genuine emotion. 'The world's going mad, son. How was Los Angeles? Apart from the bloody smog, I mean.'

'Very good,' Johnson said. 'Things are slotting nicely into place. I'll explain it all later.'

'Good, good,' Jack said. 'How's that old bastard Jimmy Luisi?'

'Fatter than you,' Johnson chuckled. 'He was getting these pains in his chest, so his doctor put him on a diet. He was moaning like hell about it.'

'Serves him right. I kept telling him to cut back on the bloody pasta.'

Jack lit a farcically huge cigar and asked Johnson if he'd like a drink.

'Too early for me, thanks, Jack.'

'Yeah, you were always a good boy like that. In that case, I'll follow your example. We can make up for lost time later. Have you seen any of the boys since you've been back?'

'That's the main reason I came to see you. I know the troubles you're having. Dennis and Steve Cody invited me to dinner Saturday night. Things are a lot worse than you think, you know.'

Jack's face dropped and he looked furious. 'I know it. I bloody know it, Carl. He hit me, you know. The little bastard actually hit me.'

'He told me.'

'So he's found an ally in that slimeball Cody, has he? Those two have always been close. I didn't think Cody had the balls for a fight.'

'He hasn't,' Johnson said. 'He just enjoys watching and then sucking up to the winner.'

'You went to school with that shit, didn't you?'

'Yeah, he was no different in those days.'

'So what's happening?'

Johnson wasn't casual in his reply, but didn't see any point in bullshitting. Looking his old mentor straight in the eye, he said, 'Dennis wants me to kill you, Jack.'

Jack's eyes widened and he sagged in his chair. 'Christ, that's nice,' he said, trying to make light of it. But he was devastated. In his own peculiar way, he still loved Dennis.

'He asked me to name my own price,' Johnson added.

With a false smile, Jack asked, 'And are you going to kill me, Carl?'

Johnson didn't answer that question, but simply gave Jack a marvellously authentic look of contempt. Jack waved a hand and said, 'Yeah, I'm sorry, boy, I should have known better than to ask you that.' He gave his cigar a distasteful look and rested it in the ashtray. 'Jesus, where did I go wrong as a father? I wouldn't mind, but Dennis was all life dealt us. Lilian could only have the one child. She couldn't . . . well, I mean, Dennis was all she could manage. How I yearned for a son, Carl. And Dennis was exactly the kind of son I didn't want. Soft as shit and just as thick. I was hard on the kid because I had to be hard on him, but I could never have disowned him. As much as the little bugger frustrated me, I always gave him the best. He was twenty-five before he got a place of his own, but he could have stayed at home if he'd wanted. I've kept the pressure on him all these years because he needs to be pushed. He's still a child in a man's body. Can you honestly imagine him running this business?'

Johnson shook his head. 'He couldn't run a piss-up in a brewery, Jack, but Cody's been sounding out the troops and he reckons most of them are behind Dennis – apart from the old guard.'

'They bloody would be,' Jack said, his temper rising. 'They're as bloody stupid as he is.' But he was alarmed and hurt. 'Shit, Carl, are things really this bad?'

'It seems so. They're unhappy with the decisions you've been making, Jack – your whole approach. They think you've lost your touch. Dennis called you an embarrassment – a dinosaur.'

Although Johnson was keeping a tight rein on his emotions, he was deriving immense pleasure from gently twisting the knife.

'The fucking little shit,' Jack said, almost comically. 'He's a weak and sad young man, Carl. He bangs me on the chin in the only brave move of his life, but he can't look me in the eye and pull the trigger of a gun. He has to get somebody else to do that. I never thought the day would dawn when I would hate my own son. But I'll tell you this, I'm going to get the bastard. Weak men can be more dangerous than strong men. They come in through the back door and you never know when.'

'He said you've got Carter and Richards on him,' Johnson said.

'Yeah, but what good can they do if most of the others are against me? They're loyal, Carl, and they're still good in a fight. But at their best, they were never sharp thinkers.'

'Dennis tells me he's confined to Brighton. What if he strays?'

'I'm going to set up a meeting with that son of mine,' Jack said darkly. 'If he misbehaves in the meantime and Carter and Richards have to take care of him, then so be it.'

'Could you really kill him?' Johnson asked. 'That's what you're thinking, isn't it?'

'Why the hell not?' Jack snapped. 'He's going to kill me, isn't he? He's had every chance I can give him, Carl. The one thing he's not going to do is take away my empire. He's not going to inherit something I fought tooth and nail for. He doesn't know what it's like to fight for something, to scratch and claw for everything you have. I've been knifed along the way, I've had the shit beaten out of me, I've been a constant target for ambitious pricks who thought they were better than me. And I've beaten them all off. I'm going to quell this revolt and I don't care what it takes. I'm going to call Dennis in, Carl. Can you watch my back in the meantime? Can I ask you that favour?'

Johnson nodded. 'That goes without saying. But first we need to think everything out very carefully. Much as I love you, Jack, I've got to say that hot head of yours has always been your one big weakness. You've asked me a favour. Now let me ask one of you. Just leave the game plan to me, okay? I'll work everything out.'

Jack smiled warmly and seemed to relax a little. 'That's fine with me, kid. Let's teach these bastards a lesson. Then we can start afresh. You and me, Carl. We'll clean house and draft the best team in the land. We'll be the kings of the beach.'

Johnson's body gave a little jerk at these last words, though he didn't know why. Kings of the beach . . . his very own description of Michael and himself in Michael's first dream. 'Sure we will, Jack,' he said. 'But in the meantime, let's go out and do some serious drinking.'

17

The 'little something' that Johnson had promised to leave Janice was a booklet on the Monterey Peninsula, crammed with colour photographs. She flicked through the pages as she sat curled up on the sofa, and for a few short minutes she was able to escape and forget her turbulent life.

She had immediately taken to Micky Lyle, who was welcomely calming and unintrusive. A quiet man, he rarely led off the conversation, yet he possessed a warmth and kindness that made her feel comfortable. He was playing cards at the table, while Michael was making a brave attempt to make sandwiches for everyone in the kitchen.

Janice could hear him fiddling about out there, as the smell of fresh coffee wafted up the hall. Michael's flat was refreshingly cool on hot days such as this, and there was a nice breeze blowing through the open window. It was a pleasantly quiet and lazy day, and Janice was surprised at how quickly she had forgotten these simple pleasures. She had been through a long and dark phase in her life where she had convinced herself that she hated simple living and the sound of silence. Happiness had been getting blind drunk, pounding her brain with loud music, and thrashing herself into a frenzy in sweaty, smoke-filled dance halls. Now she had to admit to herself that she felt at ease for the first time in many years.

Again and again, she flicked through the booklet, re-reading her favourite passages and marvelling at the Peninsula's great beauty. The names alone were magical ... Big Sur, Point Lobos, Carmel,

Pacific Grove … and Monterey itself. Was this really to be her future home? Like the summer's day in Michael's second dream, it all seemed too perfect.

When Michael reappeared, Janice and Micky giggled over his roughly cut sandwiches. Michael placed a carafe of chilled white wine and two glasses on the table, and was suddenly struck by how delicious it looked. The urge to drink had faded over the last few days, but when it did well up it bit him with a vengeance. He poured for Janice and Micky, and Micky asked, 'Aren't you joining us?'

'No, it sends me to sleep in the afternoon,' Michael said. He had bared his soul to Johnson, but didn't want the whole world to know of his problem. Micky didn't pursue the matter, and Michael wondered if Johnson had told him anyway, out of concern.

Janice was still immersed in her booklet, and, almost to herself, said, 'Is it really this beautiful?'

'Yes, it is,' Michael said. 'I've been there.'

'Me too,' Micky said.

'You pair of lucky sods,' she said. 'Is the grass really greener though, Michael? I just wonder if it's really going to get better, if all this bloody madness is finally going to stop.'

Michael shrugged. 'It's like anything else, Janice. It's what you make of it. Your dad's a shrewd and clever man. I'm sure he'll work things out. He's deadly serious about all this, you know. Once he's cleared this mess up, he's getting out of this racket. He told me that and I believe him.'

Micky winked at her and added, 'Your dad's the best I've ever met, Janice. He'll be okay.'

'But he's going to kill Jack Fossey,' she protested. 'I know the old bastard deserves it, but what if the police catch him?'

Micky laughed and tried to explain. 'They rarely catch the Carl Johnsons of this world. Strings are pulled, the word is passed around. Your dad is a pro and a well protected man, Janice. And his protectors aren't even in the firm. He's always taken good care of himself in that way. He made friends with the right people a long time ago.'

Janice nodded uncertainly, and glanced down at the booklet again.

'Maybe we'll go for a drive later,' Micky said, trying to cheer her up.

'Did you see *Play Misty For Me?*' she asked.

'One of the best,' Michael said.

'That opening scene,' she said, 'where Clint Eastwood's standing there in the early evening, looking out over the ocean ... then he drives up to the radio station at Carmel. I've always wanted to live in a place like that.'

'Carmel's a beautiful town,' Michael said. 'Maybe a little too quiet and slow for you, though.'

She shook her head and suddenly sounded sad and very much older than her years. 'No, I've had all the noise and fast living I can take. I want to leave all that behind. That's why I'm worried about Dad. He really got through to me on Sunday. I hated him for it at the time ... I've been hating him for years. But I knew in my heart I was killing myself.'

'Hey, tell you what,' Micky said, trying to cut through the maudlin atmosphere. 'Clint's got a restaurant called the Hog's Breath Inn at Carmel. All the courses on the menu are named after his movies. Get your dad to take you there, you'll love it.'

'It's a great little place,' Michael added. 'I had my picture taken outside there a few years ago. Give me a reminder and I'll dig out my old albums later and show you.'

Janice grinned and seemed to brighten again. 'Thanks, I'd like that.'

'Never give up, kid,' Micky said. 'Never throw the towel in. Keep the faith and you'll get what you want. I've been to hell and back, but I've never quit. You just can't give up, I can't tell you that enough.'

Micky Lyle had obviously led some kind of life, but, as eager as Michael was to know more, he didn't feel it would be tactful to probe. He didn't have to.

Janice, fascinated by Micky, said, 'You seem a really nice man. What makes men like you and my dad choose such a lifestyle? What makes you stand outside the law? I find myself secretly admiring you, and I don't know if that's right. I've broken a lot of rules, but I couldn't rob a bank or kill people. I wouldn't have the guts for it, anyway. I'm sorry, you don't have to answer if you don't want to.'

Micky took a long sip of wine, pushed the playing cards in front of him to one side, and rested his chin on his hands. 'No, they're fair questions,' he said. 'I first met your dad about eight years ago after I got out of the Army. I was around thirty, and the Army was the only life I'd known since I was a teenager. When I got out, I was lost. I went back home to live with my mum, and just drove her mad with my restlessness.

'My dad had died five years before and I missed him greatly. I could always talk to my old man, even though he could be a tyrant in a lot of ways. I didn't know what I wanted to do, quite honestly. I loved the Army, but I was tired, mentally and physically. Then I went to the Falklands – it seems like a million years ago now – I was right in the thick of things, and the whole damn thing just took something away from me. I still have nightmares about the things that happened out there. That's where I killed for the first time, and then the war seemed to kill me.

'There isn't a man alive who comes out of all that shit fully intact. The men you kill always come back to haunt you. You never forget that look in their eyes.'

Michael recalled Johnson's chilling story of Ernie White; the mad look in Ernie's eyes in those dark woods when he was threatening to slash his own throat, and how the eyes had nearly burst out of his head when Johnson delivered the killing blow.

'It was utter madness,' Micky reflected. 'The noise, the smells, the sheer speed at which everything happened. Once I came upon this guy . . . he was terribly wounded . . . just a bloody kid, really. He was dying, but still conscious, screaming in pain and cursing away at me in his own lingo. He knew I was there, he saw me all the time, yet he kept groping for his rifle. It was way beyond his reach, but he struggled like hell to get hold of it. He was just a mass of blood and pulp, but he never stopped trying. Instinct made me shoot him. I couldn't stand that dreadful look in his eyes. It frightened me and it made me feel guilty and ashamed.

'But he wouldn't die, and his eyes wouldn't close. The blood was oozing from his mouth and I shot him again in sheer panic. Then again, and again. He was gone by then, but I couldn't stop myself. One of my mates had to pull me away.'

Micky suddenly became conscious of what he was saying and looked embarrassed. 'Sorry, I'm wandering way off the path here.'

'That's okay,' Michael said. 'I can't even begin to imagine those sort of things. It must be awful beyond words.'

Micky nodded. 'It stays with you. It changes you.' Then he looked at Janice and said, 'But for what it's worth, I've only ever killed men in official combat. I've never robbed a bank, either.'

'I'm sorry,' she said. 'I didn't mean to imply . . .'

Micky waved a hand. 'It's all right, Janice, really. Anyway, enough of that depressing crap. When I got out of the Army, I really just wanted to clear my mind and rest up for a while. I didn't want a full-time job. I just couldn't face the prospect of punching a clock every day of my life. I was never too bright academically, so that ruled out my chances of becoming Chancellor of the Exchequer. I really just wanted something that gave me a degree of independence and some free time.

'I did a few boring part-time jobs for a few months – manual work mainly – but I couldn't settle. Then I met this guy in a pub one night who was a bouncer at the High Roller club down on the seafront – one of Fossey's joints. He said they were looking for some more muscle and got me in. What made your dad approach me, I'll never know. I mean, there was very little trouble, very few chances to show how I could handle myself. People just don't make trouble at Jack Fossey's places. Once in a while, I'd give the odd slap to some idiot who couldn't handle his drink, but it was only minor stuff. I did what I had to do, kept myself to myself, and just plodded along quietly.

'I'd heard of your dad, of course, but he was very much a mystery man. Nobody seemed to know exactly what he did and nobody asked. He just came up to me on the door one night and said, "You're Micky Lyle, aren't you?" He was smiling, but I still felt nervous. I thought I'd made some sort of dreadful mistake and Carl had come to sort me out. He offered to buy me a beer and said he'd arranged for somebody to cover for me. I just didn't know what to expect.'

Janice shook her head. She couldn't believe how remarkably little she knew about her father. Micky Lyle could have been describing a different man. 'All these friends Dad has,' she said, 'all the secret friends and secret meetings, I don't know anything about all this. He's never confided in me about anything.'

'I'm sure he's always done so for your own good, Janice,' Micky said. 'He chose his own way to hell in this life, but he never wanted to taint you. He wanted to keep you out of it, kid. I know that sounds like the old noble villain crap, but he wanted you to decide your own destiny. That's why he's trying to untangle himself now and get out of this business.'

'I could spend the rest of my life just getting to know him,' Janice said gloomily. 'I don't know my own father. He's a bloody stranger.'

'He's a good man, Janice,' Michael said. 'You'll find that out in time.'

Micky nodded. 'He's been good to me, that's all I can say. My hands were trembling when he invited me for a drink that night. But he was nothing like I'd imagined him to be. He was so cool and relaxed and pleasant. It was like talking to an old friend. He told me he'd heard some good things about me, and I didn't like to ask him where. But it was immediately obvious he'd asked around about me. He told me he needed a back-up man from time to time, and asked if I was interested. He said it was tough work that sometimes called for tough measures. He was very straight about what I was getting into and how dangerous it could be. He said he'd take good care of me, and pay me well as long as I was faithful to him in return. I didn't know the man from Adam, yet I just sensed he was genuine. I just did, I can't explain it.

'But it was something else he said that impressed me the most. And perhaps this will answer your question, Janice. He said to me, "What are you doing now, Mick? Bouncing guys for beer money at night and getting under your old lady's feet during the day. Do you want to be dependent on people for the rest of your life?"

'He told me I was a tough and single-minded man who couldn't be tied down to a specific routine, so why was I putting up with it?

He said he was giving me the chance to live by my own rules. And he didn't dress any of this up in fancy language, he was straight down the line.

'You see, I knew at once what your father meant. He was a kindred spirit. He thought the same way as me. He was offering me a freedom I'd never known, the chance to cut the chains off for the first time in my life. Looking back, I sometimes think I only really began to live after that meeting with Carl. I'd played it by the rules since day one, and life had pissed all over me. Your father saved me. He's never once let me down and I'd never dream of doing likewise to him.'

Now Michael knew who Micky Lyle was, and he was a special man indeed. He possessed an almost hypnotic air of calm and assurance. He was a man who had found his destiny, and Michael was now surer than ever that he had found his own. Never again would he go back to a suffocating office, or casually dismiss the days of his life as if they were replaceable.

Eventually, he supposed, he would come to pay a dangerous price for his new-found bravery. But now he was prepared to accept that.

18

Neil Franklin was slowly coming through his latest binge. There was no longer a day in his life when he didn't take a drink, but there were at least days when he could cut down his intake and claw his way back to a state of semi-respectability. Today was one such day when he felt so inspired. Living with his sister had helped. Unmarried, kind, and something of a wallflower, Heather Franklin had always given her brother shelter when he needed it. Guilt forced Franklin to behave as best he could in her presence. She was five years his junior, yet had assumed the big sister role since his decline, and this shamed him.

He was sitting alone now in St Nicholas cemetery in Dyke Road, his mind relatively clear for the first time in three weeks. He was smartly dressed in a blue velvet jacket and jeans, and he had trimmed his beard and washed his hair. At times like this, when he felt so good, Franklin would curse his suicidal pact with the drink. Yet he knew that he would die an early death. Even now, he had a small flask of whisky tucked inside his jacket pocket, from which he periodically took delightful little sips.

There was an important reason for Franklin's temporary rejuvenation, and that was Michael Rossi. Although well drunk during their chance meeting on the beach, Franklin remembered everything they had discussed. He had liked and respected Michael for not attempting to patronise a fallen hero. Michael had spoken of Franklin's boxing career with genuine admiration and respect.

A strange and almost mystical bond had developed between the two men. Franklin wanted to find Michael again, to talk to him properly and to apologise for his previous performance. Like Michael, he was convinced that their paths were destined to cross again, yet he didn't know why.

The dreadful nightmare that haunted Franklin's mind and soul had made the beach a place to fear, yet he constantly found himself drawn there, as if some kind of explanation for all his misery was waiting to be found.

He took a slug of whisky and began to walk briskly towards Churchill Square, the town's main shopping centre. Today, more than usual, the area was teeming with shoppers, tourists, pavement artists, and the soapbox brigade. The activists from various revolutionary parties always made a beeline for Franklin when he was more shabbily attired.

Franklin shared Michael's nervousness of crowds, and he hated the place. Quickening his pace, he headed left through Cranbourne Avenue to the welcome openness of West Street and the great twinkling sea beyond.

When he reached the seafront, he paused as ever before turning to his right. He always needed those few moments to size up the West Pier, to which he seemed inextricably linked. Like him, it was falling apart and dying, yet it was still a frightening and awesome sight. His eyes never left it as he walked briskly up the road past the Grand and Metropole hotels and then crossed over to the beach. He sat down in virtually the same spot where he had met Michael, the great pier directly to his left. He looked long and hard at it, silently begging the damn thing to provide him with answers.

He replayed the nightmare in his mind, wincing as he concentrated on the burning eyes of the man in the sea. Franklin wondered and wondered. What disturbed him more than anything in his present sober state of mind was the growing suspicion that the nightmare was a replay of something dreadfully real. Had the whole thing happened, and then become fantasy through his drunkenness and inability to deal with it? Something was very odd, very wrong, yet the harder he tried to focus his mind, the foggier things became. His head was sore and full of confused thoughts, and he tried to empty his mind and forget it all. He listened to the excited screams of children as he scanned the beach, looking at nothing in particular.

Then he heard a voice above all the others, a voice of anger. Off to his right, about a hundred yards or so, two men were engaged in heated conversation, to the point of attracting the attention of others. One of the men had his back to Franklin, but the fashionable grey suit and longish brown hair gave him away. It was Dennis Fossey. Franklin hadn't seen him in years, but he was sure of it. It was Fossey all right. He was gesticulating wildly with his arms, and the other man was trying to calm him.

The two figures were shimmering in the intense heat and Franklin squinted his eyes to get a better view. He didn't recognise the second man, a taller but stockier character with thin, greased-back hair and a large moustache. But there was something unnerving about him that held Franklin's attention. The man was clearly trying to hush Dennis, wagging a finger repeatedly and mouthing something obviously unpleasant.

Franklin was mesmerised and a strange numbness took hold of his body. All sense of sound seemed to leave him, the other people on the beach suddenly silent figures. Fear gripped him until his body began to shake, and he somehow knew what was coming next. The mystery man's attention was caught, as he stopped grilling Dennis and looked straight at Franklin. Then Dennis turned, a frightened look on his face as he met Franklin's eyes. Franklin could see all of this in the greatest detail, despite the distance between him and the two men. He didn't think this strange, because it all seemed so perfectly natural.

He wasn't concerned by Dennis's presence. It was the other face, a face of evil, that terrified him. It slowly seemed to melt like wax, until only the eyes were left; big and penetrating, expanding by the second. Franklin knew at once he had found the answer he'd been seeking, even though none of it made sense. He had found his tormentor, and it was no dream, no hallucination. But his mind and body couldn't respond to the moment. He just sat there and stared, and the terrible eyes stared back. He wanted to jump up and run, as he had done in the dream, but he couldn't.

Then there was an explosion in his ears as all sound returned, horribly loud but welcome. It jolted him from his trance and he quickly looked around to assure himself that the rest of the world was still there. He looked quickly back to his right, where the stranger was still staring back, but now turning to walk away and urging Dennis to follow him. Dennis kept looking back over his shoulder at Franklin, but the danger had passed and Franklin felt safe again.

Sweating heavily, he took his flask from his pocket and began to drink.

19

Jack Fossey didn't like walking. Crossing the road was Jack's idea of physical exertion, now that the good life had given him too much lard to carry. He suggested to Johnson that his chauffeur, Arthur, drive them around to their favourite watering holes, but Johnson would have none of it. He joked that the exercise would do Jack good, but it was all part of the careful and deliberate process of grinding the old man down and wearing him out. Johnson would walk him all over Brighton, make him sweat in the heat, get him drunk. It was to be a long, drawn-out kill, which Johnson would execute with magnificent skill, only showing his wrath at precisely the right time.

They strolled slowly through the Bohemian section of Kensington Gardens and cut through the streets to one of Johnson's favourite old pubs just off London Road. It was a traditional boozer, oldy-worldy and pleasantly cramped, with an entire wall of musty books at the end of the bar that made it feel like somebody's living-room. Johnson ordered half a lager for himself, while Jack, who rarely drank beer of any kind, went straight into his favourite tipple of Scotch and American.

On the surface, Jack seemed happy and relaxed, but his many problems were obviously gnawing at him. Like Johnson, he rarely showed his true feelings, yet he felt safe in his protégé's presence and now his defences were down.

There was a point, after some small talk, when he said, 'I've never felt as itchy as I do now, son. I don't know what I want. Up to now, I've always been sure about everything. All things fell into their proper place. I enjoyed fighting my way up. I enjoyed power – absolutely fucking loved it. I knew I was the best. I knew I could lick all the other bastards out there. But all the magic's gone. I want to pull away from it all – go and live somewhere nice and hot, and spend my days ogling the birds and being an idle sod. But it's like a bloody drug – power, I mean. I'm afraid of losing it. I don't want anybody else to have it. I'm vulnerable, Carl. The others see me as ripe for the taking. I'm not so thick-skinned that I can't see that. They think I'm too old, and perhaps they're right. I used to love this kind of challenge, but now I find it tiring.'

He threw his arms up in frustration and said, 'I mean, Jesus, who is there to take it all off my hands? Even if that toe-rag son of mine hadn't betrayed me, he'd never have been smart enough to run the business.'

'Don't look at me,' Johnson said, with a smile. He couldn't draw inspiration from Jack's melancholy. He didn't want to take his revenge on a man who had already given up. Johnson couldn't comprehend people who stopped fighting. Come the moment of truth, he wanted Jack to rage and roar and spit defiance.

Brightening up, Jack slapped Johnson on the back and said, 'Ah Christ, Carl, I wouldn't bother you with all this. You're a loner, kid. You like to go your own way. That's why I've always admired you. The one thing that irks me more than anything else is that I've got no natural heir. I was mad for a son, like Henry-the-bloody-Eighth, and look what I got.'

'Jack, I told you I'd take care of that problem,' Johnson said. 'But what you do when the dust clears, that's a decision you've got to make. You can't go on for ever. You've made your money, you've made your name. I'll clear up this shit and you can retire in a blaze of glory. To hell with the business. It'll kill you in the end, anyway. Find your hot place in the sun and enjoy yourself.'

'Yeah, perhaps you're right,' Jack said thoughtfully. 'I'm sixty-two now, I keep forgetting that. Old friends who are ten or twelve years older than me keep dying, which is hardly bloody inspiring. They've dodged bullets all their lives and they're keeling over from heart attacks. Do you remember my old pal, Jimmy Downes? Went back to being a barber when he got out of the racket. Bought his own shop.'

'Sure,' Johnson said. 'Jimmy was always good with a razor.'

'He's had to give up the booze,' Jack said mournfully. 'High cholesterol, his doc reckons.'

'And a busted liver too, I shouldn't wonder. I only ever went to Jimmy once, as a favour to you. He used to keep a bottle in a little cupboard behind the chair. I walked out of that shop as pissed as a fart that day, and Jimmy had cut everything above my shoulders except my hair.'

The two men laughed at the memory, and Johnson was jolted by the sudden realisation that he was enjoying himself. Jack had always been good company, full of rich stories about wonderful characters. Why in God's name had he betrayed Johnson so wickedly? It galled Johnson to know that for all the evil Jack had done, killing him wouldn't be easy. But it would be done, and without mercy, however many funny stories they would share this day.

'How did all this business come to a head?' Johnson asked. 'You must have had wind of it.'

Jack shrugged. 'Yeah, there were rumblings – the usual signs of the natives getting restless. People were obeying orders, but making it clear they didn't agree with me. Dennis was starting to question my decisions on business matters in his usual meek and apologetic sort of way, which I suppose was rebellious by his own miserable standards. But I didn't think he had any clout, any influence. I mean, Christ, these guys who are supposedly with him, they've laughed at him up to now. Cody especially.'

'His weakness is his strength, though' Johnson warned. 'What better than a puppet leader? He serves his purpose until you're gone, then they cut his strings and divide up the pie.'

Jack fidgeted and grimaced, unable to understand. 'It's this stupid bloody business with Bob Thompson they're all worked up about, Carl.'

Johnson nodded. 'Yeah, poor old harassed Bob on Tyneside. That's what Dennis was whingeing about in the restaurant.'

Jack gave a look of mild contempt. Bob Thompson was the least of his worries right now and he didn't regard the matter as important. 'I know you've advised me to make moves in that direction, but I can't see what all the fuss is about. The Hardy boys are just a bunch of snot-nosed juveniles. Bob must be going soft if he can't whack an outfit like that without outside help. Besides, it just isn't good business to go stomping all over another guy's manor. We don't need that kind of aggravation. There'd be too many repercussions.'

Johnson shook his head disapprovingly. 'You're missing the point, Jack, and you know it. Bob has always been a good and valued friend to us and we owe him a favour or two. He needs a few of our soldiers to help him out with this business and he's not blowing the situation out of proportion. The Hardys are dangerous. Subtle as bulldozers, but dangerous. Times have changed, Jack. The likes of you and I have never been saints, but there are certain rules we've always observed. Bob Thompson is out of the same mould and that's why the Hardys are making him look bloody silly. Those slags have no morals, no scruples, no dividing line on what's right or wrong.

'I saw the future when I was out in California. The street gangs are the bastards you've got to watch out for now. They're the ones who strike the most fear, because they'll stop at nothing. They prove it by shooting innocent bystanders from their car windows. They blow away women and children and they regard that as proof of their toughness. Bob has asked you for your help. You'd be doing yourself a power of good by showing willing. I'll talk to him myself if it makes it easier for you.'

Jack looked doubtful, but nodded. 'I'll give it some thought. Come on, let's get some fresh air.'

They turned right out of the pub and headed for the seafront. Jack, terribly unfit, was already puffing, but Johnson knew better than to underestimate the old man's staying power. Jack adored his Scotch, but could take it in great measures and control it. That's why Johnson had been surprised by Dennis's account of the old man returning home drunk and emotionally broken on the morning of Rose's death. Johnson had always believed that Jack was incapable of getting himself into that kind of state.

'Where are we going now?' Jack asked irritably, still annoyed at having to employ his legs.

'The Hole in the Wall,' Johnson replied.

'That's bloody miles away.'

'Rubbish. It'll do you good, Jack.'

'Why are you so damn intent on doing me good?' Jack grumbled. 'Man invented the car to cut out all this crap.'

Jack continued to moan good-naturedly as they made their way along the seafront. The tiny Hole in the Wall, which is tucked away in Queensbury Mews, was actually one of his favourite pubs – when he was suitably close to it. His beloved Scotch always made him nostalgic, though never soft. He had reached that stage in life where the past held more magic than the present, and he enjoyed reminiscing with Johnson about the golden days.

As he savoured his drink, he said, 'You and me should go like Butch Cassidy and the Sundance Kid, son. Shoot as many of the bastards as we can and go out like heroes.'

'Nah, you mustn't think like that, Jack. There's always something to fight for.'

'I know, lad. You of all people should know that. How have you been holding up? Do you think about Rosie a lot?'

The mention of Rose's name cut Johnson like a knife. He marvelled at Jack's nerve. The bastard actually sounded sincere and Johnson found it hard to keep his emotions in check. 'I've been okay,' he said quietly. 'I try not to think about it too much.'

'Yeah, sorry old son,' Jack said, patting him on the back. 'Listen, Carl, let's make this a really special day. Let's get disgustingly drunk and talk about the old times. We'll hit a few more places along the front, have some lunch, and then go to our favourite little dive bar.'

'Why not?' Johnson smiled. 'It's been a long time since I've had a crashing hangover. Too much temperance can be deathly boring.'

Jack roared his big laugh and ordered the same again. 'I mustn't complain, kid,' he said. 'All in all, I've had some kind of life. I think that's why I find it so hard to let go. When I was your age, I used to relish blokes challenging me. It damn nearly gave me a hard-on, truly. The first right-arm man I ever had was a guy called Roy Scott. We went to school together, Roy and me – joined all the same gangs. He was the first to accuse me of going soft, over thirty years ago. Shows you how things never change. Some toe-rag from a rival gang tried to pick a fight with me in some boozer over in the Old Steine area, and I turned the other cheek.

'He had his boys with him and it was them against me and Roy. We'd never have got out of there alive. I was pleased with myself. I thought I'd played it really well and I hadn't really lost face. So we get outside, and Roy starts giving me all this shit about bottling out. I was bloody livid. The booze was talking – it always did with Roy – and he made some crack about me not being the man to run our outfit. Well, that did it, Carl. I mean, it's not as if I liked the bastard anyway. We just happened to grow up together, like you and Cody. I challenged him to a fight right there and then. I suggested we settle it on the beach.

'Looking back, it was quite funny, really. We walked all the way to the seafront and we were cussing each other every inch of the way, but we agreed that no punch would be thrown until we got to the beach. Things were a lot more honourable in those days. It was a winter's night and bloody freezing. Roy was a pretty good street fighter and we really went at each other. But I beat him, Carl. Gave the cheeky bugger a right pounding. My lips were split in about three places and I could feel my left eye pumping up like a balloon, but I felt glorious.

'The respect I got from Roy and the other lads after that was beyond belief. The word went through the ranks that you didn't mess about with Jack Fossey, and the sudden feeling of power...' Jack balled his right hand into a tight and mighty fist, and smiled through clenched teeth '...the feeling of power was tremendous.'

Johnson looked deeply into Jack's eyes during that quietly violent moment, and once again saw the man who had ruthlessly smashed the hand of young Eddie in Preston Street.

'I've still got it in me, lad,' Jack said, glaring at his fist. 'These young idiots who are challenging me now, who do they think they are? They couldn't tie Roy Scott's bootlaces.'

As the hot day wore on and they skipped from pub to pub, Johnson kept a careful check on Jack's condition and the change was only negligible. Indeed, the alcohol and a hearty lunch had seemed to give the old man renewed energy. Johnson was the kind of cagey drinker who always appeared to consume more than he did. Lager, which he had rigidly stuck to since they started out, didn't affect him greatly anyway. On the other hand, there was nothing deceptive about Jack's drinking style. He was pouring down the Scotch and Americans like water, and it was as if they were exiting straight out of his trouser legs. Once again, Johnson found himself admiring his adversary. The doomed king was still a tough man to crack.

In the early evening, they moved to Jack's dive bar, the Blue Horizon, just a short distance from the West Pier. Johnson had always hated the place. It was a smoky, claustrophobic little den, where Jack would perch himself on his favourite bar stool and hold court with his regulars, becoming louder and more vulgar by the minute. Most of the clientele were small-time winners and losers, the kind of quietly desperate people who liked to think they were tight with the big man. They would suck up to Jack in painfully embarrassing fashion, and Jack loved it. He would denounce them to others as sycophants and lap-dogs, yet they were a comforting massage to his ego at the end of a hard day. The dive was also another of Jack's safe havens. Of all the people who had worked for him throughout the years, only Johnson had been invited there. Jack even had his own little bedroom at the back, where he would sleep on those occasions when he wanted to be alone and untroubled.

By the time he and Johnson arrived that evening, Jack's mood had become maudlin, as his attention had turned to Dennis again. One cheering thing about the Horizon was the good quality of the food, and the two men sat at the bar and ate piping hot steak and kidney pie as Jack continued to curse his son.

'I ask you, Carl, how can a boy hit his own father? That's what hurt me the most, when the bastard punched me out. I couldn't even bring myself to hit him back. I never hit him when he was a kid, you know. Did you know that? I mean, never. Sure, I gave him the odd clip around the ear, like any father, but I never beat the kid with spiked straps or any of that other brutal crap you hear about parents doing to their children.'

Johnson was content to let Jack ramble. The old man was finally slowing down and Johnson was glad. He was tired himself, but he knew that further patience was required. He would grind Jack down completely, however long it took. 'What you're trying to tell me,' Johnson said, 'is that you really love the kid.'

'Well, I never said I hated him, did I?' Jack barked, clearly embarrassed. 'Whatever he's said to you, Carl, I've never hated him. And I never expected him to be my mirror image. I just wish he'd turned out stronger – tougher. Right from the start, he was a bloody mummy's boy. He always shied away from me, as if he was afraid I was going to backhand him. He confided in Lilian about everything – even his personal problems, for Christ's sake. He'd have the occasional problem with his wedding tackle, like young boys do – a spot on his bollocks or whatever – and I'd hear all this whispering out in the kitchen and then he and his mother would disappear into the bathroom.

'It hurt me so much, Carl. The kid made me feel like a leper. I never gave him cause to fear me, yet there were times when he'd literally shake in my presence. That's why I started pushing him when he got older. Yeah, a lot of it was out of anger, I admit that. But I had to do it. The kid would have grown up a fairy. He was almost bloody effeminate in his early teens. I sent him to a bloody good school and he was useless. Christ, if he'd gone to a comprehensive, he'd have got murdered. According to his teachers, he just sat in class all day long like a vegetable. He'd never put his hand up and volunteer to do anything. I stopped going to his open days because his teachers kept telling me the same old things.'

Jack pushed his plate to one side, shook his head and said, 'I'm sorry to bore you with all this, son. I've got no other bastard I can talk to.'

'Carry on,' Johnson said. 'I'm a good listener.' He paused and added, 'Besides, I've had my own problems with Janice.'

Jack didn't react with as much as a twitch to this remark, and Johnson could feel his anger welling up again. With all that booze inside him, the old man was still utterly impassive, the consummate actor.

'Perhaps I'd have been better off with a daughter,' Jack said, lighting up a big cigar. 'Then her mother could have taken the brunt of all the problems. Boys are bad enough when they're typical boys. But when you get stuck with the kind I've got ... I mean, I'd have admired the kid if he'd smashed a few windows, let a few tyres down, punched a few other kids. I'd have whacked him for his troubles, but I'd have loved him for being a normal boy. I can't understand fucking biology. Lilian had a strong nature like me, so how come we produced a drip of a bloody son?'

Jack broke off and asked the bartender to refill his glass. 'Better take it easy, mate,' Johnson advised. 'If this is one of our serious sessions, you've got to make it through to sun-up.'

'I'm all right,' Jack said defiantly. 'I'm all right, kid. Listen, we'll grab an hour's sleep a little later, then we'll go to this great little place I've found. They stay open around the clock and we can play some poker there.'

'Anything you say,' Johnson smiled. 'But no sleep, that's cheating. I need you drunk and tired just to break even with you at poker.'

Jack's face lit up again and he gave Johnson an affectionate hug. 'Yeah, I'm a bloody great poker player,' he said proudly, and Johnson knew the remark had more than one meaning as the old man looked him dead in the eye.

20

In the small and insufferably hot washroom of the Blue Horizon, Johnson splashed his face with cold water and it felt delicious. It was gone two in the morning and Jack was at last ready to move. Johnson had thought the session would never end. For the past three or four hours, Jack had been locked in conversation with his various acquaintances, and the consequences hadn't been at all good from Johnson's point of view. The chat had slowed Jack's rate of drinking, given him a second wind, and made him buoyant again.

At least Johnson felt good in himself. He was a little weary, but otherwise he felt as he liked to at the crucial time. It always worried him when he felt too calm, but right now his stomach was tight and his nerves were tingling nicely.

He instinctively patted his breast and felt the Smith & Wesson secure in its place, but the gun would play no part in the killing of Jack Fossey. Johnson would despatch Jack in clean and fitting fashion. Walking back into the now deserted bar, he found the old man chatting away to the bartender, the gormless Keith, who looked close to falling over from boredom as much as tiredness. Keith looked profoundly thankful when Johnson said goodnight and motioned Jack towards the exit.

'Hey, look at this, Keith,' Jack chuckled. 'The kid's ready to whip me at poker. I betcha he keels over before the old man here.'

For the very last time in this grinding test of endurance, Johnson acted like the dutiful, favourite son. Throwing an arm around Jack's shoulder, he playfully kissed the old man on the forehead and said, 'Come on, Dad, come and show me how it's done.'

Outside on the pavement, Johnson feigned a violent cough. 'Christ, Jack, I don't know how you suffer that place. It's like standing in the middle of a bloody forest fire.'

Jack laughed. 'Come on, you'll be all right after a few hands of poker.'

'No, I need some fresh air first,' Johnson protested. 'Let's go and sit on the beach for a while.'

'Sit on the beach?' Jack squeaked. 'It's pitch bloody dark out there.'

'I know. It's restful on the eyes. Come on.'

They crossed the road and walked down the steps by Lewingtons, the Olde Brighton Rock and Candy Shoppe, past the children's paddling pool, and out onto the beach. 'This is bloody madness,' Jack grumbled. 'These bloody stones are murdering my feet. I don't know why this town can't have a proper beach.'

'There are just a few questions I need to ask you about Dennis,' Johnson explained. 'I'm going to start work on this problem of yours first thing.' He sat down on the stones and Jack struggled down beside him. To their immediate right, the great silhouette of the broken West Pier loomed eerily. 'Tell me about Dennis's private life,' Johnson continued. 'Girlfriends, that kind of thing.'

'What's that got to do with anything?' Jack asked irritably, still struggling to get himself comfortable.

'I'm just tossing a few ideas around in my head, Jack. Just tell me, okay?'

This was pure nonsense, a final bit of idle chit-chat as Johnson tensed himself for the moment of truth. Very soon, he would change his mood violently, stunning the old man with the force of his attack and never allowing him to recover.

'I'm about as wise as you are on that score,' Jack said. 'He hangs about with this bird called Dominique from time to time, but I don't know what kind of relationship they've got. He's never discussed her with me. That's what he's always needed, you see, a good solid wife. I mean, the kid never went out with girls in his teens. He's never gone steady with a bird. This Dominique's about the only girl he's ever been with, to my knowledge. I still wonder if he's ever had a fuck.'

'Children can break your heart,' Johnson said softly. There was a rumble of thunder and it began to spit with rain.

'That's a bloody fact, Carl. I'll tell you this much, I'd swap my Dennis for your Janice any day of the week.'

Johnson felt his body tighten and the blood rush to his face. Jack had chosen to attack, obviously gambling that Janice had told her father everything. Johnson couldn't believe his astonishing impudence.

'That little lady of yours has always held a special place in my heart, Carl. I'm sure I don't have to tell you that.'

'No, you don't,' Johnson said.

'It just saddened me when you took her away after Rosie died. It's been so long since I've seen the kid, Carl. I can understand your reasons for keeping her ... well, safe and away from all this. But I'd love nothing more than to look after her while you're away.'

Johnson now had his anger completely under control and felt almost pleasantly numb. The thunder had moved overhead and the rain was falling harder.

'Come on, kid, let's get out of here,' Jack grumbled. 'I'm all for the healthy life, but this is ludicrous.'

'No, I fancy a swim,' Johnson said, getting to his feet. Jack was in the act of awkwardly rising and nearly fell back down again. 'You what? Carl, it's pissing with bloody rain. I know we've had a few drinks, son, but let's keep things sensible.'

Johnson began to walk towards the sea and urged Jack to follow him. 'Come on, I'm serious. You're not scared of a little thunder-storm, are you?'

Jack, now a little unsteady on his feet, wearily plodded after Johnson, trying to talk sense into him. 'Of course I'm scared, Carl. That's lightning up there, boy. I can't swim anyway, you know that.'

It was then that Jack felt a strange fear. He was a shrewd and perceptive old dog, whose sixth sense didn't desert him when he was drunk. It was unlike Johnson to behave like this, even when merry; and while his mood was jocular, there was a disquieting coldness about him.

Then, as if he'd nodded off for a few seconds and missed a stop on a train, Jack was staring down the barrel of Johnson's gun. Jack's vision was beginning to blur and he felt slightly dizzy, yet he knew that all this was utterly and perplexingly real. Johnson's extended right arm was as straight as an arrow, and the gun was touching Jack's nose.

The rain was cascading off Johnson's head and body, which were blurred to Jack except for the eyes. The eyes burned fiercely and didn't blink, as if Johnson were being driven by an outside force. Jack suddenly felt a dreadful rush to his bowels as a huge flash of lightning lit up Johnson like some terrifying figure on a ghost train ride. 'What the . . .' Jack began, but before he could spit the words out, there was a huge crack of thunder and an explosion on his chin that sent him crashing onto his back. Johnson didn't want to mark the old man and had purposely 'pulled' the punch. It would be the only act of pure physical violence before the execution. Now Jack was hurt as well as thoroughly bewildered, and the alcohol had finally overwhelmed him and wrecked his orientation.

Viciously, Johnson asked, 'How much is my daughter worth to you, Jack?'

Jack was still fumbling for his words. 'Carl, what are you . . .' He was trying to get up, but his legs were betraying him and he was being blinded by the rain.

'How much is she worth?' Johnson repeated.

Exhausted, Jack dropped back onto his haunches and desperately tried to focus on Johnson. 'What are you talking about? What the hell are you doing?'

'Try five hundred quid, Jack. Is that enough for brutalising a teenage girl and buying her silence? I think that's a fucking good price personally, Jack.'

Jack was now almost shrieking in desperation. 'What are you talking about? I swear to God . . .'

'*God*, Jack? *God*? And how's God going to judge an evil shit like you? She told me, you bastard. Janice told me. And your own rotten bloody son told me what you did to Rose.'

'For God's sake, I don't know what you're on about,' Jack screamed. 'Please, Carl, please, I don't know anything about any of this. I loved Rosie, Carl, you know that.'

'Yeah, I know that now,' Johnson said. 'You loved her so much, you poured booze down her throat and tried to rape her. Then you didn't have the balls to save her, did you, Jack? This is about the spot, isn't it? Is this where you did it?'

Jack shuffled forward and lunged at Johnson, tugging desperately at his trousers. 'Who's ben telling you these things, Carl? They're not true. They're *not*. I didn't do a thing to Rosie, or Janice.'

Johnson furiously pushed him off. 'Of course you didn't, Jack. Tell me you didn't do anything to Wendy, either. You evil bastard. I respected you like a father and you savaged the only three people I've ever loved.'

Jack was now exhausted, panting and wheezing terribly. He could barely talk any more, yet still he shook his head and tried to protest. 'You're wrong, boy, you're wrong,' he gasped. 'It's Dennis, he's poisoned your mind. The little bastard, he's . . .' He fell onto his side, making sickening noises as he tried to breathe.

'Get up!' Johnson roared. A tremendously strong man, he gripped Jack by his jacket and jerked his massive body back into a kneeling position. 'On your feet, come on.'

Jack forced himself up, wavering like a shaken prize fighter, and began to weep out of sheer panic. His pathetic resistance angered Johnson even more. He turned Jack towards the sea and shoved him forward, abusing him for his cowardice. 'You should cry, you gutless bastard. You know all about killing, Jack. You enjoy it. I'm just giving you the chance to see it from a different angle.'

'You can't kill me, you *can't*!' Jack cried. 'Christ, Carl, I'm begging you.'

'Keep walking!' Johnson commanded.

The darkness and immensity of the sea terrified Jack. He had once nearly drowned as a young child and had been paranoid about water ever since. His body gave a jerk as he took the first dreadful step and the cold water filled his shoes. He turned around to face Johnson and nearly fell as he stumbled on the sloping surface. Johnson had replaced his gun and followed Jack into the water, stalking him with agonising slowness, his face expressionless.

Now close to passing out, Jack cried, 'What are you going to do?'

'Nothing,' said Johnson. 'You're going to do it yourself.'

In no time at all, the water was lapping around Jack's waist, and then his chest, and he could breathe no more. His mind was gone and Johnson was fading from his vision. He was fifty-two years back in the past, a frightened young boy of ten, struggling to keep his head above the water on a hot and crowded holiday afternoon in Brighton. The stinging salt water was in his eyes and ears and mouth, and the hundreds of people on the beach seemed a million miles away. He was looking for jellyfish, sharks, giant sea monsters and other horrors from his worst nightmares.

More than anything else, he was looking for the love and support of his father, just this one time. The old man was standing right in front of him, brutally urging his son to swim. 'I've shown you how to do it, you silly little bugger. Now stop whimpering and swim, or else you'll bloody drown.' But young Jack couldn't get his arms or legs to work and could only beg his father to rescue him. Then the water covered his head and he was lost in a terrifying blackness.

Johnson trod water for a while, as he awaited confirmation of the kill and watched Jack's body drift away. He swam the short distance back into shallow water and walked slowly up the beach as the rain continued to pound down. He didn't feel cold or wet. Just relaxed. Relaxed for the first time in two years.

21

Neil Franklin stopped again at his little cemetery on his way back from the beach. He still felt shaken by his experience, but was determined to remain in control of himself and confront it. He had been taking liberal belts from his flask of whisky, yet purely from habit. He was entertaining no thoughts of getting drunk, and because of this the alcohol was giving his mind a strange clarity.

He pulled a battered wallet out of his jacket pocket and fingered a £20 note which his sister had given him. With a twinge of guilt, he decided to buy a good bottle of whisky to get himself through the evening, promising himself that there would be no more drinking after that until he had freed himself from his nightmare. Heather Franklin was staying with a sick girlfriend in Eastbourne for the next couple of nights and Neil was glad of it. He loved his sister dearly, but had grown so accustomed to being alone that any form of permanent company now made him feel ill at ease.

Now, more than ever before, he needed to be alone with his thoughts in one final attempt to find peace of mind. Heather had left food in the fridge and Franklin had a fondness for the spare room in which he slept. It was small and warm and quiet, a sane port in a perpetual storm. That evening, he lay on his bed and drank his Scotch slowly, as he forced his mind to concentrate on his experience at the beach. He now had a face to match the eyes, but whose face? And what was the mystery man's business with Dennis Fossey? If nothing else, Franklin now knew for sure that his original suspicion was true; that the whole terrible affair had been very real.

Now he had to regain his old courage and fight an opponent he didn't even know.

He reached for his glass on the little bedside table and looked hard at the framed picture that Heather kept there. It was of Neil Franklin as Neil Shannon, smiling and victorious in the ring, during the earlier and happier part of his boxing career. Muscled and sweating and raising a bandaged right fist to the camera, he looked so young and glorious and full of life.

'Please help me, God,' Franklin said. He wasn't a religious man and he didn't know what made him say it. He sipped at his whisky, placed the glass back on the table, and felt his eyes begin to close.

Then he was on the seafront again, standing directly in front of the Olde Brighton Rock and Candy Shoppe on an insufferably hot and sticky night. Or was it early morning? He was gripping an empty whisky bottle and had no sense of time. He just felt wonderfully numb and happy. Unsteadily, he approached the steps that led down to the beach, and suddenly felt his legs sag. Stumbling forward, he dropped the bottle and clumsily tried to grab one of the rails, but viciously cracked his head on it instead. Then he was crashing down the steps, feeling little pain due to the alcohol, yet shaken by the violence of the fall and the repeated blows to his body. At the bottom, he felt blood running heavily from his forehead and into his eyes. He felt sharp pains in his back and sides as he scrambled to his feet, and everything around him was whirling furiously.

Desperately trying to clear the blood from his eyes, he staggered towards the beach, looking for a place to lie down and rest for a while. He fell heavily again on the stones, briefly losing consciousness. A piercing scream brought him to, and at first he thought it was his imagination. He was now sufficiently alert to be concerned by his heavy bleeding, yet still too drunk to know what to do about it.

Then there was a second scream, which definitely came from the water, and a man's voice shouting, 'Swim, Rose, swim, you bitch!' Franklin peered through the darkness and could hear furious splashing close to the shore. Now he forgot his own condition as he listened intently. Even in the bright moonlight he couldn't see anything, but sat up straight as if expecting some terrible confrontation. He heard something emerging from the water, but he couldn't retreat. Entranced, he clambered to his feet and walked towards the shoreline.

Blood was still splashing into his eyes, but he could make out the outline of a man less than ten feet in front of him. The man was breathing heavily, but didn't advance, as if waiting for Franklin to make the first move. Franklin walked slowly towards him, not out of bravery, but because he honestly believed he was hallucinating.

'That's right, come here,' the man said. 'Don't worry, I'm not going to hurt you.' The voice was calm, but cold and forbidding.

'Who the hell are you?' Franklin asked.

'Please don't worry,' the man repeated. 'I've had a bad accident. Please, I need your help.'

He began to approach Franklin until he was within touching distance, and in the powerful moonlight he looked like a sinister angel. Franklin's vision had cleared momentarily, yet he still couldn't believe what he saw. The drenched man was dressed in a dark suit and tie and looked as if he had just climbed out of somebody's swimming pool. He might have cut a comical figure, but for his piercing eyes and a grim countenance that was accentuated by a formidable, drooping moustache. The eyes were awful, shining brightly but cold and dead.

'Did you see it?' the man asked.

'See it?' Franklin said. 'See what?'

'Did you see it?' the man repeated.

He became a bright blur as blood flooded Franklin's eyes again, making him panic and splutter. 'Look, I can't ... I mean ...'

Before he could get his words out, the man grabbed him by his coat and pulled him forward. Franklin was close to unconsciousness again, but could feel himself being flung around violently. Although his assailant was the smaller man, his strength was awesome. Something told Franklin not to pass out and he began to thrash out with his powerful arms. He was missing wildly until he found the pit of the man's stomach with a tremendous blow. The man grunted and fell against him and Franklin instinctively swung upwards with his right fist. The second blow caught the man flush on the chin and Franklin heard him crash down onto the stones.

Now almost totally blinded by the spurting blood, Franklin tried to run, but felt his right ankle being gripped. He twisted his foot frantically and wrenched himself free, as the man began to swear and curse like a madman. 'You bastard! I'll kill you, you fucking wino bastard!'

Wiping his eyes frantically, Franklin began to run. He seemed to run forever over the hard and shifting stones, like a man wading through water, until his heart felt as though it were about to explode out of his chest.

Then he was awake again, staring at his sister's picture and the bottle of whisky on the bedside table. He was shaking and sweating and frightened. But now he had the answer.

22

Michael thought he was dreaming when he heard his phone ringing. His clock read 3.02 and he fumbled around for the receiver. He knocked a glass of water off his bedside table, and cursed as he began to recite his phone number and forgot it halfway through.

At the other end, a tentative voice said, 'Michael?', and Michael felt a chill as he knew at once that it was Franklin.

'Yes, Neil, it's me. What's wrong?'

There was silence for a few seconds and Michael thought he'd lost him. Then Franklin said, 'It's the dream I'm calling you about, Michael. I'm sorry about the time, kid, but I'm honestly not drunk. I know what I'm saying and I want you to listen to me very carefully.'

'Go on,' Michael said.

'The dream wasn't a dream, Michael. It really happened. You remember we talked about Carl Johnson?'

'Yes, of course,' Michael said, and he would never forget how he felt at that moment. He knew at once that Franklin's news was devastating.

'Michael, I can't explain all this over the phone. I need to see you. Can you be at our meeting place at about nine?'

'Neil, wait a minute, wait a minute,' Michael said. 'What's this about Carl?' Franklin was breathing heavily and clearly frightened. 'What about Carl, Neil?' Michael repeated.

'It's his wife, Rose,' Franklin said. 'I was there when Rose died. That's what I saw, I know it now. It was on the news – about her body being washed up.'

Despite the hour, Michael was now fully alert and afraid. 'The eyes, Neil . . . who did they belong to? This is very important. Was it Jack Fossey?'

'Why Fossey?'

'Was it Fossey, Neil?' Michael asked almost desperately.

'No, no, it wasn't Fossey. It's a face I've seen before, but I don't know who it is. I saw him on the beach yesterday. That's what triggered it all off. He was with that little shit, Dennis – Jack's son.'

Michael's body was now pounding. 'Tell me what he looked like,' he said, even though he knew the answer.

'Michael, please,' Franklin pleaded. 'Not now, Michael. There's so much to tell you and I'm tired and my head's spinning like mad. This isn't fantasy, Mike. It's not the ramblings of a drunk. Be at the West Pier at nine and I'll tell you all about it. This guy recognised me today, I could tell. I've got to try to find Carl. He'll protect me.'

Michael thought for a second and said, 'I'll try to bring him along.'

'What?'

'I wasn't strictly honest with you the other day,' Michael explained. 'I'm helping Carl out at the moment. Listen, Neil, forget the Pier for Christ's sake. We don't want you standing out there. Are you still at your sister's place?'

'Yeah, Clifton Terrace.'

'Give me the number. We'll pick you up there, okay?'

'Okay, Michael,' Franklin said softly. He gave him the number, suddenly sounding very tired and confused. He hung up without saying goodbye.

Michael jumped out of bed and went along to the living-room, where Micky Lyle was camped down on the sofa bed. But Micky wasn't sleeping. He was sitting up reading a book, looking as fresh as ever. 'I heard it,' he said. 'Was it somebody you know?'

Michael nodded and sat down. 'Has Carl ever mentioned Neil Franklin to you?'

'The ex-fighter turned drunk? Sure. I've never met him, but I know Carl used to help him out from time to time. Was that Franklin on the phone then?'

'Yes, and he was quite sober. I met him by accident on the beach on Saturday. Micky, I know this sounds crazy, but he reckons he knows who killed Rose and it wasn't Jack Fossey. And I believe him. Neil was on the beach that night when it happened. He nearly got killed himself.'

'Hey, hold on, hold on,' Micky said. 'I don't want to sound patronising, but Neil's ... well, the man's a drunk for Christ's sake. Carl told me he once walked stark bollock naked along the Palace Pier in protest against Brighton Council for letting the hurricane of '87 happen.'

Michael was angry and frustrated, even though he could see Micky's point. 'You just get a gut feeling about certain things,' he said. 'Micky, we've been taken in, I'm convinced of it. I think Steve Cody killed Rose and I think Dennis Fossey was behind it. Dennis wanted his old man out of the way, agreed?'

'Agreed,' Micky said, 'but that's some complicated way of going about it. Did Franklin say it was Cody?'

'No, no, Neil was before Cody's time. He never knew Cody.'

'Oh, wonderful. So this is all guesswork on your part, is it?'

'Micky, Neil says he saw the same man talking to Dennis Fossey on the beach today.'

'And it could have been anybody.'

'No, I don't think so,' Michael said, raising his voice.

'Hey, calm down! Don't go waking Janice up.'

'Neil's staying at his sister's place up at Clifton Terrace. It's a stone's throw from here. He wants to meet at nine o'clock. It's worth a try, isn't it? What can it cost?'

Micky shook his head and couldn't help grinning. 'Tell you what,' he said, 'go and make some coffee and we'll have a think about it.'

Frustrated, Michael walked out into the hall towards the kitchen. In a second that seemed to freeze in time, he saw the front door ajar, the chain off. 'Jesus, Micky...' he said, but he never finished the sentence. As he reached for the door, it flew back violently, crashing into his face and knocking him onto his back. The following horrendous moments seemed like sheer madness, doubly grotesque through Michael's blurred vision. There were two men with what looked like shotguns, bursting into the hall; there was Micky racing out of the living-room; and most bizarre of all, there was Janice, fully dressed and carrying a bag, being urged out of the door by the invaders. It was all so dreadfully sudden that even Micky, with all his skill and experience, couldn't respond fast enough.

Michael saw Micky raising his gun, but then there was an almighty crash from one of the shotguns and Micky was swept off his feet and thrown through the air. His chest turned a horrible deep red and Michael cried out as the warm blood sprayed into his face. The two men were backing out of the door as Michael – frightened but burning with anger – tried to get up and charge them. He was on his knees when one of the men surged forward again and kicked him unconscious.

23

The rain was still falling heavily as Johnson entered St Nicholas cemetery and climbed the steep path towards the church. He wasn't far from Michael's place now and was eager to know that all was well. He had felt wonderfully relaxed and sated after leaving the beach, but now he was plagued by a strange feeling of unease. He didn't know why, but as he came out of the cemetery and cut back into Dyke Road, he began to quicken his pace. Turning right into sloping Buckingham Road, he started to run. He *knew* that something was wrong.

He heard activity and saw the lights of a helicopter flashing in the sky as he neared Michael's road, and, as he turned the corner, there were police cars, an ambulance, and people in the road with umbrellas and raincoats over their nightdress. It was like a scene out of some surreal musical.

Johnson ran up the road and saw somebody being carried out of Michael's building on a stretcher. He nudged his way through the crowd and saw that it was Michael. He was conscious, and a man whom Johnson sensed was a police detective was trying to ask him questions. Johnson could see no sign of Janice or Micky Lyle. He was desperate to speak to Michael, but then the stretcher disappeared amongst a huddle of people. Johnson pushed his way through and saw the detective being pulled to one side by one of his constables.

Michael caught sight of Johnson and became agitated. He waved Johnson towards him, but as Johnson got to the stretcher, one of the paramedics put up an arm and said, 'Not now. The man's taken a serious blow to the head.'

'Where are you taking him?' Johnson asked.

'Royal Sussex County. Come on, mate, out of the way please.'

Michael became angry and shouted, 'No, he's my friend. I've got to talk to him, it's important.' He grabbed Johnson's arm tightly and pulled him in close. The paramedic continued to protest, but relented briefly when Johnson pleaded, 'Ten seconds, okay?'

Michael was desperate and highly emotional, yet clear-minded despite his slurred speech. The left side of his face had already puffed up horribly and one eye was almost shut. He yanked hard at Johnson's arm and whispered, 'They shot Micky, Carl . . . two men in masks. Janice went with them . . . door was already open . . . can't explain it.'

'What do you mean, Janice went with them?' Johnson asked, urgently. 'Is Micky dead?'

Michael nodded. 'Neil Franklin, Carl . . . go to his sister's place at Clifton Terrace. He's there now, he's got the answer. It was Cody, Carl . . . I'm sure it was Cody. Cody killed Rose.'

None of this was making any sense to Johnson and now the impatient paramedic was pushing him away. 'That's enough, pal. Do you want your mate to catch pneumonia as well?'

As Michael was lifted into the ambulance, he raised his head and said, 'Neil Franklin . . . you've got to see Neil.'

Johnson slowly backed away as the detective brushed past him and jumped into the ambulance. The rain started to crash down even harder as Johnson stood in the street, wondering what in God's name had happened.

24

Michael felt awful in just about every way. His face was terribly sore, but his physical pain was nothing compared to his mental torment. It was now five thirty as he tossed restlessly in his bed in the casualty ward of the Royal Sussex County hospital, some two hours after the explosion of violence in his flat. Once in a while, he would fall into a light sleep and the horrific pictures would fill his brain again, jolting him back to consciousness. His mouth was insufferably dry, his brain hopelessly scrambled. All he could do was twist and turn and take frequent sips from the water at his bedside.

Since having his tonsils removed at the age of five, Michael had hated the mere smell of hospitals. He had been lucky with his own health, but had been deeply disturbed as a youngster by frequent hospital visits to his beloved grandfather, who was withering away from cancer. Michael had watched a giant of a man shrink away to a weight of five stones before the end eventually came. He had inhaled the strong aroma of medication and listened to the coughs and cries of other dying people in the ward. And he had felt ashamed at wanting to run away from them.

By contrast, the ward Michael was in now was almost totally quiet. Nobody was even snoring. Through a gap in the curtains that surrounded his bed, he could see the night nurse writing busily. Occasionally, she would clear her throat, and Michael would welcome the sound. He looked at his plastic wrist band, which bore his name and number, and as he finally drifted into sleep, the band became a gleaming Swiss watch, the kind of watch he had dreamed of owning all his life. He was holding his arm up to the light, proudly admiring the immaculate timepiece from every angle.

It was an hour after closing time at Johnson's restaurant at Monterey harbour on a blissfully cool and calm summer's night, and Johnson was laughing in the background. 'Jesus, Michael, what a week you've had,' he said. 'You look like a kid on Christmas morning.'

Johnson was sitting up on the bar in T-shirt and jeans, a glass of cold beer in his hand, swinging his legs playfully. Michael, Janice and Neil Franklin were spread out around a large round table, laden with beer and food and a huge poster of the Beach Boys. Johnson had named the restaurant Surf's Up, after the Boys' 1971 album, and they were all celebrating Michael's birthday and a successful first day's trading.

'And you deserve it, old pal,' Johnson said, raising his glass. He winked at Janice and Franklin. 'You know, I think this is the first time I've seen old Michael genuinely relaxed. I mean, here's a guy who'll invent a problem if he hasn't already got one. Little over a month ago, he was standing ankle deep in empty whisky bottles, moaning about his dead-end job. Chuck your job, I told him. Chuck your mortgage. "I can't Carl, I can't," he kept saying. Now he's met the great Brian Wilson, got himself the finest Swiss watch in town, and managed a busy restaurant without getting pissed and insulting the clientele.'

Michael laughed at Johnson's mimicry. 'Okay, okay, you're right,' he conceded. 'I'll try not to invent any more problems. And I'm profoundly grateful for the watch. Seriously, Carl, it's beautiful.'

'Hey, come on, let's not get all sloppy,' Franklin said. 'Where are we going to hang this damn poster?' He was slightly drunk, comically so. He looked as happy as he'd been when Michael had first dreamt of him dancing on Sunset Boulevard.

'Right above the bar where Dad's sitting,' Janice suggested. 'We've got to give the Boys pride of place.'

'So be it, kiddo,' Johnson said. 'Bring it over, Michael.'

As Johnson was hanging the poster, Michael happened to glance over at the main door and saw the silhouette of a large man. It was motionless, more like a black cut-out that had been stuck to the window pane. Michael immediately felt uneasy. 'What's up, Michael?' Franklin asked.

'I don't know,' Michael said. He nodded at the door. 'I was just wondering what that guy out there's playing at. I thought he was going to ring the bell, but he's just standing there.'

Johnson turned to look. 'As long as it isn't that nut we had in here earlier.'

'Let's see what he wants,' Franklin said, careful to take his beer with him.

'Neil, be careful,' Janice warned. 'It might be some lunatic.'

'So was that other guy,' Johnson said. 'White as snow and he kept telling me he was Muhammad Ali.'

Franklin waved a hand dismissively as he walked somewhat unsteadily to the door. He had only got halfway when the window pane blew out with tremendous force. He staggered back and fell as the glass fragments showered over him, and Janice jumped up and screamed at the grotesque figure standing in the doorway. Michael felt his legs turn to jelly and grabbed at the bar to support himself. He looked at Johnson and, for the first time ever, he saw fear in his eyes.

The man – or creature – was hideously cloaked in seaweed and slime and was crawling with maggots. Only its eyes were clearly visible, blinking slowly and taking everything in. They carefully surveyed each of the people in the room and, for some ten or fifteen seconds, there was no sound, no movement. The eyes settled on Johnson and the words that followed confirmed Carl's worst fears. 'Hello, Carl, I was told I could find you here.'

Johnson walked slowly around to the front of the bar, and nodded knowingly. 'Hello, Jack.'

Janice suddenly became hysterical and screamed. 'Dad, it can't be him. He's dead. It *can't* be him.' In panic, she slammed herself back against the wall, cracking her head hard. The blow rendered her unconscious and she slid slowly down the wall as Michael rushed to her aid. 'Oh, Carl, I am disappointed,' said the ghost of Jack Fossey. 'I was rather hoping that Janice would be happy to see her Uncle J again. Don't mind if I come in, do you, son?'

The stench that came from Jack was horrendous, and Franklin nearly vomited when the big man reached over and opened the door with a maggot-infested hand that had been chewed clean through at its centre. As Jack walked slowly towards him, Franklin scrambled to his feet and yelled, 'Get away from me, Fossey. Don't you dare touch me.'

Jack laughed. 'Come on now, Neil, I have no business with you. You never did me any harm, old son. No, it's poor old Carl I've come for. He owes me.'

Jack opened the jacket of the beige summer suit he had been wearing when Johnson drowned him, and performed an almost comical twirl. 'Don't you think I'm a picture of sartorial elegance, Carl?'

Seeing the look of disgust on Johnson's face, Jack dropped his joker's mask and his tone became savage. 'Don't turn your nose up at me, boy. Have you any idea what you've committed me to? I'm at the bottom of the sea forever. That's my punishment for something I never did. The bastards keep me in a constant state of panic, you see. I'm dead but I'm made to feel like I'm drowning all the time. I'm gulping for air every second. But now they've given me a holiday, Carl. I've been granted my one and only wish.'

'And what's that?' Johnson asked.

'You, old son. You. You're coming with me, Carl. You're going to choke and gasp for air and look at this face of mine for all eternity.'

Michael noticed the beads of sweat beginning to trickle down Johnson's face, but his voice was calm and measured when he said to Fossey, 'You were a good friend of mine, Jack, and I made a dreadful mistake. I did the most terrible thing a man can do. I trusted the words of people I should have known better. But I can't bring you back and you can't drag me into your world.'

'Yes, old son, you really were suckered, weren't you? You of all people – the cool one, the great judge of character. I told you what a bastard my son was. I kept telling you he was as guilty as sin when I was covered in shit on that beach and begging you for my life. As for believing Cody ... well, honestly, Carl. Sadly, old son, you still haven't heard the worst of it.'

Jack laughed, and, thrusting a finger at Janice, said, 'Ask that little slut, Carl. She's the one who betrayed you.'

A look of horror flashed across Johnson's face and, as he looked across at Janice, Jack shuffled menacingly towards him with open arms, welcoming him to Hell.

25

It was still raining violently when Johnson reached Franklin's flat, and he had to press the buzzer six or seven times before rousing him. Franklin, dressed only in his underpants, was sleepy and smelled of alcohol, but he was coherent. Clearly shocked at seeing Johnson so early, he led him into his little bedroom, and Johnson sat down in a chair at the end of the bed and told Franklin what had happened at Michael's place. Franklin was devastated and needed a few moments to collect his thoughts.

'God, I'm so sorry,' he said. 'I only met Michael the other day, but he's a good kid and he's been nice to me. I never knew Micky Lyle, but I know you always spoke well of him. Jesus, I hope your daughter is okay.'

Johnson nodded impatiently and said, 'Michael told me you had the answer, Neil. What did he mean by that? This is bloody important.'

'I know that, Carl. That's why it's hard for me to explain.'

'Well, try your damn best,' Johnson snapped. 'I killed Jack Fossey this morning.'

'What?'

Johnson lit a cigarette and looked hard at Franklin, wondering if explaining the situation was at all worthwhile. 'Listen,' he said, 'you don't know Steve Cody, do you?'

'No. Only heard of him.'

'He's – he was – one of Jack Fossey's men. Before Michael was carted off to the hospital, he told me he was sure Cody killed Rose. He said you had the answer.'

Franklin nodded and suddenly looked frightened. 'Yes, I do,' he said slowly. 'I think I know who your Mr Cody is now.'

'So tell me, Neil.'

Franklin reached for the bottle on his bedside table and Johnson quickly grabbed hold of his arm. 'I mean, without resorting to that bloody stuff. Christ, man, it's not even dawn yet.'

Franklin looked ashamed, and shrugged apologetically. 'I told Michael about my dream,' he said, 'just like I told you. He was the only one who didn't laugh at me. He's got insight, you see. He had a gut feeling.'

Johnson was finding it hard to contain his temper. 'Listen, Neil...'

Franklin put up a hand. 'Hear me out, Carl, please. Believe me, I wondered if I was going fucking mad myself. But you see, it wasn't a dream at all. I just convinced myself it was. On the beach today – shit, it's yesterday now – I saw Dennis Fossey. He was having this violent argument with this big guy I'd never seen before. And suddenly, this guy turns and looks at me ... I mean, he was quite a way away, but it was like he was two feet in front of me. His eyes were the size of saucers ... burning, terrible eyes ... the eyes I'd seen in my dream. And that triggered it, it cleared my mind.

'I came home last night and everything came back to me. I really was on the beach that night, Carl, the night Rosie was killed. He was the one who did it. I heard him shouting her name when they were in the water. Then he was in front of me, saying he wouldn't hurt me, saying he needed my help. Then he just went berserk. He was going to kill me. I managed to struggle free, and I ran and I ran and I fucking ran. I seemed to run forever until I got to this phone box. I dialled 999 for an ambulance. They took me to the hospital and kept me in 'til the next day. I made up some bullshit story about what had happened to me. I was too scared to tell the truth.'

Franklin was trembling and he looked longingly at the bottle on the table. Johnson grabbed it and poured a short measure into the glass. 'Go on,' he said, his tone now kinder. Franklin took a big slurp and grimaced as the burning alcohol hit home. 'Let's get one thing straight, Carl,' he said. 'I was drunk that night, as usual. I fell down the damn steps on my way to the beach and cut my head badly. The blood kept running into my eyes and I was dizzy and I was drunk, and ... but I saw the bastard, I touched him, I fought with him. It happened. As God is my witness, it happened.'

'This guy,' Johnson said, 'I mean, apart from the eyes, what else can you tell me about him?' He knew now that Franklin was telling the truth and was simply awaiting the dreadful confirmation.

'His moustache, Carl. He had this big, walrus-like moustache, like the old-time Western gunslingers. Is that Cody?'

'It's Cody,' Johnson said quietly. 'Jesus Christ Almighty ... Cody and that shit Dennis set me up.'

He got up and paced around for a few seconds and then sat on the bed next to Franklin. 'Neil, how come all this suddenly came back to you?'

'It's crazy,' Franklin said. He pointed to the picture of himself on the table. 'Before I fell asleep, I was looking at that and thinking about a time in my life when everything was fine. I just asked God to help me. It's all as clear as a bell now. I've just been blotting it out of my mind all this time. Fear, I suppose ... shock, the booze, whatever. I'm so sorry, Carl. I could have saved you so much grief if only ... well, if only I'd stopped drowning myself and acted like a man. It was the dream that made me leave Brighton and start drifting. I knew I had to leave this bloody town. Fucking good thing I did. Cody would have had me by now.'

'It's not your fault,' Johnson said quietly. 'I was conned, Neil, absolutely taken in.' He closed his eyes and made a fist, squeezing until his knuckles were white. 'I've always trusted my judgement, my gut instinct. It's never let me down before. Christ, I've been charging around like a bull in a china shop. When Cody told me Rose had been pushed, I stopped thinking. I was so hell bent on getting the bastard who did it, I believed everything I was told. I don't even know what to think about Janice. It was weird, the way Michael described that part of it, as if she went voluntarily. I just don't know what the hell's going on anymore. I don't know what other lies she's been telling me. I've got to talk to Michael. Jesus, Neil, I'm so damn tired.'

'There's nothing you can do for now,' Franklin said. 'You must sleep, Carl. Here, get out of those wet clothes and take my bed for a few hours.' He gave an embarrassed little chuckle and added, 'It's clean, man, honest.'

Johnson nodded wearily. 'Listen, don't get pissed on that stuff,' he said. 'I need waking at around seven thirty.'

'What will you do?' Franklin asked. 'About Cody, I mean.'

'I'll do to him what I shouldn't have done to Jack,' Johnson said coldly. 'Him and that spineless coward Dennis, and any of the others who get in my way. They've got Janice, I know it. I'm going to get them all, Neil.'

26

A few hours' sleep didn't soothe Johnson's unrest. There was so much rage within him. He wanted to rush out and find Janice, he wanted to get Cody and Dennis Fossey. Yet he couldn't make a move until he had talked to Michael. He was reluctant to phone the hospital, because the police would be asking Michael questions as soon as they could. Michael had Johnson's mobile number and Johnson decided to get back to the Grand Hotel and wait for him to call.

Johnson declined Franklin's offer of breakfast. Feeling too tense to eat, he simply gulped down a glass of milk. 'Listen,' he told Franklin, 'I'm going to need some time to resolve all this. Who else knows you're living here?'

'Nobody,' Franklin replied. 'Why?'

'Well, I know it's going to be bloody tough on you, Neil, but I want you to stay here until I call you. Now he knows you're back in Brighton, Cody's going to be looking for you. Just keep all your doors locked and don't answer to anyone. I thought Michael's place was safe, but the bastards cottoned on to that. However tough it gets, however long you have to sweat it out, I don't want you to leave this place without my say.'

'Don't worry,' Franklin said. 'Right now, I don't have the slightest desire to venture out.'

'Not now you don't,' Johnson warned. 'But it's hard for anyone to stay locked up for long. Have you got enough food?'

'Yeah,' Franklin chuckled, 'my sister's left me half a supermarket as usual.'

'Does that include booze?'

'No, but she's got some tucked away if the going gets tough.'

'Look,' Johnson said, a hint of anger in his voice, 'I didn't mean it like that. I can't stop you from drinking, Neil, but for Christ's sake be careful. I don't want you getting pissed and wandering down to the beach for a breath of air.'

'I'll be okay, I promise. I'll have the odd shot, but I'm not looking to get bombed, honestly.'

Johnson strongly doubted that, but had no time to play babysitter. Franklin could only offer him some dry underwear, so he was forced to climb back into his wet clothes, which pissed him off even more. The rain had stopped by the time he left at around eight thirty and another mercilessly hot day was in prospect. He still felt exhausted as he began his walk back to the Grand Hotel. The past twenty-four hours had seemed like three days and his tired brain tried to unravel the confusing chain of events.

It was Janice who worried him the most, because it was logical to suspect the worst. Michael's words kept coming back: 'Janice went with them.' They hardly implied that she had been kidnapped, or had the concussed Michael simply phrased it like that? How had Micky Lyle's assassins come to know of his whereabouts? Why was Michael's door already open? Was Dennis Fossey still in control, or had Cody ordered the hit off his own bat? How and when did they plan to contact Johnson? After despatching Jack Fossey, Johnson had phoned Dennis from the beach to tell him the job had been done, but that was a good half hour before the violent events at Michael's flat. Dennis had never been good under pressure, yet if he had known of the imminent raid, his tone hadn't betrayed it. More than anything, how did Janice fit into this whole puzzle?

When Johnson walked into his room, he threw himself face down on the bed, trying to rid himself of the terrible buzzing and pounding in his brain. He didn't want to fall asleep again, but when he opened his eyes it was eleven o'clock and he was furious with himself. He was being weak and sloppy and this was no time for such lapses. He hurriedly showered and shaved and changed into fresh clothes, and he was drinking orange juice and taking heavy drags on a cigarette when his phone rang.

It was Michael, thank God. He sounded weary and emotional, but reasonably coherent. 'Jesus, Michael, are you all right?' Johnson asked, almost laughing with relief. There was a lot of noise in the background, and Michael sounded distant when he said, 'Yeah, I'm okay, Carl.' There was a pause and then his voice became much clearer. 'It's okay, I've found a place out in the hall here where I can talk. They're hoping to let me out today.'

'Are you badly hurt, Michael?'

'No, no. I was concussed, but I wasn't badly injured. I'm just a little dizzy. Did you see Neil? I don't know what to do, Carl. Everything's gone wrong, hasn't it?'

'It's a bloody mess,' Johnson admitted. 'What the hell happened last night? Can you tell me exactly what happened?'

'Yes,' Michael said, his voice cracking a little, 'I can remember. It happened so fast, but I can remember. It was so strange, Carl. None of it made sense. Micky and me were arguing . . . Neil had called just after three and told me he'd been on the beach when Rose was killed. He said the man who tried to kill him wasn't Jack Fossey. He wanted me to meet him this morning, but Micky wouldn't have it. But I knew Neil was right, Carl. I *knew* he was right.'

Michael was raising his voice in his emotional state and Johnson said, 'Come on, hold yourself together. I've seen Neil, I know the score. I'll make things right, believe me.'

Michael was silent for a few seconds, then continued his story as if Johnson hadn't said anything. 'I was going out into the kitchen and the front door was open. Only slightly, but it was clearly open. Someone took the chain off. I always keep that damn chain on, even when I'm on my own. Shit, it just happened so fast . . . so fast. The door smashed into my face and I went crashing. There were these two guys in balaclavas. They had shotguns . . . sawn-offs, I think. One was taller than the other, but that was all I noticed. I saw most of what happened, but my vision kept going funny. I saw Micky with his gun, but then there was this terrific bang and he was flying through the air. It was terrible, Carl. It was the worst thing I've ever seen. There was blood everywhere and it was splashing all over me.'

To his shame, Michael began to weep, and for a split second he thought he was going to vomit. He tried desperately to stop the

171

flood of his tears, but his stomach was convulsing and he couldn't catch his breath. He wanted to drop the receiver so that Johnson wouldn't hear, but it seemed to be cemented to his hand.

Johnson gave him a few seconds and then said softly, 'Michael, come on now. You've never been through an experience like this before. There's no shame in crying. But you've got to tell me everything, kid. If I'm going to nail these bastards, you've got to tell me all you can.'

'None of it made sense,' Michael repeated. 'It was Janice, Carl. I mean, she wasn't forced out. She was screaming, but she was expecting them . . . she was all ready to go. Dressed and carrying a bag. She gave me this strange look . . . this terribly guilty look. I was so furious. Shit scared as I was, I was raging mad. I tried to charge the bastards and that's when one of them rushed forward and kicked me – the shorter one. I thought they were going to kill me. Why didn't they kill me?'

'They weren't there to kill you,' Johnson said. Michael had told him the one thing he didn't want to know. 'Are you absolutely sure about Janice? You took a bad hit. Are you sure it happened like that?'

Michael paused for another few seconds before saying, 'I'm sure of it, Carl. I'm sorry. Everything was spinning, everything was going mad. But there are certain things you remember . . . certain things that just bang home and stay in your brain.'

Johnson's mind flashed back to Janice on the beach at Greatstone on that mad Sunday, and the great emotion of their reunion. The feelings of fury and sadness he had experienced then were swamping him again now. While he wasn't naive enough to believe that their relationship was perfect, Johnson had thought he had regained his daughter's affection and respect. Now this. What the hell was she up to and why? Most chilling of all, had she been involved in some terrible way in the death of her mother?

Johnson's mind was racing again and he wondered if he was reading too much into everything. He wondered if Michael, with blurred vision and massive shock after seeing Micky Lyle's bloodied body hurling through the air, had indeed imagined the next sequence. Then he cursed himself for his wishful thinking.

He became conscious again of Michael's faint voice. 'Carl? Are you still there, Carl?'

'Yeah, I'm still here.'

'What about Jack Fossey? Did you . . .'

'He's gone. I'll tell you about it later.'

'The police have been here, and I don't know if I've said the right things. They were asking me about Micky's gun.'

'What did you tell them?'

Michael let out a big sigh. 'I just pleaded ignorance. I told them Micky was an old acquaintance I hadn't seen for a long time. I said he'd just dropped in by chance and asked me if he could crash for the night. I said I had no idea he was carrying a gun. I told them I was just going out to the off-licence to get some beers, when these guys burst in. God, Carl, I was struggling. I don't know if they believed me. I just don't know. I was getting confused and they just kept pumping me with all these questions. I thought they'd never leave. They want to speak to me again when I get home.'

'Just stick to your story,' Johnson advised. 'Don't deviate from it, Michael. Don't get smart. You'll only get yourself into trouble if you start adding or subtracting little bits and pieces. You're totally ignorant, just like you said. Micky suddenly came back out of your past and the rest is a mystery. Micky was a smart boy. He never got himself into trouble, he was never known to the police, so we've got no problems there.'

Michael was still trembling and trying to stop himself from breaking up again, and Johnson sensed it. 'Michael, are you going to be all right? You can pull out if you want to. I won't think badly of you. It's got nothing to do with cowardice, you've got to understand that.'

Michael felt awful. He desperately wanted to last the course, even though he had already surpassed his own expectations. He didn't want to shrink back into anonymity, travelling to Horley every morning and vegetating in that god-awful office with its rotten air conditioning. Carl Johnson was his inspiration, his lifeline, yet he could feel Monterey and the Beach Boys and all things golden slipping through his fingers.

Until his recent dreams, Michael had never had any reason to believe he was psychic. Yet the dreams were too vivid, too frightening to be ignored. And in the last two – on the beach at Carmel and in the restaurant at Monterey – Johnson had been a gruesome victim. As much as he tried to fight against his instincts, Michael was depressed by his growing conviction that Johnson was going to die in this steaming Brighton summer. He couldn't tell Johnson this, but there was something else he couldn't keep secret. Michael had lost his nerve. He was shaking now as he had done at the height of his alcohol addiction, and he couldn't stop it.

'Carl, I'm sorry,' he said, 'but I don't think I can be in the thick of the action any more. I'll do anything else I can to help you and I'll never let you down. But I can't ... my nerves are shot, Carl. I'm shaking like hell and I keep wanting to shit myself. That shotgun going off ... the blood ... poor Micky dying ... you see it all the time in films, you read about it in the papers. But it's different when it's real ... to an ordinary bloke like me, anyway. It's not my world. I'm out of my league. I'm scared out of my wits and I can't lie to you about that.'

'Michael, it's okay,' Johnson said. 'I got Micky to look after you and Janice in the first place because I wanted you out of the way. That's the whole stinking point of all this. It *shouldn't* have happened. I'll stay in touch with you, don't worry. Just go home and get some rest. Keep thinking of that place of ours at Monterey, okay? We're nearly there. Even if it's just you and me, we're going to do it.'

'What about Janice?'

Johnson sighed heavily and said, 'I don't know, I really don't know. I'm going after Cody and Fossey. They've got the answers to all this.'

'I don't think I'm going to be able to sleep at nights, Carl,' Michael said. 'What if these guys come back?'

'They won't come back, Michael,' Johnson assured him. 'You're safe as long as I'm around. If they kill you, they'll know they'll have to contend with me. They came to get Janice, I can't get away from that fact anymore. There's just no other explanation for it. Wait for me to call you, okay? I'm going to be out and about for a while.'

For a few blissful moments, Michael felt calmer and safer, and he was compelled to ask Johnson a silly but necessary question. 'Carl, are we still going to be kings of the beach?'

Johnson shivered at the words. 'What made you say that?' he asked.

Michael chuckled and said, 'It's stupid, I know, but that's the expression you used in that dream of mine I told you about. You were lying on the bed in our hotel room on Sunset Boulevard and you said to me, "Nobody can touch us any more, Michael. We're the kings of the beach." You were waving this big gun around you called Barbara Ann – a really big gun – not the one you carry.'

Johnson sounded disturbed when he half-jokingly said, 'That was some spooky dream you had, Michael.'

'Why?'

'Oh, it's probably nothing. It's just that Jack Fossey used that expression yesterday – kings of the beach. That's the same dream where I said I was afraid of getting to Monterey, right?'

'Yes,' Michael said nervously. 'Two out of two, eh?'

'Three out of three. I've got a big silver gun in my collection. I call her Barbara Ann. You ought to set yourself up a stall on the Palace Pier. You've got special powers.'

Michael felt himself go weak again. He didn't want to hear any of this. He didn't want special powers, the golden touch, whatever. He wanted to go to bed at night and not be afraid. He didn't want to see into the future and smell death all the time. He had wanted to tell Johnson about his latest dream, where the hideous Jack Fossey had pointed his great accusing finger at Janice, but now he couldn't bring himself to do it. 'It was a dream, Carl,' he said. 'It was just a stupid dream.'

Johnson laughed and said, 'Nah, it's an omen, Michael, I can tell. You're my lucky charm, kid. With you by my side, I can live for ever, right?'

'Right,' Michael said. And when he rang off, tears flooded his eyes again.

27

Stay put, Johnson had told Neil Franklin. All Franklin had to do was lie low for a while, hold himself together, and everything would be all right. He thought it would be a cinch, for he had everything he needed. His sister's fridge was more than well stocked and booze was plentiful. She had given up trying to hide that from him, since he always found a way of acquiring alcohol anyway.

Yet it wasn't nearly enough. He had grown accustomed to a rambling lifestyle and his years of freewheeling had led to a natural love of the outdoors. He welcomed the cosiness of his little bedroom at the end of the day, but being shut in for too long a time made him fidgety and eventually panicky. Even drinking lost its romance when he couldn't share it with fresh air, the smell of the sea, and the reassuring noise of the outside world.

By midday on this now sweltering Wednesday, Franklin had drunk a bottle of brandy on an empty stomach and had moved on to his second. He reflected on the promise he had made to Johnson about not getting drunk, and he felt guilty; but not guilty enough to stop drinking. Like most drunks, Franklin was only plagued by guilt during those first terrible moments of rare sobriety. He had tried feebly to occupy himself since Johnson's departure. He had watched some TV, listened to the radio, and even played himself at chess until the booze had destroyed his ability to think straight. For the most part, he had simply stretched out on the sofa, dressed only in a pair of shorts, as he sipped at his brandy and sank into that ever pleasant state of numbness.

The feelings of pleasure were short lived. As Franklin made

serious headway into his second bottle, he became restless and irritable. He took his bottle up to his bedroom and tried to sleep, but even with all that alcohol inside him he was wide awake and full of energy. It didn't help that his room overlooked the sea, which twinkled back at him invitingly. He tried his utmost to think sensibly. He was aware of the dangers that lay in wait if he ventured beyond his front door. He turned Johnson's advice over in his mind, trying hard to focus and see the logic of it. But the brandy was shouting at him to go out, assuring him that he could come to no harm on such a beautiful day.

His mind was made up, and he moved fast before having second thoughts. Unwittingly, he climbed into the outfit he had worn when he met Michael on the beach – black T-shirt, worn jeans, battered trainers, and his favourite black trenchcoat. He willingly sweltered in the trenchcoat in such weather, curiously regarding it as a good luck charm despite all the grief he had suffered. Besides which, it was practical, with large, deep pockets that conveniently concealed a bottle or two. He stuck his bottle of brandy inside one pocket, roughly pushed his hair back without even looking in the mirror, and set off.

What little breeze there had been had dropped and the heat was now severe. But Franklin was oblivious of it, just glad to be out of his stale and suffocating prison. Despite his new confidence, he was still pulled towards the tormenting West Pier, instinctively taking the quickest route into Western Road, and then turning left into Preston Street, which sweeps down to the sea.

Franklin loved the atmosphere of Preston Street, with its many restaurants and the gorgeous smells of cuisine in the air. He was in that early state of drunkenness where everything in the world would normally seem fantastic; yet he thought of poor Michael Rossi in hospital, of Jack Fossey floating somewhere in the sea, and of all the dangerous consequences. And he worried for his old friend, Carl Johnson.

Halfway down Preston Street, Franklin glanced across at the former site of Jack Fossey's hamburger bar, from where the big man's tentacles had once reached out and terrorised Brighton and beyond. Franklin had hated Fossey for letting him rot in prison, yet now he had no anger in him at all. Fossey was dead, and, in a strange sort of way, it was if he'd never existed. Yesterday's man, yesterday's papers ... irrelevant now.

When Franklin hit the seafront, he crossed the road and made straight for the beach, where he thought he would sit for a short while and finish his second bottle of brandy. The beach was packed with people, which made him feel safe. Surely Cody wouldn't come looking for him here. Yet even the alcohol-toughened Franklin had stepped beyond his limit on this occasion. It was rare for him to actually feel drunk, but now, as the sea lazily winked back at him, he was overcome by drowsiness and that delicious desire to sleep for ever. He looked at all the children and mothers and fathers playing in the sea, and they became hazier by the second. Like every stubborn drunk who fights off unconsciousness for as long as he can, Franklin wearily lifted the bottle to his mouth one more time, and savoured the burning brandy sliding into his stomach...

For the umpteenth time in his life, he awoke with a frightening jolt, wondering where he was and how much time had lapsed. It was considerably cooler and the beach was virtually deserted. He reached for his bottle, but it was gone. He panicked and started cussing, threatening all manner of violence against the thieving bastard who had snatched it. Then he became aware of a scruffy young kid standing a short distance in front of him.

'Are you all right, mister?' the kid asked.

'Yeah, I'm all right,' Franklin snapped, and then, in almost comical desperation, added, 'Listen, kid, you haven't seen a bottle of brandy around here, have you?'

'Nah, but there's an off-licence in Preston Street,' the kid replied.

Wonderful, Franklin thought, remembering that he was carrying exactly twenty-seven pence right now. 'Do you know what the time is, kid?'

'About half five – and I'm not a kid. I'm eleven tomorrow.'

Damn it, he'd been asleep for almost five hours.

'Twenty to six, actually,' said a voice from behind.

Franklin jumped, and when he turned his head, there were three figures towering over him, their faces obscured by the bright sunlight. Yet he could still make out the big moustache on the man in the middle. Shielding his eyes, Franklin slowly got to his feet. He looked around for the young boy, who had seemingly vanished off the face of the earth. Now he could see the three men clearly, and for the first time – finally – he could look into the eyes of the menacing Steve Cody in the clear light of day.

To his surprise, Franklin felt no fear now, only a burning anger that was fuelled by the presence of Dave Richards and Kenny Carter, who had beaten him senseless and left him for dead a drunken lifetime ago. Cody and Richards were dressed in sober grey suits and ties, as if they had just stepped out of a convention. Carter, as ever, was the odd one out, with an eyesore combination of maroon jacket and blue slacks that were reluctant to make the acquaintance of his shoes. It was Carter who had long riled Franklin the most. Short, squat, with closely cropped hair, Carter resembled a ferocious bulldog. In reality, he was the typical thug, who was the first to pull the trigger as long as he was in safe company. Richards was taller and much leaner and not nearly as intimidating in appearance. But he had balls, and Franklin admired him for that.

But what about Cody? What was Cody made of? Franklin's sleep had done him good. He was still drunk for sure, but he didn't feel it. Had his senses been scrambled, he might have fled in panic, but his head was clear and he found himself quite looking forward to this confrontation.

'Always wise to keep track of the time, Neil,' Cody said, smiling. 'You never know who might creep up on you. Had too much to drink again, have we?'

'What do you bastards want?' Franklin seethed. 'You want a fight? Okay, let's have a fight. Right here and now.'

Cody feigned a hurt expression and held up his hands. 'Neil, Neil, calm down, mate. I'm genuinely concerned about your health. I mean, the last time we met down here, you were pissed out of your brain, bleeding like a sieve, and then you hit me. Twice, Neil. You weren't very sociable that night.'

'I seem to recall you were trying to kill me at the time,' Franklin said.

The three men laughed at Franklin, and then Cody suddenly became serious and frighteningly cold. 'Yeah, I'm afraid that's the tricky bit, Neil. You should have stayed out of Brighton. When you got away from me that night, I thought to myself, what the hell. He's drunk, he's mad, and his memory's probably shot to hell anyway. Oh, I had a bloody good look for you. But I reckoned you'd either left town or boozed yourself to death somewhere. Then you came back, Neil. You couldn't resist coming back, could you? By God, when I saw you yesterday, I thought Christmas had come early. I didn't even know you were a member of the old firm until Dennis told me.'

'I knew it was you,' Franklin said. 'I looked into your eyes and I knew it was you.'

Cody nodded knowingly, and for a few seconds the two men shared something which neither could explain. 'Yeah, I know,' Cody said quietly. 'I could tell instantly. You weren't even sure I was for real, were you?'

'No, not until then,' Franklin said. 'So let's get it over with, Cody. I guessed you'd come mob-handed, but I've met your two friends before.'

Cody nodded and chuckled. 'Mmm, they told me. I don't know, Neil, it seems that every time you run into our little gang you get some sort of hiding for your troubles. Sorry about the lopsided odds, but I can't afford to screw up this time.'

'Well, from what I've heard of you, Cody, three against one is pretty brave by your standards.'

'Don't make a scene, Neil. We've got a nice comfy car waiting for you up top, so let's all take a slow walk. I don't want to draw attention to this little party of ours, but I'll take the risk if you're dumb enough to start swinging.'

Franklin weighed his options and decided that Cody was right. Man, how he wanted to slug the bastard. But if people came running, then Kenny Carter, for one, would be crazy enough to take his chances with a gun.

'Okay,' Franklin said, 'let's do it your way.'

Cody motioned him to walk ahead and the four men made their way up to the steps and began walking towards the pier. Temptation was killing Franklin as they weaved slowly through the crowds of people on the King's Road. Cody, right by his side, sensed his frustration and said, 'Stay sensible, big man. All these people will make one hell of a bloodbath if Kenny goes apeshit.'

They crossed the road short of the Palace Pier, just before the Hospitality Inn, and Franklin's heart sank as they headed up a deserted little back street away from the safety of the seafront. Cody stopped him when they reached an old red car that looked as though someone had taken a baseball bat to it.

Figuring that he might as well have some fun, Franklin turned to Carter and said, 'I suppose you're the proud owner of this piece of shit, are you, Kenny?'

Always easily baited, Carter bristled. 'Get the fuck in and shut up.'

As Franklin turned his back, he was lost in blackness as Carter drew his gun and viciously cracked him across the head with the butt. Carter grinned at Dave Richards and said, 'Help the man in, Dave. I've done my bit.'

When Franklin regained consciousness, he instinctively reached for his neck and the irritating, trickling blood. But his hands wouldn't work, and it was a few fumbling seconds before he realised that they were tied behind his back. Blood seemed to be every-where, running down the sides of his face and drip-dropping onto his clothes. His head was pounding violently, and in his confusion he thought momentarily that he was back on the beach with Cody on that black and violent night.

Then his eyes began to slowly clear and he saw a blurred sign for Hassocks as they sped along. In panic, he tried to straighten up, but his legs were tightly trussed, and it was then that reality hit him. Kenny Carter was sitting beside him on the back seat, grinning like the cat that got the cream. Dave Richards was driving and Cody was leaning over the passenger seat, toying with a gun. Cody smiled and said something that was just a distant drone to Franklin. Carter elbowed Franklin hard in the ribs and said, 'Pay attention, champ.'

'What?' Franklin slurred.

'I said, I'm sorry about the knock on the head,' Cody shouted. 'Just being precautious, Neil. We fancied a drive into the country, but we got the impression you didn't want to join us.'

Carter giggled at this remark and bounced up and down in the seat like a kid having an accidental orgasm. 'Don't worry about bleeding all over the car, Neil,' Cody said. 'We can afford a new one. This is the sort of battered number that serves a useful purpose before finding its way over a cliff.'

Franklin was trembling with anger at Cody's arrogance. Cody embodied everything that was evil, a cruel coward with no semblance of a heart. In the ring, Franklin had joined battle with many different men, most of them good, others from the wrong side of the tracks. Yet they had all been men of honour and courage, true warriors. Now he was defenceless against the kind of spineless adversary he yearned to tear apart. 'You're a gutsy man, Cody,' he said. 'How long did it take you to kill a sick woman in the sea that night?'

The remark hit a raw nerve. The cocksure smile vanished from Cody's face and he nodded at Carter, who crashed his right fist into Franklin's jaw. It was a sudden and savage blow, yet Franklin barely felt it in all his rage. Cody leaned right over his seat and said, 'The question is, how long is it going to take me to kill you? How do you think I should do it, Neil? How should a fighting man like you die, eh? A bullet in the head like dear old Freddie Mills? Now there's a sensational way to go. Nah, too quick, too easy. We can think of something better for you.'

Franklin shrugged and said, 'I'm no longer worried about what happens to me, Cody.'

'Oh, noble stuff, Neil, noble stuff.'

'You'll get yours,' Franklin added. 'You'll have to answer to Carl Johnson eventually, and you're not in that man's class. He'll find out the truth.'

Cody laughed and exchanged knowing looks with the others. 'From who, Neil? You're the only one who can tell him. I'm sorry to say good old Carl has already served his purpose. He killed Jack Fossey this morning, while you were probably tucked up in some shit-hole sleeping off another great binge. He phoned in the good news to Dennis. I must give Dennis great credit there, useless shit that he is. He got quite emotional the other night, telling Carl how Jack had killed Rosie. Pity you didn't get the chance to tell Carl the real version, but then that's why you've got to go. We don't want you spoiling things, Neil.'

'How do you know I haven't talked to him already?' Franklin asked.

Cody shook his head. 'No, I don't think so, matey. I don't think you've seen Carl Johnson for years. I think you're just a drunk who's fantasising. Dennis reckons old Carl sounded just a touch too gleeful this morning. He thinks he's got his man. Now we just need to . . . well, I'm sure you know.'

Franklin played along, looking suitably deflated. 'Yeah, I think so. Dennis gets a bullet as well and you're suddenly the big chief, right?'

'That's about it,' Cody nodded. 'Shame about Dennis, but can you honestly imagine a loser like him being the big chief of anything?'

'You must have a big hold on Dennis,' Franklin said.

Cody laughed. 'Yeah, I've done my homework. I've been doing it for a long time. It hasn't been easy, I'll tell you that – playing the loyal blockhead all these years. That's my strength, you see. That's how Jack Fossey thought of me. That's how your old pal, Carl Johnson, thinks of me – the bone-brained plodding foot soldier who's just good at making up the numbers. Well, fuck all that, man. You're looking at the uncrowned king. I'm going to make this outfit of ours the best there is. Nobody is ever going to laugh at us again. It's just a matter of tying up the loose ends now.'

'Why did you kill Rose?' Franklin asked. 'If I'm a dead man, there's surely no harm in telling me.'

'I don't have to tell you anything,' Cody snapped. 'I hate drunks like you, Neil. You sober up for ten minutes and you're suddenly full of insight and a million questions. You're better off when you're pissed and falling around on the beach. Give the man a drink, Kenny.'

Carter reached down in front of him and pulled up a litre bottle of Bell's Scotch. 'It'll numb the pain of your wound,' Cody said mockingly, as Carter screwed the cap off.

The sun went in briefly at that point and Franklin experienced the strangest feeling. He no longer had any doubt that he was going to die on this hot and brooding day, yet he couldn't have felt calmer. He had peace of mind at last, and just yearned to be free of his shackles so that he could have one glorious last fight. He wanted to reward Carl Johnson and Michael Rossi for the kindness they had shown him by doing these bastards some kind of damage, however small. He was glad to be bleeding, to be on the rack. He was approaching death, yet he couldn't have felt more alive.

Carter roughly clamped a hand on the back of Franklin's neck and jammed the bottle to his mouth, but didn't meet any resistance. Franklin willingly and calmly gulped down the whisky, welcoming it as fuel to his fire.

Even Carter was surprised at the big man's placid acceptance and eased his grip. 'I should have known better, Steve,' he said. 'This is like putting petrol in a bloody car.'

'Let the man breathe awhile,' Cody instructed. 'We don't want a fast finish here, boys. Let's savour it.'

The sun came out again and streamed through the car, and for a few seconds all Franklin could see of Cody were those saucer-like eyes. But now Franklin was glad to meet the dreadful stare. His adrenaline was pumping at an exhilarating, almost alarming rate, and as the whisky pleasantly burned his insides and charged his brain, the car seemed to move along ever faster. He couldn't see the road signs, the other cars flashing past, or any of the outside world as the bottle was held to his mouth again, almost gently this time. Cody was the centre of his whole universe, and now those eyes were fearful, not fearsome. Cody was staring at Franklin with what appeared to be an odd mixture of puzzlement and admiration, as the big man chugged down the strong alcohol as nonchalantly as other people consume water. Again, both men could feel that strange link, where each could seem to tell what the other was thinking.

Cody shook his head very slightly and said, 'You're enjoying this, aren't you?' There was no sarcasm or contempt in his voice. Rather, he seemed to be paying Franklin a reluctant compliment.

'Yes, I am,' Franklin replied flatly. 'Do I get a fighting chance, or are you going to keep me trussed up like this?'

'You'll get your chance,' Cody said.

Franklin looked in the driver's mirror, and Dave Richards, who hadn't uttered a word, winked and gave him a simple nod of acknowledgment.

'If the bastard can stand up for long enough,' Carter said, utterly unaware that the other men had moved onto a higher and more complex plane.

'Yeah, this is just the prelude,' Cody said. 'Have you ever seen a bullfight, Neil? I mean, actually been to a bullfight?'

Franklin shook his head and had to suppress a smile as specks of his blood spattered onto Carter's garish slacks. Carter loved his clothes, even though he had no dress sense, and was too dumbstruck to react with his customary violence. 'No, I haven't,' Franklin replied. 'Felt as though I've been in a few, though.'

'The way they soften up the bull,' Cody said with relish, 'now that's a real art form – like violence itself. It's something you can never teach all the bleeding heart liberals who infest our society today. You watch those picadors with their lances . . . they have to weaken that bull to just the right degree. That's what we're doing to you right now, Neil. Priming you for the big fight. After all, you're a big bull.'

'So you see violence as an art form, do you, Cody? Even needless violence?'

Cody looked disappointed, like a teacher whose shining pupil had suddenly come off the rails by asking a dumb question. 'Don't be silly, Neil. A fighting man like you should understand what I'm saying. It's the great dividing line between the weak and the strong. Always has been, always will be. It's in all of us, Neil. It's just that some poor bastards never find the courage to pull the trigger. But they still love going to the pictures on a Saturday night and watching Schwarzenegger blow away anything that moves.'

'And you see yourself as a Schwarzenegger,' Franklin said.

Cody shrugged and playfully aimed the gun at Franklin's head. 'I don't see myself as anyone. But I've got the guts to pull the trigger.'

Franklin motioned to Carter for another slug of whisky and Carter tipped the bottle to his mouth in mild astonishment. This wasn't quite the way it was meant to be. Now Franklin became purposely insulting. 'I love the way guys like you throw around words like *guts* and *courage*,' he said. 'Yeah, I suppose it takes some balls to pull the trigger, even when you've got a couple of guys to cover for you. Most people could never fire a gun, but they're not lesser people because of it. But there are different levels of courage, Cody. And you'd get chewed up at the highest level in no time.'

Cody began to smoulder and reached across to ram the barrel of the gun into Franklin's chest. 'You think so, do you, Mr Franklin? Perhaps you'd care to explain that before this thing accidentally goes off.'

Carter, excited that proceedings were back on his own basic level, grabbed Franklin's hair and said, 'Do you want me to hit him, Steve?'

'Shut up,' Cody commanded. 'I want Neil here to elaborate.'

Franklin was now enjoying himself immensely. Bloodied, battered and boozed up, he felt very much the warrior and was revelling in the role. His life had a purpose for the first time in years, yet he had no fear of death. First, he would rile these buffoons as much as he could. He loved Cody's bullfighting analogy, since Franklin saw himself as the picador of the piece. Who was really tormenting who? Wasn't Cody the raging bull right now? Cody pulled slowly back, and with a flick of the gun invited Franklin to continue.

'Okay, let me give you an example,' Franklin volunteered. 'Forget Carter and Richards for a minute. They don't exist. It's just you and me, sitting opposite each other at a table. My hands and legs aren't tied, and you know I'm the kind of big guy who can knock you senseless with one punch. Forget the picadors and the lances and all that other bullfighting shit. It's one on one. That gun of yours is smack in the middle of the table and the man who survives is the one who grabs it first. How's that for a scenario, Steve? Would that situation give you the same kind of rush? Would you be bursting to go for the gun, or would you be cool enough to work out a compromise and quietly walk away? Or, as I suspect, would you simply shit yourself and beg for your life? Jesus, I was drunk and half dead on the beach that night and I still damn nearly took your head off.'

Cody's face was reddening by the second, but before he could react, Carter grabbed Franklin again and said, 'Pull the trigger, Steve. Kill the bastard now and let's finish this shit.'

'I told you to shut up,' Cody shouted. 'Stay out of this. God, Neil, you're rich, I'll give you that. You're like all the great psychologists who can't manage their own lives – a drunken screw-up who's great at lecturing other people. You're fucked yourself, but you know how everybody else ticks. You don't know anything about me. I've spent years clawing my way to the top of the tree. Being nice to prehistoric monsters like Jack Fossey and irresponsible airheads like his dopey son. What have you done in all that time? Jesus, man, you couldn't even hack it in the ring, and that was the last time you did anything worthwhile.'

'I could have done better,' Franklin conceded quietly. 'But as long as I was actually in that ring, I never quit. That's what it all comes down to, Cody. You think you're good, but you've never been on the ropes. Frankly, I don't think you'd have the balls to even get in the ring.'

Cody was stung again, but knew he was being baited and held his temper. 'Yeah, well, call me a boring practical bastard, Neil, but as long as I'm holding the gun I won't have to climb into any ring.'

Franklin turned to face Carter, knowing he would get the reaction from him that he sought. 'And what about this short-arsed little fashion show here, Cody?'

Carter couldn't believe Franklin's nerve and began to literally shake with fury. He grabbed Franklin violently by the shirt and yanked him forward until their faces were almost touching. 'You're full of shit for a man who's got no hand to play,' Carter seethed. 'You're dead, Franklin, do you understand that? And I'm going to drag it out for as long as I can.'

'Let him go, Kenny,' Cody ordered. 'We're almost there, you'll get your chance then.'

Reluctantly, Carter slowly released his grip, and Franklin feigned submissiveness as he began to draw back. This brought a smile and a cocksure nod from Carter, and Cody visibly relaxed again. Neither was prepared for the explosion of violence and chaos that followed. Summoning all his formidable strength, Franklin crashed his huge head into Carter's face, cutting his forehead deeply and sending his blood spraying all over the car. The shock made Cody jump so hard that he cracked his head on the roof and dropped the gun. Richards lost complete control of the car for a few seconds, as it veered out of the fast lane and was nearly rammed by a lorry. As Cody reached over the seat to retrieve the gun, yelling madly at Carter to do something, Franklin lunged forward and attempted to butt him. But Carter had grabbed hold of the bottle and smashed it so hard into Franklin's face that it shattered completely. The blow knocked Franklin back in his seat and into unconsciousness, his nose and cheeks horribly cut.

'Do it now, Steve!' Carter screamed. 'Kill him now!' His eyes were bulging out of his grotesquely bloody face and the words came out in an almost girlish shriek. For a few mad moments, Cody felt himself being swept along and his finger pressing the trigger. But it was Carter who frightened him more than Franklin, and he slammed his hand hard into Carter's chest. 'Shut up, you idiot. Get a hold of yourself, for Christ's sake.'

'Look at me! Look at me!' Carter screamed. 'Jesus Christ, Steve, I'm bleeding to death here.'

'You're not bleeding to death,' Cody said. 'Tie something on it. Use your imagination.'

Dave Richards spoke for the first time and said, 'That crazy drunk could have killed us all. No more of this nonsense. When we get to the field, it ends.'

28

Earlier that Wednesday evening, at around five o'clock, a restless and pained Michael Rossi had left the suffering confines of his flat, knowing that he had to get out, but not knowing what he wanted to do. In all his life, Michael had never felt as lost and disoriented as he did now.

Things had been going so wonderfully well. Meeting Carl Johnson again had given him the kind of high that booze never had. Now the bubble had burst and the magic of Monterey seemed a mere dream again. He recalled his dream of Sunset Boulevard, when Neil Franklin had danced happily in the street and the whole world had seemed so fine; and he wished that somehow, some way, he could now be instantly transported to that kind of paradise.

Johnson had assured Michael that he wasn't a target, yet as Michael stood at the bottom of his steps, he nervously looked up and down the street for strange people, a strange car, anything that didn't seem right. It was deathly quiet, another oppressively hot day drawing to an end. Michael's feelings were so jumbled. He was jumpy, fidgety, sweaty ... almost exactly the way he used to feel after one of his great binges. He imagined evil men with guns coming out of the trees, yet a part of him wanted a bullet. If it was quick and painless, then what the hell. It would end the pain and the dreadful sense of emptiness.

Michael was on painkillers for his swollen and throbbing face, yet the medication had made little difference. He had checked out of the hospital just after noon, and, having no money on him, had then faced the long walk home. The heat of this torrid summer was now driving him mad. As he trudged along the coast road past Brighton Marina and up to the Palace Pier, everything around him had been almost bizarrely calm and still. The traffic had clogged and crawled and the sea had looked as unreal as it does on those cheap postcards – the wrong colour and utterly motionless. He had taken a short break on the pier, smoking a cigarette and dreamily watching the seagulls and the people floating past, and it had struck him that his reunion with Johnson there that previous Saturday now seemed ages in the past. Now there was nothing to revive his spirits.

Then there had been another visit by the police in the afternoon, which had put more unwanted pressure on him. He had followed Johnson's advice and pleaded ignorance from the outset, but he was no actor, and he could feel himself coming apart inside. The officers had been pleasant enough, but they had kept hitting him with the same probing and relentless questions and Michael had been too dizzy and confused to judge his own performance. Had the policemen thought he was lying, or just upset? They would come back again, that was for sure, and Michael dreaded the next grilling.

He began to walk down the road, knowing in his heart what he was going to do, yet teasingly telling himself that he could still turn back. Around the corner from his flat, there was a convenience store and a grocer's shop; and in between them there was an off-licence, which had long been a comforting little haven for Michael, for more than the obvious reason. The off-licence was a family concern, run by a warm and lovely lady called Jean Parris and her son, Sammy. Jean had increasingly taken a back seat since the sudden death of her husband, Max, a couple of years ago. Always disturbingly gaunt and thin, Max was a placid and kindly man whom Michael had got to know well and enjoyed chatting to.

Then, one Sunday morning, a hung-over Michael wandered along to buy his hair of the dog, and young Sammy – who couldn't have been more than twenty-three – was there instead of his father. His mind trained solely on the bottles of vodka directly behind Sammy, Michael felt wearily obliged to make conversation and asked of Max's whereabouts. 'My dad died during the week,' Sammy replied, with embarrassment more than self-pity. Michael couldn't believe it and never did find out the cause of Max's death.

He liked Sammy a lot and simply didn't feel he could ask. In his own shock and embarrassment, he just blurted, 'Christ, kid, I'm so sorry.' Sammy smiled appreciatively, and from that point on the two men seemed to share a special friendship.

Michael pitied the terrible luck of one so young. Just a year or so after his father's death, Sammy, a keen and fanatical amateur footballer, suffered a broken leg and was told he could never play again. Michael shared Sammy's love of all sports, and even on the gloomiest days, he came to thoroughly enjoy his visits to the little shop, where Sammy always had his portable TV on. Sammy had a special passion for American football, which Michael had followed for years on the American Forces Network. Michael was a fan of the San Francisco 49ers, while Sammy supported the Miami Dolphins, and each would jokingly insult the other's team throughout the season.

Now, on this terrible day when he needed such welcome shelter, Michael walked into the off-licence and Sammy wasn't there. The TV was off, the atmosphere cold and empty. A straight-faced guy whom Michael didn't recognise looked up and said, 'Yes?'

'Is Sammy about?' Michael asked.

'On holiday with his mum,' the guy replied bluntly, looking as if he'd rather be somewhere else himself. He gave Michael a look of great impatience, as if to say, 'Come on, pal, buy something and get out of here.'

And, suddenly, Michael felt stripped of all hope. He wanted to punch the guy, but what would that achieve? He was too tired anyway. He cared about nothing right now, especially his own health. 'I'll take a bottle of the Chekhov vodka,' he said. He had spoken the magic words and he wouldn't change his mind. To hell with the consequences. To hell with how he felt tomorrow. He wasn't going to sit through this rotten evening with pain and loneliness as his only companions. If the booze and the painkillers sent him into a permanent sleep, so much the better.

When he got back to his flat, Michael went through the familiar old routine that preceded his drinking sessions, carefully placing everything he needed on his big table by the window; his favourite glass, his favourite little coaster, cigarettes, ashtray, and all his spare change. He counted the change, and was delighted to discover that he still had enough left to buy another bottle if this one didn't knock him kicking. It was tight, but he could still make it without a visit to the bank and he always got a strange kick out of running that close to the edge.

Then he broke the seal on the bottle and poured his first drop of alcohol for four days. He always adored that golden moment. The very first glass, when the bottle was still gloriously full. It was almost orgasmic. He took the first gorgeous sip, and at once he could feel the tension leaving his body and the physical pain subsiding.

29

The Volks miniature railway runs from the Palace Pier to Brighton Marina, and as Carl Johnson sat on the little train, deep in thought, he was too preoccupied to be bothered by the young girl at his side who kept trying to spear him with her ice-cream.

It was around half past three, some two hours before Cody and his men would haul Neil Franklin from the beach, and Johnson's mood was as dark as this classic summer day was bright. Dressed entirely in black, even his clothes were at odds with the weather. Not all men blessed with good looks and charisma are conscious of their good fortune, and Johnson was one. Even at school, Michael Rossi always envied Johnson's ability to emerge from a rain-sodden rugby field covered in mud and still looking as handsome as hell.

Now at the peak of his powers, this quiet and dangerous man looked devastating as he braced himself for the final battle of a career that would read like fiction to most people. As the train trundled slowly towards the Marina, where he would confront Dennis Fossey and Steve Cody, Johnson instinctively patted the gun under his jacket for reassurance, in the way that normal men feel for their wallets.

When he had phoned Dennis to tell him of the kill, shortly before making his way back to Michael's flat, the sound of Dennis's voice had only riled him more. In fact, as Johnson sat there now with his own feelings, it struck him that he wanted to kill Dennis more than Cody. Once upon a time he had pitied Dennis, but no more. Johnson was a natural born warrior, a man of pride and honour, and every trait of Dennis' character now sickened him; the man's cowardice, his treachery, his weakness, his galling vanity.

Dennis had moved into the Marina a couple of years ago, buying a plush flat so that he could rub shoulders with the kind of transparent, jet-set characters who had always mesmerised him. Now a very wealthy man himself, he was still in awe of the rich and influential, the worst possible example of a poor and humble boy becoming an insufferable snob. Johnson recalled Jack Fossey telling him that Dennis wanted to buy a boat. 'Jesus, Carl,' the old man had complained, 'the kid gets seasick when he takes a bloody bath.'

Dennis hadn't even been able to respond properly when Johnson told him his father was gone. Dennis had instigated one of the worst crimes that man can commit. Had he acknowledged the kill with a word or two and simply hung up, Johnson would at least have had a modicum of respect for him. Instead, he made Johnson's stomach churn with his fumbling stab at remorse. He had asked how, where and when before feigning a breaking voice and asking Johnson if his father had suffered. Then he had attempted to lay a trap with insulting clumsiness.

'I know you want to get out of the business and I appreciate your feelings on that,' Dennis had said. 'You made your position clear when we last met, and I'll honour our agreement if you still feel that way. I just think it's a great waste of your talent, Carl. I was as angry as you were in the restaurant the other night and I didn't appreciate some of the things you said to me. But things are different now. Think of the great things we can do together. None of us wanted it to happen like this, but it had to be. Believe me, Carl, I looked at all the options, but this was the only way. I want you on the team. My original offer is still open – any damn thing you want.'

Purposely, Johnson hadn't uttered a word throughout this diatribe, and Dennis had begun to sound increasingly embarrassed and ill at ease. 'Listen, Carl,' he had said finally, 'Steve and me have got a lot of things to work out, so we'll be here for the best part of the day. Come round later and we'll have a few drinks and talk about things.'

'Not interested,' Johnson had said. 'The job's done and there's no need for us to meet again. Remember what I told you about crossing me, Dennis.'

194

He had hung up at that point, leaving Dennis to worry and wonder. That's the way Johnson wanted it. Unexpected, he would now explode on Dennis and Cody with shocking suddenness.

30

For a few delicious moments, Neil Franklin thought he was in heaven when he opened his eyes. Flat on his back, he was staring up at a wondrous blue sky; deep blue without a wisp of cloud. Birds were singing loudly, and, as he turned his head, luscious green fields ran for as far as he could see. On the hills in the distance, there were two windmills, which suddenly disappeared from Franklin's vision as the blood from his wounds flooded his eyes and brute reality hit him once again.

'Welcome to Hassocks,' Cody said from behind him. 'Pretty little place, isn't it, Neil? Such a shame to have to slop blood all over it.'

Franklin wiped his eyes and rolled over, and the blurred figures of Cody, Carter and Richards were standing there like three gun-fighters about to draw. Franklin could feel the blood oozing out of his face and he didn't realise how seriously his injuries had weakened him until he tried to get to his feet and fell back again. He expected laughter, but now he could see the three men clearly, and they were stock still and expressionless.

Cody had his hands on his hips, his gun tucked into his waistband, but it was Carter who presented the most sinister sight. He was glaring at Franklin like a man possessed and had seemingly made no attempt to stop his own bleeding. It was as if he were using the blood as a spur, as it ran off his face and soaked into his clothes.

Franklin made it to his feet on his second attempt, but he could feel himself wavering. He silently begged God to renew his strength, so that he could produce the grandstand finish to his life that was now everything to him.

'Nice and quiet here,' Cody said. 'Now we can have that bullfight we were talking about. Think you can take my two boys here?'

Franklin nodded. 'I've waited long enough for the chance. How exactly do you plan to play this one, Cody? Is it a fair fight, or are these jokers going to pull knives on me as soon as I make a threatening gesture?'

'That's up to them,' Cody said. 'I want to see how good you are, Neil. Kenny here has even volunteered to even up the odds for you. I reckoned two against one would be fair, because you're the great fighter. But Kenny wants to take you on his own. He's upset because you messed up his looks.'

'And what's my prize if I beat them both?' Franklin asked. 'Do I get to mess up your looks as well?'

Cody smiled and shook his head. 'Oh Neil, be realistic. One way or another, you're going to die in this field, you know that. This little exercise is just for our mutual satisfaction. For me, it's fun. For you, it's one last chance to regain your self-respect before you go to that big boxing ring in the sky. Whatever the result, you get a bullet. I'm the chairman and chief executive, Neil. I've got the right to cheat.'

Despite the gravity of Cody's words, Franklin's eyes wandered to the grotesque figure of Kenny Carter, who suddenly seemed a different man. Not the man who would normally recoil from such a confrontation. Not once did Carter take his icy gaze off Franklin, and Franklin knew that this bizarre showdown now meant every bit as much to his opponent.

'So let's cut the shit and get on with it,' Carter roared. Franklin gave him a little nod as he removed his blood-spattered trenchcoat and threw it to one side. Carter removed his own jacket with such fury that he almost completely ripped off one of its arms. Then he was running at Franklin at terrific speed, and Cody and Richards were no less startled than Franklin by the suddenness and savagery of their man's attack. Up to that point, this amazing scenario had been as slow burning as a shoot-out scene from a Sergio Leone western, and it seemed somehow inappropriate that the moment of truth hadn't been prefaced by a dramatic pause.

Franklin was far too slow for Carter's rush, as the smaller man rammed his head into Neil's chest and sent them both crashing to the ground. Carter was a madman completely out of control, and he swore and cussed madly as he lay on top of Franklin and thrashed punches at his arms and sides. But the vicious onslaught only served to stoke Franklin's own fires, and now at last he was in his element. Still a formidably strong man, he grabbed Carter's arms and shoved him off with almost contemptuous ease.

Carter was on his feet in a flash and caught the rising Franklin with a tremendous kick in the shoulder. But Franklin had long passed through the pain barrier and simply accepted the punishment while awaiting his moment. Carter's madness had given him exceptional strength and a fearlessness which Franklin hadn't believed he possessed. Once again he charged forward with reckless abandon, but this time Franklin was ready. Swinging his mighty right arm with perfect timing, he caught Carter directly under the chin, literally lifting him off his feet and dumping him on his back. Carter was spreadeagled and out to the world, his body still, apart from his left foot which twitched rapidly with a mind of its own.

Dave Richards, poker-faced as ever, showed no concern, but Cody was clearly stunned by the breathtaking speed at which one of his soldiers had been despatched. He nervously waved Richards on, and Richards immediately put some distance between himself and Franklin, backpedalling away to buy a little time.

Franklin now required all of his concentration, because he knew exactly what to expect. Richards was an anything-goes streetfighter whose speciality was the knife, and now he was brandishing the switchblade that had been his constant companion since his earliest days as a criminal. The blade was a distraction in more ways than one to Franklin, reflecting directly into his eyes. Yet it was Richards who was put off his stroke as Cody lost his composure and shouted, 'You're fighting a drunk who's out on his feet, Dave. Finish the bastard, for Christ's sake.'

Richards was a cool old professional who rarely showed his emotions in the heat of battle, but he was visibly irritated by Cody's childish outburst. Lanky, gaunt, and suitably battle-scarred, Richards was a more dangerous proposition than Carter, simply because of his deceptive calmness. There were no insults from Richards, no attempts to out-psyche his opponent. Franklin began to circle him, content to let his adversary make the first move. The two men moved to within striking distance and Richards made a few probing thrusts. Feeding greedily off his pain, Franklin almost wished for another wound, and it was as if Richards purposely obliged him as he made his first significant charge and inflicted a deep cut on Franklin's left arm.

Now Franklin was blind to the knife, as the cut galvanised him into a furious attack. He didn't even try to grab the switchblade as he rushed at Richards with all the glorious abandon of a warrior who is ready to meet his maker. As Franklin came thundering in, Richards almost totally buried the switchblade in Neil's left shoulder, yet the savage strike had all the effect of a toothpick. Using all his strength, Franklin barged Richards back and then doubled him over with a tremendous blow to the stomach. Richards let out a mighty groan, and as he struggled desperately for his breath, he looked up at Franklin through shocked and frightened eyes.

Even in his fighting days, Franklin had been an inherently gentle man who had never possessed the so-called killer instinct. Yet now there was nothing but hate and rage in his heart, and he showed Richards no mercy. Hooking his punches with all his old skill and precision, he rained in a succession of blows that had Richards jerking in all directions like a puppet. When Franklin finally stopped punching, Richards hung motionless for a second before pitching face down into the grass.

Cody was clearly devastated. He had badly underestimated Franklin, totally confident that Kenny Carter would put paid to the old drunkard, and that Richards would merely play the role of trusty reserve. Yet now Franklin had destroyed both his soldiers in an awesome display of power. Even though he was the man with the gun, Cody was now gripped by fear and uncertainty and could feel his body freezing up. He had never experienced these sensations before. His arms and legs were paralysed and without feeling, yet his heart was thumping so violently that he was fearful it would explode. Franklin was moving slowly and almost lazily towards him, and in a classic twist of fate it was now Cody who was being tormented by the piercing eyes of the predator. He knew he held the advantage. He knew the damn gun was in his waistband, within inches of his grasp. Yet he couldn't move. He simply couldn't move. The sweat was pouring from him and soaking his whole body, but he couldn't even raise a hand to clear the stinging drops from his eyes.

Franklin stopped within a foot of Cody and stared long and hard into his face. This was the quivering wreck of a man who had scared and haunted him for so long, and suddenly Franklin realised how foolish he had been. He really had nothing to fear at all and there were many more years in which to make amends and fall in love with life again. He was no longer a man with a death wish, but he was still full of fire and wanted to punish Cody severely for all the misery he had caused.

'So now you're on the ropes,' Franklin said. 'It's that moment we were talking about, Steve. We're sitting at that imaginary table and one of us has got to go for that gun. You've already got it, but can you use it? When you aimed that thing at my head in the car, you said you had the guts to pull the trigger.'

Cody loathed himself for showing his fear. He had always believed he could handle this kind of situation. Like Michael Rossi, he had yearned for it. Yet here was his biggest test and he was shaking violently and falling apart. The part of him that so desperately wanted to be a hero was telling the coward to grab the gun and pull the trigger, but the gun might just as well have been ten miles out of reach. Knowing that he was hopelessly beaten, he searched for the faintest sign of mercy in Franklin's eyes, but there was none. Rooted to the ground, he could only watch as Franklin slowly reached across and pulled the gun from his waistband, and then pressed the barrel to his forehead.

'Tell me how it feels,' Franklin commanded. 'You've always found these kind of games great fun, Steve. So tell me how it feels when the gun is in somebody else's hand.'

Virtually blinded by sweat, Cody could only see blurred images, and what little strength he had left was rapidly draining away. He could stand this humiliation no more and almost wished for the loud crash that would signal a merciful bullet going into his brain. As he fell to his knees, he lost all control of himself and began to urinate.

His fear and his anger merged as he began to cry uncontrollably and shout obscenities at Franklin.

To his surprise and distaste, Franklin was unmoved by all of this, his disgust at Cody so intense that it had swamped his humaneness. 'You're useless,' he said quietly. 'You've ruined my life and you're so damn small and useless.' He pulled the gun away from Cody and held it up. 'Look at this thing, for Christ's sake . . . a .357 Magnum. That sums you up, Cody. No balls, so you carry a miniature cannon in your pocket. You remind me of the average short-arse who drives a bloody great car in the hope his prick will grow as big.'

Cody rubbed his eyes with his shaking hands and looked at the sleeping bodies of Carter and Richards. 'Get up, you bastards!' he screamed in panic. 'Get up!' He looked at Franklin and yelled, 'Do it, then. Kill me. Bloody well kill me. It'll be the only worthwhile thing you've ever done, you drunken bastard. You're the one with all the analogies, all the bloody fancy scenarios. What if this, what if fucking that. Well now you've got the gun, Neil. So do it. Kill me.'

'Yes, I suppose I really should,' Franklin said, raising the gun and taking aim again. 'But you see, Steve, it would be the same as treading on an ant. There's no thrill in treading on an ant. No real purpose. Killing you would make me sicker than I already feel. Besides, you're going to die anyway, I can promise you that.'

Franklin wiped some blood from his face and held out his reddened hand. 'You're the only one here who hasn't shed any of this. I want you to wear some of mine. I want you to smell it and taste it.' As Franklin smeared the blood on Cody's face, Cody heaved as if he were about to vomit, but nothing would come. He had expended all his anger and now he could only weep silently in shame. He screwed up his eyes, covered his face with his hands, and slumped forward, his head coming to rest on Franklin's feet. Franklin stepped back and looked at the prostrate figure, and suddenly his anger was gone and he just felt sick. There was so much beauty around him, yet it had been horribly scarred by everything that is bad in life. For a few moments, he wondered what he would feel like if he blew a hole in Cody's head and he shuddered as he imagined it.

As he stood there in the vast and now deathly quiet fields, bathed in evening sunshine, Franklin didn't know whether he could stop drinking, whether he could start a new life and fade quietly into the mainstream. He simply knew that he could stand no more violence, no more blood, no more terrible nightmares. He just wanted it to be all over, at long last.

He could look at Cody's quivering figure no longer. He dropped the gun down into the grass and walked over to retrieve his trenchcoat. He now looked upon that bloodstained coat as a trophy and he pulled it on with pride as he began to walk away, not really knowing what to do next or where to go.

He was taking a last look at the windmills, which really weren't that far away but seemed to be in another perfect world, when Cody screamed out his name. Franklin turned, and he was strangely conscious of doing so slowly, rather than spinning round in alarm.

Cody was lying on his stomach, clutching the gun with shaking hands and taking direct aim. 'Jesus,' Franklin thought, 'isn't it just the way.' Yet he couldn't have felt more relaxed during those last few seconds, before the terrible bang rang out and echoed around the fields. Birds flew from the trees as the bullet crashed into his chest, and he longed to lie in the cool and delicious grass and savour the last few seconds of his life.

He was dead before he even started to fall.

31

Johnson was in the Marina and it was typically crowded and
overwhelmingly hot. He slowly weaved among the sweating and
sticky people as he edged closer to Dennis Fossey's flat, taking in
every body, every face. Everyone looked irritable and pained as they
pretended to enjoy themselves in the time-honoured British way.
Husbands and wives snapped at each other, stressed mothers barked
at their young children.

Johnson couldn't feel the heat. He never could at a time like this.
His blood seemed to turn to ice, producing a wonderful calmness
that enabled him to move with ease and think with remarkable
clarity. He had now recovered all his old strength and composure.
Gone was the sense of confusion and desperation that had earlier
threatened to tear him apart. He knew exactly what he had to do and
had every confidence in his ability to close this one last brutal chapter
in his life and start afresh.

Nevertheless, he wanted a few quiet minutes to finally prepare
himself. Thirsty, he walked into a nearby pub where he ordered an
orange juice and found himself a quiet little corner. He was
watching the boats and collecting his thoughts when there was a
sudden commotion outside. Johnson couldn't see what was going
on, but there were raised voices, a woman screaming and above it all
the slurred voice of a man yelling abuse.

Johnson jumped up, almost knocking over his drink. It was the
voice of Dennis Fossey. Johnson cautiously walked outside, and to
his right, sitting on a bench in the square as large as life, was Dennis.
Bare chested, barefoot, and wearing only a tatty pair of blue jeans, he

was clutching a bottle in one hand and waving away a small group of irate people with the other.

Johnson seriously wondered if he was seeing things. He glanced around for Steve Cody, Carter, Richards or any other familiar faces, but he recognised nobody. Dennis was quite horribly drunk and his language was foul. A fat man in an ill-fitting T-shirt, which revealed his tremendous belly, was wagging a finger at Dennis and saying, 'That's no reason for pushing my kid. Don't ever lay a finger on my kid again.' He was trying to be brave but he was inching away from Dennis all the time, as were the rest of them.

'Get the hell out of here!' Dennis roared, and the crowd hurried back and began to disperse as he got to his feet and staggered towards them. Johnson cringed in disbelief as Dennis gestured violently with his bottle and yelled, 'Do you bastards know who I am? Do you know my name? Dennis Fossey, man. Dennis-bloody-Fossey. I can wipe you all out with one phone call!'

Johnson had to get him inside fast, before the police or local security or any other form of officialdom came raining down on him. He carefully and briskly approached Dennis, who had slumped back down on the bench. Clamping a hand on the back of his neck, Johnson whispered, 'Don't make any more noise. Get up and start walking.'

Dennis jumped violently and his eyes rolled back in his head as he tried to focus on Johnson. There was a tremendous lump coming up under his right eye and bruising and dried blood around his mouth. He looked as though he hadn't shaved for about three days. 'Carl?' he spluttered. 'What the ... I thought...'

'Pick up the damn bottle and just walk with me,' Johnson said. 'Where's Cody? Tell me where Cody is or I'll finish you right here.'

For a brief moment, Dennis seemed to sober up. He stopped walking, looked Johnson straight in the eye and said, 'It's too late, Carl. It's all over. It's the end.'

32

Michael had fallen asleep on the sofa after drinking half a bottle of vodka, and when he came round it was quarter past seven. He hated coming out of a drunken slumber, because he always imagined it to be later than it was. Consequently, the time was a pleasant surprise. He had only been out for an hour or so, the sun was still bright and warm and there was still plenty of booze left in the bottle.

He got to his feet, lit a cigarette, which tasted awful, and filled his glass. He cursed himself as he did so, but he never could give up on a bottle that was already open. As he sipped gratefully at the harsh vodka, Michael was conscious of things not being quite as they should. He couldn't put a finger on it, but he knew it wasn't his drunkenness. Outside in the street, people were walking past and everything was in its proper place. Inside his flat, the atmosphere was strange, not at all right. It was as if everything had been shifted onto a different plane while he slept.

A strong breeze was blowing up the hall and into the living-room, yet he knew that he hadn't left his back door open. The breeze carried the faint smell of cigar smoke and now Michael grew fearful. He knew he wasn't alone and the vodka couldn't numb the tremors that began to go through his arms and legs. He kept an old police truncheon under his bed, and after another hearty swig from his glass, he padded quickly into his bedroom to get it. From his bedroom window, he could see part of the patio, and as he peered through the nets, he could see clouds of blue smoke lingering in the still air.

He was now desperately scared and began to shake violently. There had been many previous occasions in his drunken stupors when he had been frighteningly lost or disoriented, but this was something quite different. Was he hallucinating? Was he losing his sanity? He remembered a chilling story one of his schoolteachers had once told him about the French writer, Guy de Maupassant. Maupassant had apparently arrived home one night to disturbing noises in his house, and then watched in horror as his furniture – tables, chairs, everything – came dancing down his garden path.

Michael's curiosity outweighed his fear, and as the sweat ran off his face and plopped on the carpet, he peered down the hallway and saw the kitchen door wide open. He was into the kitchen when a deep voice from the patio said, 'Come along, Michael, I've been waiting for you.'

Michael stopped dead, and in an instant his fiery body turned icily cold. Impossibly, it was the voice of Jack Fossey, the voice that Michael had heard in his terrible nightmare of Monterey. He had never met or even seen Fossey, for Christ's sake. The man was dead, anyway. How could this be real? Michael couldn't make the final steps to the patio. His legs had gone to jelly and he was having to clutch at the sink to keep himself upright.

The voice spoke again and this time it was smoother and more assuring. 'Don't be afraid, Michael. You know who I am. Come and sit with me. There are important things to be said and done.'

Michael walked unsteadily to the kitchen door and stared incredulously at the huge fat man seated at his patio table. Bathed in the early evening sunlight, Jack Fossey was dressed in a white suit, white tie and white shoes. Everything about him was immaculate, his whiteness almost blinding. His big legs were crossed and he was gently pouring Scotch into a magnificently sculptured tumbler that was as beautifully perfect as the rest of this mad scene. His big cigar was resting in an elegant ashtray and Jack continued to pay careful attention to these details, not turning his big, ruddy face to acknowledge Michael's presence.

Michael felt himself mouthing something, but then he was overcome by a terrible dizziness and crashed backwards onto the kitchen floor. He was looking up at the ceiling, which began to fade, and in seconds he was sitting opposite Jack, not knowing how he had got there. Jack was sipping at his whisky and looking at Michael with a faint smile. Michael wished he were sober, because then perhaps he would be able to make some sense of this. He couldn't clear his head and now he was beginning to feel faintly sick. It was almost as if Fossey was reading his mind when he said, 'I'm disappointed in you, Michael. I thought you'd knocked the booze on the head.'

'This isn't bloody happening,' Michael blubbed, in sheer panic.

'Yes, it is,' Jack said calmly. 'You know it is.'

'You can't possibly be alive,' Michael protested. 'Carl told me that...'

'And Carl was right. Did I say I was alive? Why shouldn't I be dead, Michael? Who says that dead men don't walk in their sleep? Who says they don't feel lost and empty and feel pain? You're disgustingly drunk, but I can assure you you're not seeing things.'

'What the hell is this all about?' Michael asked. 'I just can't... I don't understand...'

'Calm down, old son, calm down,' Jack said, smiling. 'I didn't come here to hurt you, Michael. As strange as it may seem to you, I've come to help you and Carl. I can understand your fear. I can understand you getting the wrong impression of me, after my behaviour in your dream. That was a very accurate and perceptive dream, by the way. You have a rare gift, believe me.'

'Why perceptive?' Michael asked nervously.

'Oh, not in the sense that I had come back to drag Carl under with me,' Jack assured him. 'No, your perception of *me*, Michael – the way I looked. Very accurate. When I first woke up, I was looking in some horrible, distorted mirror under the sea. And I could see my face chewed away, crawling with maggots and scum and everything. I don't honestly know why I'm here, old son. If you're looking for a logical explanation, I can't give you one. I suppose it's a chance to make up for my so-called sins in life. I always thought I was a bloody decent bloke actually, but never mind. What made you start hitting the booze again?'

Michael shook his head violently. 'This is fucking absurd. I've finally gone mad.' He started to rise from his chair and couldn't believe what happened next, as Jack leaned across and gave him an almighty slap in the face.

'Now do you believe I'm for real?' he thundered.

The stinging in Michael's already throbbing face was certainly real enough, and now his disbelief had turned to plain fear. Jack's face was a picture of fury and Michael remembered the big man's legend and the awful things he had apparently done to people.

'Listen,' Jack said, lowering his voice again, 'if I'm just a pissy, half-baked ghost, how come you felt that?'

Close to breaking, Michael threw up his arms and pleaded. 'I'm sorry, I just don't understand. I don't understand anything anymore. Nothing makes sense. Everything's gone wrong and I don't know what to do.'

Jack looked disgusted. 'You can put it right. You can stop drowning yourself in vodka every time a minor crisis comes along and put it right. You're the most important part of the jigsaw now, Michael. Carl still doesn't know all the answers and he's running into serious trouble. He came back into your life and pulled you out of the mire. Is this your way of saying thank you? Keep drinking the vodka, boy. Keep quitting on yourself. And when you're finally an old man and life suddenly becomes precious to you, I hope you'll be able to look back and convince yourself it was worth it.'

Michael was silent for some seconds as he shamefully wiped tears from his eyes. 'It all seemed to be going so well,' he finally said. 'Carl took me out of a life of drudgery and into something which scared me, but excited me. For the first bloody time in my life, I felt important. I felt my life had a reason at long last. The other day, we got into a fight in some pub at the beach. I knocked out some giant of a guy, and I felt so damn proud of myself. Carl didn't say a word. He just nodded at me and that meant more than words. It meant everything to me.'

Michael was talking dreamily now, in the unwitting assumption that Jack knew everything. 'Then, last night, when those two guys came bursting into my flat and shot Micky . . . the whole thing just became a horrific nightmare. The shots, the blood spraying every-where . . . Christ, I realised just how far out of my depth I was. I'm not brave at all. I don't belong in that world. I wanted to cry, I

208

wanted to vomit, I wanted to shit myself. I was so scared. When that bastard turned to kick me, I didn't think he was going to kick me at all. I honestly thought he was going to blow my brains out.'

Michael dreamily fumbled for his bottle and his cigarettes, but realised they were back in the living-room, which seemed miles away. 'You don't need those,' Jack said quietly. 'Carry on.'

Michael chuckled quietly to himself and said, 'Before all this blew up, my life was orderly, boring, the same thing day after dreary day, and I hated it. But it was cosy and safe. Like every quiet and dull man, I secretly yearned to know if I had the balls to deal with danger, or whether I would be shamed and just run away from it.

'As a kid, I watched Gary Cooper in *High Noon* every time they showed it. For me, that was the ultimate when it came to a test of a man's courage. The bad guys getting off the train, the time ticking away . . . and Cooper was all on his own.

'When I knocked out that guy in the pub, I thought I'd cleared that hurdle like a champion. Christ, how I deluded myself. Last night I was in a different league and I felt like a stinking coward. I was a misfit . . . the quiet and dull man completely out of his element.'

Jack tut-tutted and shook his head. 'Michael, my old son, you really are dreadfully tough on yourself.'

'No, I knew it for sure when I was in the hospital,' Michael said. 'I always hated hospitals . . .'

'Ever since you were a boy, when your grandfather was dying,' Jack said.

Michael was jolted out of his trance. 'How the hell did you know that?'

Jack shrugged, still bemused himself by the powers he had acquired since his demise. 'I just know. This isn't the time to question anything, there are no rules or boundaries between us. Tell me more about the hospital, and what you felt.'

'To my surprise, I enjoyed it – almost loved it. Lying in that bed, it was like being a child again. My mother was the last person who really loved me and made a fuss of me. I was in dreadful pain, I couldn't bloody sleep. But I was safe and warm, and that feeling of safety was so wonderful.

'I had this sweet Irish nurse who called me Michael. Not Mr Rossi, but Michael. God, I felt like I wanted to stay with her forever. She reminded me of the one and only true girlfriend I ever had, a lovely girl called Elaine. I lost her because of what the drink was doing to me. Stupid bastard...

'I dreaded coming back here, back to the violence and that dreadful smell of death. As long as I live, I'll never forget those bastards storming in and Micky Lyle getting shot. I'll never forget the feel of his blood. This isn't my home anymore. I've got to get away from this place. I just want to start my life all over again, in a place where nobody knows me.'

Michael felt a strange relaxation coming over him, as he gave full vent to his feelings and desires. All his life, he had found difficulty in expressing what he felt, for fear that people would laugh at him. Now he didn't care. He certainly didn't care what Jack thought, because Jack probably wasn't there anyway. Michael remained convinced that this was either delirium or insanity. If it were the latter, then at least he had no further cause to worry about the laughter or ridicule of others. What was so scary about insanity? After all, if you said something crazy, people could only accuse you of being insane.

'I'm not sure what I really want,' he said, still not addressing Jack specifically. 'I mean, I don't actually know what I want to do for the rest of my life. I just know certain things, from my gut feelings. I don't want to live in towns and cities anymore. I don't want to keep drinking myself silly to cope with all the pressures of that kind of life. I want a quiet place far away, where I can look out of my window at a meadow or a river. I don't want violence in my life anymore. I don't want to feel compelled to turn on the news at six o'clock every night and hear of some old lady being savagely murdered for a few pennies. But there's really no way out, you see, because you can never have it that good. Sooner or later, the ugliness encroaches again and you can't keep running forever. Reality makes you sick, but you can't deny it, can you?'

'No, you can't,' Jack answered firmly. 'I'm glad you still realise that.'

'But I can't take it anymore,' Michael said. He was exasperated,

210

because he knew he was going down a one-way street. He wanted this magical vision of Jack Fossey to produce a magical solution and he knew in his heart that there wasn't one.

Jack suddenly banged a fist on the table. 'Well, it's about damn time you learned how to take it,' he roared. 'Christ, it might as well be Saturday all over again. You're blubbing to me the way you did to Carl – whining about your bloody misfortunes, as if you're the only person on earth who's ever felt pressure.' He began to cruelly mimic Michael. 'Help me, Carl. I want to get better, Carl, honestly. I can't go on living this kind of dreary, rotten life.'

The words chilled Michael. How did Jack know all this? 'Well, congratulations,' Jack said. 'Four days later, you're already back to your dreary, rotten life again. I don't doubt you feel guilty about it, but that's not good enough. Carl has made the effort to save your life and promised you a new one. You owe him, son, and now's the time to pay off. I'll guide you as best I can, but I can't do any more than that. You've always wanted to be like him, haven't you?'

Michael smiled through his tears. 'Yes, always. I look at Carl, and I see a great rock that can't be broken. I always wanted to be like that.'

Jack sighed and looked sincere. 'I can't tell you how all this is going to turn out, Michael. The one thing I know for sure is that the angels will be with Michael Rossi. And I want you to use that knowledge as your strength, your magical weapon – your Excalibur, if you like. Do what you must do, Michael, and you will come out of this all right, I promise you.'

'Will the dreams persist?' Michael asked. 'I know you know, Jack, so tell me the truth.'

Jack nodded gravely. 'Yes, you will dream again. Just try to keep your mind on reality, though. These dreams are trying to crush you and you've got to fight them off.'

'But are they telling me the truth? Are they just dreams, or something more sinister? Christ, they're so frighteningly vivid.'

For the first time during this bizarre meeting, Jack looked uncomfortable. 'There's an element of truth there,' he said delicately. 'That's all I can say. Pay attention to them, but don't let them influence your judgement.'

There was silence for a few minutes, as Jack sipped quietly at his whisky and Michael attempted to digest all that he had been told. 'Why are you helping me, Jack?' he finally asked.

Jack chuckled softly. 'So that I can rest in peace of course,' he replied. 'I'm not pretending I don't have selfish motives, Michael. Listen to me, now. It's important that things are put right. This is a wicked, evil business and Steve Cody is a wicked and evil man. And it's not over yet. The guilty have to be punished and good has to prevail. Does that sound funny coming from an old bastard like me? I did some bad things in my time, son, but nothing like any of this. I want to help you and Carl and I don't want Micky Lyle's death to be in vain. I want justice for Rosie. You know I didn't kill her and Carl knows that too now, which is some comfort to me. I had nothing but love and respect for Rosie. And I never hurt Janice. Never.'

'You mean you didn't ... at the bungalow in Greatstone...'

'Not guilty. I wasn't even there.'

Michael rubbed his face, trying to clear his muddled mind. 'In my dream of Monterey,' he said, 'you pointed at Janice and said she was the one who'd betrayed Carl.'

'The girl's no good,' Jack said coldly. 'She has a hatred of her father which is evil in its intensity.'

'We got along well during the short time we spent together,' Michael said. 'She seemed so lost. Her emotions seemed so genuine.'

'Oh yeah, she's a clever bitch,' Jack said contemptuously.

Perhaps it was because he remembered Janice fondly that Michael was stung by this casual remark. Who was Jack Fossey to condemn such things as violence and betrayal? He had been a villain all his life and now he was playing God. 'What about Neil Franklin?' Michael asked, unable to conceal his bitterness. 'You use the word "evil", yet you treated that man despicably.' He fully expected Jack to erupt again, yet now there was shame in the big man's eyes.

'Yes, I did,' he conceded. 'I was coming to him. I've left him until last for a very good reason. Neil is every bit as much in my thoughts, you must believe that. Perhaps more. My business was everything to me when I was alive and it blinded me to so much in life. You've seen the gangster films. A mobster kills his own brother and says "It was just business", as if that forgives everything. Then he goes to church the next fucking morning and thinks he's a model Christian. Well, business stinks, Michael. But for business, there were so many people I would love to have made friends with, instead of alienating or destroying.

'I liked Neil, if you can believe that. He had the same heart, the same fighting qualities I've always admired in Carl. Jesus, how I yearned for a son with those qualities. I wish my Dennis had been a Neil Franklin, booze habit and all. I've lost them both, you see. I'm hoping this will be the final spur for you, Michael. I can tell you're still not convinced by all of this. In fairness, I suppose it does seem like another of your bizarre dreams.'

Michael knew for sure now that it was no such thing. His body had suddenly chilled in the cooler evening sun and things were no longer muddled or out of focus. He knew that Neil Franklin was no longer alive. He didn't need to seek confirmation of this, but simply enquired, 'What happened to him, exactly?'

Jack looked into his glass and said quietly, 'He died a short while ago. Cody, Richards and Carter took him to a field in Hassocks...' He paused to catch his breath and Michael saw a single tear run down his cheek. 'I honestly can't explain it, Michael. Suddenly, I was just there, watching it all. I was up above somewhere, looking down on the whole scene, but I couldn't speak. I couldn't shout out. I couldn't physically do anything to stop it. I saw Neil fight with a passion that made me weep. I thought he was going to come out of it all right. He beat them all, he was glorious. Then Cody shot him and you should have seen the look in Neil's eyes. I've never seen a man so utterly at peace with himself. When the bullet hit him, he seemed to embrace it. Then he closed his eyes and fell almost gracefully.' Jack nodded and smiled sadly. 'Yes, I wish I had been Neil Franklin's friend.'

Michael felt as if he'd been kicked in the stomach for the umpteenth time. When he desperately needed some kind of lift, his world was becoming blacker by the minute. Micky and Neil both gone, so violently and without justification. How he had admired those men. How they had offered him strength and hope when he had most needed it. Jack had accused him of being self-pitying, yet he had tried to rebuild his life during these last several days and God – if there was a God – had already torn down the foundations.

He tried to picture Neil, dying the way Jack had described, and he felt a surge of pride for the man he had met only once, yet who had been a friend. 'If he goes to Heaven, I hope they'll greet him with a malt whisky,' Michael said.

'What do you mean?' Jack asked.

Michael grinned. 'When I met him on the beach, he was glugging this really cheap whisky. There wasn't even a label on the bottle. It could have been bloody rocket fuel for all I know. He said his favourite tipple was malt whisky when he could get it.'

'The question is,' Jack said, 'when we've finished here, are you going to go back into that private little world of yours and glug some rocket fuel yourself?'

Michael shrugged. 'I want to, I can't lie about that. I've tasted the forbidden fruit again and it was good. I feel absolutely awful as a result of it, but alcohol never stops tasting good, even when you have to stop to puke it all back up. That's the awful thing about it. I sometimes think it's worth all the pain that comes with it. Yet if I could look into a crystal ball and discover I was never going to drink again, I think I'd be the happiest man alive. I want that, Jack, I really want it. I know I've got to try a lot harder. Brian Wilson did it and so can I.'

'He did, and yes, so can you.'

'You've heard of Brian Wilson?'

'Indeed I have. Carl told me of the times you and he used to listen to the Beach Boys at his house. They were golden days in your life, but the golden days didn't have to end there, any more than they did for Brian. Orbison's the other guy I liked. The Big O. Now there's a man who experienced some tragedies in his life, but he never stopped fighting back. But Wilson was the best, better than Phil Spector and all of them – the king of the Sunset Strip. He worked long and hard to get his life back, Michael, and you've got to do the same.'

'I know,' Michael said. 'His music moves me like nobody else's. I've got his new album, and he does new versions of "The Warmth Of The Sun" and "Wonderful". There's an added poignancy to those songs now. They're so beautiful, they almost break my heart. He wrote "The Warmth Of The Sun" the day Jack Kennedy got shot. Do you remember "Wonderful"? The original version was on an album called *Smiley Smile*. There was a picture of a little house on the cover, deep in the forest, and there was a big smile on the front of the house. I always wanted to walk into that forest, smell its freshness, hear the birds and all the little animals. Then I'd go into the little house, my house, and be safe and secure. Nobody could touch me there. And I know now that there's no such forest, no such house. I can't run and I can't hide any more. I never did find a true hiding place.'

Jack reached across and gently placed a hand on Michael's shoulder. His touch was warm, comforting, very real. 'Listen, Michael,' he said, 'this may be your one and only adventure in life. You're a quiet man by nature and you may go back to leading a quiet and monotonous life. But you're wrong to take that as a sign of failure. You're an honourable man with a big heart and you believe in right and wrong. And there's nothing at all wrong with that. Don't keep drowning all the good things in booze. Don't be found lying dead on your bed one of these days, with no one to care for you or give you a decent burial. Don't rack up so many debts with God that you're left in the kind of limbo I'm in now, repaying them for Christ knows how long.

'The emptiness I feel is dreadful, Michael. I know I'm here, but I don't know where I'm going to be next. I'm just shunted from one place to the next and everything in between is a blank. I haven't rested since that god-awful water sucked me down. Drowning was the one way I never wanted to die. I felt everything. I was conscious of every little detail. And that's the way it's been ever since. I can see everything that's behind me in the most incredible detail, yet only some of what's ahead. I don't know whether I'm being punished, or whether I'm lucky to be floating around like this instead of burning in some terrible place. Everything seems real, I'm as much flesh and blood as I always was. Yet some time before I came to you, I saw my body washed up on the beach, just a way up the coast, and a bunch of little kids standing all around me. One of the heartless buggers was poking me with a stick.'

Michael couldn't help chuckling at that. 'Jack, however things turn out, I'll try my best to change,' he said. 'I'll do all I can to help Carl, I promise. Can you tell me one more thing?'

'What's that?'

'What about Dennis? Do you know what becomes of him?'

Jack nodded sombrely. 'Dennis won't be a further problem. You'll see.' He was clearly in no mood to discuss his son anymore and awkwardly changed the subject. 'Listen, Michael, I want you to stay here for another hour or so when I'm gone. Carl will call you from the Grand Hotel and ask you to meet him there. That's when the ball will start rolling. Don't fall asleep in the meantime, okay? Have a shower, get yourself into shape.'

'Are you going now?' Michael asked.

'In my own time,' Jack replied, sounding a touch embarrassed. He gave Michael a certain look and added, 'Look, I prefer to be alone when I make my departure, okay? I don't stare at you when you're sitting on the throne having a crap.'

He winked and gave a little smile, but Michael was far too scared to appreciate the humour. He felt his body begin to pound again as he stepped back into his kitchen and allowed Jack his privacy. Drained, scared and defeatist, Michael now had to somehow lift himself to fight his greatest battle of all. Did Jack Fossey know the eventual outcome of all this? Michael suspected he did, and the worst part of it was not knowing who would be slain and who would be saved.

33

By the time Johnson had hauled Dennis Fossey over to his apartment block, Dennis had lapsed into semi-consciousness and become a dead weight. He stank terribly of booze and sweat and urine, the front of his slacks still wet.

The security guard was one of those conscientious types who was full of questions. He had seen Dennis stagger out and now wanted the full story. Johnson explained he was a close friend and spun an elaborate tale about Dennis falling into a depression after a death in the family. As the guard wavered, Johnson applied just the right degree of urgency and said, 'I think he's gearing up for another piss. Do you want him to do it here?'

Before slumping into his sleep, Dennis had tearfully told Johnson that Cody had left, like every other friend he'd ever had. He had seemed sincere, but Johnson still had his doubts. 'Listen,' he said to the guard, 'Mr Fossey had a guest earlier. Did you see him leave?'

'Indeed I did, sir,' replied the guard. 'It's never too difficult to remember some of Mr Fossey's guests, if you'll pardon me for saying so.'

'Big guy with a moustache?' Johnson suggested.

'That's him, sir. Hard to miss that one, if you get my meaning.'

Once outside the apartment, Johnson dropped Dennis like a bag of tiresome shopping and quietly let himself in. The apartment, expansive and beautifully furnished, reeked of alcohol. Although the place wasn't a wreck, certain things had been upset, suggesting that Dennis had either been stumbling around in his drunkenness or had been knocked about. The TV set had been knocked over, the large sofa was askew, and a couple of empty bottles were on the carpet. Everything else, strangely, was immaculate, and bore the touch of a houseproud woman.

Johnson found the bathroom, dragged Dennis inside and hauled him into the shower. Disgusted at how a man could get himself into such a state, Johnson turned on the cold tap and hastened Dennis's revival with several sharp kicks to the ribs. Dennis snapped to almost immediately and began coughing and swearing violently. 'Shut up,' Johnson ordered, 'shut up.' Beginning to feel the pain, Dennis implored Johnson to stop, his tone changing from that of an angry man to a whining boy. 'Please, Carl, for fuck's sake... Cody's already beaten the shit out of me.'

Johnson relented, turned off the tap and hurled a towel at Dennis. 'Dry off and get in here.' Marching into the lounge, Johnson pulled up a chair and sat and waited for Dennis to catch up. Dennis was still very drunk and disoriented, and almost comically toppled over as he entered the room, still dripping wet. Johnson didn't help him as he crawled and stumbled over to the sofa. Shivering violently, he made a fumbling effort to fling the towel around his shoulders and sat up as best he could. 'I thought you said on the phone ... I thought you told me ...' He was slurring badly and couldn't get the sentence out.

'Just shut up for a minute and try to pull yourself together,' Johnson said. 'I'll ask the questions and when you've got your mouth in gear you can give me the answers. That way, we might just wrap this thing up before nightfall.'

But Dennis couldn't help talking. Though Johnson didn't yet know it, Dennis was in a suicidal frame of mind and was desperate to bare his tortured soul. 'This is only the second time in my life I've been drunk, Carl.' He managed to spit out these words without fumbling and repeated them to reassure himself.

'Yeah, I can tell you need to practice more,' Johnson said. 'Where's my daughter, Dennis? Where's Janice?'

Dennis ignored the question. 'The first time was when I raided the old man's drinks cabinet as a teenager. I was with a mate of mine. I did it to get even with Dad, you see. He'd taken me to this bloody rotten pub with some of his bloody rotten friends and bought me my

218

first beer. I took a sip and I hated it and I wouldn't drink the rest. So you know what the old man did? He called me a little fairy in front of all his friends and just humiliated me for the rest of the night. When we got home, he gave me the whole thing about what an embarrassment I was to him and . . .'

'Yeah, well, your old man's dead now, so he won't bother you any more,' Johnson said.

'Fuck you, Carl,' Dennis spat, and suddenly he was roaring at the top of his voice. 'Mister bloody cool, aren't you? Mister balls of steel. Well, you fucking listen to me, you smooth bastard.'

Johnson bolted from his chair, raced over to Dennis and punched him flush in the mouth. Yet the heavy blow had little effect and merely fuelled Dennis's anger. 'Come on!' he urged. 'I'm used to this shit, man. I took enough of this shit from my father.'

'Where's my daughter?' Johnson yelled, slapping Dennis repeatedly about the face. He could have been hitting a dummy. Dennis sat there and took it all. Then he began to laugh uncontrollably.

Johnson saw now that Dennis was a seriously sick and desperate man, and slowly backed away. He sat back down, waiting for Dennis to blow himself out. Yet still Johnson couldn't feel pity for the man before him; only hate and contempt for all the misery his cowardice had caused.

When Dennis recovered his composure, he began to speak matter-of-factly, as if this violent interruption had never taken place. Johnson's blow had started his mouth bleeding again, yet he seemed oblivious of the blood as it dripped off his chin and gently splattered onto his chest. 'Raymond Smith, that was my mate's name. Christ, I was so proud Raymond was my friend. He was the best fighter in the school. None of the other kids messed around with Raymond Smith. He used to sit next to me in Maths class. He just seemed to like me for some reason. He *respected* me. I knew nobody would ever dare touch me as long as Ray was there. I told him about the old man's drinks cabinet, and I took him back home one lunchtime and we dared each other to raid it and get drunk. It was probably the only brave thing I ever did. That drinks cabinet was so special to the old man — sacred, you know? Not something that belonged to the family. It was like some kind of monument in the corner of his study, something you didn't dare touch. We got pissed as farts and then threw up all over the carpet.

'I was still ill in my bedroom when the old man got home that night and I'll never forget how he burst into the room. I was bracing myself, ready for it. I'd heard Mum pleading with him not to go mad, but I knew the worst was going to happen. He was roaring like a fucking great lion. He almost tore the door off its hinges when he kicked it open and his face was purple. I expected violence, but nothing like the kind of shit that followed. He beat me with his fists, he kicked me, he did everything. I was panicking like hell, because it seemed I was bleeding from everywhere on my body. I was down on my knees at one point and he was banging my head against the wall. My mother had to jump on his back and beat him with her fists to get him to stop.

'I just blacked out. He wouldn't even let Mum call an ambulance, because he was shit-scared of the consequences. He got this doctor friend of his – some half-baked quack who owed him a favour – to look me over. All my life, that incident has haunted me. I bet the old man told you he never hit me, right? Yeah, he liked to tell everyone that. It's a fucking lie.'

Dennis had been staring into space during this rambling tale, but now his tired and bloodshot eyes focused on Johnson for some kind of reaction. But there was no warmth in Johnson's face, no hint of understanding or compassion. 'What do you want, Dennis?' he asked. 'Do you want my forgiveness? Do you want me to tell you a rough childhood is justification for everything that's happened since? Whatever the old man's failings, you're worse than he ever was. You're a coward, and you're an evil coward. You're the worst kind of murderer. You killed two people without getting a drop of blood on your hands. You lied to me, Dennis. About everything. And now I'm going to put you in hell for it.'

Dennis laughed. 'I'm in hell already, can't you see that?'

'You put yourself, there, Dennis. Nobody else did. Where's Cody?'

'Gone. Out of my life for ever, I hope. All my demons are gone now ... the old man, Cody. Now I can just go to sleep and never wake up again.'

'Where *is* he?' Johnson repeated. 'Stop talking to me in riddles. I don't give a shit what you do to yourself once I'm gone. But I'll get the truth first, however many more lumps I have to put in that sweet little face of yours. I want Cody, Dennis. I want my daughter. I want the whole bloody story and you know how far I'll go.'

'Get me a drink,' Dennis said. 'There should be another bottle out in the kitchen.'

'You've had enough to drink. And I've had enough of people drinking. Everywhere I go, I seem to bump into emotional cripples who need a glass of Scotch in their hand for courage.'

'Please get me a drink,' Dennis pleaded, begging now instead of demanding. He leaned forward and held his tired and aching head in his hands. 'Get me a drink, Carl, and I'll tell you the whole thing. No more bullshit, no more self-pity, I promise. I'll tell you everything and you can do what you want to me after that. I've had enough.'

Dennis was through with his life and Johnson knew it. These were the tired and emotionless words of a man who simply wanted to unload the last of his burdens before signing off. Johnson went into the kitchen and quickly returned with a bottle of whisky and a clean glass. He poured the drink for Dennis, who was still trembling so violently that he had to grip it with both hands. Johnson pulled his chair closer and sat down again. Dennis needed no prompting this time. He shuddered as the whisky went down and said quickly, 'Steve's got Janice.'

'Where?' Johnson asked.

'I honestly don't know, Carl. He wouldn't tell me.'

'Is she okay?'

'I think so. I don't think Steve would hurt her.'

'How the hell do you know?'

'Because Janice is his girl, Carl. She's been his girl for ... Christ, ages. He's crazy about her. God, you never knew, did you? You never had the vaguest bloody idea. Face it, Carl, you don't know the first thing about your own daughter.'

This hard truth cut Johnson deeply and he wanted to lash out at Dennis and finish him right there and then. He didn't need a moral sermon from a man who couldn't even look after himself. 'Listen,' he said calmly, 'I asked you for the truth and that's all I want. I don't want your opinions, your judgement, or any other little asides. Are you straight on that, Dennis?'

Dennis, with nothing more to lose, looked challengingly at Johnson for a few seconds, but then nodded sheepishly. He shivered and drank some more of the warming whisky.

'How long?' Johnson asked. 'How long have they been...'

'A long time. Before you went to the States. Nobody knew except me. Then Rose found out, and that's what started it all ... the whole bloody nightmare. One big trail of lies, deceit and destruction. She was careful to keep it from you and the old man because she thought either one of you would probably kill Steve. Then, after you'd taken Janice up to Scotland, Rose called me and asked me to bring Steve over. She wanted to have it out with him and that's when it all turned nasty.

'You call me an evil bastard and you're absolutely right. I was always weak, always scared. Right from a kid, I just wanted my own life, away from all this. This rotten business and my lack of courage made me evil. But I'm nothing compared to Cody. You don't know how evil that man can be. Last night's fiasco was Steve's work. Kenny Carter and Dave Richards shot your friend Micky Lyle. They weren't working for the old man like I told you. The old man thought they were, but they were working for us. Janice called Steve from Michael Rossi's place and told him where she was.'

'Why?' Johnson exploded, jumping up. The force of his sudden eruption jolted Dennis, who thought that Johnson was about to set on him again. But Johnson could find no outlet for his anger. He punched the air in frustration and paced around like a caged lion. Talking to himself more than Dennis, he said, 'She seemed so happy when I brought her back here. It seemed she'd forgotten all her troubles. We were happy together for the first time in years. How the hell could she do this to me? Does she really hate me that much?'

'Because she's as hateful as Cody, Carl, that's why,' Dennis said. 'And you can be a loyal father and beat the shit out of me for saying that, but it's true. She hates you, man. She always has. She blames you for ruining her mother's life. In her eyes, you killed Rose.'

'*She* killed her,' Johnson roared. He stormed at Dennis, knocking his drink flying and clamping a hand on his throat. 'I know that bastard Cody did it, Dennis. And that makes Janice just as guilty. Neil Franklin emerged from his great slumber and told me everything.'

'Wrong, wrong, wrong!' Dennis yelled, slapping Carl's arm away. 'The one damn thing Janice doesn't know is that Steve killed Rose. We told her the old man did it, just like we told you. For all her bad ways, she adored her mum. She's mad about Steve, but he always knew he could never tell her the truth about Rose's death. He knew that would be the one thing that would break her and drive her back to you.'

Johnson sat down again, trying to make sense of everything. Quietly, he asked 'Where's Cody now?'

'He went to pick up Carter and Richards. They went cruising to try and find Franklin. We saw him at the beach yesterday, standing out like a big sore thumb. Cody couldn't believe it.'

'I know,' Johnson said, 'Neil told me. That's when his memory clicked back into place. He'd blocked it all out before that.'

Unable to find his glass, Dennis swigged straight from the bottle and shook his head. 'Bloody amazing, that was. Steve never knew Neil. When he met him on the beach that night, he thought it was just some old wino who'd probably be dead by now. I remember him scouring the seafront for Neil for days afterwards, just to make double sure. He seemed to put it out of his mind after that. He really believed it was no problem. Christ, the look on his face when he saw Neil yesterday. I couldn't believe it myself. Neil didn't have his beard back in the days when he was working for the old man, but he's such a big and striking bastard. I knew it was him. It was all we needed. Another massive fucking problem. Steve figures he won't be hard to find again. He seems to have given up on hiding himself.'

'He won't find him,' Johnson said. 'I've got him locked away.'

'I hope you're right, Carl.'

'Screw you, Fossey. Don't give me bloody sympathy now.'

'God damn it, Carl, it's not sympathy. There's just no bloody point to it all anymore, that's all. I tried to tell Cody that before he went berserk today. Everything's gone wrong. It's all over. He wanted to be the big boss, he wanted to knock off the old man, you, everybody . . . but it all got out of hand and went horribly wrong. He shared my hatred of the old man, but he knew he didn't have the balls to kill him. He needed the best in the business to do that and he knew he had to wait for the right time. When we knew you were coming back, he got the idea to pin Rose's death on the old man. He knew that would be like showing a red rag to a bull.

'But he's not a leader, Carl. He hasn't got what it takes. He's too greedy and he panics under pressure. Now he's lost it completely. He's found his courage too late in the day, if you can call it courage. And now he wants to sweep away everything in his path. Christ, he thinks he's in a bloody cowboy film. The three of them are coming to get you tomorrow, Carl. Janice told Steve you planned to be around until you'd settled your account. He gave her some bullshit about having to talk business with you. He's going to call you to set up a meeting.'

Johnson didn't seem greatly bothered by this. 'Tell me something,' he said, 'when they came to get her last night, did she know they were going to kill Micky Lyle?'

Dennis shook his head firmly. 'No, Carl, I swear it. Nor did I. The version Cody gave me was that Janice was supposed to slip out at a certain time and meet Carter and Richards halfway. That was another major bloody disaster. Steve said that Janice took the chain off and then got cold feet. Carter and Richards panicked when she didn't show up and decided to storm the place. Steve said Janice was hysterical about Micky getting shot.'

Johnson sneered and said, 'Yeah, how tremendously moving. I'm supposed to believe she's been a wide-eyed innocent through all of this, am I?'

'No, Carl, I never said that. She's obsessed with Cody, but there are things she wouldn't do for him and Cody knows that. He's not stupid, Carl, he doesn't tell her everything.'

Johnson was silent for a few seconds as he stared down at the floor. 'The bastard knew she was at Greatstone all along, didn't he?' he said. 'Tell me about Greatstone, Dennis. I've heard Janice's version and now I want yours.'

There was a new tone of menace in Johnson's voice and suddenly

Dennis felt sick again. He could feel the whisky sloshing around in his stomach and he gingerly placed his bottle on the floor. 'Tell me what happened to Wendy,' Johnson demanded. 'It wasn't your father who bundled her into that car. The old man was never there, was he?'

'No,' Dennis said quietly. 'He never knew Janice was at Greatstone. No, we set that one up too. Well, I mean, it was Steve's idea. Janice hated it when you moved her down there. She told Steve straightaway and begged him to get her out. He couldn't do that, of course, but she asked him if he could get rid of Wendy. Christ, those two fought like a pair of cats.

'Well, Steve jumped at that. Right away, he saw it as another chance to poison the old man in your eyes. He was doing anything he could to stoke the fire. He filled Janice's head with all sorts of romantic rubbish. Stories of power and money and all that crap. He told her if he could frame the old man and turn you against him, he'd gain control of the firm and the sky would be the limit. Well, that turned Janice on, the thought of Steve being the boss over her own dad. She got off on that kind of thing, it excited her. And she didn't like the old man, of course. He never hurt her in any way, but he always found a reason to touch her or give her a little cuddle. You know what I mean, Carl, you saw it often enough. It was all perfectly harmless, but Janice thought he was a dirty bastard. He gave her the creeps. It was her idea to make up the story about the old man getting violent with her. Yeah, she enjoyed inventing that one. Of course, Steve didn't tell her that killing you was part of the overall plan.'

'So what happened?' Johnson asked. 'What did that gutless wonder do to Wendy?'

Dennis shook his head. 'It was a disaster. A complete botch-up. The simple plan was to get Wendy out of there, pay her off and send her back home. Simple. Should have been a stroll. I mean, Christ, Cody thinks he's Marlon Brando in *The Godfather* and he couldn't even handle that.'

'Get on with it,' Johnson said irritably.

'Actually,' Dennis said, 'Janice didn't have to change the true story that much, apart from substituting the old man for Steve. I went down there with Steve when she called us and the place was a mess. Carter and Richards were with us and Steve told them to wait in the car. Things had quietened down by the time we got there, but it was obvious there'd been some kind of almighty fight. Wendy was just sitting there on the settee, but she was clearly freaked out. I looked into her bedroom and there was cocaine all over the place. All the money you sent Janice, that's where it was going. Wendy took men back to the house, she was doing all kinds of things. Janice said when she was bombed she'd get absolutely hysterical. She'd just go mad and play loud music right around the clock.'

Dennis reached down for his bottle again and Johnson snapped, 'Leave it. Just try to relate one disastrous story in your life without a drink, Dennis.'

Dennis sighed like a child who'd been told he couldn't have any more sweets. Looking slightly desperate, he asked, 'Can I bum a smoke off you?' Johnson threw him his cigarettes and lighter, and Dennis sucked down the first drag of nicotine as if it were life-saving oxygen. 'Anyway,' he continued, 'Steve asked Janice to go into her bedroom. He told her we wanted to talk to Wendy alone and the atmosphere suddenly got very edgy. Wendy didn't know us from Adam and she was panicky anyway from being so far out of it. She kept asking Janice who we were, and then Janice got nervous and started saying she didn't want any more trouble or anyone to get hurt. That only made Wendy worse.

'Steve was in an absolutely foul mood and I didn't like the way things were going at all. I just seemed to know right there and then it was all going sour. Steve managed to usher Janice into her room and Wendy was getting really loud. He told me to keep her quiet, but how the hell do you keep a mad woman quiet? I tried shaking her but that made her worse. Steve was furious when he got back and told me to get out of the way. As I let Wendy go, she just flew at Steve and started scratching and slapping at him. Steve grabbed her by the neck and punched her full in the face, and when she crashed to the floor I honestly thought she was dead.

'Janice rushed back into the room and kept asking Steve what the hell he had done. There was blood pumping out of Wendy's nose and now Steve was flaming mad. He kept telling Janice Wendy was only unconscious, but Janice kept making a commotion and he slapped her in the face and started shaking her. He told her to go and pack Wendy's things and then he told me to clean up Wendy's face. He said we'd walk her up to the car as best we could, and if anyone saw us . . . well, hopefully, they'd think she was pissed or something.

'There was nobody around, thank Christ, and we bundled her in the back of the car. Steve told Janice to clean up the bungalow and said we'd be in touch. She was still pretty strung out and the whole atmosphere was just . . . frightening. But I thought we were home and dry at that point. Wendy was still spark out and the plan was to drive her up to London, put the frighteners on her and pay her off. Steve had promised Janice he wouldn't hurt her. I mean, God, money was all Wendy wanted. She didn't need Janice or a sleepy little place like Greatstone. Steve figured it wouldn't be hard to buy her silence. We hadn't been driving for that long when Wendy came around, and she just started going crazy again. It was pure hysteria. She wasn't saying anything in particular, just swearing like hell and lashing out at everyone. Carter and me were sitting on either side of her on the back seat, and Steve kept shouting at us from up front to get her under control.

'Dave Richards was driving and Wendy lunged forward at one point and grabbed him round the neck. He damn near lost control of the car and that was when Kenny Carter went mad. You know what an evil temper that bastard's got. He stopped messing about trying to grab Wendy and just lost control completely. He punched her in the face and knocked her unconscious again, but he wouldn't stop. He just kept punching her right in the face until her blood was spurting all over the car, and we were all shouting at him to stop. I tried to get him off her, I swear I did, but it was like trying to stop Mike Tyson in full flow.

'Dave stopped the car and Kenny stopped hitting Wendy all at once, as if he suddenly realised what he'd done. We were out in the middle of nowhere, halfway across Romney Marsh, and there were suddenly a few seconds of total quietness when I remember looking down at my clothes and seeing they were soaked in Wendy's blood. Then her head flopped against my chest and fell in my lap, and I thought I was going to vomit. I got out of the car and stumbled into a field, but I couldn't bring anything up. I was heaving and shaking and I knew he'd killed her. I knew Kenny had killed her. I wanted to tear my shirt off and get all the blood off me, but I knew I couldn't. I kept looking around for any sign of people, any traffic, because the others were making a real bloody din.

'Dave had pulled Kenny out of the car and was giving him a right slapping around the face. Then Steve tried to go for Kenny, and Dave had to keep them apart. I just snapped and yelled at them all to shut up. I asked them if Wendy was dead. I asked them to check if she was dead for Christ's sake, even though I knew. I doubt if anybody could have survived a beating like that. It was Dave who leaned inside the car and checked Wendy out. He was the only one with a cool head. He seemed to take forever over it. Then he shook his head and said to Steve, "She's gone". Well, that just made things worse. Kenny tried to justify his actions by saying she deserved it and Steve lost his temper and tried to go for him again. It was like watching a bunch of schoolkids blaming each other for smashing somebody's window.

'I walked away from them, further into the field, and that's when I finally threw up. I could feel the warm blood on my shirt, pressing against my belly, and I just fell down on my knees and puked. I knew then there was no going back, that the whole rotten thing had gone too far and there was no way out.'

'There's always a way out,' Johnson said contemptuously, galled by Dennis's self-pitying expression. 'If you had any steel in your spine, you'd have ended it right there and then.'

Dennis covered his eyes wearily and said, 'I couldn't, you don't understand.'

'Then make me understand,' Johnson snapped. 'Where's Wendy now? What did you evil bastards do with her?'

'I don't know where her body is, Carl, I honestly don't. I only ever asked Steve once after that day and he told me to forget about it. He said he'd never tell me because I'd lose my nerve and let it slip to someone.

'When they'd all calmed down a bit, Steve and Dave started discussing the options, but it was all in hushed tones and I couldn't pick up much. I just heard Dave Richards telling Steve not to worry,

228

that he knew a safe place. Dave and Kenny lifted Wendy's body into the boot of the car and Steve grabbed some rags and wiped up the blood inside. He kept telling me to keep my eyes peeled, but I was just sitting there in the grass in an absolute daze. I couldn't concentrate on the road or anything else. Everything was blurred and hazy in the heat and it was hurting my eyes.

'I wanted us to get caught. I wanted someone to pull up and ask us what the hell we were doing. But I knew that wouldn't do any good, because the boys were tooled up and it would have led to one almighty carnage. It was a do-or-die situation and I know they would have blasted anyone who interrupted them. Steve came across and threw me a spare T-shirt he had in the back of the car. He asked me if I was okay and I told him I wanted to kick the hell out of Kenny for doing what he did. He told me it was done with and now we just had to limit the damage. Those were his words – limit the damage. He'd obviously heard that somewhere, like all his other favourite sayings. He told me to get my jacket and shirt off and throw them in the back.

'I tried not to look at Wendy when I got back to the car, but I couldn't help it. She was lying there all limp, blood all over her . . . her face horribly smashed. I just felt . . .'

'I don't want to hear it,' Johnson said. 'I don't want to know how bad or how guilty you feel about any of this. I'm not your priest and I don't want your confession. You're an unlucky man, Dennis. Do you know why?'

Dennis shook his head. He was still fearful of Johnson's quiet rage, yet he wanted the torment to end. He wanted Johnson to take the gloves off once and for all and pound him into a permanent sleep, shoot him, knife him, whatever. Johnson knew this when he said, 'Because, logically, I should put you out of your misery by beating the life out of you as Carter did to Wendy. But that's a fate you don't deserve, Dennis. You've bared your soul and now you want your release. And, as always, you want somebody else to do the hard part.'

'I just want to die,' Dennis said, close to breaking again. 'I don't expect forgiveness for the things I've done. I just want my life to end.'

'Fine,' Johnson said coldly. 'Then when we've done here, do the honourable thing. I suppose suicide requires a brand of courage, if that's what you're looking for.'

Dennis tipped his head back and stared at the ceiling, as if trying to find the answers there. 'I wish to Christ Steve Cody had never come into my life. He didn't say a word on the drive back to Brighton. He just sat up front stuffing his face with chocolate bars, as if it had never happened. The drive seemed endless. I just wanted to get back to Brighton and get out of that hot car. There's no direct route from Greatstone and we were in traffic jams the whole time. The others didn't seem at all worried, but I kept thinking we were going to get stopped. We had a dead body in the back of the car. It didn't seem real. Carter was driving me mad, chewing gum and making slapping noises with his mouth. He just didn't ... I mean, there was no feeling there at all. It just didn't register on him ... what he'd done. Steve and Dave kept whispering to each other but I couldn't hear them. I didn't want to hear them.

'When we got back to Brighton, they let me out at the Marina and Steve told me not to worry, that he'd handle the rest. I didn't ask any questions. I was tired and sick and confused, like I was in another world. I just went home and went to bed.'

Dennis gave Johnson a quick glance to gauge his reaction, but Johnson was staring into space and said nothing. He got up slowly and went into the kitchen to pour himself a glass of water, and then walked over to the window behind Dennis, where he took long and measured sips as he peered out at the harbour. Dennis, disturbed by the sudden quietness, said, 'That's all I know about Wendy, honestly. Only Steve ... I mean ... only he can tell you...' Nervousness was making him talk for the sake of talking and he quickly bit his tongue.

'Oh, I'll find out,' Johnson said quietly. 'I'll make that bastard tell me. Is this something else he kept from Janice?'

'Yes. As far as Janice knows, Wendy was taken back to London and told not to show her face again.'

Johnson sat down and suddenly looked tired and lined as the sun passed over his face. He had been bemused and hurt by so much since his return to Brighton. He wondered if he was old before his time, too set in his ways. It was Janice who had cut him the deepest.

'What the hell ever made her get stuck on Cody?' he asked. He seemed to be thinking aloud and Dennis wasn't sure whether he should answer.

'The old man dropped by the house one night a long time ago when you were away,' he ventured. 'Just to see that Rose was safe and well, like he did when you weren't around. Steve had been helping him out that day and tagged along. I joined them there later, and Janice could hardly hide her fascination for Steve. God alone knows what she saw in him, but he obviously struck a chord and he played it up to the full, preening and showing off like a bloody schoolboy. I don't know how, but they obviously arranged to meet and kept it hidden from Rose – for a time anyway. It was while Rose was drinking heavily, and she wasn't always ... well, you know. Steve would bring Janice up to my place every once in a while, and I made it known that I didn't think it was a good idea. I told him there'd he hell to pay if you or the old man ever found out.'

'But Rose found out.'

'Yeah.'

'Tell me what happened,' Johnson said. 'Tell me exactly what happened the night Rose died.'

34

Dennis sighed and expected another rebuke as he reached again for his bottle of whisky. But Johnson let it go this time, and Dennis took a long, greedy hit on the bottle. 'Like I said, Rose called me the day after you took Janice up to Scotland. She sounded straight – I mean, not drunk or anything – but she was very angry. She said she needed to see me that evening and told me to bring Steve along. I asked her what the problem was, but she wouldn't elaborate and she emphasised that Steve had to be there. Well, of course, it was Steve she really wanted to see. She just didn't want to confront him alone, I suppose. I sensed she'd found out about him and Janice in some way. Steve sounded edgy when I asked him and he asked a lot of questions, but he agreed to come along.

'He came over to me around ten o'clock that night, and all the way over to your place he was asking me if I thought Rose knew. I told him it didn't sound too good, and he seemed to get more nervous by the second. He was saying there was no way he could let you or the old man find out, that he had to find a way of winning Rose round. But he didn't seem paranoid about it. Christ Almighty, he didn't strike me as a man who was considering the ultimate act. I didn't think he was capable of anything like that anyway, not until everything started to come apart. He went quiet for a while, then he told me to stop at an off-licence. He came back with this bag which he quickly slung on the back seat, as if he was hoping I wouldn't notice it.

'I asked him what he'd bought and he said it was a bottle of vodka. He said it was Rose's favourite, that it would maybe loosen her up and make her more reasonable. I told him not to be so stupid. He knew Rose's condition, he knew she'd only recently been treated for her drinking. I told him he couldn't be sure she knew anyway. He didn't argue with me. He didn't say anything. He just sat there and brooded the rest of the way.'

Dennis was now feeling tired; physically tired and tired of talking. His head ached and every muscle in his body felt unbearably sore. Making himself more comfortable, he slid down onto the floor with his back against the sofa, and took a deep breath as he reluctantly relived the tragic night that had ruined so many lives. 'As it turned out, Rose had already been drinking when we arrived. There was no sign of a bottle or glasses, but her breath smelled strongly of alcohol. She was very much in control though, not at all drunk at that stage. She was very cold, very brusque, and quite obviously trying to hold her temper. She led us into the kitchen and asked us to sit down. Well, it was every bit as bad as I'd feared. Worse in fact. Rose opened a drawer and pulled out this letter and slammed it down on the table in front of Steve. She said it was the most filthy thing she'd ever read and asked him for an explanation. Steve just wasn't expecting her to produce something like that. It was one of the few times I've ever seen him lost for words.

'It was his own bloody fault. It was a love letter he'd written to Janice. It was highly intimate stuff and written in the crudest fashion. I mean, really crude in a sexual way, you know? I got a sneak look at it later on and you only had to read a sentence or two to get the general gist of it. He was telling Janice what he'd like to do to her. It was the kind of crude shit fifth formers write. Steve sort of apologised as only Steve can, and then cancelled it all out by going on the offensive and protesting that it was a private matter between him and Janice.

'Well, that did it. Rose went mad and really read him the riot act. She asked Steve if he could even imagine the consequences of you or the old man finding out, and Steve looked as worried as I've ever seen him. He asked Rose if Janice or anybody else knew about her finding the letter, and she said no. It was the quiet way he asked her ... I guessed he had something terrible in mind.

'Then the lucky bastard got his break. Rose was ranting and

raising her voice more and more when she suddenly wobbled and grabbed hold of a chair. I thought she was going to crash over onto the floor and I jumped up and grabbed her. She was holding her head and gasping, but she got her breath back when I sat her down and seemed to recover a bit. She was trembling violently and pointed at Steve's bag and told him to pour her a drink quick. I said I didn't think that was wise, but Steve said we all needed a drink and he grabbed some glasses and poured the vodka.

'I pushed mine to one side and told Rose again not to drink. As God is my witness, Carl, I really did. Steve told me to shut up, but it didn't make any difference anyway. Rose grabbed the glass really fast and drank it down in one go. It steadied her up and Steve poured her another one. I just wanted to get out of there, but I didn't know what the hell the fucker was going to do. Rose wanted to know how long he'd been seeing Janice, and Steve suddenly became the great diplomat. He gave her all this flannel about how much he loved Janice, but he didn't want to cause anybody any grief. He told her how much he respected her feelings, how much he respected Janice and you and the whole world-and-his-brother. He assured Rose he would call Janice discreetly when she got back, and end the affair in return for Rose's promise not to take it any further.

'Rose seemed to calm down and things were beginning to look good again. Then the booze seemed to hit her really fast and she became confused and irritable. She said she needed some air. She said she was having trouble breathing and couldn't think properly. It was a horribly sticky night and Steve said we should all get a breath of fresh air, and suggested a drive down to the beach. I didn't like the idea of that at all and I tried to talk Rose out of it. I told her she was strung out and it wasn't a good time to discuss all this.

'Steve was giving me some really shitty looks. He just cut right in and said, "Come on, Rose, let's go for a drive." Rose went to get her coat and Steve put the bottle of vodka back in the bag, ready to take with him. I asked him what the hell he was playing at and he was furious. He told me to shut up and stop panicking. "I'll handle it" he said. He said that twice, maybe three times, but he wouldn't tell me what he meant by it. Rose sat in the back of the car on her own and didn't say a word. None of us did. I had all the windows open and it was still like a furnace in there. I drove to the seafront and past the Palace Pier, and as we were approaching the West Pier Steve told me to stop.

'I noticed Rose was finding it hard to keep her eyes open and Steve reached across the seat and said, "Come on, Rose, let's go for a little walk." I was going to get out but he grabbed my arm and told me to go home. He said he'd meet me back at my place later. I told him no, I wasn't going to do that. The situation was getting dangerous and I was really scared shitless at that point. I thought he was going to start his bullying again, but he eased up and told me everything was going to be okay. He said he'd let Rose clear her head, then they'd straighten things out and he'd walk her back home. He promised me, man. He said he'd be committing suicide if he did anything silly. I didn't believe him, but I knew he wasn't going to let me hang around anyway.

'I drove home and started hitting the drink and just waited and waited. I must have got home around midnight and it was pushing three o'clock when Steve finally turned up. He'd walked all the way and he looked like hell. From the moment I saw him, I knew what he'd done. He was surprisingly calm about it actually, either calm or in a state of shock. He was still wet and asked me for a bathrobe. Then he casually started to tell me what had happened, like a guy describing his round of golf. I told him I didn't want to know, I told him it was a mad thing to do. But he said this was his big chance, the shot he'd been looking for at toppling the old man. He said it had been easy, that Rose had virtually done it all herself. She'd gone downhill really fast after I'd left them and didn't even seem to know where she was. Steve said she was slurring badly and was changing her mind all the time about what she wanted to do. She told Steve she wanted to go somewhere for a drink and he offered her the bottle, but she wanted to be around other people. He took her to some club and she really started hitting the booze and getting loud and abusive.

'Steve said that when he finally managed to pull her out of there, she started nagging him to take her down on the beach. She said she wanted to go swimming. Well, that was the perfect opening for Steve. He just let things follow their natural course from there.'

'Tell me anyway,' Johnson said. 'I want to hear it all.' He could feel the tears in his eyes, but was damned if he was going to let them out and show them to Dennis.

'He didn't have to kill her as such,' Dennis said. 'At least, that's what he told me. The version he told you and Rossi the other day – when he said the old man did it – was pretty much the way it happened. Rose just went crazy and started running pell mell for the water. Steve said she was taunting him, taking her clothes off and inviting him to . . . well, sort of asking him if he had the balls to do to her what he did to Janice. Steve just kept following her until they were quite a way out, and then she, well, she just suddenly got into trouble and began to flounder, and . . .'

'Yeah, I know,' Johnson said quietly. 'That's exactly the way I killed your father. Killing's still the word for it. I wanted him to feel that same sense of panic and desperation. He got drunk and then he drowned himself. I didn't even have to give him a shove. Perfect poetic justice. Or so I thought.'

Dennis lit another cigarette with still trembling hands and said, 'Yeah, Steve was proud about that part of it. That's the word he used – perfect. He said he'd never once had to touch Rose. Mind you, I could tell he was troubled about something, and that's when he told me about running into some drunk. He had a big mark on his chin and I asked him what the hell had happened. He said it was a big guy honking of alcohol, who had suddenly gone mad and belted him a couple of times before running off.

'That was Steve's version of the story, anyway. He said he'd tried to talk to the guy, because he was afraid he might have seen what had happened. Then he sort of dismissed it. He said the guy was bombed out of his brains and probably wouldn't remember any of it. But I knew he wasn't convinced, and it's haunted him ever since . . . never being certain, never knowing for sure. I know for days afterwards he'd cruise Brighton with Carter and Richards, looking in every shit-hole in town for Neil.

'I think he became more relaxed about it as time went on. He told me more than once that Neil had probably died somewhere, but it was bloody strange, you know . . . Neil *did* haunt him. Sort of became part of him. I mean, you know Steve. He's not the deepest of men. Yet he said to me once, "If that bastard's still alive, I wonder if he remembers me? I wonder if he sees me in his dreams, because I see him in mine".

'Anyway, he'd done it, and that night he told me his master plan – how he'd wait for the right time and then put the old man in the frame. Christ, he waited and waited. Two years, man. I didn't think Steve had that kind of patience, but he insisted the time had to be right. Then he'd recall you from the States to do the necessary work. And all the time he'd use me as his cover.'

Dennis laughed self-mockingly. 'It was to be *my* master plan, you see. My big strike for ultimate power. The bastard used me like he used you. It was utter madness, doomed to failure right from the start. I hated my father, but I never wanted him dead. I never wanted anybody dead in all my life. I was doing pretty good until all this. I hated being under the old man's thumb, but I had pretty much everything I wanted.'

Johnson could take no more of this. 'So why the fuck did you go along with it all?' he exploded.

'Because I had no bloody choice,' Dennis shouted, banging the floor with his fist. 'The bastard had me over a barrel. He's had a hold on me since . . .'

'Since when?' Johnson thundered.

Dennis swallowed hard and shook his head. Now he was about to tell Johnson the one thing he had been dreading the most, something that only Cody knew. 'Look,' he said, 'a couple of years ago Steve and me were in the Old Steine area, just drinking at various places and larking about. I thought he was a true friend in those days, somebody I could trust. The weather was like it is now. Hot and sticky. I'd had enough and we were about to head back home, and that's when it happened.

'There's a well-known gay pub down there, just a way back from the seafront, and this young guy suddenly comes staggering out and falls straight into my arms. He bashed into me so hard, he nearly knocked me over. He was clearly out of his mind on something. He was crying into my chest and gripping hold of my arms, and his own arms were covered in needle marks. Then he lifted his head and looked into my eyes with the most frightened expression I've ever seen. His face and body were so dreadfully wasted, I didn't even recognise him at first. Then he said my name very softly and it hit me. Jesus, then he said it again, and then he kept saying it, louder and louder each time. He went mad, throwing his arms around my neck and kissing me, and I couldn't move. I wanted to throw him off but I couldn't get my body to work. I saw Steve staring at all this with a funny smile on his face, and I was sort of shaking my head and pretending I didn't know what it was all about.

'Then I got really angry and threw the bastard off me. He went crashing into the wall and fell to the ground, and then he went berserk, shouting all kinds of abuse at me. I was still acting for Steve's sake and I said something like, "Let's get out of here, this guy's insane." But I knew I wasn't fooling him. He'd found out something and he wasn't going to let it go. It was too much to bear and I felt myself breaking up.

'I started to run, leaving Steve behind me, and I ran so fucking hard I felt I couldn't stop. When Steve finally found me, I didn't even know where I was. I was slumped down against a wall in some stinking back alley and I couldn't stop myself crying. He sat down beside me, playing the compassionate big brother, and I thought at long last I had somebody to confide in. I didn't have the strength to lie about myself anymore, so I told him everything.'

Dennis took another drink from his bottle and smiled at Johnson. 'You were close to my old man over the years. I'm sure at one time or another he must have discussed the mysterious lack of female company in my life. He discussed it with just about every other bastard.'

'He mentioned it from time to time,' Johnson nodded.

Dennis laughed, not so much a nervous laughter now but one of resigned relief. 'Yeah, well, it wouldn't have done the old Fossey family image a lot of good if I'd come clean about that side of my life. I once read that Queen Victoria refused to acknowledge the existence of lesbians. The old man was never quite that blinkered, but he did believe that a good cure for the average fairy was a bullet through the balls.

'This guy who ran into me that night . . . his name was Ricky. I met him at a gay club I used to go to from time to time and I felt sorry for him. He seemed very lonely, without a friend in the world, and he'd recently lost his job. I gave him some spending money and paid his rent for a while, but I quickly learned he was one of those neurotic types who couldn't be helped. He always drank pretty heavily, but then he started doping and getting into really heavy drugs. I found some stuff in his room and I knew I had to ditch him.

'You know what the old man was like with drugs. That was the one thing he wouldn't tolerate, whether it was business or recreation. The relationship was getting uncomfortable anyway. I always drummed it into Ricky that I wanted it kept under wraps, but he was a chronic motormouth when he was high. Christ, it was like trying to train a puppy.

'When I finally told him it was over, I had to threaten him with all kinds of mayhem if he ever dared talk about me. By that time he knew who my father was and I told him what the old man did to people who upset him. It was still an ugly business, though. I don't think he was ever stupid enough to drop my name anywhere, but that didn't stop him calling me up at all times in the morning. Sometimes he'd just abuse me, other times he'd get emotional and just break down and cry.

'Finally, I changed my number and it stopped. He never chanced coming to my place, thank Christ. And from then on I steered well clear of the kind of places where he might pop up. The way he was destroying himself ... well, I got to thinking maybe he'd killed himself, OD'd or something. I actually hoped he had. I hadn't seen him for nearly two years until that night with Steve.'

'So what did Steve do about it?' Johnson asked.

'Well, he had me where he wanted me, didn't he? He was fairly subtle about it at first. He gave me all that shit about looking after me as long as I looked after him. I knew at once what that meant. He'd never made any secret about wanting to be leader of the gang some day, and he knew I had no real ambition in that direction. But of course, he knew I carried enough clout to help him. Yeah, old Steve always wanted to be leader of the gang. That's the word he used – gang – as if we were all still a bunch of kids in the playground.

'It wasn't so bad at first. The kind of favours he asked me for in the early days were no big deal. But Rose's death changed all that.

Fortune smiled on the lucky bastard and opened the door. But for that, he wouldn't have stood a cat in hell's chance against the old man. The night he came back to my place after Rose had gone, that's when it got really nasty. I kept telling him I'd have nothing to do with what he had in mind and that's when he said he'd tell the old man about my great secret. The old man and everyone else.

'Christ, I couldn't bear the thought. I just couldn't bear it. The old man's wrath seemed so much worse than any other kind of punishment. Steve grabbed hold of me and asked me if we had a deal, and I said yes. And I knew then that we were both on our way to hell.'

'And that's it, is it?' Johnson said.

Dennis nodded very wearily, like a dying man about to take his last breath. 'That's it. There's nothing more I can tell you.'

Johnson got up and walked over to Dennis. Standing right above him, he said, 'Tell me again. In your heart of hearts, do you think Cody will hurt Janice?'

Dennis shook his head. 'Not unless he's gone right out of his mind. If he's scared, if he's totally lost it, who knows? I told you he was crazy about her, but mad people sometimes kill for love, don't they?'

'All right,' Johnson said edgily, not wanting to think about that possibility. 'What's the bastard's plan for tomorrow? You said he was going to call me. Do you know when?'

'No, I don't, honestly. Just be there. He'll make the call and he'll make the meet, because killing you will convince him he's got balls.'

'And what about you?' Johnson asked. Even now, even though he felt strangely calmer, there was a part of him that still wanted to beat the very life out of Dennis.

'I'm going to sleep,' Dennis said. 'And this time I won't have to wake up and face another day. I'm really no threat to you, Carl. You can leave me alone now.'

Johnson understood. And without making another gesture, without saying another word, he walked out.

35

Michael walked the short way into his kitchen to splash some water on his face, and when he stepped back onto the patio, Jack was gone. So had his glass, his ashtray and any hint of cigar smoke.

Drunk as he was, Michael felt remarkably fresh and alert. He had seen the big man, he had talked to him. All of this had really happened. He knew now how a sane man must feel when he drives past a field on his way home from work and sees strange little creatures climbing out of a spaceship.

Michael kept wondering why he felt so much better than he should, and it was because the throbbing in his head and face had gone. Completely. He no longer felt tired and washed out, but more alive than he had in years. The water hitting his face had perked him up even more, and he returned to his living-room and waited for the call from Johnson that Jack had promised. Michael didn't doubt at all that it would come, and it did, at around a quarter to nine.

Johnson sounded tired but very calm. 'Tell me you're feeling better than I am,' he joked, 'because I've just had the kind of day you don't want to hear about.'

Michael felt great hearing Johnson's voice, knowing that he was well. His fear had left him and now he was hungry for excitement again. 'I want to hear about it,' he said. 'I'm a lot better, Carl. When do you want me there?'

'Well, yeah, I do actually,' Johnson said, sounding surprised. How did Michael know? 'I took the chance of booking you a room.'

Not knowing how to explain himself, Michael said merely, 'Jesus, Carl, I've got so much to tell you.'

Johnson paused before saying, 'Yeah, me too, but not over the phone. Are you sure about this, Michael? Are you sure you want to get involved again?'

'Absolutely sure,' Michael insisted. 'You might think I need locking up when I tell you what's happened, but I know I've got to be a part of this.'

Johnson laughed. 'Christ, kid, what are you on? You haven't had another of those weird dreams of yours, have you? Listen, be here at ten and come straight up to my room. Get a cab, okay?'

Michael wanted to tell Johnson that Neil Franklin was dead, but how could he explain that without relating the whole remarkable story? Besides, he was grateful for the hour or so that he had, needing that time to prepare himself adequately for the next chapter in this weird and wonderful saga.

He went to his table, lit a cigarette and slopped a generous measure of vodka into his glass without hesitation or guilt. He wondered if Jack Fossey was watching him and he didn't care. He had never felt as strong and purposeful as he did right now, and for once it had nothing to do with the alcohol in his bloodstream. He knew this because the booze was no longer burning his chest or kicking at his insides. It was going down like water without scrambling his thoughts or blurring his judgement. He would drink no more after this one last special treat, and he knew that too. It was as if he were being guided now, wrapped in a protective armour that nothing or nobody could pierce.

He drank down the vodka, and, almost without thinking, went to his tape deck and put on 'Til I Die' by the Beach Boys. Beautiful and haunting, it had always been one of his favourite Brian Wilson songs. As he stepped into the shower and the cold water washed away the last of his doubts, he softly sang along to the lyrics which seemed to so accurately reflect the state of his own life.

Wilson had written the song during the early days of his slide into depression, comparing himself to a cork on the ocean, a leaf on a windy day, a rock in a landslide. The great man had lost his way, yet his music was still achingly beautiful.

Michael thought of all the things he wanted to be from now on – strong, proud, respectable, loyal – and then savoured the song's gorgeous and repetitive ending, where the final words are repeated over and over until they fade away.

36

Some time before Michael Rossi was released from his personal hell, Dennis Fossey had ventured deeper into his own. Yet while Dennis felt as though the weight of the entire world was coming down on him, he too had at last found an inner peace. He had continued to drink heavily after Johnson had left, finishing the bottle with a vengeance, and then squeaking with child-like glee on finding another full one tucked in his bed of all places, as if Santa Claus had placed it there.

He positively ripped his way through this one, taking huge mouthfuls as he staggered around the room, bumping into the walls and occasionally breaking into laughter as he lost his balance and tumbled over. He wanted to fry his brain now, to soak it and numb it to the point where he could burn out all the whirling shit and concentrate on the task of severing his lifeline. As the alcohol and the thrashing of his body made him sweaty and deliciously delirious, his mind began to spew out snapshots of the people who had touched his life.

Naked and within touching distance of freedom at last, Dennis spread his arms and looked up at the revolving ceiling as he spun round and round. He saw himself as a boy again, innocent and smiling, standing on a station platform with his mother; his wonderful, gentle, protective mother, the only person he had ever truly loved. They were on a visit to her sister's, which he always loved, because Auntie Joan spoiled him rotten. The sun was shining, and in his beautiful drunkenness Dennis could almost believe he was back in that warm and perfect world.

Then the black clouds began to gather and the happy picture was smashed by visions of his father and the shallow man that the boy Dennis had become. It was the day Dennis had raided his father's drinks cabinet, and the old man was beating him all over again, making him beg for his life. Dennis felt his mother's pain more than his own, as she cried and screamed and hurled herself at her rampant husband in her fury. Dennis's emotions were hitting both ends of the scale now, as he was jerked between despair and elation. He wept as he recalled the beating and then laughed maniacally as the magic picture show switched to his one moment of glory, his only act of bravado, when he had hit the old man square on the chin. Christ, how wonderful that had felt. Why had he been able to muster that kind of courage only once in his life?

Now the alcohol was really punishing him hard and the visions that remained were painful. There was Cody's face, satanic and intimidating, grinning knowingly back at him; there was the screaming voice of Ricky, his one-time lover, breaking up over the phone and begging Dennis not to abandon him.

Dennis whirled himself around even faster, the sweat now flying from his hair and his body as he tried to will the bitter memory out of his mind. Every part of him seemed to be on fire and he could no longer put out the flames. He saw Carl Johnson racing towards him and felt the pain again of Johnson slapping his face.

Then Dennis stopped dead, putting a hand to his face to try to halt the madness. The moment was right. He knew it instantly. Now was the time to stop all the craziness and make his exit. Utterly drunk and acting on his instincts, he staggered out to the kitchen and pulled open the cutlery draw, cutting two of his fingers on the utensils as he searched for his favourite knife. He found that richly ironic, considering what he had in mind, and he started laughing again. He found the knife, a small Kitchen Devil, and felt a rush of excitement as he gripped it tightly in his bleeding hand. He stumbled back into the bedroom, laughing harder as he bounced rubbery-legged off the walls as he went.

There was no great dramatic pause before Dennis committed the dreadful act. Standing before the full-length mirror that stood at the end of his bed, he was disgusted by his reflection. With two savage slashes, he cut clean through the tendons on each wrist, too far gone to feel the pain. As the blood began to run, he made a fist and smashed the mirror with a series of frenzied blows. Climbing onto his bed, he began to swathe his body in the blankets and sheets when his scattered senses were jarred by the smell of cigar smoke. Dennis spun round like a frightened child and peered out through the open door into the living-room. 'Dad,' he said, 'is that you, Dad?'

Then he fell back exhausted, curled up his body and embraced the permanent sleep he had craved for much of his muddled and wasted life.

37

Michael got to the Grand Hotel at about ten o'clock, and all the way down in the cab he had felt the adrenaline pumping through his body with frightening force. He had talked incessantly to the cab driver, and his animated state had nothing to do with the vodka he had consumed. That was the strange part of it. He had forgotten to brush his teeth and take his usual quota of strong mints before leaving – an ingrained habit for years – yet the taste and smell of the alcohol had gone completely from his mouth. He was high on excitement but not at all fuzzy or detached. After so many years of destructive drinking, Michael knew his system so well, and it was as if he'd never bought the bottle of vodka at Sammy's place. He found this disquieting, but it intrigued and thrilled him. He checked in, parked his bags in his room and went along to meet Johnson.

When Johnson opened the door he'd just taken a shower and was bare-chested and wearing only a pair of slacks. He looked tired and tense, but he smiled on seeing Michael and playfully cuffed him round the neck and pulled him inside.

The room, though large, was hot and muggy, and Michael noticed that the main window was only partially open, as if Johnson was trying to feed off the punishing atmosphere. Michael was just so pleased to see him again. When he shook Johnson's hand he had the stupid desire to hug him. He didn't want his great friend to die. He wanted him out at Monterey, running his restaurant, free of all his demons and ghosts.

'So you've got a lot to tell me, kid,' Johnson said, giving Michael a gentle poke in the stomach. 'I think you'd better go first. You look as pumped up as a fighter coming out for the first round.'

Michael noticed that Johnson was drinking iced water and said, 'I could do with some of that.' Johnson poured him a glass and then stretched out on his bed, looking pained as he eased himself into a comfortable position. Michael pulled up a chair close to him, and before he could speak Johnson said, 'I've been trying to raise Neil since I got back here. I told the silly bastard to stay home and I bet he's gone wandering.'

'Neil's dead,' Michael said suddenly. He had no proof of this, of course, but he was so sure. And he knew now that there could be no more secrets, that he had to tell Johnson about his meeting with Jack Fossey and his dreams of Monterey and Carmel that he had kept to himself. If Johnson ridiculed him and thought he was back on the drink again, then so be it.

Michael took one gulp of his water and then talked and talked and told Johnson everything. He related his dreams in every detail, acted out his bizarre conversation with Fossey, and spoke with such calm conviction that Johnson didn't once interrupt him. Michael chain-smoked five cigarettes and when he'd said all he could think of, the room was bathed in a suffocating blue haze. He didn't ask Johnson what he thought but simply took another drink and waited for his response.

Johnson smiled and let out a deep breath. Seconds passed before he spoke but his own words were equally as sure. 'I can't doubt you, Michael. I've never seen anyone look as intense as you do now. I know you're telling me the truth. I'm either as fucking mad as you are or I was right about you having that special gift. It all tallies. It all fits into place with some of the things I found out myself this afternoon. Old Jack was right about Dennis taking care of himself. I got his whole confession today. Then I left him to die like his old man.'

Johnson told Michael about his meeting with Dennis, but it was when he recounted his last day with Jack that Michael saw him crack for only the second time. This time, however, Johnson's lapse was so much more protracted and painful that it was unbearable to watch. His guard dropped completely and his grief was so shocking that

Michael wanted to cover his face and ears and shut it out. He had felt this way to a lesser extent on the seafront on Saturday, when Cody had told Johnson about Rose. But he wasn't going to be overwhelmed now by the kind of shame he had felt then. Never again was he going to be a coward, running away from every little problem whilst expecting his heroes to take it all on the chin and never buckle. When Johnson had shed his one tear on that hot and horrible day, Michael had felt let down, just as he had when his grandfather was dying from cancer in hospital.

He refused to turn his eyes away from Johnson now, seeing him for the first time as a real human being with a breaking point like anyone else. Tears ran down Johnson's face as he said, 'I always liked him, you know. Right at the end, when I was sticking that gun in his face and leading him down to the water . . . I still didn't want to kill him. He'd killed Rose, I was convinced of it, and I still wanted to forgive him. I just wanted to beat him and beat him in frustration and keep asking him why. He was begging me for his life, he was falling about and crying like a kid who's lost his father. All through it, something didn't feel right and I could feel the doubts overwhelming me. He just kept protesting his innocence in a way that seemed so utterly genuine. I was wavering, I wasn't sure any more. I should have pulled back then.

'Christ, Michael, I'm so used to killing I can't haul myself back from the brink any more. When he drowned, you see, it was a job well done. I was proud of myself. I was back in control again and so damn pleased about it.

'He wasn't marked, you know. His face wasn't marked and it should have been. There should have been a blotch, a bruise, something. Janice told me she punched him full in the face in her fairy story about Greatstone. I spent a day and a night with the man before I sent him to his grave, and it only occurred to me afterwards that his face wasn't marked. Christ, look at the trail of devastation . . . Jack, Micky Lyle and now Neil.'

Desperate to console his friend, Michael floundered for words. 'I got caught up in it too, Carl,' he said. 'When Cody gave us all that bullshit on Saturday, I wanted to go out there and kill Jack Fossey myself. The man was just a name to me but that's how strongly I felt.

With you, it was personal and even worse to bear. I've got to know you better than I've ever known you before these last few days, and I know how you pride yourself on being in control. But you can't odds something like that, Carl. You can't expect to be on your top form and think logically when someone has just told you your wife died like that. All these things you've told me about Dennis, all he told you about Cody, you couldn't have known. How could you have known? You weren't even there for most of the time. We both thought Cody was still the same blockhead he used to be at school, the coward who was all mouth. We'll get him, Carl. Whatever it takes, we'll get him. I promise you that.'

Johnson had been staring at Michael intensely and nodding, yet his mind was clearly on what lay ahead. Embarrassed by his show of emotion, he rubbed his eyes, scuffed back his hair, and took a deep breath. 'I still don't know what to think about Janice,' he said. 'Dennis reckoned Cody wouldn't hurt her, but he seemed to have his doubts. It's as if that bastard is trying to kill everything that's a part of my life.'

'He's definitely calling you tomorrow?' Michael asked.

'Yeah, according to Dennis. He didn't know what time but I would guess it will be early. We'll just have to sit tight and wait. Are you happy with that?'

Michael nodded. 'Whatever it takes, Carl. When the time comes, just tell me what to do and I'll do it.'

'I was going to ask you if you know how to handle a gun,' Johnson chuckled, 'but that's a silly question. Jesus, that's a sign of what this racket does to you. You get so used to toting guns and knives around, you ask people things like that like you're asking them if they can swim. How would you feel about it? If it came to the crunch, I mean.'

'Christ, I honestly don't know,' Michael said. 'I just don't know. I suppose if I had to . . . well, I hope I'd pull the trigger instinctively.'

'Nothing can prepare you for killing another human being,' Johnson said sombrely. 'I'm telling you that right now, Michael. I hope it's something you won't have to do. Some people can't do it anyway, even when they know the other guy is going to kill them. You had first-hand experience of seeing a man die when those bastards took Micky out. But something as terrible as that still doesn't compare with firing the gun yourself. You can watch every Peckinpah or Tarantino movie a thousand times over. That's cartoon stuff. As you said to me yourself, it's different when it's real.'

Johnson got up and walked over and opened the wardrobe. He rummaged in his sports bag and pulled out the Smith & Wesson he had shown Michael in his flat. 'Here,' he said, throwing it over, 'it's not loaded, don't worry. Hold it, feel it, get used to it. I'll explain the mechanics later, that won't take too long.' He dug deeper in the bag and held up a second gun, a mighty thing that Michael immediately recognised.

'By God, that's a Magnum 44,' he said. 'I've never actually seen one for real before.'

'Catch,' Johnson said, and Michael was shocked by its weight as it thumped into his hands.

'Jesus, I can barely lift it,' he marvelled.

'It's not what I call a regular kind of gun,' Johnson said. 'It's okay for special occasions. And if I'm going to blow a hole in Cody I may as well do it in style. That one's been good to me, but you have to know how to handle it. The recoil can knock you off your feet if you're not ready for it.'

Michael thought back to his dream of Sunset Boulevard and asked 'Have you still got Barbara Ann?'

'Yeah, I've still got her. I call that one there Wild Honey.'

'Brian Wilson/Mike Love, 1967,' Michael said. 'Those songs bring back so many happy memories for me. Life seemed more fun in those days, although I probably didn't think so at the time. I changed schools that year and started growing up for the first time. Among other things, I met a charming bastard called Steve Cody.'

'The past always seems better,' Johnson said, 'but you can't live there. It's like people who always try to tell you the summers were longer in those days. They forget all those picnics where they had to pack up at half-time because it was chucking with rain.'

Johnson climbed back onto the bed and drank down the rest of his water. He ran a hand down his chest and it was covered in sweat. 'I like summer, Michael,' he said thoughtfully. 'I like the sunshine and the flowers and the pretty girls. I even like being hot like this.

Summer always comes around, that's what keeps me going. It's what kept me going as a kid when my old man was terrifying the hell out of us at home. All that shit always seemed so much worse on cold winter nights when it got dark so early.

'I need some sunshine in my life now, Michael. I've been around violence and darkness all my life. I want it to end tomorrow. I want it to stop right there. I want a life of peace. When I was driving around the Monterey Peninsula, I sat on the beach out at Seal Rock one day, and that was the first time I'd felt at peace with myself for years. Christ, man, I wanted to sit on that beach for the rest of my life.'

His mood grew melancholic. 'I really miss Rose, Michael. We were a funny pair, it was a funny marriage really. I mean, we weren't at all luvvy-duvvy, we didn't smother each other all the time, all that crap. But we had something, you know. It was a strange bond between us, but it was a strong one and we were both aware of it. We were both tough but we were always tied. I could have loved her a lot more than I did. *Should* have loved her a lot more than I did. I should have been around a lot more, yet she was loyal to me. She reserved the right to curse me up hill and down dale but, by God, she'd savage anyone else who did the same.

'There were so many things I loved about her. She was all woman, totally feminine, but I loved her toughness. She'd sit around watching the fights and the football with me, the kind of things a lot of other women don't do. And she knew as much about it as I did too. She liked to eat and drink and take long walks ... she just loved life. Too damn much in the end. I don't think she ever hid behind the booze, she just loved it like everything else.

'Except one day, she just couldn't stop it anymore. She didn't turn into a mess or anything. She always took good care of herself, looked her best and all that. Some people drink like fish and it all seems so natural. That's the way it was for her. Christ, I was always so busy I hardly noticed anyway. Until the rubbish went out at the end of the week and I'd count the bottles in the sack. Then I knew she needed help, some kind of treatment. But that never worked. The kind of work I do makes it necessary for me to shut a lot of other things out of my life, and I suppose I chose to ignore the fact that

Rose would eventually kill herself, that she'd go like that in some way or another.

'To my shame, I just gave up on family life when she died. Janice was torn apart and raging at me for everything that had gone wrong, and I just thought, "Fuck it, I don't need this". I dumped her on Wendy, which was a pretty lousy choice to begin with, and just . . . well, virtually disowned her for a while.

'I could only think of Rosie, Michael. She was the only one who mattered to me. And suddenly she wasn't there anymore. The rain was crashing out of the sky the day they buried her, and when they started shovelling the mud onto her coffin it occurred to me that all I'd ever done, all my life, was stare death in the face. I was glad to get away at that point. Jack had some business for me out in the States and I just made the next couple of years a kind of working holiday. Then Cody called me when I was in Los Angeles and that's when it all started again.'

'Do you get lonely?' Michael asked.

'What do you mean, for women?'

'For anyone.'

Johnson shrugged. 'Oh yeah, sometimes. We all do, but then I was always a loner and you get used to it. I was lonely even when I had Rose. She knew what I did but there was still a large part of myself I had to hold back. Yeah, there are times when I feel great emptiness, just like you.'

He laughed self-consciously. 'Sexually, it seems to have killed me totally. I remember one night in Los Angeles. One of Jack's friends out there is a guy called Jackie Guardino. I mean, Jackie's a nice guy, but very basic, you know? It's just like him to think, "Gee, the poor guy's lost his wife, he's probably dying for a fuck". So he invites me to one of his clubs, this really ritzy place in one of the nicer parts of town, and he fixes me up with this Amazon of a girl who looks as if she's made of plastic.

'Jesus, it was awful. This girl was all over me right through the evening, groping my balls and sticking her tongue in my ear, and I'm sitting there feeling as cold as ice. I should have ducked out, but I ended up going back to her place and it was a disaster. She worked on me with everything she had and I couldn't even get a hard-on.

Then she started getting shitty and asking me what was wrong with her, and I just didn't have the energy to explain it all. I'd seen her kind of world a thousand times before. That rich, upmarket world which still manages to be as seedy and sickening as trying to screw some old slapper in her bedsit behind the railway station. Only difference is you get a snort of cocaine beforehand instead of a cup of tea.

'When we get to Monterey, that's the kind of world I never want to see again. My own daughter's already been tainted by it. I entrusted her to a woman I thought had given up all that nonsense, and I find out she's running a bloody brothel. There doesn't seem to be an area of my life that's been untouched by that kind of poison. I want to exterminate it all tomorrow, shut it out for ever.'

Michael picked up the Smith & Wesson and began to caress it again, and he could feel his heart thumping as he did so. 'Then I suppose you'd better take me through this,' he said. He wanted to ask, 'What if it all goes wrong?', but if Johnson was thinking about that possibility, he wasn't showing it, and now didn't seem the right time to be negative.

'It's going to be tough, Michael, but try to get a few hours' sleep tonight,' he said. 'Don't feel too bad if you can't. It's good to be tight, it's good to be nervous. Don't forget what I told you about fear.'

38

Michael couldn't sleep of course. His system hadn't slowed down and he was now scared by the way his whole body was violently beating. He could hear the steady thumps in his chest, and his sweating body had made his bed wet and impossible to settle in. He counted three hours going past on his little bedside clock and then he gave up and went to the bathroom. He splashed himself with cold water, walked back into the bedroom and smoked a couple of cigarettes as he peered out of the window at the quiet sea. He looked up the road at the ghostly West Pier and cursed the damn thing for ruining Neil Franklin's life. At times like this in the past he would have cleared out the contents of the mini bar, yet he wasn't craving for alcohol.

He poured himself a glass of water, turned on the TV and sat up on the bed. He didn't even know what he was watching and he was convinced he was still awake when static momentarily broke the picture and changed it completely. The camera was panning slowly up the Santa Monica Pier in Los Angeles, and then the picture broadened to take in the beach. The sea looked beautiful and at long last Michael could feel his body slowing down and giving him relief. The picture changed again to a large beachfront motel called the Bay Inn, and Michael jumped as he saw Neil Franklin standing outside, holding a bottle of his favourite brew and trying to hitch a ride. He was barefoot and wearing an open white shirt and a pair of old jeans.

Then Michael was being swept off the bed and into the picture until he became a part of it. He was standing just up the sidewalk from Franklin and he could feel the chilly ocean breeze cooling him down until he felt quite shivery.

'Neil!' he shouted and he signalled Franklin to join him. Franklin waved and began to walk up the road, drinking from his bottle like a saddle-weary old cowboy who had just breezed in off the trail. 'How come you're thumbing a ride?' Michael asked. 'We're meeting over there at Chez Jay's.'

Franklin shook his head vigorously and said, 'Nah, not me. I'm spooked by this meeting, Michael. It doesn't feel right. Haven't you heard the news?'

'What news?'

'I just heard it on somebody's car radio. Dennis Wilson died this afternoon. They found him in the water at Marina Del Rey.'

What in God's name is he talking about, Michael thought. Seeing the puzzlement on Michael's face, Franklin started gesticulating like the Englishman abroad who simply talks louder when he's not understood. 'Dennis Wilson of the Beach Boys – Brian's brother.'

'I know who he is and I know he's dead,' Michael said irritably. 'How much of that stuff have you had, Neil? Dennis died eleven years ago.'

'I'm telling you he died this afternoon,' Franklin insisted, now getting worked up himself.

Michael felt the same sense of detachment he had experienced when talking to Jack Fossey and he was suddenly frightened. 'What year is this?' he asked.

'Oh, and I'm supposed to be the piss artist around here,' Franklin said sarcastically. 'It's 1983, pal, and I can even tell you the day – Wednesday, December 28. Listen, seriously Michael, I'd rather not go to Chez Jay's. It was one of Denny's favourite places, you know that. I feel funny about it, it just doesn't feel right.'

'It'll be all right,' Michael assured him. 'Carl and Jack are there. They want to talk to us.'

'You don't look too confident about that,' Franklin said. 'In fact you don't look too hot at all. Have you sorted out what year it is yet?'

'I'm okay, Neil. Let's go.' But Michael was feeling increasingly nervous.

They crossed the road to the small and dark bar of Chez Jay's on Ocean Park Avenue, and Johnson and Jack Fossey were already there, sitting in a booth and chatting away very amicably. Jack laughed when he saw Franklin and said, 'Christ, kid, aren't you cold like that? I know it's not the same in winter out here but that's still an adventurous ensemble for December.'

'Hey, talk to this guy, not me,' Franklin said, giving Michael a playful cuff around the head. 'He hasn't started drinking yet and he thinks he's in 1994 already.'

Franklin and Michael sat down and Michael noticed how well Johnson looked. He looked fit and full of life and was obviously enjoying Jack's company. 'Me and the old man have made it up,' he told Michael. 'I told him I was really sorry I drowned him.'

Jack roared with laughter at this and said, 'He's going to buy me a pair of water wings in case I fall in the bloody sea again.'

The bizarre humour and the laughter was disturbing Michael and upsetting him. It was frightening and unreal. He still didn't feel a part of all this and his eyes kept wandering out to the street. He knew that something was lurking out there but couldn't remember what.

'Hey, Michael, cheer up,' Johnson said. 'I've spoken to Cody and he's come to his senses. He's going to drop off Janice any minute now. Then we're all going to bundle into a car and drive up to Monterey.'

Michael felt himself nodding but his body was beginning to pump again as it had done back in the hotel room. Christ, he could still remember being in that hotel room in Brighton and everything that had led up to this. What the hell was happening to him now? 'Neil just told me Dennis Wilson died this afternoon,' he mumbled.

'Avenge it,' Johnson said, making no sense at all.

'That's right, Michael,' Franklin said. 'Go get the bad guys.'

'What?' Michael gasped. 'What do you mean?'

Jack Fossey leaned forward, a big cigar clenched between his teeth. 'This is it, Michael,' he said gravely. 'This is the test of your courage you've been looking for all your life. I don't mean punching out some punk in a pub. I mean life or death. Can you pull the trigger like Carl taught you?'

Johnson was suddenly holding out the Smith & Wesson. He

patted Michael on the shoulder and said, 'We don't owe Cody any favours after all he's done to us, Michael. Shoot him. Once Janice is inside, shoot him. Do it for us and the original Beach Boys – Brian, Carl, Dennis, Mike and Al.'

'Then we can all be free, Michael,' Jack said. 'You've always wanted to be free, haven't you? Free of all your shackles, free of all the mental torture that's been twisting you inside out for years. Imagine a great cornfield, Michael. Imagine all that yellow corn stretching for miles under a clear blue sky. Imagine running through it without a care in the world. The time has come, kid. Uncover the cornfield and smile. Now is not the time to be a dumb angel.'

Michael could feel everyone's eyes on him, and the dreadful burden of duty made him want to hold his head and scream out. Quickly, he grabbed the gun and walked briskly out of the dark little bar into the bright light. A large limousine with gleaming black windows was pulling into the kerb right before him. It seemed to sit there for an eternity and Michael began to sweat and shake. Then a door opened and Janice was smiling and rushing into his arms, the soft perfumed fabric of her dress pressing delightfully into his face. 'Get inside quick,' he whispered to her. 'Do as I say and get inside.'

Cody had got out of the car and was walking towards Michael wearing his familiar, sickening grin. Janice began to tremble in Michael's arms, as if she knew what was going to happen next, and she broke away and fled inside. 'Michael, how are you?' Cody gushed, opening his arms as if expecting a bear hug. Then he stopped, looking at first anxious and then amused. 'Shit, Michael, what are you doing with a gun? You'll shoot your damn foot off if you're not careful.'

'Shut up,' Michael said, as he raised the gun and levelled it at Cody's head. 'I'm going to kill you, Cody. I've got to. It's the end, don't you see? It's all over. Finally, it's all over.'

'No, you can't do it,' Cody said quite casually. 'Not you, Michael. This isn't your world, it never was. Let me show you something.' He backed up to the car, opened the back door and pulled a sawn-off shotgun off the seat. He smiled devilishly as he held it up. 'Now this is my idea of a real gun, junior. And I've got the balls to pull the trigger. That's what it all comes down to – pulling the trigger. I mean, there's little point in the President holding the magic numbers for the big bang if he can't bring himself to press the button. And you can't pull that trigger, can you, Michael? You can't.'

Cody walked slowly forward, aiming the shotgun at Michael's chest. Michael's outstretched arm was now shaking violently and all the feeling had gone out of it. 'You can't,' Cody taunted. 'You can't pull the trigger.'

Try as he did, Michael couldn't. His arm slowly came down and as Cody's shotgun thundered and blew a hole in his chest, he was looking up at a cloudless blue sky and falling gently into the great and wonderful cornfield that Jack Fossey had asked him to picture.

Before darkness enveloped him, a series of images passed almost leisurely before his eyes. He saw a sea of police officers, whirling madly before falling into their appropriate places as the pictures took shape. They were milling around Dennis Fossey as he slept peacefully in blood-soaked blankets; they were on the beach, urging a group of young children to stay back as they huddled round to gawp at the washed up and bloated body of Jack Fossey; and they were in the once quiet and unstained field at Hassocks, where the mighty body of Neil Franklin had finally come to rest.

Then the images began to fade and Michael Rossi was back on his hotel bed in Brighton, finally able to sleep for a few precious hours before the biggest day of his life.

39

The calmness Michael felt when he awoke to the sound of his television proved deceptive. It was around six thirty, the kind of time he dreaded when he was going to the office, but now he welcomed it. The dream seemed only a few minutes old and he could recollect every painful detail.

Johnson had suggested they meet up at eight o'clock but Michael hadn't the slightest inclination to sleep on. He wasn't going to cower from anything this day and immediately pulled back the curtains to let in the light. Brighton was still waking up and everything was in its proper place. For a few sleepy seconds he found it hard to believe that Johnson, Franklin and Jack Fossey weren't still in the room and that the palm trees of Los Angeles weren't outside. Even the television had gone back to showing its usual bland and trite terrestrial images. One guy was whacking another over the head with a giant foam saucepan and the studio audience was roaring its head off.

Lighting a cigarette, Michael sat on the edge of his bed and was nearly sucked into analysing the whole crazy thing. Not wanting to entertain any negative thoughts, he quickly shut the dream out of his mind and it was then that he felt the awful knot in his stomach which made it an effort to breathe.

It was sheer nervous tension, yet there was no sweating, no trembling of the hands. This he couldn't quite believe. He always trembled the morning after consuming a full bottle of vodka. And if the Jack Fossey who had visited his patio hadn't been real, he knew the vodka had. Even so, he managed to cut himself shaving, which stupidly irritated him and added to his edginess. However this rotten day was destined to end, he just wanted everything to feel right beforehand.

Damn it, he thought. He had shaved, showered and dressed and it still wasn't seven o'clock. All his life he had hated hotel rooms. Whatever the time of year, whatever the facilities available, they were always insufferably stuffy and overbearing. They had been one of the great banes of his life when he had been drinking a pint of vodka a day. In fact he couldn't help chuckling at the memory. He'd get up extra early to get his full quota in before breakfast, take a cold shower in the misguided belief that it would ease his sweating, and still melt before making it to the breakfast room. On one business trip, to his eternal embarrassment, it had been so bad that a colleague had nearly called him an ambulance in the belief that he had malaria.

Michael watched the news for a while, but even the local bulletin carried only a brief mention of Micky Lyle and nothing on the Fosseys or Neil Franklin. He wondered when Jack's body would be washed up, because he knew it would happen exactly the way he saw it in his dream, exactly how Jack himself had described it. More than anything, he wanted Neil Franklin's body to be quickly found. He didn't want the big man to lie out there in that field, alone and ignored as he had been for much of his life.

Michael had been alone with his agonising thoughts for long enough and he was relieved when Johnson called him at ten to eight and asked him to come along. Johnson had told him to dress casually so that he could feel loose and comfortable, and Michael had chosen his favourite beige jacket, grey T-shirt and jeans. Although not an overly suspicious man, he always felt easy and comfortable with this mix. He despised suits and ties and anything restrictive. They felt like some kind of mental strait-jacket, which was one of the reasons he loathed his time at the office. He was a journalist and the company made him dress like a damn civil servant.

Johnson was dressed in similarly casual fashion but typically looked so much more immaculate. Apart from a fresh royal blue shirt, he was wearing the same combination as he had when skilfully driving Dennis Fossey to self-destruction. Johnson's black jacket, hanging on the wardrobe, seemed to have a formidable presence of its own as Michael gazed at it.

Johnson was taking breakfast and the sudden aroma of bacon and eggs made Michael feel queasy. Johnson grinned when he saw his friend's expression. 'Take that jacket off and sit down,' he said. 'I know your stomach's jumping but try to get something inside you. It's important. Wherever that bastard Cody is right now, he's feeling as tight as us.'

'He hasn't called yet?' Michael asked.

Johnson shook his head contemptuously. 'We may have to wait around here awhile, so don't get too worked up,' he said. 'Come on, eat something. If you puke it later, fine.'

Michael normally loved bacon and eggs but as Johnson plonked a helping onto his plate it resembled a mountain. He suddenly felt like a boy again, forced to eat one more mouthful before being allowed to leave the table. He managed more than he thought he'd be able to but had to keep taking gulps of coffee just to make it slide down his throat. 'How did you sleep, Carl?' he asked.

'Not so good,' Johnson admitted. 'I won't sleep again until I've wrapped this up. I just rest as best I can. My mother always told me that if you just lie there and don't fidget around, you're still doing yourself some good. I don't know if that's true or not. She had a whole bunch of theories like that. What about you? Any more dreams?'

'No,' Michael said quickly. 'No, nothing.'

Johnson gave him a certain look but didn't pursue the point. Michael fidgeted and said, 'I'm worried about the police, Carl. I mean, if they come back today and find I'm not there . . .'

'Don't worry about that,' Johnson said quickly. 'Forget about everything else until we've finished this business. I didn't go into any of this lightly. I've considered all the eventualities. If you come out of this on your own you'll be okay, believe me.'

'Christ, Carl, don't talk like that,' Michael said nervously.

'You have to think of everything at a time like this. Just don't worry about it. Concentrate on today and believe you'll still be around tomorrow. Do everything I tell you today. Don't question my judgement. Don't question anything. Just do it. You'll find your instincts will take over at a certain point. Once the nerves have gone, it's like swimming or riding a bike.'

Michael nodded uncertainly and got up, sick of the smell of food. The bacon and eggs were lying in his stomach like a brick. As he sat in a chair and read the newspaper, he noticed how calm and measured Johnson was as he busily prepared himself. There was a quietness about him that was admirable, but frightening.

Cody's telephone call came at ten past nine and the sudden bleeping of the phone didn't seem to unsettle Johnson in the least. He picked it up and said 'Yeah?' as wearily as a man who knows there's a double glazing salesman at the other end.

'Morning, Carl,' Cody said cheerfully. 'I thought I'd give you a call and let you know the state of play.'

'I know everything, Cody, so let's skip around the bullshit,' Johnson said. 'Your pal Dennis filled me in on all the details.'

Cody laughed and said, 'Yeah, shame about old Denny. I went back there last night and he'd cut himself terribly shaving. He never did get quite accustomed to being a man, did he?'

'Is my daughter still alive, Cody?'

'Carl, honestly, what a cruel question. Dear Janice is the love of my life, didn't Denny tell you?' He gave a little laugh and added, 'She's not here right now but she's safe.'

'So what do you want?' Johnson asked.

'Slight change of plan there, Carl. I was going to pop by the Grand and show her off, but I think I'll feel a little safer on neutral turf. Besides, if push comes to shove and guns start going off... well, it might lower the tone in a place like that. I won't insult your intelligence by telling you not to come armed, because me and the boys are. But it's important we have a little chat first and we don't want Janice to get caught in the crossfire, do we? Remember an old haunt of ours, The Chandelier, on Marine Parade?'

'I remember.'

'Nice, dark old-fashioned boozer. Always reminds me of one of those old Western saloons where Clint shoots up the villains.'

'Well, you're the villain, Steve, so I should be careful.'

Cody laughed almost maniacally. He surely couldn't have been drinking at this time in the morning, yet while his speech was unimpaired, he sounded as if he'd been hitting something. Johnson didn't need additional complications and this worried him.

'Old Bruce Hales is still running the place and he owes me a favour,' Cody said. 'He's opening up early especially for us. The party starts at ten sharp in the main bar. I suppose you'll be bringing your quiet little friend Michael Rossi with you.'

'Does that concern you?' Johnson asked.

'Oh, come on, Carl. Michael's a nice enough boy but he's not exactly the Sundance Kid. You'd better tell him to wear an old pair of trousers. Ten o'clock, old pal.'

Cody rang off and Johnson gave a little grin and told Michael the details. 'We'd better get going, then,' Michael said.

Johnson patted him on the cheek. 'We've got forty minutes, champ. Nice and easy does it.'

40

Johnson got the two guns which were now in their holsters, and helped Michael to put his on. Johnson had taken him extensively through each step last night and now patiently repeated the whole procedure, asking him if he had any questions. Michael shook his head, feeling there was no point anyway. He had grasped the basics, but right now his brain wasn't in the mode to absorb great detail.

When the time came, the two men checked out and loaded their bags into Johnson's car. Neither mentioned Janice. Michael knew that Johnson was thinking of her more than anything else but felt it best to leave him with his thoughts.

As they pulled out onto the seafront on another cloudless and hot day, Michael looked out at the West Pier, the beach, the sea, the people. All had somehow played their part in this remarkable chapter of his life. He thought once again of his meeting with Neil Franklin, when the big man had happily supped at his whisky and told the story of his life. All that was in the past now, gone for ever, irrelevant. It all came down to whatever would unfold just a short drive away.

Michael pondered on how infuriating life can be; on how you overlook all the little things until something awful appears on the horizon. Then you take in every detail, hug it, love it and never want to let it go. There were so many of these little things that he was joyously beginning to embrace again now that he had finally driven the demon drink from his system. Shit, he thought, now I'm liable to get killed.

His nervous system was done no favours when they stopped in

heavy traffic just short of the Palace Pier. One of those people who had to talk when he was jumpy, Michael asked Johnson, 'Why do they call this pub The Chandelier?'

'It's got a big chandelier,' Johnson replied, not intending to be sarcastic. He caught Michael's uncertain expression and added, 'No, I mean, it's a really massive thing. The whole building is strange, almost like a miniature church. There's this incredibly tall ceiling in the main bar and the chandelier is smack in the middle. I'm surprised you've never been there on your rounds.'

'Perhaps I did and I forgot,' Michael laughed.

'I've never liked it myself. It's a dark, spooky sort of place. Bloody appropriate, I suppose. See it on the left up there?'

'Yeah, I've seen it before. I just never dreamed it would become so special.'

'A guy called Bruce Hales runs it. He's been doing us favours for years. He hates Cody but he feels safe with me, so maybe that's a small help.'

The Chandelier was just a short way up Marine Parade and didn't look any less depressing in the bright sunshine. There was a large car park directly in front of the building, containing just two cars: an old but immaculate maroon Jaguar and a black Ferrari. As Johnson pulled in he nodded at the Ferrari and said, 'That's Cody's latest little number. The dickhead always drives that kind of thing when he's trying to look inconspicuous.'

'What about the Jaguar?' Michael asked.

'Belongs to Hales. He's had it for years.'

Johnson stopped the engine and took a good look around. There was a flight of wooden steps leading up to the main entrance of the pub, which looked eerie and lifeless. 'Oh well, better get it done with,' he said.

Michael's whole body was racing again and he wasn't at all sure about any of this. 'How do you know they're in there?' he asked.

'They're in there,' Johnson said. 'Cody wants to talk. He wants to gloat before he pulls the trigger. He's not going to hide in the bushes and hit us from out here.'

'What about Janice? How do we know they've got her?' Michael was panicking. He knew it and suddenly felt terribly inadequate.

'We don't,' Johnson said. 'That part of it rests entirely in his hands. Listen, this is my affair, Michael. If you feel uncomfortable about this, stay here. Better still, go home.'

Michael wasn't sure whether Johnson had intended to sound so sharp but he was stung and a little insulted by the remark. 'No,' he said quickly, 'if I do that I may as well die anyway.'

'Stay one step behind me all the way, but stay close,' Johnson advised. 'Watch everything I do but don't pre-empt me. However frightened you get, wait for my move.'

They got out of the car and walked up to the entrance, and Michael was suddenly aware of the quietness all around. The tiniest sound seemed to carry an echo and their footsteps sounded like gunfire as they climbed the stairs. The door opened before they reached the top and Kenny Carter quietly motioned them in. His face was horribly swollen and bruised from the punishment he had taken from Neil Franklin, giving him an even more psychotic countenance.

As the bar opened up before him, Michael was in awe of its size. Dark and awesome and hauntingly punctuated by shafts of sunlight, it seemed intent on stoking his fear and swallowing him up completely. There were portraits of his favourite boxers on the walls, but this was otherwise a cold and unwelcoming place. The distance between the door and the bar seemed like miles. Dressed inappropriately in a long grey raincoat and jeans, Carter was training a sawn-off shotgun on Johnson and Michael and began to slowly back up to the bar as they followed him. Johnson stared at him but didn't utter a word. Up ahead, two men were standing with their backs to the bar and a third was sitting at a table to the right. However, through the sunlight and the shadows, Michael could see no sign of Janice and now he felt that the door was slamming shut on him and Johnson with every step they took.

Everything became brutally clear when they stopped about ten feet from the bar. If they only but knew it, they were standing directly beneath the huge chandelier. Michael would later wonder why it hadn't dawned on either of them to look up and whether Cody had counted on that. Michael could now see that the man in the chair, whom he took to be Bruce Hales, had been terribly beaten and was barely conscious. He was slumped back, his mouth bleeding heavily and one of his eyes nearly closed.

Johnson acknowledged Hales with a gentle nod and then turned to meet Cody's baleful stare. Cody and Dave Richards were casually leaning against the bar, and between them on the counter were two shotguns similar to the one Carter was carrying. Carter moved in on Cody's right side, leaving Cody in the centre, like a proud sheriff with his two marshals. Richards looked as gross as Carter with his injuries from his encounter from Franklin, and was scruffily attired in a crumpled chequered jacket and old denims.

Cody was at his slickest and smartest for what he was convinced would be his grand coronation. His heavily greased hair was combed back severely and his formidable moustache immaculately groomed. Dressed in a black jacket and waistcoat, white shirt and black trousers, he bore a resemblance to the legendary Wyatt Earp. Michael looked into Cody's eyes, as he had done during their schooldays, as he had done when they had met again on Saturday, and saw the same cruel being. On Saturday, in less intimidating circumstances, he had wanted to lash out and punch the bully who had caused him so much misery at school. Now his desire for revenge was no less but his bravery was fast deserting him.

As he stood slightly back from Johnson, Michael could feel the sweat beginning to slowly trickle out of his hair and down the side of his face. He was becoming hotter by the moment, the sweat dampening his clothes, and he was praying that his discomfort wasn't too visible to the others. The dreadful shaking, which was still very much a mental obstacle to him, was beginning to spread through his whole nervous system, and in his desperation he was straining every muscle in his body to try to keep it at bay. It made him so angry, yet he was afraid to curse it in case it punished him even more. Hold on, Michael kept telling himself. Hold on. As one bead of sweat fell to the floor, he could hear it actually explode.

The sound of Johnson's voice was welcome and gave him the chance to divert his concentration. 'Where's my daughter, Cody?'

Cody's stony expression broke into a broad smile. 'Don't be hasty now, Carl. She's here and resting quite safely. I said I'd bring her and I'm a man of my word.' He was now looking at Johnson in the way that a young autograph hunter gazes at his favourite film star. 'My God, the great Carl Johnson!' he exclaimed, with quite genuine admiration. 'I'm going head to head with the great Carl Johnson. Admit it, Carl, you didn't think I had it in me, did you?'

'I'll admit I didn't think you'd come this far,' Johnson acknowledged. 'But things are really the same as they always were, Steve. You still need a guy on either side of you to stop you falling over.'

Cody tried to take the jibe well, but it clearly hurt. 'Well, I see you've brought your own back-up man, so it's only three against two. Unless poor old Michael melts first.'

Carter cackled at this remark and gave Michael such a contemptuous look that it proved curative rather than destructive. The rage Michael felt began to slice through his fear, yet constructively so, calming him and giving him back his confidence.

'Poor old Michael will be fine,' Johnson said. He nodded at Bruce Hales and said, 'What was all that for? Did Bruce forget to bow when you walked in?'

Cody simply couldn't resist taking the bait any longer. 'Yeah, Bruce is learning respect,' he said hatefully. 'Like you and Jack and Dennis and Franklin, and everyone else who thought I was just an obedient bit player. Times change, Carl. The old order's gone now, you're the only one left. I've waited and waited and now it's my turn. I think I've eaten more than my fair share of crap over the years. I watched Jack Fossey for years, man. Sitting up there on his big mountain like a great fat buddha, doing nothing but getting fatter and richer. I ran around doing errands for him and his wet son for longer than I care to remember.

'Then there was you, the great untouchable. Mister Big, treating me like the office flunky who makes the coffee. Well, I'm inches away now, Carl. It ends here and it ends for you. Christ, you still can't see it, can you? Even your daughter hates you. I've actually got her blessing to put a bullet through your brain. That must really piss you off.'

If Johnson felt pain at this remark, he didn't show it. 'I don't believe you,' he said. 'She's done some bad things but she wouldn't go that far. I think that's what's eating at you, Cody. I don't believe you've got her blessing at all.'

Cody was suddenly enraged and he slammed his fist down on the counter. 'Yes I have!' he roared, sounding like a guilty schoolboy protesting his innocence. 'She loves me. She *idolises* me, man. She'd do anything for me.'

Now it was Cody who was sweating, and as he ranted, Johnson caught the faint smell of alcohol coming off his breath. 'Bruce, get us some Scotch up here,' Cody demanded. Hales was drifting into sleep and didn't hear him, which angered Cody even more. He banged on the counter several times and yelled, 'I said get some fucking Scotch up here, you dozy bastard.'

Hales jumped and nearly crashed over the table as he panicked and struggled to his feet. Michael could hardly bear to look at his injuries and wondered how one man could so savage another. Hales gripped the bar to balance himself as he shuffled round into the serving area.

Now raving and clearly out of control, Cody pointed a finger at Johnson and said, 'Janice is my queen, that's what she is. She's going to be my wife and stay by my side. All my life I've wanted a woman like that and I'm not going to let her go. She adores me and that's what you can't live with.'

Slowly, Johnson could feel things moving his way. Even the po-faced Dave Richards was now looking disturbed by Cody's wild and erratic behaviour. 'Then let me hear that from her and we can get down to settling this,' Johnson said.

'She's an angel, young and pure,' Cody said, his face and moustache now glistening with sweat. 'That's why she's resting with the angels at the moment. Only the best for her, you see.'

He grinned pathetically, as if he were about to burst into tears, and raised his eyes skywards. At that moment Johnson felt a light tap on his shoulder, quickly followed by another, and then saw a small drop of blood splatter on the floor. As Bruce Hales clumsily placed a bottle of whisky on the counter with a loud bang, Johnson looked up at the great chandelier for the first time. He didn't see the awful vision at first, but like one of those trick pictures that holds another picture within, the chandelier revealed its terrible heart. Janice's body was weaved through the elegant glass, as if suspended there by invisible strings. Johnson went to cry out but then her body was hurtling down on him, like an angel that had been shot out of Heaven. Her white, blood-soaked dress billowed out and in the final split second of her descent she seemed to almost float. Michael caught only a fleeting vision of this as Janice fell into her father's arms and knocked him heavily to the floor.

A massive explosion then took Michael into another dimension, where everything was suddenly wonderfully clear and thoroughly logical, for all its sickening rawness. Bruce Hales had grabbed one of the shotguns on the counter and blown half of Dave Richards' head away. Richards was falling sideways into Cody, throwing Cody and Carter into panic and disarray. Cody had been hit by most of the blood and fragments from Richards' horrific injury and was crying out in shock. Carter was the first to recover and fired straight into Hales' chest, hurling him clear through the open flap door of the bar. Michael didn't think about pulling his gun out of its holster; it simply happened. As he fired at Carter he could see his bullets hitting home and blood spurting from Kenny's left shoulder.

Michael had forgotten about Johnson in these fast and mad exchanges, but then there was the crash of Johnson's Magnum and Carter was bouncing off the bar like a rubber ball, before crashing face first to the floor. The Magnum's roar had sounded like a cannon in Michael's ear and for a few vital seconds it broke his concentration. Too late, he saw the shotgun in Cody's hand, and before he could warn Johnson, the cartridge had been fired. It smashed into Johnson's left arm, causing terrible damage and knocking him to the floor. Michael took aim at Cody, but now Cody was charging forward, making his break for freedom, and seemed immune to Michael's bullet which cut into his belly. He was on Michael in a flash, knocking the Smith & Wesson from his hand and sending him crashing. Michael was convinced his life was now ending as he felt his chest and stomach being viciously kicked, but Cody chose to keep running, the shotgun and its last cartridge still firmly in his grasp.

Jolted out of his cocoon of concentration, Michael was devastated by the carnage around him as he lay on his side clutching his stomach. For a moment or two, he couldn't react to it. Johnson was writhing and crying both in agony and grief as he clamped his bloodied arm around Janice's body. 'Help me up!' he cried. 'Help me up!'

Winded and in terrific pain himself, Michael was floundering.

'Come on!' Johnson shouted. 'Don't let him get away, Michael. Don't let the bastard get away.'

His desperate words spurred Michael to ignore his own discomfort and help his friend to his feet. He shuddered as he saw the damage to Johnson's arm and said, 'Carl, you're too badly wounded. Stay here, *please*. I'll get him for you. Stay with Janice.'

The advice was pointless, since Johnson could no longer hear him. Carl motioned at the Magnum on the floor and said, 'Pick it up, pick it up. Give me the gun.'

Michael was close to tears as he retrieved the mighty gun and placed it in Johnson's hand, helping him to grip it. 'Look after her,' Johnson said. 'Stay here and look after her. I don't want . . . I don't want anybody to touch her.'

As Johnson stepped outside, he could see Cody a short way up ahead, limping along Marine Parade and heading for the Palace Pier. Johnson took a couple of deep breaths that seemed to revive him. His pain was severe but his wound wasn't making him feel drowsy or weak. His first few steps gave him the confidence to increase his speed and soon he was jogging, ignoring the blood that was now oozing out of his arm at an alarming rate. Nothing else mattered to him now. He had passed into a one-way tunnel which only he and Cody inhabited. He wasn't thinking about Janice or Michael, the fading dream of Monterey or life or death. He didn't notice the people he passed, who were gasping in horror and hurrying out of his way, or the slowing of the traffic in the street as motorists began to notice the bizarre chase. Johnson had to hunt Cody down and kill him. It was that simple, that brutal, just as his life had always been.

Michael couldn't keep his promise to Johnson. Janice was dead and Carl was alive, and Michael had to do what he could to help his friend. His body was throbbing from the violent kicking Cody had given him but he picked up the Smith & Wesson and forced himself to run. Unlike Johnson, he couldn't block out all the awful events that had gone before and he wanted to let out a great roar of anguish as he ran ever faster down Marine Parade.

Cody had lost a lot of blood from Michael's bullet and was slowing all the time as he passed the Sea Life Centre just across the road from the Pier. He was nearly knocked down by a car as he willed himself on to the Pier's entrance, his vision now failing him.

People began to scream and bump into each other as they realised what was happening and tried to get out of the way. Cody could hear police sirens as he stopped right beneath the Pier entrance and turned to face Johnson, who was coming across the road to meet him. Johnson's own sight was now troubling him and he drew closer to Cody than clear vision and judgement would have demanded.

Michael had nearly caught Johnson and saw the two men squaring off. Cody was exhausted and being torn apart by the demons inside him. Hideously cloaked in the blood of Dave Richards, he looked like the lone survivor of a holocaust. He had come so far, right to the brink of glory, and still he couldn't vanquish the one man he admired as much as he hated. Everything was wrong, everything had fallen apart around him, and now the crown had slipped from his grasp forever. He was alone again, just as he had been in the field at Hassocks with Neil Franklin, and he felt just as small and terrified.

This time he found the courage to raise the gun, but as he levelled it at the blurred image before him, the final shot that Carl Johnson would ever fire crashed into Cody's chest and lifted him off his feet. Cody's finger stroked the trigger of the shotgun before he took flight and Michael cried 'No' as Johnson's body flew back from its force and slammed to the ground.

People were screaming and weeping and car horns were going off as several vehicles collided in the mad chaos. Michael dropped his gun and threw himself down at Johnson's side, gasping at the massive wound in his chest. Amazingly, Johnson was still alive and fumbling for something in his pocket. He pulled out the silver dollar he had carried for so long and pressed it into Michael's hand. Michael grasped it tightly as Johnson smiled at him and passed away.

With tears streaming down his face, Michael got slowly to his feet and walked across to Cody, who blinked once and murmured, 'You pulled the trigger,' before the life went out of him.

Michael looked around for some kind of comfort, some kind of help in all the melee. A police car screeched to a halt behind him, and two officers were running towards him when a young boy's voice snapped him out of his trance. 'I saw it, mister,' said the boy, who couldn't have been more than ten. 'I saw it all. I know it wasn't your fault.'

Michael looked at the boy, fresh-faced and tanned and so full of glorious innocence. He was clutching a junior surfboard and trying to console Michael with a shy and desperate smile. He looked so familiar, like a little angel who was meant to be in this place at this time all along.

Michael smiled back and asked, 'What's your name, son?' He knew the answer to the question, but had to hear it for his own salvation.

'Brian,' the boy replied. 'Brian Wilson. What's yours?'